The Girl Who Cheated Death

AL AN B AKER

ISBN: 9781089869443

Published by Baker Venture Group, LLC

For my wife.
You're my biggest fan, my harshest
critic, and everything else in between.

Contents

KATE BLASTED THE HORN a second time as I wearily opened my eyes, letting in the morning light. She had called me ten minutes before to say she'd be picking me up, but I'd decided to go back to sleep instead of getting ready.

I rushed out of bed, grabbed the first pair of pants and shirt I could find, and went to the bathroom. I was half-ready when I heard the doorbell ring. I knew right away it was Kate, most likely tired of waiting in the car.

Another five minutes passed as I rushed out of the bathroom, finished dressing, and hustled downstairs. Kate was waiting for me at the foot of the stairs with an anxious look on her face.

"We gotta go, Allie," she said.

My real name was Alexandra. Most people called me Alex, but Kate always called me Allie. She had been my best friend since middle school, even though she was the prettiest and most popular girl in school, and I was far from either of those. She was sporting a pair of designer jeans and a tight red shirt. The color complemented her flowing, sandy-blond hair and hazel eyes quite nicely.

"Where's my mom?" I asked Kate as I put on my shoes.

"She just left with Bailey. She said they're going school shopping," Kate said. Bailey was my six-year-old sister. She and I were separated by twelve

1

years and three miscarriages. I remember how happy my parents were when she was born, and even though my dad really wanted a boy, he still cried when he first saw her.

"Is that the best outfit you can find?" Kate asked, surveying my clothes.

I looked down at my blue T-shirt and jeans. "Well, without really knowing why we have to rush to go to breakfast, I didn't have time to find something cute."

As we left my house, Kate said nonchalantly, "No rush. I'm just really hungry."

I knew better though. Kate was up to something, but I brushed it off. This was the last Saturday before our senior year of high school started, and I planned to enjoy it as much as possible. Spending the morning with Kate was a great start.

Summer in southeast Michigan was often very warm, and that day was no exception. The sun was shining brightly in a cloudless sky. As we entered Kate's car, the clock on the dash read five past ten.

"So are you coming to Morgan's party tonight?" Kate asked as she started the car.

"I guess," I said. "But I promised Bailey we would build a fire in the backyard tonight."

Kate smiled. "She is so cute. We can go after that." Kate turned on to the main road, leaving my subdivision.

"That's a plan," I said. "So are you going to tell me why we're in such a rush?"

Kate kept her eyes on the road. She was driving faster than usual; that was apparent.

"No rush," she said.

I just rolled my eyes and tuned the radio to a pop station. Two songs later, we arrived at Kate's destination, the Coney Island, a diner clear across town. We had passed at least three breakfast places on the way. Kate parked the car in the first spot she could find.

"Let's go," she said, hopping out of the car.

I followed, knowing that Kate's hurry probably involved a boy. She'd been on the prowl ever since her boyfriend broke up with her a few months earlier. I had never had a boyfriend, even though a few guys had asked me out. Kate, on the other hand, always had a man.

The hostess seated us in a booth near the center of the restaurant. I watched as Kate surveyed the place as if she were casing it before a robbery. I just smiled.

"So what's his name?" I asked.

She looked past me. "Jeremy. He's at the corner booth behind you, with Carl."

"Carl?" I said, turning in their direction.

Kate grabbed my hand. "Don't make it obvious."

I turned back to look at her. "Whatever. You're the one that dragged me out of bed and sped over here to see a guy. How'd you know they'd be here, anyway?"

"Michelle was just here, and she texted me that they walked in right as she was walking out," Kate said.

"Why is Carl with him?" I asked. Carl had been a classmate and friend since middle school, and he was the last boy to ask me out. He had done that last semester, and even though Kate urged me to go out with him, I just couldn't. I liked Carl but just as a friend. I wanted to keep it that way. Of course, his proposal had seemed to put a wedge between us, and we'd been nervous around each other ever since.

"Guess he's showing him around town. Jeremy just moved here from Lansing. Everyone is saying he's really cute. Plus, I think his family is rich. His dad has a BMW, and his mom drives a Range Rover. Their house is nice too; we drove by it."

"You drove by? What are you, some kind of stalker?"

"Well, no. Michelle called me like a week ago and said that Jeremy was washing his dad's car in the driveway, and…well, she had told me about him before—how cute he was—and so I picked up Amy, and we drove by. He had his shirt off."

"You're such a freak for driving by there. I bet he saw you staring at him."

"He did the second time," she said, laughing.

"The second time?" I couldn't believe it. "You're so embarrassing!"

"Whatever. I had to go back that way after we stopped at 7-Eleven; it was on the way."

I just shook my head. At that moment, our server approached our table, and we gave her our orders.

Just after she dropped off our water and coffee, I saw Kate's face brighten with a smile. She was looking past me, in the direction of Jeremy and Carl. "They're coming this way," she said without moving her lips.

I didn't turn my head until they were at our table. "Hey, Carl," I said.

"Hey, Alex, uh…" He stammered for a second. "This is my friend Jeremy."

I looked over at Jeremy and gave him a smile. "Hi," I said. He was good-looking, for sure, with dark eyes and even darker hair. He stood about six feet tall.

"Hey," Jeremy said, smiling politely. His voice was deep.

"This is Kate," Carl said, and they exchanged hellos.

"I heard you're new in town," Kate said to Jeremy as she brushed her hair back behind her ear with her right hand and smiled cutely. She was so good, I thought.

"Yeah, we just moved here from Lansing," Jeremy said. "My father just got promoted at Ford. He's an executive."

Jeremy said "executive" nonchalantly, but we were all impressed.

"How do you like Crescent City?" Kate asked.

Jeremy smiled, but it was directed at me. I couldn't look him in the eyes, so I stared down at the table.

"Here, there are more trees," Jeremy said. "Other than that, it's about the same."

We all nodded in unison, and I looked up again and saw that Jeremy was still looking at me.

"So you girls want to join us tonight?" Jeremy asked.

Kate looked at me, biting her lower lip. "Yeah, sure. What's up?" she said.

"Jeremy's throwing a party at his house," Carl said. "Morgan is going to cancel hers, and everyone from school is going to be there."

I just nodded, and Kate said, "Nobody told me." I knew this bothered her a little. She prided herself on always being in the know on the comings and goings at Crescent City High School.

"Well, we just confirmed with her like an hour ago," Jeremy said. "I bet she just hasn't had a chance to tell everyone."

"OK. We'll be there," Kate said, looking back at me and smiling.

"Cool. See you girls later," Jeremy said.

I looked up at Carl and smiled. They both said goodbye, and I followed Jeremy's eyes until he and Carl turned and walked away. Just before Jeremy exited the restaurant, he glanced back in my direction, and we locked eyes again for a fleeting moment. Then he was out of sight.

I felt my stomach flutter. His image seemed to linger for a few seconds on my retinas.

"Allie, that boy likes you," Kate said, breaking my trance.

"Kate, I told you that Carl's just a friend," I said, refocusing on my coffee and then taking a sip.

"No, I'm talking about Jeremy."

I looked at her skeptically. "No way."

"I swear he was looking at you the whole time we talked," she said.

I brushed it off. I'd kind of gotten that feeling too, but I couldn't convince myself that it was true. Here I was, sitting next to the prettiest girl in school, and I was the one getting the stares from a cute boy. That just seemed impossible. By the time we finished breakfast, Kate had locked me into going to Jeremy's party.

***

My mother and Bailey got back from shopping in the late afternoon. My father was spending the day with my uncle Rick, who was my mother's brother. Rick and my father had been best friends since high school, and that was how my parents got together. I always had the feeling my mother was jealous when my father and Rick hung out. She hid it well, though, and there really wasn't much she could complain about; my dad was a loving husband, Rick was awesome, and it all fit together so nicely.

I had gotten permission to go to Morgan's party, so I didn't mention the change of plans to my mother. She was very inquisitive about my personal life, and I figured the mention of a new boy in town would spark up a line of questioning that I wasn't ready to answer. At first, she had cautioned me about boys; that was back in middle school. As the years went by and she noticed that I generally stayed away from them, she encouraged me to at least give someone a chance.

During freshman year of high school, I involved her in my personal affairs, telling her about some of the guys I was interested in. That, I later learned, was a big mistake. I loved my mother more than anything, but there were some things she just didn't need to be a part of. The pinnacle of my embarrassment came at a parent-teacher conference. The boy I'd told her I liked, Danny, was there with his parents. She went out of her way to introduce herself and talked me up as if she were a saleswoman in a used-car dealership and I was her best late-model sports car. I wanted to die.

Bailey walked into my room as I was trying on different outfits to wear to the party.

"Aliss!" she said. Her lisp prevented her from making some sounds. It was cute, though.

"Hey, Bailey," I said as she gave me a hug.

She looked at my hand with a frown. "You forgot your bracelet."

"I'm sorry," I said and walked over to my nightstand. Next to my clock was a bracelet Bailey had made for me the week before. It was one of those beaded ones with the lettering in the middle. It read "Alex & Bailey," and it matched the one I had made for her, which read "Bailey & Alex." I put it on.

"Don't forget about camping today," she said. She called it camping, but all we did was build a fire in the backyard.

My eyes widened. I had forgotten. "OK, but I have to leave early. I have somewhere to go."

Bailey pouted. "You have to stay all night like last week. You promised."

I felt bad. "I can't. How about we do it tomorrow? I promise we'll camp all night."

She looked disappointed and for a second didn't say anything. Then she said, "OK, but you better not change it, or I am going to be very mad."

I smiled. She was way too mature for her age.

Finally, I found the right outfit to wear and put it aside. Then I went downstairs, where my mother had dinner ready. We ate together, summing up the day's events, which included her shopping trip with Bailey. She also reminded me that my curfew was midnight and that my father planned to take us all to the wave pool the next morning, but we had to be up and out the door by ten. This was exciting news for both Bailey and me.

After dinner, we watched a movie together, but my mind kept drifting to Jeremy and the party. I watched the clock intently. Kate would pick me up at nine, and as the hour approached, my nervousness increased.

Looking back now, I wish I had just stayed home. What I didn't know was that it would be my last opportunity to spend the evening with my family. Had I known, I would've spent the night watching movies with my parents and roasting marshmallows with Bailey. I would've kissed them all a thousand times and hugged them so tight they would've had to yell at me to let go. I would've told them that I loved them and how much I would miss them. But most of all, I would've said goodbye.

KATE WAS WAITING FOR ME outside. I hurriedly finished getting ready and rushed out the door to meet her. I could tell that she was pleased with my choice of outfit; she gave me a coy smile as I entered her car.

"Nice shirt," she said.

I thanked her, but the truth was that I was very uncomfortable. Along with a pair of skinny jeans, I had on a V-neck short-sleeve red shirt that I felt was two sizes too small. She had told me to make sure I put on something formfitting and not the "baggy shirts you always wear."

We arrived at Jeremy's house just before nine thirty. Cars filled his driveway and lined the street in front of the house. The lights were on inside, and we could see the silhouettes of many bodies through the curtains that covered the front windows.

"Are you sure you can't stay past twelve?" Kate asked as we stepped out of her two-door Ford.

"My dad will kill me. Last time I stayed out past curfew, he called me like a thousand times," I said.

"Well, that only gives us like two hours," Kate said.

I adjusted my tight shirt as I exited the car. "You're the one that made me come in the first place. Plus, my parents know I'm with you. They'd be mad at both of us."

Kate sighed. "OK. But if it's a really fun party, you can take my car, and I'll catch a ride."

I just shook my head and smiled. "What are your plans? You going to lock in this Jeremy guy in one night?"

"No," she said defensively, "but I wanna have a good time. I've been single for like three months now."

"Whatever, Kate. God forbid you go longer than three months without a man in your life."

"Get a boyfriend, and then you can talk."

"I'm waiting for the right guy. I don't wanna rush it."

We reached the front porch, and Kate turned to me. "You have no idea what you're missing. There's more to life than books and bonfires, you know."

I shrugged and rang the doorbell a few times. I wasn't sure if anyone would hear with the music blaring inside.

A few seconds passed, and the door opened. It was Jeremy, with those deep, dark eyes; that silky, soft hair; and a smile that could light up an entire town. Music was playing inside the house, and a few people squeezed past him in the foyer.

"Thought you girls weren't coming," he said, still smiling brightly.

"Thanks for having us," Kate said with a smile.

"Of course. Thanks for coming. All your friends are here," he said. Then he looked at me. "Alex, right?"

Hearing him say my name made my stomach flutter. "Yes," I said nervously.

"Come in," he said and ushered us in.

The music was much louder once we entered. Directly in front of us was a beautiful winding staircase leading upstairs. To the right was the dining area, and to the left was a living room filled with gorgeous furniture that looked as if it belonged in a palace. His house was even better looking on the inside than it was from the outside. Teenagers were everywhere. It was very apparent that girls outnumbered boys—if I had to guess, I'd say at least by two to one.

"Nice house," Kate said to Jeremy, speaking loudly over the music.

"Thanks," he said. "The fridge is stocked, and there are snacks if you want them. There's a bunch of people out by the pool, if you like it quieter."

As I passed Jeremy, his eyes never left mine. I was so shy that I had to look away.

"I'm setting up a keg outside. I'll be back around," he said, and with one last smile directed at me, he turned and headed through the dining room.

Kate took me by the arm and pulled me close to her. "Oh my God, Alex," she said into my ear. "For sure he likes you."

Her words sent shock waves throughout my entire body. "What?"

"He was eyeing you the whole time we were talking. You can't tell me you didn't notice that."

"Whatever. He was trying to be nice," I said, but I was lying. I had noticed, and I wondered how red my cheeks were at that moment, because the room had just gotten a few degrees warmer.

We mingled for a few minutes, saying hello to our friends. Well, they were mostly Kate's friends. My thoughts never left Jeremy. My stomach was doing somersaults at the thought that he indeed liked me.

Kate grabbed a can of beer, and I just had a bottle of water. I had never drunk alcohol in my life, and Jeremy or not, I was not about to start now.

After about twenty minutes of mind-numbing bass from the music, I approached Kate.

"Let's go outside," I said loudly into her ear.

She was talking to a few girls who were sitting on the couch in the living room.

"You go. I wanna hang out here for a minute," she said with a devilish smile.

I just rolled my eyes. I knew what she was thinking, but it was loud in there; Jeremy was not the only reason I wanted to step outside.

I walked back through the house. A hallway connected the living room to a large family room. I was in awe of the richness of it all. The furniture, the paintings—everything just looked so expensive.

In the family room, there was a very large TV on the wall, in front of a sprawling sectional. The room had a really high ceiling with an intricate chandelier. More teenagers were scattered about on the sectional and standing around near the TV. On the far wall was a beautiful mosaic fireplace, and to the right French doors opened to the backyard.

The yard was big. The pool, large in its own right, was dwarfed by the seemingly endless expanse of lawn. There were chairs and tables everywhere, all occupied by teenagers with red plastic cups, undoubtedly filled with alcohol.

Next to the pool, Jeremy was tending to the keg, pouring beer for his guests.

In front of him was a large awning covering a wicker outdoor couch set. A few people were sitting there, and a single armchair was unoccupied. I walked over and took a seat. With all the bodies moving around him demanding their cups be filled, Jeremy had not noticed me.

It was much quieter outside, although the music was still audible. I smiled at the two guys sitting on the love seat to my right. I didn't recognize either of them; one was a skinny little thing with glasses, and the other was a fat guy wearing a white shirt that had a cartoon on it.

"Hey," the skinny guy said.

"Hi," I said.

The fat guy didn't even look in my direction.

A minute of silence passed, and just when it appeared the skinny guy was going to say something to me, a blond-haired girl approached.

"Hey, Steele," the fat guy said loudly to her.

"Hi, Al," she said.

A fat guy named Al. I wondered if his real name was Albert. I found this pretty amusing, and I smiled to myself.

"Sit down," Al said, motioning to a recently vacated chair directly across from me.

She sat down and gave me a smile. "I'm Kiley," she said. "Jeremy's cousin."

"I'm Alex," I said.

"Like Alexandra," the skinny guy said, his smile revealing crooked teeth.

"Yup," I said.

"That's a cool name. I'm Steve," the skinny guy said.

"Nice to meet you, Steve."

I looked over to Al to introduce myself now that the ice was broken, but he was busy chugging his beer. After he drank, he turned to the blonde and said, "So, Kiley, your family gonna come live here or what?"

Kiley smiled politely. She had a pretty smile, I thought.

"No, we like Lansing. They said since your dad got the job at Ford, they would give my dad a promotion."

"That's cool. So he's making more money?" Al asked.

This question annoyed me a bit; of course, he was making more money. For what other reason does someone get a promotion?

"Yeah, I guess," she said politely, but she appeared uncomfortable.

"Did you see the house?" Al asked Kiley, letting out disgusting belch.

"Yeah. It's nice," Kiley said.

Al took another chug of his beer. It was at that moment that I realized he was Jeremy's brother. They looked alike, though at least a hundred pounds separated them. But Al was his brother, all right. I looked over to Jeremy and couldn't believe the difference.

"You know, if you wanna stay the night, we have a guest room," Al said to Kiley, smiling. "Right next to mine."

"That's OK, Al." She seemed more uncomfortable than ever and changed the subject. "Say, what's on your shirt?"

Al looked down to his chest, apparently having forgotten what he had on. He looked up and smiled proudly. "It's Dilbert," he said, puffing out his chest to her. "Read it."

Kiley had a look on her face that said she wished she hadn't asked. Al straightened the shirt over his more-than-generous male curves, and for an awkward moment, she read it.

Then she smiled and said, "That's funny."

"It's hilarious," he said.

I looked over to the skinny kid, who seemed annoyed.

"You wanna read it?" Al said.

For a moment, I didn't realize that he was talking to me.

"No thanks," I said.

"C'mon. It's hilarious. What, you don't like cartoon comics?"

"No, I like them, but just in newspapers."

Al looked at me quizzically.

"I don't think they belong on people's shirts. It's kinda stupid," I said.

Al appeared offended. "How's that stupid? People wear all kinds of shirts. Cartoon shirts are no different than wearing a shirt with your favorite band or football team on it."

"I don't agree. Cartoon shirts are stupid," I said. This guy was really getting on my nerves.

"How? How are they stupid?"

"They just are," I said, preparing myself to get up.

"You're stupid," he said, and he laughed at me.

I felt myself getting angry. "No, people who wear shirts with cartoons on them are stupid. The concept of having a cartoon on your shirt is even dumber. People have to stare awkwardly into your chest while they read it, and whether or not they find it funny, they have to pretend to laugh. All the while, they feel like idiots. You'll never see anyone with half a brain wearing one of those shirts." I stood up, fuming. "And you shouldn't call people you've never met stupid," I added as I turned to walk away.

He was taken aback; they all were.

"Dyke," Al said to my back.

"Albert!" Kiley yelled. She was about to say something else, but hearing his name made me burst into laughter.

The three of them just looked at me as I laughed.

I looked up and saw that Jeremy was looking in my direction. He smiled, and I smiled back, still chuckling at Fat Albert. I almost heard the "Hey, hey, hey" callout in the distance.

I walked over to Jeremy.

"Seems like you're having a good time," he said.

"Great," I said.

"Was my brother giving you a hard time?"

"Who, Albert?" I said, smiling.

"Yeah," Jeremy said. He appeared to get the joke. "He's a dick. Don't listen to a word he says."

He reached for a red plastic cup. "You wanna beer?"

I shook my head. "No, no, I don't drink."

Jeremy seemed impressed by that. "Me either," he said.

"Yeah, right. You have enough booze here to satisfy an army."

He shook his head, putting the cup back on the table. "No. I have vices, but alcohol is not one of them. It gives me really bad headaches."

He took a few steps back and pulled a green bottle from a large metal bucket of ice. He shook off the excess water and handed me a cold, glistening, glass bottle of sparkling water.

"You'll like this," he said. "It's good."

"Thanks," I said, taking the bottle.

"You wanna tour?" he asked, smiling and gazing at me with those eyes. "Of the house?"

For a second, I was frozen—barely able to respond. "Sure," I said, willing the word from my mouth.

"So you obviously have seen the backyard," he said as he motioned around.

"Nice," I said.

"The yard is twenty thousand square feet, and the house is almost four thousand."

"Wow," I said, but really, those dimensions meant nothing to me. I didn't even know how big my house was. I knew it was much smaller than this one. Even his yard made mine look like a parking space in comparison.

"Follow me. I'll show you inside."

As we walked around on the main floor, he pointed out all the expensive stuff they owned and provided the corresponding values. There was a grand piano in the study that was worth over $10,000. Everything was so elegant and nice; it was very impressive.

He then walked me upstairs. I locked eyes with Kate on the way up. She was still on the couch with her friends, and she gave me a rather presumptuous smile—as if I were about to walk upstairs with this guy and do something. I rolled my eyes at her. She couldn't be serious.

All five of the bedrooms were upstairs. Jeremy and Albert each had his own. There was one guest bedroom and their parents' room. The fifth room was set up as an art studio. It was a very nice room overlooking the backyard. His mother was a painter; canvases stood on the floor, leaning against one of the walls.

Jeremy showed me in, and we walked over to the art. I could feel Jeremy's deep, dark eyes on me as I studied them. I came upon a piece I liked. It was of a woman who was standing and looking out a window. The perspective was from behind her; the viewer saw only her back. She had on a red-and-white-flowered sundress, and there was a single empty chair to her left. The back of the chair was facing her.

"This one is really nice," I said.

"She's contemplating suicide," Jeremy said.

"What? Really? How do you know?"

"I don't know, but that's what it looks like to me. You see, my mother is one of those purists when it comes to art. She won't tell us what the real meaning is behind her work. She says that true art has multiple meanings, and each person takes something different from it. I told her that it looks like the lady wants to commit suicide, and she appeared to like that, so I figure that's what it is."

I studied it for another moment. "I think she got stood up—you know, like by her husband or boyfriend. She was sitting in the chair, looking out the window, waiting for him to come home, and he didn't. Now she's so anxious she can't even sit down, and that's why she's standing and looking out the window."

I looked at Jeremy. He was looking over the painting again. "Yeah, but you see, the chair isn't facing the window. I bet you that above her, there's a noose that she hung up, and she's about to hang herself by kicking the chair out from under herself."

We stood in silence for a moment, both looking at the painting.

"Let's go to my room," he said, breaking the silence.

My heart stopped. No boy had ever invited me to his room before, and now the best-looking one of them all just casually put it out there as if it were nothing.

"Sure," I said before I even had the chance to think about it.

We left his mother's studio and walked a few steps to his room. It was a large room, much larger than mine. He had rich mahogany bedroom furnishings and a computer desk. A few sports posters hung on the walls. A half-open door led to a bathroom.

"Wow, you have a bathroom," I said.

"Yeah, it's nice. In our last house, me and Al had to share one. It was annoying. My dad found this house. It has a bathroom for every bedroom except the studio room."

He smiled at me. I melted at the sight of him, and my cheeks likely turned red.

He pulled out the chair from his computer desk and offered me a seat. I sat down. He walked over to his dresser and pulled a wooden box from his top drawer.

"So I'm guessing that since you don't drink, you like to do other things," he said with a devilish smile. He sat on the edge of the bed, facing me.

"What do you mean?" I asked.

"Smoke," he said. He opened the box and pulled out a small, hand-rolled white cigarette. It was twisted on both ends.

"No, I don't."

He was already lighting it up. He took a few puffs of it and extended it to me. He glared at me, and I was powerless.

I took the cigarette from him and said, "I haven't really done this for a long time. Last time, I got really sick."

"You'll be OK," he said. "Just drink the water right after you take a few puffs. It'll help with the coughing. This is the best stuff around, really expensive."

I lifted it to my mouth and took a puff. As I exhaled, I coughed uncontrollably. The sparkling water did help. I could feel my chest contract, pushing out the unwanted smoke.

I gave it back to him. He smoked until I was done coughing and then gave it back to me. He didn't cough one bit; he must do this a lot, I thought.

The next few puffs were a lot smoother. I still coughed, just not at the level I did at first. The sparkling water was a lifesaver, as the taste of this stuff was almost unbearable. I looked at Jeremy, who was smiling approvingly. I smiled back.

"I always said the nondrinkers had the most fun. I would much rather be high than drunk," he said as he took another passionate puff.

"I never really was high before," I said. "Last time I did this, I just got sick and nauseated. I felt a little funny, but it was never like people said it was. So I figured I wasn't high."

"This stuff," he said with a deep voice as he held in a large inhalation, "this is straight from Cali." He exhaled. "Ah, the best stuff indeed."

I looked around the room. Smoke danced around us as I took another sip of sparkling water. "Don't your parents get mad that you smoke in the house?"

Jeremy laughed and leaned in. "No. They smoke too." He laughed some more.

"Really?" I was shocked. "But isn't your dad an executive at Ford?"

He smiled at me and took another puff. "Yeah, and I bet all his executive coworkers smoke too. Here," he said, handing me the cigarette again.

I shook my head. "I can't."

"C'mon," he said, giving me a smile that made me warm inside. "Just one more puff. Here. I'll even hold it for you."

Unable to resist his urging, I bent forward, and he put the cigarette gently to my mouth. His warm fingertips pressed lightly on my lips, and my entire body started to tingle.

I inhaled another puff, and he promptly covered my mouth with his other hand. "Now hold it in," he said, smiling.

I did, and I felt my lungs contracting, wanting to push the unwanted smoke out. After a few seconds, when he saw that I couldn't take any more, he released his hand, and I let out a deep breath.

I coughed for a second and felt tears forming in my eyes. I had not smoked enough of anything to really confirm whether this stuff was "the best," but so far, it seemed pretty good.

"Now, that was a real puff," he said as he put the cigarette to his mouth and finished it off.

Jeremy gazed at me for a long moment. I was uncomfortable with his stare and did everything except look in his direction.

"So I'm guessing you don't have a boyfriend," he said.

I shook my head. "No," I said.

"I had a girl back in Lansing, but I broke up with her when we moved," he said.

"That must have been hard."

He smiled to himself. "No, she was a total…well, you know what. She was always thinking that I was cheating on her. And she was too needy, always wanting attention and stuff like that."

I just nodded. I had nothing to say to that. Having never had a relationship myself, I really couldn't add much to the discussion.

"It's better. I think I wanna just have a good time for a while, you know?" he said.

"Yeah, I like being single too," I said.

"What about you? Who was your last boyfriend?"

I smiled. "Nobody."

He seemed surprised. "Really? Never?"

I shook my head. "No."

He seemed to like this. He leaned in and said, "So are you a…"

I shook my head no, as if he were implying that I had some type of terminal illness. Even though I was a virgin, I was not about to admit it.

He nodded acceptingly and said, "Cool." Then he stood up. "I'm gonna go put this out. Make yourself comfortable."

He got up and headed to the bathroom, closing the door behind him. I got up and walked around his room. He had so many nice things—his bed, his computer, and even his trash can looked like they were purchased at high-end stores.

On his dresser, there was a miniature replica of the stone statues on Easter Island. It looked as if it had been carved by hand. I stared at it for a while, and for a split second, I thought the face of the statue smiled at me.

I was suddenly struck with a realization: I was stoned. My entire body felt numb, and things around me just did not seem right. It was as if I were watching myself from another place, and my body was moving around under the command of some other consciousness.

I lay on the bed and stared at one of the posters on the wall. It was of a man in a black jersey and helmet. He wore the number forty-two. He was hitting a guy in white and blue who had a star on his helmet and was jumping for a football. It looked very painful.

There was the flush of a toilet, and then the bathroom door opened. I immediately sat up. Jeremy said something to me, but I was still concentrating on the men in the poster.

"Alex, you OK?"

"Huh?"

"I was asking if you wanna go back down or just stay up here."

"No, I wanna stay. I don't feel like going down right now."

Jeremy stood in front of the bed. He wasn't looking at my face when I looked up at him; he was surveying my body.

"You know, I have condoms in the drawer," he said, smiling.

Condoms? Suddenly, I awoke from my daze. Was he serious? We'd known each other for like two minutes. "Probably better that they stay in the drawer," I said, starting to get up. "Maybe we should go downstairs."

"C'mon," he said, holding me by the shoulders. "Just relax. Plus, it's noisy down there. Sorry I said that."

I nodded and sat back down on the bed.

Jeremy was still smiling as he watched me closely. Then he took off his shirt. Shivers ran through me as he exposed his hairless, broad, perfectly formed chest. His stomach was flatter than concrete, and his arms looked as though they were carved out of stone. I stared a moment too long and then looked away, embarrassed. He noticed me staring and seemed to enjoy it.

"C'mon, Alex. You are the prettiest girl I've seen since we moved here, and since I saw you this afternoon, I can't stop thinking about you. I mean, we don't have to go all the way, but we can make out a little, can't we?"

I kept my eyes off him, but I was fully aroused. Nobody had ever called me the prettiest anything in my life, and now the prettiest boy I'd ever seen had just said it. And he was standing two feet away with his shirt off. I wanted to faint.

I looked up at him and knew instantly that, just as before, I was powerless to say no. He leaned in, moving toward me, and I fell back on the bed. As his face closed in on mine, I pulled away. He kept moving forward, and I kept moving back. Finally, we were both on the bed, and my back was up against the headboard. He let his muscular, warm body slowly fall over mine, and then our lips touched.

I don't know whether it was the drugs or him or a combination of the two, but fireworks were going off inside and all around me. I had kissed a boy before, but it had been nothing like this.

Our tongues met, and I melted. With my eyes closed, I was lost in some other existence, some other state of mind. I was not myself anymore, and whatever control I had was now lost.

I allowed myself to lie flat as he adjusted himself over me. He pressed himself on me, and his weight and strength locked me down firmly on the mattress. As our bodies rubbed against each other's, tiny shocks of electricity exploded from every nerve ending. He left my mouth and started kissing my neck. Before I knew it, his hand was over my breast, and he was rubbing it on the outside of my shirt. I let him go on. My eyes were still closed, and I was enjoying every second of it.

It was not long before my shirt was off. Frankly, I had no idea how it happened. We were both breathing heavily and rolling around on his bed.

Then, as he was on top of me. I felt his hand go into my pants, and I jumped, breaking the passion. "What are you doing?" I exclaimed.

Still kissing my chest, he didn't respond. Instead, he jammed his hand deeper until it was between my legs.

"No!" I said, this time yelling as I tried to pull his hand away.

"Chill out!" he said, forcing me down, and then he stuck one of his fingers inside me.

It hurt, but I didn't scream. Instead, I looked over to his nightstand

and found my glass bottle of sparkling water. With my left hand, I pushed him back, and with my right, I swung the bottle so hard at his face that it shattered on impact.

"I said no!" I yelled as blood gushed from his face.

He clenched his face with both hands and let out a bellow of pain.

He yelled obscenities as I gathered my shirt.

I ran to the door and looked back at him on the bed. His head was still buried in his hands, and blood was dripping onto his bedsheets from between his fingers. I slammed the door behind me and quickly put on my shirt.

He yelled again, but I couldn't make out what he was saying; I was already rushing to the stairs. Kate was still with her friends on the couch. She hadn't seen me come downstairs. The music was so loud that I doubted anybody had heard the noise.

Embarrassed and upset, I ran out the front door.

The night was cooler now, and the music faded as I closed the door. I felt myself starting to cry, but I held the tears back. I started walking toward the street, and then a voice came from behind me. It was Kate.

"Alex, are you OK?"

I didn't turn around. I just kept walking down the walkway. I was high, and I felt violated. I didn't want to face her. I wanted to be alone.

"Alex?" she called again. I heard her steps behind me.

"I'm fine. I'm just gonna go for a walk," I said, but my voice cracked as though I was about to cry, and I knew she didn't believe me.

She ran around me, stopping in front of me, and we faced each other. I couldn't look her in the eyes. Now the tears began to pour out of me. She pulled me into her chest and hugged me.

"Honey, what the hell happened up there?"

I didn't respond. I just sobbed, my head resting on her shoulder.

"What did he do to you?" she said, her voice taking on a more alarmed tone. Kate knew I was a virgin and that I wanted to wait until I was married. She was the only one who knew that.

"He tried to stick his finger…" I said between sobs. "Well, he did actually get it in…" A few more sobs came, and I couldn't finish my sentence, but I knew Kate got the idea.

"That bastard!" she said. "Stay here. I'm gonna go tear him a new one."

"He's bleeding," I said as she let go of me and started for the house. "I broke a glass bottle on his face."

Kate froze and stared at me when she heard this. At first, she looked confused. Then she smiled. "Hell freaking yeah. Are you serious?"

Her smile made me smile, and I nodded.

"Stay here. I'll go see what's going on, and then we'll get the hell out of here. You did the right thing. Don't be upset."

She turned and went back into the house. I wasn't sure I'd done the right thing, and I was very upset.

Still half-baked from the drugs, I looked up at the half moon shining brightly in the sky and resumed walking away from the house.

I crossed the street, reached Kate's car, and sat on the curb next to it. It was dark. The only light came from the evenly spaced streetlights along the somber residential road. I was happy that I was not sitting directly below a light; the solitude of the dark was comforting.

I pulled out my phone. It was thirty minutes before midnight, and my father would be calling soon. I thought hard about how to handle it. Kate would likely be back in a few minutes, and if I wanted to be home on time, I could do it. But I didn't feel straight enough to face my parents. There was just no way. They would take one look at me and know something was wrong.

Images formed in my head of the scenarios that would likely play out if I went home right away, and they all seemed to end badly. I'd be grounded for months. I knew I should've stayed home.

Kate trotted back from the house. She saw me next to her car and cut across the street, walking in my direction. She appeared to be smiling, which gave me comfort. Hopefully, the damage to Jeremy's face wasn't so bad.

"He'll be OK," she said, a little short of breath. "I tore into him pretty good."

"How's his face?" I asked.

She leaned against the hood of her car, catching her breath.

"It actually was not so bad once the bleeding stopped. His cousin, some blonde—"

"Kiley," I said.

"Is that her name? Well, she's a nurse. She looked at it and said it was nothing major. A few stitches and it'll be fine." Kate paused. We looked at each other in silence for a second. There was something else at the tip of her tongue, but it was apparent that she was having a hard time saying it.

Then we heard some noise coming from the house. I looked over and saw Jeremy coming out the front door. He was holding something up to his face and was surveying the area.

"He wants to apologize," Kate said.

"So you told him no, right?"

Kate did not answer, and with that, I had my answer. Tore him a new one, she'd said. What a bunch of crap. She was probably in there playing peacekeeper. Typical Kate. Now I was fuming.

"I don't wanna talk to him!" I snapped. I said it loudly enough so he could hear. I watched as he turned and came in our direction.

I looked at Kate. She was speechless. "Let's get out of here," I said, standing up and walking over to the passenger door.

"Alex, he just wants to say he's sorry." She was still standing in front of the car.

"What's he gonna say? 'Sorry, Alex, for sticking my finger up your pee hole, but you know I was all high and blah, blah, blah,'" I said, doing my best dumb-guy imitation.

I looked over to Jeremy, and he was close. I got into the car. Kate turned to him and met him at the driver's door. All the windows were rolled up, and I could not make out what they were saying. As Kate turned to get into the car, Jeremy ran around the front; I eyed him the entire time.

He knelt outside my door, tapping lightly on the glass. Kate started the car. I refused to look in his direction.

"Alex, roll down the window, please, just for a second," he said and tapped the glass one more time.

The glass came down. I looked over to Kate, her left hand on the power-window button. I scowled at her, and she looked past me.

"Jeremy, she doesn't want to talk. Maybe another time. We're going home," Kate said as she shifted the car into gear.

"Alex, please, let me explain. I'm sorry I got carried—"

As angry as I had been a minute earlier, those words drove me insane. I turned and stared right into his eyes. He had a blood-drenched rag pressed to his face.

"Let me tell you something. You think you're hot, but you're nothing.

You thought I was some whore you could meet, drug up, and have your way with. Well, you were wrong. Guys like you make me want to puke. You always blame your dumb-ass moves on drugs or alcohol when in reality, you are all a bunch of nasty pigs that can't keep their things to themselves. If you ever try to talk to me or look at me again, I'm going straight to the police and telling them what happened tonight."

His mouth hung open. The towel he was holding to his cheek seemed to get redder.

"Oh, and by the way, I forgot to return the favor for that finger you gave me." I lifted my right hand and gave him my middle finger from inside the car. Kate drove away right on cue, before he could say a word.

She was laughing hard as we made a right turn on Michigan Avenue. I tried to laugh along with her, but I was shaking with anger.

"Alex, honey, maybe you should stay away from pot. Makes you feisty— not that I don't like it," she said and resumed laughing.

"How do you know I smoked?" I asked, confused.

"Are you serious?" She laughed some more. "You and him reek."

"Don't take me home yet," I said, as it was obvious that she was heading in that direction.

"I have perfume you could put on. They'll never notice."

"No. I still feel funny, and I keep going in and out. I'm afraid I might say or do something, and they'll know for sure."

She put her right hand on my arm as she steered with her left. "Honey, it's called being paranoid. I swear, if I didn't smell it on you, I would have no idea."

"Really?"

"Yeah. I swear. Actually, when you first came out, I had no idea. When we hugged, I smelled it on you, and then I smelled it on Jeremy when I went inside. I didn't know until then. Honestly, you could have fooled me."

This was hard to believe. I felt as if the world around me was contorted and moving both slow and fast at the same time. Everything was just not right, and my mind couldn't put two and two together.

"How about now, when I'm talking to you? Am I fine?"

She smiled. "Oh yeah, you're more than fine. C'mon." She dug her hand into the center console and pulled out a bottle. "Spray some in your hair, and you'll be fine."

I took the bottle of perfume and closed my eyes. I gave it a couple sprays, and suddenly the air around me smelled of sweet roses. I took a few deep breaths as Kate turned onto my street. She was right; I would be better off going home on time than having to explain why I was late. She made her way to my block and stopped in front of my house. Except for a porch light, my house was completely dark.

"Alex," Kate said, "don't worry about him. He's a dumb ass. I just can't believe he did that to you."

"I'm not gonna think about it, and honestly, this whole thing has turned me off to parties. I think I'd rather stay home."

"No," Kate said, sounding concerned. "This is isolated. There are nice guys out there. Look at your dad and how happy he makes your mom. Wouldn't you want that? They met in high school. You never know; the next guy that comes along could be the one for you. You just can't lock yourself in your room for the rest of your life."

"Maybe not the rest of my life, but honestly, I need some time. Jeremy practically raped me. He's lucky I didn't call the cops."

Kate let out a little laugh. "Well, you did bust his face open."

That made me smile.

"OK, well, I guess I'll see you. We're going to the wave pool early tomorrow, so I'll need to go get some rest."

"Have fun, honey," she said, giving me a hug.

I left her car and hesitantly walked up to my front door. Once on the stoop, I looked back at Kate. She gave me a wave and drove off.

I opened the front door quietly; inside, it was dark. Occasionally, my parents stayed up on Saturday nights, but luckily this was not the case. I was instantly filled with a sense of relief.

I tiptoed through the foyer and into the dining room. Quietly, I put my purse and keys down on the table. On the couch, in the family room, I could see that my dad was fast asleep with the television on.

I tiptoed up to the bathroom and then to my bed. Once I was under the covers, all my nervousness left me. I was safe.

I tossed and turned for hours. The combination of drugs and the events of the party had left me restless. Sometime between three and three thirty in the morning, I fell asleep.

IT WAS PAST NINE IN the morning by the time my eyes caught their first glimpse of morning light. Next to me, sleeping soundly, was Bailey. She had on her bathing suit and a pair of oversized sunglasses. I was suddenly struck with a sense of urgency; I had overslept.

Not sure what to do first, I got out of bed and looked around the room. The events of last night seemed like a distant memory, and my altercation with Jeremy only a dream. I didn't have time to think about it, so I rushed to the bathroom across the hall and took a shower.

Bailey must have heard me, because she was waiting for me in the hallway when I exited the bathroom holding a white towel around me with another one over my head.

"You're late," she said, her face filled with disappointment. "You slept too much, Aliss, and now we can't go to the wave pool."

I walked by her to my room, avoiding eye contact.

"I came at seven thirty and then eight thirty, then I was tired, and I slept next to you because you wouldn't wake up. You sleeped too much. Were you drinking beer?"

I was putting on my bathing suit and paused, puzzled by where she could have gotten that information. "Why do you say that?"

"What, you drink beer? 'Cause Daddy said to Mommy that he doesn't want you to drink beer when you go to a party. Mommy said you don't drink beer."

I smiled and shook my head.

"Daddy said he doesn't want you to go to the parties and that there are boys, and they give you beer so that they can sleep next to you."

"Bailey!" I said, shocked. "When did Daddy tell you this?"

Bailey giggled. "He didn't tell me, but I sneaked downstairs and I heard him tell Mommy yesterday."

I finished putting on my clothes and knelt down, facing Bailey. "What did we tell you about sneaking around? It's bad. You can't listen to big people's conversations. They aren't meant for you. It's very rude."

Bailey seemed to take this in stride and turned, pulling my hand.

"OK, sorry. Can we go now? It's late, and Daddy is already mad at you."

"Bailey," I said, pulling her back to me.

"What?"

"I never, ever drank beer, and I never will, OK?"

She smiled. "OK." Then she trotted off.

I finished getting ready and went downstairs, where I was met with suspicious stares from my parents.

My dad was sitting at the kitchen table reading the sports section of the paper, and my mother was grilling my eggs. I poured myself a large cup of coffee and sat down next to my dad. He looked up at me and gave me an amused smile.

"Come home late last night?" he asked.

This was an obvious trap he was trying to set. He was sound asleep when I got in; there was no way he could have known what time it was. Of course, if I had come in late, I'd be guilted into admitting it, because I would've had no idea when he fell asleep.

"No. I walked in at twenty minutes before midnight," I said, taking a sip of my coffee. "You were asleep on the couch." I smiled.

He smiled back. "Well, you overslept. I was worried. You know what this means, right?"

I rolled my eyes. My dad and his ultimatums. "No wave pool."

Bailey let out a gasp of disappointment when she heard those words.

"Dad, it's only ten. They can't be filled to capacity yet," I said.

"It's a forty-five-minute drive, and by the time we're done eating breakfast and loading up the car, it'll be twelve. It's also the last Sunday before school starts and hot outside. We needed to be up by eight thirty and out the door by ten if we ever had a chance."

"Can we at least try?"

My dad took a sip of his coffee and flipped a page of the sports section.

"Please, please, please!" Bailey said, looking at him expectantly.

"No," he said, shaking his head, still looking at the paper. "I'm not driving forty-five minutes just to find out that the pool is packed and they won't let us in."

Bailey and I let out concurrent sighs. I felt so bad. Bailey looked dejected, and she had been so excited about going.

A few minutes of silence ensued as my mother gave me my breakfast, sat down next to me, and started eating.

"So how was your party last night?" she asked as she put butter on her bread.

I hesitated. "It was good. Very loud."

"Well, did you have fun? Meet any new people?"

"Yeah, there were a lot of people there. Kate and I mingled."

My mother nodded and then took a bite of her toast. I took the moment she would spend chewing to think of something to say that would change the subject.

"How about Willow Park?" I suggested to my father. "They have a pool, and it's rarely full."

My father seemed to agree. "Yeah, that's what I was thinking."

Bailey didn't like that at all, and her lower lip curled outward like the unrolling of a tightly wound rug. "I wanna go to the wave pool," she said.

"Honey, you heard us. We can't drive forty-five minutes just to turn back. There's nothing near that park. We would waste two hours of the day if they don't let us in," my father said.

Bailey lowered her head, her lip still in the "I want what I want" position. Reluctantly, she drank her juice.

We finished breakfast. There were no more questions about the party, but I knew that later today I would have to face my mother's probing questions about what I did or didn't do. Because she met my father in high school, she was convinced that there was no other way to meet your soul mate. What she didn't realize was that she grew up in a different time.

What happened with Jeremy last night was a prime example. After that encounter, I was all partied out for a while.

We loaded up the car, and as forecast by my father, it was almost noon. Willow Park was about twenty minutes away. Many family memories had been made there. It had a large, clean pool. The park must have been ten miles from one end to the other and filled with open fields and plenty of trees. We never really went on family vacations, but we did a lot of one-day trips. It was fine for me. While I was often envious of the kids who came back from Christmas break with tans and citing the excessive heat they'd had to deal with during their tropical excursions, I was just as happy know-ing that my parents loved each other and loved us.

Our blue minivan made its way onto the freeway, heading west. Bailey was in a booster seat to my right, and I was sitting behind my father, who was driving. My mother was in the passenger seat. The gentle hum of the engine increased once we got onto the expressway. With my headphones connected to my iPod, I was lost in music land. Bailey was playing on her Nintendo DS.

It was a nice day—would have been perfect for the wave pool. The forecast said it would be almost ninety degrees.

We drove along the expressway for ten minutes without any problems. Suddenly, my body was jerked forward. The car had slowed abruptly, and looking over my father's shoulder, I could see what seemed like miles of cars backed up.

"What is it, Dad?" I asked, taking off my headphones.

"Probably an accident," he said, sounding very annoyed.

We were in the center lane, and my dad bullied his way over to the right. In the distance, I could see the sign for the next exit.

"Hon, I'm gonna need you to start up the navigation," my father said to my mom.

"Are all these cars going to the park, Daddy?" Bailey asked. "Is the other park going to be closed too?"

"No, honey. We're still on the freeway. Nobody is gonna be at the other park," Dad said.

My mother was digging through her purse. "I think I left my phone at home," she said.

My dad let out a sigh and unbuckled his seat belt. As we slowly crept closer to the exit, he dug deep into his right pocket and produced his cell phone.

My mother took it and started the navigation. Bailey resumed playing her game, and I decided that I would go back to my music.

I watched as we slowly passed the cars to our left. Most of them were filled with families, all probably doing the same thing we were, and not a happy face among them.

We finally arrived at the exit, and my father turned right. I found that odd, because almost every other car was turning left. We found ourselves on a two-lane road, surrounded by cornfields and the occasional house or barn.

We drove along one road for a while, and then we turned onto another road, and then another. By the third turn, I knew we were lost. My mother and father were bickering about something in the front, their voices muffled by my music. Bailey was looking up from her Nintendo, concern all over her face. She hated it when they fought.

I looked down at my iPhone and changed the song. I looked up and heard a loud screech, followed by my mother screaming.

The crash came from the right. I barely had time to turn my head when our van was tossed about. First we spun, and then we flipped. I heard the sound of glass shattering mixed with the screeching of metal on concrete. Most of it I would only remember later, as my body went into deep state of shock.

As our van finally came to a stop, everything went dark. The world was still, and when I opened my eyes, I was terrified, as I hung upside down, suspended by my seat belt.

Bailey was next to me, motionless. A red paint covered her entire body. Her side of the car was smashed against her, and she appeared much closer to me than she had been before.

I started to cry. I tried to scream, but the pain was too great. I tried to turn my head, but I couldn't; I was trapped by the seat belt.

The smell of iron and burning rubber filled my nostrils. My breathing got heavier and labored. I tried to unbuckle myself, but it was too difficult to move my arm. I looked over at Bailey again. She still had not moved. I tried to scream again. I let out a small yell, but she did not budge, not an inch.

Then I heard footsteps, and suddenly I was filled with a rush of enthusiasm. Someone was here to save us, save Bailey and my parents. The steps came closer and closer as I hung, barely able to breathe, in the overturned vehicle.

With everything I had, I turned my head to the back window. It was shattered, and I could make out two feet standing outside. Whoever it was had on a pair of dress shoes. I watched the figure crouch down like a baseball catcher. A man peered in, saying nothing. As my eyes focused, I could see that he was in a three-piece suit. The fabric had thin, white pinstripes. He had an olive skin tone and a goatee. Oily black hair fell all the way to his shoulders. On his side was a gold chain that led up to his right hand. He was holding what looked like a gold pocket watch.

"Help," I sputtered. A sharp pain ran through my chest as the words left my mouth.

The man looked at me, perplexed. It was as if I were speaking a foreign language that he didn't understand.

"Please," I said as the pain in my chest overtook me and I started to cry.

The man didn't react. He looked down at the gold watch, and with his right thumb, he pressed one of the buttons on the top. He then looked up toward me and Bailey.

"Victor Drummond, your hour has arrived. Do you accept?" the man said in a loud, bellowing voice.

"I accept," I heard my father say from the front seat.

In shock, I turned to the front seat. My father's right hand was visible, but the rest of him was not. He was covered by his seat and the mangled remains of my mother.

"Patricia Drummond, your hour has arrived. Do you accept?" the man said from behind me.

I watched in horror as my mother's blood-drenched head suddenly split in two and another head protruded upward, clean and bloodless. "I accept," she said.

Terror stricken, I tried to scream, but the pain in my chest overtook my efforts. I was barely able to breathe. My heart pounded furiously in my chest.

"Bailey Drummond, your hour has arrived. Do you accept?" The man bellowed again from behind me.

I looked over to Bailey and watched as her head split in two and turned in the direction of the man.

"I accept," she said.

Forgetting the pain, I forced my head and body around and looked back at the man.

"Please," I said.

He once again looked at me. This time, I think I saw concern on his face. He looked down at his gold stopwatch and looked up at me again. Then he put the watch into his pocket.

He pulled out a rope, and with a flick of his wrist, one end split into three. The rope took on a life of its own. All three ends started moving in midair, slithering like snakes in our direction.

I closed my eyes in fear as the three rope ends came toward me, and when nothing happened, I opened my eyes. The three ropes ducked in and around the car. One stopped at Bailey; the other two went to the front seat, one for my father and one for my mother.

I looked back at the man, who was waiting and watching as the ropes found their marks.

"What..." I said, the pain too strong for me to finish my sentence.

The man stared at me intently. His face bore a grim expression, and for the first time, I noticed that his eyes were completely black. They stared at me, and fear coursed through my veins. His skin turned a light shade of gray, and as he opened his mouth slowly, his cheekbones seemed to triple in size. His snarl revealed matching rows of sharp, pointed teeth. He uttered a loud, snakelike hiss at me, sending shock waves throughout my body. I not only heard the sound, but I somehow also felt it deep within myself. It bored into me as though a spear were being driven through my core.

I screamed. Even with all the pain, shortness of breath, and rapid heartbeat, I screamed louder and more hysterically than I'd ever screamed before. Then everything went dark.

4

THE NEXT FEW WEEKS FELT like months. I remember the ride in the ambulance. The medic was talking to me, but I couldn't comprehend a word he was saying. I was in and out of consciousness, waking at the sudden jolts of pain in my side as the ambulance veered in one direction or another.

I would not wake again until a few days after that. My first memory in the hospital was of a tall white man—he was older—staring down at me. He appeared to be eight feet tall, and his voice was muffled and barely audible. The pains I felt were still there, but they were fainter, less pronounced.

Over the next week of intermittent consciousness, I would see many more figures walking into the room and standing around my bed. They all smiled and said words that I could not hear or comprehend.

One evening—I would learn later that it was the second week of my hospitalization—I woke up more conscious than I had been since the accident. Suddenly, I was vaguely aware of my surroundings, but I was deathly afraid. I looked around the room, and I saw him again. It was the man from the accident, the man in the neat three-piece suit and the long, greasy, black hair. He stood in one corner of the room and just stared at me. I began to scream and convulse in equal amounts of fear and anger. I threw my hands into the air toward him, as if I could reach him from twenty feet away, and I yelled at the top of my lungs.

An alarm rang out behind me, and three nurses in blue rushed in. With the nurses holding me back, I struggled to get off the bed and get to him. He remained there, just staring at me grimly. I struggled for a few moments, and then I was out like a light, once again alone in the darkness.

I woke up in a dream. I was sitting at a round white table. To my right was Bailey, directly across from me was my father, and to my left was my mother.

I looked down at myself, dressed in a flowery pink sundress. The wrist-band that Bailey and I had made the week before the accident was on my right wrist. I looked over at Bailey, who was smiling. She had on the match-ing bracelet and a perfectly white sundress with a matching white ribbon in her hair. My parents were also dressed in white, and they bore the same loving smile that Bailey did.

"Hi, Alexandra," my mother said. "How are you?"

I smiled. "Good."

I looked around. There were many tables evenly spread out around us. We were outside, the sky was blue, and beyond the tables was an ocean. The sound of waves suddenly became audible as they crashed against the beach. The breeze came in from the water and caressed my face, warming my body.

"Where are we?" I asked, looking around at my family.

None of them answered. Each just looked at me and smiled.

"We miss you," my mother said.

I nodded in agreement. I looked at Bailey and my father, who just smiled at me.

"We have a new house, Aliss," Bailey said, her voice like a melody.

I smiled. "Yeah? Is it nice?"

She smiled and nodded.

"How long can you stay?" I asked.

"Not long," my father said.

"Can I come?" I asked.

He smiled and shook his head. A sense of comfort came over me none-theless. I saw deep into his eyes. There was no fear in them, no suffering, not a hint of discomfort. They all had the same look.

"Will you come back?" I asked.

Again, no response; just a smile.

After another minute, my father said, "We're proud of you, Alex."

"Proud?" I asked quizzically.

"Very," he said.

I took one last look around the table. Something told me it was time to go. I smiled at Bailey and my parents.

"I love you guys, and I miss you," I said.

"We miss you too, honey," my mother said.

The dream ended, and I woke up in my bed at the hospital. The room was dark, and I immediately looked over to the corner where the man had been standing. Nobody was there.

Carl was sitting on the chair next to me. Flowers were scattered around my room, and he was reading a book. He didn't notice that I had opened my eyes.

"Carl," I called out to him faintly. My chest still hurt, but it was much better than before.

He darted up from his chair, a smile on his face. "Alex," he said, standing at my bedside.

"What happened?" I asked.

"You were in an accident—"

"No. To my family. What happened?"

His face was somber. He did not respond.

"They're dead, aren't they?" I asked.

He nodded his head in dismay.

Tears began to fall from my eyes.

"Your uncle Rick wanted me to call as soon as you came to. He's been here a lot. You've been out for a while."

I sobbed as sorrow filled me.

"The bastard that hit you guys—he lived."

I looked at him, bewildered.

"Where is he?"

"He's here, but they have him in another part of the hospital. He was being chased by the cops. He was in a stolen car. The police said that they tried to pull him over, and when he saw the lights, he sped away. They said that they chased him for miles. He was going like eighty when he hit you." Carl bit his lower lip. He looked furious. "He was some drug dealer or something, wanted for who knows how many crimes. The news said that he was seriously injured—paralyzed, I think—and that he's barely holding on."

I couldn't understand it. So many times, I'd heard on the news that a drunk driver had killed a family and walked away uninjured. I was so furious that I wanted to find him and finish him off myself.

"News said that he would be tried for first-degree murder. Too bad Michigan doesn't have the death penalty. That bastard deserves to die," Carl said.

More tears fell from my eyes as I stared directly in front of me.

"How do you feel?" Carl asked.

I looked up at him, annoyed by the question. "How do you think I feel?" I snapped.

He recoiled. "I'm sorry, I just meant—"

"It's OK," I said, immediately feeling bad for him. "Can you leave me alone, just for a few more days? Tell Rick I'm OK for now and that I just want some time. I don't want any visitors."

He nodded. "Is there anything I can get you?"

I shook my head and lay back against the pillow. After a few minutes of silence, he left the room. I spent most of the next few days crying and sleeping. I turned away every visitor who came to my room and ignored those who wouldn't leave. I wished I were dead; I wished I were with my family.

I WOKE UP ONE MORNING TO the sound of a child crying outside my door. It was dark, and the analog clock on the wall was broken, frozen on twelve thirty, so I had no idea what time it was. In fact, I didn't even know what day of the week it was.

I'd had a dream the night before; it was about school. I was naked and walking the hallways, and nobody seemed to notice but me. I ran and ran but couldn't find my way out of the building. Finally, I just found a closet to hide in, and that was when the dream ended.

Every day that passed, I wished I could go back to that dream with my family next to the beach. I replayed every second of it in my mind a thousand times. I wondered why I was so docile, why I didn't hug them or kiss them or at least touch them. As I'd think about it, I kept coming back to the feeling I had throughout that dream; I'd felt so safe and secure. I'd felt as though nothing in the world could hurt me or my family, and I somehow knew they felt the same way. I saw it in their eyes; it was a comfort, a sense of knowing, and a sense of absolution that I had never seen before.

As the days passed, my grief leveled off, but new emotions started to stir in me, mainly hate and regret. I hated the man who had done this to us, and I wanted him dead. One of the nurses finally told me his name, Manuel Alderas. For hours, I concentrated on that name, and the only thoughts that surfaced were that he needed to die, and it had to be a brutal death, the same way he had killed my family.

I couldn't help thinking that it was my fault. If I had not overslept, we would never have been on that road. We would have been heading in another direction, going to the wave pool.

Using the button on the side of my bed, I raised the head of my bed up and looked around the room. For the first time, I really paid attention to the details. A small tube television hung in one corner, adjacent to a large window. The floor, walls, and ceiling were all some shade of beige. I was alone in the room, and directly in front of me was a whiteboard that told me what day of the week it was. It was Tuesday. It also told me that my nurse's name was Brandy and that my doctor was Khan. There were some references to medications, but I lost interest.

Just under the window was a bench, and on it were a pillow and blanket. I thought about Carl, Rick, and Alicia, Rick's wife. Kate had come a few times early on, when I was still in a coma. Carl had told me that. But I hadn't seen her since. Rick came after work and stayed most of the evening. He put up with my bitching and crying and just sat idly by, offering as much comfort as he could. Alicia came and went a few times, but she had two small children at home, and it was difficult for her to stay long.

Mostly, I preferred just being alone. With people around me, I was constantly reminded of my parents and Bailey. It was such a surreal thought that I would never see them again. I had not fully comprehended it and really had no idea how long it would take me to accept it or if I would ever accept it at all.

Of course, solitude came with a price; the horrific memories and images of the man in the three-piece suit plagued me. At some point in the past few days, I'd convinced myself that the man didn't exist, that he was just an imaginary figure I had manifested at a time of great anguish and pain. Some part of me couldn't believe that—couldn't accept that simple dismissal of something that looked and felt so real. I feared and hated him in equal measures. I wished the nurses hadn't sedated me that day; I would have attacked him and torn his head off.

I wondered who he was, but each time the thought occurred to me, I became afraid and immediately pushed it from my mind.

As I sat in bed, I looked at the corner by the door where he'd been standing a few weeks ago. He had been there, all right; I knew he had been. He was so real—real as the bed I was on, the walls, the window, everything. He was real. I had seen his oily black hair in rich detail; his black eyes; the way he hissed at me; all of it. It was all real.

I wondered if I should tell people about the man, wondered what they would say. I ran through the scenarios in my mind. Of everyone I knew or could tell, Kate seemed to be the best choice of all. She always put my mind at ease and would know exactly what to say. Yet she was not around. I hadn't seen her since the night before the accident. She was conspicuously missing from my life.

I looked over to the beige phone on the nightstand next to me and thought about calling her. I would invite her over for lunch, just as we used to do, except it would be in a hospital and not at my house. She would cheer me up, tell me all kinds of stories of the first few weeks of school and all the new boys she was seeing or about to see. It would be fun. As I reached for the phone, though, I hesitated. Why hadn't she come? A voice inside me asked. Why wasn't she the one sleeping next to me on the bench under the window? Why hadn't she brought me breakfast that I wouldn't eat or one of those teddy bears that say Get Well? She was my best friend, and I almost died a few weeks ago. These thoughts troubled me greatly, and I stopped myself from calling her. I decided that if she wanted to come see me, she would have to come on her own.

A blond nurse walked in. Her long silky hair was pulled back and tied in a neat bun. She smiled warmly at me, and I barely cracked a smile back to her.

"Good morning," she said. "You're looking better."

I nodded.

"How's the pain?" she asked.

"It's much better. It doesn't hurt anymore when I breathe—it's been like that for a few days—and my right arm feels better too."

She smiled. "OK, well, now that you're feeling better, we might try to walk around the hallways a bit. It's important for your coordination, after a closed-head injury like you suffered."

I looked at her in confusion. "Closed head?"

"Yes. You probably are just getting your bearings, but you hit your head pretty badly on the left side. The doctor will be in shortly, and he can give you more details."

I lifted my left hand to my head and felt the left side of my face. For the first time, I felt the rough surface of my skin and the lack of hair above my ear. Instead, there was a bandage surrounded by bare skin.

"Can I have a mirror?" I asked.

The nurse was typing something on the computer next to me. "Sure," she said, her eyes not leaving the monitor.

She walked out of the room, returned with a mirror, and handed it to me. I held it in front of me and turned my head to the right, exposing the left side of my face.

The hair on the left side of my head was partially shaved off. The bandage looked horrendous, and I guessed that what was underneath was even more unappealing. The skin on that side of my face looked to be healing, but it was still red and bruised in places.

"Why didn't I notice this before?" I asked her.

She shook her head with a solemn expression. "That happens a lot. You had a very traumatic accident, and…well…you had many other things on your mind. Dr. Khan is coming in an hour or so and said he wanted to talk to you as soon as he could. It's amazing that you survived. The doctor said it was nothing short of a miracle."

I looked at her with surprise. A miracle? How could that be? It had been some time since the accident—I guessed at least three weeks—but at no time had I felt that I was about to die. Then again, the first few weeks after the accident were just a blur.

"What injuries did I suffer?" I asked.

"Dr. Khan will go over that with you when he arrives," she said.

"Why can't you just tell me?"

"You have to discuss that with the doctor."

"Brandy, right?" I asked, now thoroughly annoyed.

"Yes."

"You know exactly what's wrong with me and what I've been through, and you can't just tell me? I don't get it."

"They don't let the nurse do that. It would be like giving a medical opinion. It's illegal."

I clenched my teeth. "OK, well, if it's illegal, then it's illegal. It just doesn't make any sense. I have to ask questions to a guy I see once a week. I bet he doesn't even know my name."

She smiled, and I could tell that I was preaching to the choir. "He's very good," she said, "and I'll make sure he knows your name before he comes in."

She finished checking all the tubes and wires attached to me and walked out. A miracle, she had said, and nothing short of it. Although a few days ago I had wished that I'd died, now the thought scared me.

Dr. Khan was a very good-looking man. He had silky brown hair that fell just below his ear and was clean-shaven. His face was young and tan. A dimple showed on his right cheek every time he moved his lips.

He stood over me, looking down at a clipboard he pulled from the slot at the foot of my bed. He was reading the information intently. I just stared up at him, admiring his long eyelashes and gentle, handsome features.

"You had an episode about two weeks after the accident. Do you remember that?" he asked without looking up from the clipboard.

"Yes," I said.

"What do you remember?"

I breathed deeply, and my heart rate began to increase. "There was a man standing in the corner of the room. He was staring at me," I said.

"Which corner?" he said, now looking up.

"That one." I pointed to the corner next to the door.

He looked at the corner for a moment and then looked back at me. His kind brown eyes were fixed on mine. "And what did he look like?"

"Well, I think it bears mentioning that he was at the scene of the accident. He was the first person there, and I think he took my family away," I said.

The look on Dr. Khan's face told me that I wasn't making sense. He probably thought I was crazy, but what did he know, anyway? He was not a psychologist.

"Had you ever seen this man before the accident?"

"No."

He lifted the clipboard and started writing something. I waited until he was done to ask, "Do you think it had something to do with my head injury? Maybe I'm seeing things." I tried my best to sound normal to him.

"It's very possible. I want to have some more tests done to determine if there was any neurological damage we didn't pick up. Everything we've seen so far has seemed normal. Then I'll have a therapist come see you. You've suffered a great trauma, Ms. Drummond, both physically and emotionally, and we want to take every precaution. Also, I need you to try to walk around as much as possible. One of the nurses will assist you at first until you build up your strength, and you should let them know if you have any pain. You need to build up the strength in your legs."

"What if I see him again?" I asked.

"Well, if it's while you're here, tell one of the nurses. If it's anywhere else, immediately go see your therapist or primary care doctor. The therapist will elaborate some more on this issue."

I breathed easy; all this made perfect sense. I had been in a traumatic accident, and I'd suffered a head injury. Of course I was going to see things. I was surprised that he was the only image; I bet other people had to suffer through multiple hallucinations.

Dr. Khan asked me a bunch more questions, and I responded to them. He jotted down my answers on the clipboard.

"Well, Ms. Drummond, I will come back in a few days to see how you're doing. We will be moving you out of the ICU now that it appears that you are doing a lot better. You really should be grateful. You came back from a very serious injury. You've exhibited great strength and made a remarkable recovery."

He said this to me with an air of drama, as though he were the narrator in a movie. The words resonated with me.

"Thank you," I said.

There was a brief silence as he continued writing on the clipboard.

"You know, this is the first time I remember seeing you, even though I'm sure you've come many times."

He smiled. "We have actually spoken a few times. However, I believe you were delirious at the time."

"Really? How delirious?" I asked, shocked.

"Well, it was right around the time you had your episode that you state was caused by the man standing in the corner. You went back into your coma for one day, and then you seemed to wake up, but you were not very lucid. You went on and on about things that none of the hospital staff could understand. In any case, we decided to have your family speak to you about it. It was troubling at the time, but you seem to have recovered nicely."

I didn't quite understand, but it appeared that he didn't want to elaborate. So I changed the subject, asking, "What about my stitches? When will they heal?"

"It looks worse than it really is," he said. "We only shaved a very small area, and your hair should cover it up. You had a cut above your ear that seemed to be caused by hitting your head on the car window."

His words took me back to the accident. I didn't remember hitting my head, but I did remember the moment just before the accident, when my mother screamed. A shiver ran through me.

Dr. Khan stood in silence for a second, waiting for me to say something. When I didn't, he asked, "Do you have any other questions for me?"

I hesitated, not sure how to ask my questions, then said, "The nurse said it was a miracle I survived. Was I that badly injured?"

Dr. Khan nodded his head solemnly and said, "I was here when you were brought in, and I remember looking at you. Your face was so pale white and you had lost so much blood. We were all so amazed you just kept holding on. I really have no idea how to explain it."

"Wow," I said. "Can't say I remember any of it, but I'm really glad you're my doctor."

He gave me a warm smile. "Anything else you'd like to ask me, Ms. Drummond?" he asked.

"Just call me Alex," I said. "And, no thanks, you've been really helpful."

He bowed his head slightly and smiled brightly. I half smiled back, and he left the room.

Shortly after he left, I fell asleep. I woke up the next day, sometime around ten in the morning. My nurse, Allison, brought me breakfast, which I barely ate.

I spent the rest of the morning watching daytime TV and shelving my problems. For the first time since the accident, I actually spent a waking minute not thinking about my family or the tragedy. Instead, my thoughts were consumed by whether the price of a vacuum cleaner was above or below $132 and whether the contestant on *The Price Is Right* would win a new car. I marveled at the simplicity of the game and wished that I could be a contestant. Considering how much I hated shopping, though, I guessed I would not get very far.

I took a nap at about three in the afternoon, and when I woke up, Carl was sitting on the bench under the window. He was reading a book. It looked like a Stephen King.

"Hi," I said.

He looked up, startled. "Hello."

"How long you been here?" I asked.

He put the book down on the windowsill next to him. "About an hour, maybe less. How're you feeling?"

I breathed deeply, and no pain came from my chest. "Better," I said. "They said I should be out soon. The doctor was really nice."

"Yeah, he's done a good job. He was around here almost every day in the first few weeks."

"I wish I could remember. Dr. Khan told me I was talking, but I don't remember any of it."

Carl just nodded silently.

"Dr. Khan said something about me being delirious. I don't understand what he meant."

Carl looked away from me. He looked uncomfortable.

"Do you know what he's talking about?" I asked him.

He nodded. "Yes. I was here the whole time."

"OK, so what did I say?"

"Do you remember anything from that time?" he asked, still not making eye contact.

I thought hard but couldn't remember a thing. In fact, I could barely remember the accident. The only vivid memory I had was of the man in the three-piece suit.

"I don't remember anything," I said.

"I think it's better we don't talk about it, Alex. If you can't remember, then it doesn't matter," he said.

I looked at him intently. "Why do you say it like that? What did I say?" I asked.

He walked over to an armchair next to the window on the other side of the room. He sat down and folded his arms. With the increased distance between us, he was able to look at me.

"You yelled and cussed a lot. The doctor said it was typical. You cussed out Kate, you know," he said, his voice was cracking.

"What?" I asked in utter shock.

"You called her some pretty bad names, and you said some pretty bad things to your uncle and his wife. You just kept going on and on anytime one of us would enter the room." Now his eyes were locked on the floor in front of him. "It was like…it was like you were possessed or something. Then you went back into the coma."

I was stunned. My face was numb, my arms and legs limp. I couldn't believe what he was saying.

"How could that be? I don't remember any of it," I said, dumbfounded.

Carl shrugged and then looked up at me. His eyes were red with tears. "You said some pretty bad stuff about me." He was shaking. "But I wouldn't leave you like they did. I wasn't gonna give up. We were all very scared, Alex." He wiped a tear from his cheek.

"What was I saying?" I asked, but a part of me didn't want to know.

He shook his head. "I don't want to repeat it, Alex. You said some really bad things."

"Like what?" Now I was thoroughly confused.

He held back his emotions and swallowed hard. A moment went by, and he didn't say anything. He just stared at the floor blankly; he was thinking. Then he raised his head and said, "You told Rick that he and your dad were…" He was unable to finish his sentence.

"Were what?" I asked.

"Well, um, gay," he said, choking on the last word.

I was shocked. Gay? What kind of thing was that to say?

"Carl, are you sure?"

He nodded.

"What about you? What did I say about you?"

He shook his head and stared down at the spot on the floor he had been eyeing a second ago.

"I'm sorry," I said. Now I was getting ready to cry.

A moment of silence passed, and then Carl spoke up again. "Something else," he said.

I looked at him in anticipation. "What?"

"I would sleep here on the weekends, and during your coma, in the middle of the night, you would talk out loud really quickly for like two seconds. At first, I disregarded it, but then you did it again. I was asleep, and you woke me. Both times you did it, it was late at night."

He paused and took a deep breath. "So then, like, two weeks ago, I decided to stay up all night and listen to see if you would do it again. Around three in the morning, you did. The only word I was able to make out was 'Azrael.'"

I was thoroughly perplexed. "Azrael?" I'd never heard the word before. I was not even sure it was a word.

He nodded. "Yes. I don't think anyone else heard you. I looked it up on the Internet. It means something."

"Really? What?" I asked.

"It's the name for the angel of death," he said.

I felt as if I had been hit in the face with a hammer. Until that point, I had not given any consideration to who the man might be; I'd just wondered whether he actually existed.

"Are you OK?" Carl asked, taking notice of my sudden shock.

"I saw a man," I said. "He took my family, and I'm sure he was here at the hospital once. Those nights you heard me talking, I was dreaming about him. Now you tell me I was saying the name for the angel of death while I was in a coma."

Carl looked at me, stunned. For a moment we didn't say anything. Then he asked, "What did he look like? How did he take your family?"

"With a rope," I said. "The rope had a mind of its own, and it attached to them. I didn't see him pull them. He made a scary face, and I couldn't look anymore. He was in a three-piece suit. He had long, oily black hair, and he wore a gold watch. The suit had really faint pinstripes on it. The vest too. He had a goatee, a short one."

Carl was mesmerized; he seemed to be in deep thought.

"He looked normal at first," I said. "But when he noticed that I was looking at him, his face turned into a monster. It was so scary. I screamed so loud, and—"

"You screamed?"

"Yes," I said.

"Alex, you almost died. You broke four ribs and punctured a lung. You could barely breathe on your own when they found you. Are you sure that was not just a dream?"

I thought for a moment. He was right. I remembered how much pain I had been in. Maybe I had passed out right away, and everything I remembered about this man was really a dream.

"It was so real. I don't know," I said helplessly. "Now you tell me I said his name. How could that be?"

"Did you know that Azrael was the name of the angel of death?" Carl asked.

"No," I said quietly, staring at the corner of the room where the man had stood.

"You could have read it somewhere—you know, in a book—or heard it in a movie," Carl said.

I just shook my head in dismay and looked at Carl. He was deep in thought. I was more worried now than I'd been before. Being crazy and having visions was one thing, but Azrael being real and haunting me was something else altogether. Based on the look on Carl's face, I knew we were thinking the same thing: it hadn't been a dream.

6

Rick and Alicia called and said they'd be coming by around five. They were very happy to hear I was doing better. I felt bad. Carl had told me that I had said some bad things about everyone and that no one could stand to be around me. It was going to be hard to look Rick in the eye knowing what I'd said about him.

Carl had said something else that disturbed me the more I thought about it. He'd said that I knew things about him that he did not realize I knew. Was it possible that what I'd said to everyone was true? That would mean what I said about Rick and my father was true. It couldn't be, though. Two grown men with wives and kids—how could they be gay? It made no sense to me. These thoughts made my stomach turn as if it were in a blender.

As five o'clock approached, my nerves began to consume me. I wanted to call Rick and Alicia and tell them that I was not feeling well and that I would prefer if they came tomorrow. Then there was Kate. No wonder she'd stayed away. I was a monster, and she was just helpless. I thought about all the bad things I must have said and wanted to cry. I looked at Carl, who appeared to be reading. But I bet he was using the book as an excuse to not talk.

"What about Kate?" I asked.

Carl held the book to his face for a second, avoiding the question. Then he looked up.

"Alex, I think it's better if we don't talk about it. Why do you need to know?"

"Carl, I want to know so I can apologize. It's not right," I said.

He sighed and stood up from the bench. He put the book on the windowsill and started to pace in front of my bed; he appeared to be deep in thought.

"It's not a calculus problem, Carl. Just tell me what I told her."

"It's not that," he said. "Kate was the first person by your bedside, even before me. She was also here when you opened your eyes the first time. She was here for you all along. Now you're saying that this guy who took your family came here and was standing in that corner." Carl pointed to the corner as he paced. "If you're saying that you saw him that day when the nurses had to sedate you, then it was a few days after that incident that you started to speak. If all this is true, then my guess is that you probably were possessed or something like that. I mean, we looked it up. This guy or thing—he's like a demon."

"So?" I asked, not following his point.

"So who cares what you said? It wasn't you. I still say you should apologize to everyone, but tell them that you don't remember a thing and that you had no idea what you were saying."

I breathed deeply. He made sense. Maybe I should move on—although it was killing me not to know every detail. I couldn't apologize for things I didn't mean to say. Worse, maybe it was better that I didn't know. This whole gay thing with my dad and Rick was really bothering me. Why add more to the pot?

"You're probably right," I said.

Carl seemed to like my response and gave me a smile. "Yes, and I accept your apology for everything you said about me. Although it was all true."

"All of it?"

He nodded, and I knew there was something on the tip of his tongue.

"Every word, good and bad," he said. He stopped pacing and was standing at the foot of my bed.

"Good?" I asked, wondering where he was going with this.

He smiled and looked me squarely in the eye. "I love you," he said.

I was taken aback. "Eh..." But I couldn't say anything else. An awkward silence followed.

Carl broke the silence. "When you were going through that phase, you told me that I was your...well, let's say you used a four-letter word, and that I loved you and that you never noticed me and that I would never have a chance. All that was and is still true. I've loved you since we were in middle school. You are the prettiest girl in the world, and you don't even know it. You are strong and confident. The way you laid out Jeremy—that was crazy. No other girl in school could have done that. I promised myself I would tell you as soon as I had a chance."

Now I couldn't look Carl in the eyes. He was the first boy ever to say this kind of thing to me, and to be quite honest, it made me blush. Carl had always been a part of the picture. My mother liked him, and everyone at school seemed to like him. The only problem was that I never liked him, let alone loved him. I could never understand why. He was almost a perfect guy. The fact that he had spent so many sleepless nights right here, next to me, for the past month said so much about him. But love was not in the cards for me, at least not now.

"Carl, you're the greatest—"

He smiled and shook his head. "I know how you feel, Alex. I'm OK with it. Just because I love you doesn't mean you're obligated to love me back. That's not how it works. I'm gonna stick around, and you tell me how you feel when the time comes. If the answer is that you don't feel the same way, I'll be fine. The mistake I made was entering the friend zone with you. I should have just asked you out in sixth grade."

"The friend zone?" I said, a little confused.

"Yes." His voice deepened a few octaves. "There is a fifth dimension beyond that which is known to man. It is the middle ground between light and shadow. It is an area which we call the Friend Zone."

"I don't get it," I said, smiling.

"*The Twilight Zone.* Hello," he said.

I shook my head. "You're such a nerd."

We laughed for a few moments, and Carl volunteered to go get me some food. This sounded like a really good idea, so I took the offer and instructed him to get me a burger from somewhere good. He gave me a smile and walked out.

***

I had fallen asleep when the knock on the door came.

"Hello," Rick said.

"Come in." I sat up in bed.

Rick walked in, flowers in hand. Alicia was behind him. Rick was a tall man, thin, and always neatly dressed. Alicia was a blonde with blue eyes. She was fighting, and losing handily, I might add, to drop her baby weight. Even with the extra pounds, she still looked pretty. She carried it very well.

"How are you feeling?" Rick asked hesitantly. Looking at their cautious stares, I couldn't imagine what I'd put them through.

"Fine," I said, smiling my best "everything is all right" smile.

"You look good," Alicia said.

"As good as a girl can look with stitches on the side of her head," I said.

Alicia smiled. "You should be thankful. We're all glad you made it out alive, honey."

"I'm sorry if I said anything that offended you guys," I said. The words just burst out of me.

They looked at each other and smiled nervously.

"Carl told me. Well, he left out the details, and frankly, I don't remember any of it, but I said it, and I'm sorry."

Rick gave me a smile. "You don't have to apologize. We know that wasn't you."

"I don't know who it was. This whole thing has really taken a toll," I said.

"Just hold on a little longer, honey. The doctor says it won't be much longer before you get out of here," Rick said.

I sighed. Although the past few weeks in the hospital was barely a memory, my body was telling me it had been too long.

Rick and Alicia sat down next to each other on the bench under the window. They eyed me as if I were a wild animal that was out of its cage. I could tell that I would have to do a lot more talking to convince them that I was feeling better.

"Can I come live with you guys?" I asked.

"Of course," Rick said. "We already have a room ready for you—bed set and everything."

I thought about my family and our house. I thought about my bedroom and longed to be back there.

"Also," Rick said, "there is a lot we have to do, you know, for the probate court."

"Court?" I asked.

"Yeah, well, your parents didn't have a will, and all the things have to be sold, including the house."

"What?" I was alarmed. "They can't sell the house. That's my parents' house."

"I'm sorry, Alex, but there's a large mortgage on it, and the home is barely worth what is owed," Rick said. "You won't be able to pay the mortgage in order to keep it. There's really no other choice."

"What about all our things?" I asked.

"You can keep those, but there's really not much of anything else. Your dad had a life insurance policy that lapsed because he stopped paying it. His job had one on him, but they said that was only in the event of death on the job. The son of a bitch that hit you guys didn't even have insurance, and now he's basically a vegetable."

My stomach was turning, and I wanted to cry. All this talk was making me sick. I could tell that Rick noticed.

"Don't worry, Alex," he said. "You can come live with us, and we'll take care of you as long as you want. Honestly, I don't care if you never move out."

I nodded, still very concerned, but knowing that I had a roof over my head did comfort me.

Carl came in at that moment, a greasy bag of food clenched in each hand. He had gone to Mitchell's, where the best burgers in Michigan—and, if you asked me, in the country—were made. It appeared that he had gotten enough for everyone.

"Hey, guys," he said, smiling as he placed the burgers on a tray.

"Hey," Rick said.

"Let's eat while the burgers are still hot," Carl said. He dug through one of the brown bags.

Usually, I could not eat more than one burger, but that night I was able to scarf down two without any problem. Each bite was more satisfying than the last, and as I filled my stomach, I started to feel better. I looked around at Carl, Alicia, and Rick as they were finishing their meals. They were my family now. With the exception of Kate, they were all I had left.

Carl was looking down at his food in his lap as he ate. Maybe I could learn to love him. Maybe in time we could be married and have kids and all that. Nobody else had done what he had, not even my own uncle. He was willing to take all the horrible things I had to say and suffer with me through near death, all because he loved me. I wished I could say that I felt the same for him. I wished I could fall in love as he had and make another person the center of my life. But I would be lying if I told him I loved him, and he knew it.

He looked up at me and smiled. I smiled back.

A FEW DAYS PASSED, AND I was moved upstairs in the hospital. I was now sharing a room with an old lady. As I was rolled in, she didn't so much as look in my direction. Nobody was there with her, and she was flat on her back, watching a soap opera. They said I would be out in a few days, and I was growing very impatient. Dr. Khan had come to see me every day for the past three days. He said he really was happy with my progress and wanted to get me out as soon as possible. Kate still hadn't come, and I hadn't called her. Carl offered to call her for me, but I vehemently opposed it. When I first heard the news of how I had acted toward everyone, I felt really bad for her, but a part of me wondered why she hadn't stuck by me as Carl had. Ultimately, I decided that I would go see her as soon as I was out of the hospital. While Carl didn't tell me what I had said about her, I figured it must have been really horrible to keep her away from me for so long.

I slept soundly the first night in my new room and woke up early the next day, a Sunday morning, to the sound of voices outside my door. There was a clock right in front of me; it was seven in the morning. I looked over to the old lady to my right. I had not spoken to her since I had gotten in the room and wanted to wish her a good morning. The curtain that separated us was out of the way, and I could see she was sound asleep, so I would have to wait. Carl had wanted to stay the night, but I'd sent him home. He'd stayed from Friday to Saturday, and I felt kind of awkward seeing him sleeping next to me. I did promise myself that I would give him a fair shake, but seriously, sleepovers were way down the line.

I stretched and let out a big yawn as I sat up in my bed. I was seeing a psychiatrist, Dr. Reynolds, and he had told me that every morning, I should try to remember everything I could since the accident. Everything since last Tuesday was clear as day, and so was everything before the accident. However, between the accident and the past Tuesday, I could barely make out a memory. It was as though I were trying to watch a movie that was blacked out by the cable company: every once in a while, a picture would form, but it would quickly disappear in a pattern of squiggly lines. For about twenty minutes that morning, I strained to remember anything. Nothing came to mind, so I stopped trying.

I called the nurse to let her know I was awake, and she brought me a breakfast of eggs and a blueberry muffin along with some coffee. The coffee was terrible, but it was the best I would have until Carl arrived. I made a mental note to remind him to grab me a cup when he called to tell me that he was on his way.

I ate my breakfast and watched Sunday morning's finest compilation of old cartoons and religious programming. Halfway through my eggs, just as I was going to take the first bite of my muffin, I suddenly froze with fear. I was looking down, but in my peripheral vision, I saw a man wearing all black in the doorway. It was him.

My right hand, holding the muffin, was shaking, and I could feel my heart rate increasing. I didn't look up; I couldn't look up.

The man strode into the room as though he owned the hospital. His shiny black shoes against the vinyl floor made a deep wooden sound that sent shudders through my body. I continued to stare down at my plate, holding the muffin just inches above it. He walked right by me and stood at the foot of the old woman's bed.

I was short of breath. My chest hurt from the pounding of my heart. I wanted to run, but I felt faint and weak. I closed my eyes and told myself that he wasn't there. I told myself I was just dreaming and that all this would be over as soon as I woke up.

Suddenly, an alarm went off right next to me. It was coming from the machine next to the old woman's bed. I was startled, and my reflexes forced me to look up. I locked eyes with the man. His pitch-black eyes gazed at me sternly as he held the gold watch in his right hand. Three hospital staff rushed into the room, but I barely noticed them, as I was entranced. Nobody but me seemed to notice that he was there as the alarm bells rang. Staff members yelled orders back and forth and ran in and out of the room. I couldn't break my gaze with him, and had he not looked away, I would have fainted.

"Isabelle Nelson," the man in black bellowed above the noise. "Your hour has arrived. Do you accept?"

I looked over at the old woman. A second head rose out of the head that rested on the pillow. The face on the raised head was much younger, and she said, "I accept."

I looked back at the man. He pulled the light-yellow rope that I had seen before. Its end did not break apart as it had before. It just slithered through the air and fell on the old woman's right hand. The man tugged on the rope, and I watched in shock as another person was pulled out of her. She was a much younger person, and she wore an all-white dress. The man started for the door, his gaze on me. I watched as he trotted past my bed with the woman in white floating behind him, tethered by the yellow rope. They left the room.

"She's dead," one of the hospital staff said.

I flipped onto my side, facing away from them, sending my food flying in all directions. I was still shaking, and my heart pounded like a drum. I closed my eyes and tried to calm myself down, but I was stricken with fear.

"Are you OK?" A woman said from behind me.

I collected myself enough to respond, my eyes still closed. "Yes. Just a bit shaken up."

"OK," she replied.

It was about twenty minutes before I got over the shock of seeing the man. Once I had enough courage to open my eyes, I kept looking at the door, waiting for him to return. The old woman, Isabelle, was wheeled off, and an empty bed was positioned beside me, ready for its next occupant. I began to cry. I was afraid and alone and wanted my parents more than anything.

I fell asleep sometime around nine in the morning and woke up a few hours later. Carl was sitting in the wingback chair to the right of my bed. He smiled when I opened my eyes. I didn't smile back.

"Doing OK?" he asked.

I shook my head. "No."

He looked cautious. "Why?"

I took a few deep breaths. Then I said, "He was here a few hours ago."

Out of the corner of my eye, I saw Carl dart to his feet. "What!" he exclaimed.

I turned my head and looked at the empty bed to my right. "He took the old woman who was in that bed. She died. I saw the whole thing. It was terrifying. He kept looking at me, and I was so scared. His stare…it's frightening."

Carl didn't say anything. I looked up at him; he looked very concerned.

"He pulled her…well, I guess her soul out of her body with that snake-like rope I told you about. Her soul was really young looking, and she was wearing white. I had a dream a few weeks ago that I was with my parents and Bailey, and they were all wearing white too. You think that means they are all going to heaven?"

Carl shrugged. "I guess."

"What do I do, Carl? I'm scared. What if he comes for me next? What if he pulls my soul out of my body and just kills me? He looks at me like he is going to do that, like he is really angry, and he's just waiting for the right time. I wish I'd just died," I said. Tears started falling from my eyes.

"Alex, you can't say that. All this—it's gonna get better. Think about it; the only time you saw this guy or thing or whatever it is, people died next to you. I mean, how many times is someone going to die right next to you? Maybe that's the only time you'll ever see him, or maybe you'll never see him again. In any event, you can't wish death on yourself."

He made sense, but I was still very worried. "I don't know, Carl. Something else is going on. He looks at me so harshly, like he's mad at me. He haunts me. Every night, I have nightmares about him. I get the feeling that he's after me."

The room fell silent. Carl paced in front of my bed. "Well," he said finally, "you can't tell your doctor about this. He'll think you're crazy."

"Maybe I am crazy," I said.

"No way. You saw this guy come when a lady died. You know his name; you mumbled it in your sleep. There's no way you could have known that. He's real, and you're able to see him somehow."

This made sense to me too. How could I have known his name? Of course, assuming that *was* his name. And I had seen him when people died. Maybe the other time I'd seen him was just my imagination. The dreams could simply be my own fears coming out. It was all so confusing.

"Maybe you're right," I said. "I'm just shaken up by all this. I really want to get out of here. I want to go back to school and start living a normal life again. Maybe I can put all this behind me and forget about it."

Carl nodded. He seemed pleased by my words. He reached out and took my hand. He stood over me, looking me in the eyes and giving me a gentle smile. Although it was very small and faint, something fluttered in the pit of my stomach as I stared into his eyes. I smiled back and clenched his hand tight against my chest.

"Sorry," I said.

"For what?"

"For whatever I said to you when I was going through that phase, and for not giving you a chance to be my boyfriend, and for turning you down when you asked me out."

"You don't have to—"

"No, I do. I have to because I was wrong."

He smiled. "Apology accepted."

"Thanks," I said. "And as soon as I'm home, I expect you to take me out, maybe to a movie."

He nodded. "Of course."

8

THE LAST FRIDAY IN SEPTEMBER was to be my final day in the hospital. I had missed a whole month of school. Even though I was a month removed from the accident and I had made much progress, I was still in some pain. It was early morning, and I was sitting up in bed, watching the news. Dr. Khan had come by the evening before, and he said that I could leave sometime in the afternoon. He suggested that I meet with my psychiatrist, Dr. Reynolds, one more time before I left.

Regardless of what was going on, though, I'd made a lot of decisions over the past few days, and I planned to stick to them. First, I decided that Carl was right; I would not tell Dr. Reynolds about my most recent encounter with Azrael. I needed to live a normal life, and I didn't need a psychiatrist telling me I was crazy.

I also decided I would do my best to move on. My life had taken a turn for the worse, and I was about as low as any person could be. However, I had to push forward and make the best of it. My family would want that for me. I remembered what my father had said by the beach in my dream. "We're very proud of you." He'd said it as though he knew something, and the more I thought about it, the more I understood. He was willing me on, telling me to live my life and make the most of it. The looks on their faces told me that they were fine, happy, secure, and in no pain. He was proud I had survived, I was going to move on, and I was going to be the person he had raised me to be. I didn't want to let him down.

The last thing I decided was that Carl would be my boyfriend. I was not going to let myself stop me from having someone, especially when I needed it most. I had kissed three boys in my life, the last one being Jeremy. Carl would be my fourth, and I hoped he would be my last. I was starting to feel something for him, and although it was not the immediate passion I had once felt for Jeremy, it was something, and that was a start. He had shown me over the past few weeks that he really did love me and that he would always be there. In time, I thought, I would feel the same way. In time, I thought, I could fall in love with him and get married and maybe have kids.

It was about nine in the morning when I heard a knock on my door.

"Come in," I called out.

The door opened. I expected Dr. Reynolds; instead, Dr. Khan walked in.

"Good morning, Ms. Drummond," he said. He wore his white lab coat over a pair of Dockers and a light-blue button-up shirt.

"Hello," I said.

"As promised, we are going to discharge you this afternoon. Dr. Reynolds called me early this morning and said he had an emergency, and he'd have to fly out. I told him I'd come by and see how you were doing and report back to him."

I smiled, and he smiled back. I was very glad he was there instead of Dr. Reynolds.

"Well, I think I'm going to be fine," I said. "I still have some pain, but I really want out of here."

Dr. Khan walked over to the wingback chair and sat down. He crossed his legs. "What about the man you spoke of—the one you saw walking around? Are you still seeing him?" he asked.

"No," I lied. "Not since the last time I told you. I've had a few bad dreams, but everything has been just fine."

Dr. Khan looked over to the still-empty bed next to us. "The nurse told me you were here when the patient in this bed died. Do you remember that?"

I nodded.

"Did you see anything then? You know, the man—did you see him?"

I took in a deep breath and nervously said, "No. I was just shaken up."

He sat up in his chair, uncrossed his legs, and looked me straight in the eye. I could tell that he knew I was lying. "One of the nurses told me she saw your face frozen on something, and you followed it across the room until your eyes arrived at the door. She said it was as if you were in a trance, but you were not looking at anything—just a blank wall. Do you remember that?"

I could feel my heart rate increase. Dr. Khan noticed that immediately on the heart-rate monitor on the screen. I couldn't say anything; I didn't want to.

"Alex, I hope you don't think I'm trying to give you a hard time, but I need to know if you saw anything. It is very important to your—"

"So you can put me in a crazy hospital?"

"No, of course not. Frankly, based on what you have told me, I'm inclined to believe you," he said.

Now I wondered if *he* was lying. "You believe me?" I asked.

He nodded. "I'm very religious, and I believe in the angel of death. Carl told me you mumbled Azrael in your sleep. That's his name in many cultures and religions around the world; it's one of his names where I come from. So if you tell me you saw a man appear when people died right next to you, I could believe that. If I didn't, I wouldn't be trusting my own faith. Of course, science cannot explain any of this. But if we are going to work to make you better, we need to know."

I looked at the doorway and hesitated for a moment. I contemplated telling him another lie, but I couldn't think of anything that would make any sense.

I looked back at Dr. Khan and said, "He walked out that door with the woman's soul. I saw him this time. I watched him pull her soul right out of her body. Before he did it, he asked if she accepted that her hour had arrived. She said yes, and then he took her."

"He asked her to accept?" Dr. Khan sounded confused.

I turned to look at him. "Yes. He asked my family too. He has this deep, powerful voice and this rope that can move like a snake. He looks at his gold watch before he takes the person."

By the look on his face, Dr. Khan was amazed. "That's a great bit of detail; do you see him clearly?"

"Clear as I'm seeing you right now. He has long, oily black hair and a black goatee. I even hear his footsteps as he walks. He's as real to me as anyone else."

Dr. Khan thought for a minute. "Why would he have to ask people to accept if they're already dead? That goes against most religious beliefs. Once you're dead, you're dead. There really isn't much to accept or deny."

"Well, he said it to everyone he took. He says people's names and asks if they accept, and they say yes. Then he takes them. I can't explain it." I let out a big sigh and dropped my head back on the pillow. "You know, maybe I am crazy. Maybe you should tell Dr. Reynolds to commit me and be done with it. Who knows?"

Dr. Khan was silent for a moment. I was staring up at the ceiling, so I could not see his reaction.

"Did you see this guy before the patient in the bed next to you died?" he asked.

I thought about it. I remembered that he had stood in the doorway, and he froze me. I was not sure whether the woman was dying before he came to the door. I closed my eyes and returned to the scene. After a moment, I was sure of the answer.

"Yes, he was in the doorway before everything happened. He walked past me and stood right there." I pointed at the space at the foot of the bed next to us. "Then everything went crazy. He took his eyes off me only to look at his watch and call out to the woman. It was like I was in a trance."

"What does he say exactly when he calls out?"

"It's been the same each time. So for the woman, he said, 'Isabelle Nelson, your hour has arrived. Do you accept?' And that's when they reply with yes."

Dr. Khan raised an eyebrow to this. "Did you know her name was Isabelle Nelson?"

I shook my head but I hadn't considered this at all. Maybe I had heard someone else say it before, but I couldn't remember.

I looked at Dr. Khan, who was rubbing his chin and appeared to be in deep thought.

"You think maybe your head injury gave you some ability to see him?" he asked after a long pause.

I shrugged. "Maybe."

He went back into deep thought for another moment, then said, "You're not crazy; no way. How could you have known the woman's name or that she was going to die? If you assume that you are making this guy up, then how would you know to manifest him before a woman right next to you dies? There is no way."

"Well, what about the time he came to the hospital when I was in intensive care? Since then, I have had bad dreams every night. Why would I see him then? Nobody died that day."

"That was very early in your recovery. That could have been a manifestation. The dreams—well, there is nothing you can do about them. You can't control your dreams."

"How about the feeling I get that he is after me, like he might come to me one day and just take my soul? I really think it's going to happen."

Dr. Khan shook his head. "Well, we all die, but I don't think he has the power to do that. If he did, he would have done it by now. This Azrael—or angel of death or whatever you want to call him—in all the Abrahamic religions, he has no power to kill. He is just a servant of God. I think therapy is going to help you out a lot in dealing with this. I will tell Dr. Reynolds that you are having bad dreams, but I won't mention the last encounter."

"Will he think I'm crazy if you mention the encounter?"

"Let's just say he doesn't really believe in religion, so his interpretation of the events will be purely scientific."

I smiled. Now I had two people on my side, Dr. Khan and Carl. This made me feel comfortable. Moving forward, I would always have someone to talk to.

Dr. Khan got up from his seat and pulled my chart from the clipboard slot at the footboard of my bed. He jotted down some notes, and I watched him quietly. For the first time, I noticed that he wore a wedding band.

"You're married?" I asked once he had stopped writing.

"Ten years in February. I have two girls too."

"Really?" I asked, amazed. "How old are you?"

He smiled. I could tell that most people reacted the same way to hearing this news. "Thirty-eight. I look much younger, I'm told."

I smiled. "No offense, but if you put on a pair of jeans and a T-shirt, you could pass for one of my classmates at the high school. It's OK, though. It's a good thing."

"Thanks." He reached into his coat pocket with his right hand and pulled out a business card. "This is my card. My office hours are scattered, depending on whether I'm in the hospital. Just call ahead and schedule an appointment anytime you want to talk. Mostly, I want to know if this Azrael pops up again. If he does, come see me right away."

I nodded and took his card. In raised, gold letters in the top, right corner, it read Ameer Khan, MD. The address and other information was in the middle, along with the Crescent City Hospital logo.

"I appreciate it, Doctor," I said as I put the card on the nightstand next to me.

"Of course. See you soon," he said.

We said our goodbyes, and he left. I felt better than I had felt since the accident, and I would be out of the hospital by the afternoon.

Seeing that I had some time to kill before I would be discharged, I thought I'd take a nap. I lay on my side and closed my eyes. Before I fell asleep, I made one more promise to myself. No matter what happened, I wasn't going to let Azrael ruin my life. I wished him gone and drifted away.

9

Rick and Carl came to get me in the afternoon. We packed up all my stuff, all the gifts and flowers, and headed out the second the nurse said we could go.

I was ecstatic that I was leaving. It felt so good to put on a pair of jeans and a T-shirt, to have the cool breeze caress my face as I was wheeled out of the hospital through the automatic double doors, and to be with family once again.

I was still very weak, and my chest, head, and left arm still hurt. I took care getting into the car with Carl's help. Rick loaded the back of the SUV. In line with my promise to myself, I sat in the back of Rick's SUV with Carl, and I held his hand the entire ride. I could tell he was nervous; his hands were clammy, and he didn't say a word the whole ride. Rick and I exchanged some information about some of the things I needed to do for the probate court, most of which I barely understood.

Rick and Alicia's red-brick bungalow was nestled in a nice little neighborhood in Crescent City. It was just off Michigan Avenue, and the road that led to their house was winding and lined with trees. Although Rick was being particularly evasive about the sleeping arrangements, I figured my room would be the upstairs bedroom. I had been in it numerous times before; Rick had stored his guitars in it, along with his sports gear, CDs, books, and all the other pre-Alicia memorabilia that Alicia wished had stayed pre-Alicia. He had always told me that all women wished they had one of those wands that were used in the *Men in Black* movie to erase memories. That way, as soon as a guy said, "I do," they could delete every happy thought he had ever had that was not a product of his current relationship.

Alicia had taken the twins to the doctor for a checkup, and the house was empty. Rick and Carl brought my modest suitcase and all the flowers and gifts into the house. I insisted on walking without any help, and I was pretty proficient. Rick and Carl led me upstairs, and once I was at the top of the stairs, I was amazed by the sight.

"Oh my God!" I said loudly, my eyes beginning to water.

They had transformed the attic into one of the nicest rooms I'd ever seen—new paint, new carpet, new window dressings, and new furniture. All my clothes were neatly hung in the closet and folded in the drawers of my all-new bedroom set. There was a small TV right in front of my bed and a desk with my computer on it. There was a pink-and-white-striped comforter on the bed with matching pillows. On my nightstand was a card.

Rick and Carl stood by and smiled as tears fell from my eyes. I walked over to the nightstand to pick up the card. I wiped my eyes and read what it said.

> *Welcome home, Alex. Consider this your home forever. We will always be there, no matter what happens, and we all love you very much. We all lost something not long ago. Now let's get through it together, as a family.*
>
> *Rick, Alicia, and Carl*

Reading this just made me cry more, and I sat down on the bed. Carl came and put his arm around me. I nestled my head into his shoulder. After a few minutes, my tears subsided.

"Let's go get some burgers and milkshakes," Rick said as soon as my tears stopped. I laughed at this. He always knew how to lighten the mood. He knew I hated verbal confrontations, and to share any more sentiment than was on that card would just make me feel uncomfortable.

"Let's do it," I said, sniffling and wiping my face with my T-shirt.

Carl smiled. "Sounds great to me."

I looked at Rick. "Can you give us a minute before we go? I want to talk to Carl."

He smiled and nodded. "I'll be in the car. Don't take too long. I'm starving."

He left the room, and I listened intently as his footfalls descended the stairs and crossed the first floor to the front door. Carl just sat next to me, his arm still around my shoulders and a perplexed look on his face.

I lifted my left hand to Carl's face and turned it into my own. For the first time in my life, I initiated a kiss with a boy. He was notably surprised, but he settled into it after a moment. We kissed for what felt like an hour. To me, I was not just kissing him; I was letting out every ounce of anxiety that had built up in me for the past month. Every pain, every worry, and every fearful thought I had was fluttering away as our passion ensued. He tried to pull away, but I wouldn't let him. I held him by the back of his head, and our tongues jostled about like swords. He never once moved to touch my body; both of his arms remained neutrally around my shoulders.

I finally let him go. His face was tomato red. I smiled. He smiled back, unable to hold my gaze.

"I guess that means we're boyfriend and girlfriend," I said.

He laughed. It sounded like a relieved laugh. "I guess."

"Let's go," I said, jumping up to my feet.

He remained planted on the bed, his hands crossed in his lap. "I'll meet you down there. I need a minute," he said.

I held in my laughter as best I could, and without another word, I left the room. Last time I had given a guy an erection, it hadn't turned out so well, I thought. Better quit now while I was ahead.

Rick was waiting in the SUV. He gave me a coy smile as I climbed into the passenger's seat.

"Where's Carl?" he asked.

"He was right behind me. Maybe he stopped to use the bathroom," I said nonchalantly.

He nodded, and we were silent for a moment. Then he said, "You know, we're serious. You can stay here as long as you need—forever, even. I know you're turning eighteen this year. Don't think that means you have to go."

"I know," I said, looking out the window at a female neighbor raking some leaves three doors down.

"And whenever you're ready, we can go visit…" He paused, but I knew what he was talking about.

"I want to go today, after we eat," I said before he could finish. I kept my gaze out the window as I spoke, watching as the woman raking the leaves lumped them into a large brown bag.

"And we can do all the other stuff, the probate paperwork with the attorney, when you're ready," he said.

The woman filled one bag and set it aside. She bent to get another bag, and then, directly behind her, I saw him. It was Azrael, and he was staring at me. I was taken by surprise and jolted so far back in the car seat that my hip hit the gearshift.

"What is it?" Rick exclaimed as I turned my face away and covered my eyes.

I breathed deeply and settled myself down. He wasn't going to win, I told myself. I raised my head and looked at Rick. He was looking at me with great concern.

"Are you OK, Alex?" he asked, his hand on my shoulder.

I turned and looked back toward the woman. She was loading the second bag of leaves. Azrael was no longer visible, if he'd ever been there to begin with.

"Fine," I said. I heard Carl trotting down the porch steps. "Just jumpy from the accident." I kept my eyes on the woman. "Just need some time, you know?"

Carl got into the back seat and closed the door. The car was silent.

"Everything OK?" Carl asked.

"Great. Let's go get some burgers and shakes," I said.

Rick started the car, and I kept my eye on the spot just beyond the woman. As we backed out of the driveway, Azrael was visible again. He was still staring at me.

"Can you go down this way?" I pointed in my direction.

"Sure, I guess. Alex, are you sure you're OK?" he asked.

"Yeah, just do it, please. It's important," I said.

He turned in that direction, and as we rolled down the street, Azrael's gaze never left mine. He was standing on a lawn that was two doors down from the woman raking her leaves. As we approached, his black eyes followed me the whole way. I stared back at him intently. I wanted him to know that I wasn't afraid.

"What are you looking at?" Rick asked.

"Nobody," I said, my eyes still fixed on Azrael's gaze.

"Is it him?" Carl asked from the back seat.

"Yes," I said.

Rick was driving slowly, and he slowed even more as we approached the lawn where Azrael stood. "Who are you talking about?" he asked.

"Stop here," I said, once we were in front of Azrael.

Rick stopped the car and started talking, but I didn't hear him. My eyes were fixed on Azrael's, and I couldn't move. His pitch-dark eyes seemed to speak to me; they pulled me in. I felt as though I were floating in the air. The world around me was still and calm. My heart beat slowly, calmly, as though even it was mesmerized by the gleam in those eyes. I saw my family, deep within him, past the darkness of his stare. They were floating; their lips were moving, but I couldn't make out what they were saying.

Azrael smiled, and I smiled back. His sharp teeth showed between his parted lips. It was a devilish smile, a seductive, entrancing smile.

I was shaken out of my daze. I turned my head and looked from Rick to Carl. Concern was painted on their faces.

"Are you OK?" Rick said again.

I nodded, still in shock. Azrael wasn't going to win, I told myself.

"I'm fine," I replied. But I wasn't fine; I was scared. I tried my hardest not to be, but I was—more than I had ever been before. Terror consumed me, swallowed me up, and engulfed my senses. He had pulled me in with a simple stare. What else could he do? What other terrible tricks would be at his disposal when he got me alone?

"Let's just get out of here," I said, looking at the road ahead. As we drove off, out of the corner of my eye, I could see that Azrael was still standing on the lawn; he was still smiling.

10

W E WENT TO A CHAIN burger place called Red Stripe. It had the best milkshakes, and the burgers weren't half-bad, either. Even with the shock of seeing Azrael, I devoured my food as though I were competing in an eating contest. It was amazing how much I missed about everyday life after being stuck in a hospital for a month.

We finished eating at a quarter after six in the evening. Rick and Carl did most of the talking, as I was deep in thought throughout the meal. I was thinking about Azrael and what my next step would be.

Carl and I exchanged many knowing glances as we ate. I could tell that he wanted to ask about what had happened. I explained to Rick that I was not myself and that I thought I had seen someone in the house we'd stopped in front of. I also told him that I would rather not elaborate, and I made it a point to look at Carl when I said that so that he would not press the issue any further.

We left the restaurant and made our way toward the cemetery. A part of me didn't want to go. The thought of seeing concrete slabs on the ground with Mom's, Dad's, and Bailey's names on them was unsettling. I had thought about this trip often, and each time I'd come to the same conclusion: I was afraid of closure. I feared the idea of spending the rest of my life without my family as much as I feared Azrael. I had never wanted to believe that any of this had really happened. I'd never once admitted to myself that it was true, even when it was happening right in front of me. Seeing those gravestones would be that final piece of evidence my conscious mind needed to convince my subconscious mind that this was not a dream—that it had all really happened, and it was as terrible as I thought it was.

We turned onto the cemetery's winding road. Rick was driving slowly, and graves passed us one after another. I looked out my window at all the dead. The graves seemed to continue on forever on either side of the road. Every few yards, there would be a statue or a small structure that looked like a house.

We came to a stop just before the road made a wide loop to the left to take us back in the direction we'd come. I looked over at Rick; he had a solemn expression. "Just over there," he said, pointing. "If you want, we can leave you alone."

I thought for a moment and decided that it was best that way. "Please," I said.

"You see that statue, the white one? Just about ten feet to the right of it, if you are facing it," Rick said. "Take as much time as you need."

I nodded and got out of the car. I had taken a sweater with me when we left the house, and as expected, the weather was colder as the sun started to set. I opened the rear door and took the sweater from the back seat. Carl gave me a small smile of encouragement. I just nodded and closed the door.

It was about fifty yards away, and each step felt as if it were uphill at a forty-five-degree angle. My legs told me to turn back and forget all this, that I wasn't ready. My brain was shut off to all thought. It had no idea why I was putting myself through such a trauma. It was my gut that urged me on. It said that I had to do this, that the first step to moving on was right there in that cemetery.

My father's gravestone was the first one I saw. His name was printed at the top. Victor Drummond, it read in bold capital letters, 1974–2013. At this sight, my eyes filled with tears. "Daddy," I said, choking.

I turned my head slowly to the right and found my mother's gravestone. It said her name and the same years. I cried harder now, barely feeling able to move. Like the gravestone, I was planted there for a long moment, tears pouring from my eyes as I stared at her name.

For a very long time, I didn't look at Bailey's marker. I didn't want to. I didn't want to see her name etched in stone with only six years separating her first year from her last. I could see it out of the corner of my eye—even make out the first letters of her name. My heart was pounding rapidly, and tears ran from my eyes. Once I gathered up the courage, I held my breath and turned my head.

I had watched so many movies in which people went to see a loved one's grave and conversed as if the deceased were right next to them. I did nothing of the sort. Instead, I fell to my knees and started wailing. I buried my head in the sleeves of my sweater and cried harder and louder than I ever had before. I crawled on my hands and knees to Bailey's stone and hugged it as if I were hugging a person. The tears poured out of me like raindrops from a dense cloud.

After about ten minutes, I was all cried out. My eyes were crusty, my heart rate had slowed, and I was no longer gasping for air.

I sat back on the ground, looking at the gravestones. I revisited the dream I had had by the beach. I saw my parents and Bailey dressed in white, the smiles on their youthful faces, and heard the conversation. "We're proud of you," my father had told me, and although it confused me at first, I think this visit to the cemetery told me what I needed to know. They wanted me to move on, to go on with my life and do great things, be an adult. I wanted all those things too.

"I won't let you guys down," I said to the quiet, cool breeze that blew in my direction. "I promise."

I sat there for a long while. The sun was setting behind me. I thought about all the great memories we had together. I thought about all the trips to the park; the cookouts in the backyard; and the one family vacation we took to Disney World when Bailey turned three. I thought about my mother and how she had always been there for me. I regretted shutting her out of my personal life and wished I could have shared so much more with her. If I could go back, I would tell her all about every boy I had ever liked—every detail.

I thought about my father and all the fun we had camping up north. I thought about all the things he taught me and how much time he spent with me. I thought about how much love we had, and how perfect it was.

I thought about Bailey and how she made me smile every time she said something. My biggest regret would be not seeing her grow up and become a woman. I wished they were all next to me one more time. One more family hug and kiss. The cool breeze picked up slightly as that thought crossed my mind. I smiled.

"Goodbye," I said to the gravestones. "I'll be back soon."

I got up from my knees and started walking back to the car. I was much lighter now; the weights around my ankles had been taken away. My brain was calmly processing all the information, and it was telling me that everything was going to be OK. My gut had been right all along; I guessed that was why most people found it so trustworthy. For the first time since the accident, I felt ready to move forward.

Of course, as ready as I was to move on, life had other plans for me. What I thought was the end of a long road was only the beginning of an even longer journey—a journey that would test every one of my beliefs to the point of insanity, a journey that would change everything.

11

I SPENT MOST OF THE WEEKEND getting ready for school. Carl had all my homework neatly organized in five folders, one for each class. I had two more "classes" called co-op, which were not actually classes. The deal was that I had to get a job, and I'd be excused from school for the first two hours of the day. Only seniors could join this program, and I had been looking forward to it since I first heard about it in sophomore year. I was never a morning person.

Carl spent all of Saturday and most of Sunday up in my room, helping me with my homework. We kissed on and off, and he told me that he loved me again. I didn't respond, again; but I did give him a long kiss after he said it.

By Sunday evening, all my homework was caught up, and I was feeling a lot better about myself. I wasn't the best student in the world—I mostly got by with Bs and Cs, but I had never failed a class, and I didn't want to start in my senior year.

We spent the evening with Rick and Alicia; the twins were with Rick's parents. They took us out to Applebee's, and we all stuffed our faces. By the end of the night, I was spent. Carl gave me a final, long good-night kiss on the stoop before going home. I retired at around ten and slept soundly. Counting that night, it was the first time I had gone two nights in a row without dreaming about Azrael. It was also the first time I had felt safe for two nights in a row.

My first real class after co-op started at ten in the morning. Of course, I was hopelessly unemployed, so I had to get up early and meet with the co-op coordinator, who would help me find a job.

Seven in the morning was an ungodly hour. My alarm rang promptly at that time. It was a very loud alarm—the buzzer sounded as though it were warning everyone of a fire or an invasion by a foreign enemy. It did the trick, though; it brought me out of my slumber within seconds. Even with nine hours under my belt, I still felt as though a force greater than gravity was pulling me toward my comfortable bed and pillow. It was seven-thirty by the time I finally got out of bed, and by then, I was already running late. I hustled to the bathroom downstairs and got dressed as quickly as I could.

Rick was drinking coffee and reading a paper at the dining room table. I paused for a second as I came into the room—he reminded me of my dad as he sat there. I pushed the memory aside and went over to the coffeepot.

"Morning," he said with a smile.

"Morning," I said, pouring myself a cup. "Sorry I woke up late."

"That's OK. It's technically the first day of school for you. Anyway, I have good news."

"Really? What?"

He waited until I sat down with my coffee.

"I got you a job," he said. "You can help work the phones at the construction site. The girl quit last week."

"Really?" I said, very excited. Rick and my father had worked construction together for years, and when I was younger, my father took me to their job sites a few times. From what I remember, there was a trailer on the site that they all called the office, and I would spend the whole day there with whoever was handling the phones. I always thought it would be a fun job.

"Yes, you'll be handling calls and coordinating schedules—stuff like that. It should be really easy for you. You're very smart."

I smiled. "Very smart" was a bit of a stretch, but I wasn't going to argue.

"I can't wait," I said. "Let's go to school and tell the coordinator so I don't have to wake up this early again. I'm so happy," I said. I stood up, hugged Rick, and kissed him on the cheek.

After I finished my second cup of coffee, we got into the car and drove to school. My appointment with the co-op coordinator was at eight, and we walked out of the house at a quarter past eight. As we drove, Rick said he'd wait for me in the parking lot. After I gave the coordinator all the job details, we'd go to the International House of Pancakes and have breakfast.

After a ten-minute ride, we arrived. Crescent City High School was a very large school. Even though Rick parked at the very front of the circular driveway, it was still a long walk to the administration offices. I hurried along the empty hallways. Classes were in session, so nobody was supposed to be in the hallways without a pass from a teacher. I walked into the main office and was greeted by a student who was working there. She sat behind a very large brown desk that had neat stacks of paper organized all over it.

"Hey," she said as if she knew me. I wasn't sure who she was.

"Hi," I said.

"Alex, right?" she said with a slight smile.

I nodded. "Yeah. I have an appointment. Sorry I'm late."

She waved off my apology. "Don't even mention it. After everything that happened, we're just glad you're back."

I nodded again. "Thanks."

"No problem. By the way, I'm Lisa. I'm a junior."

"Nice to meet you," I said, shaking her hand. "Now I know why I didn't recognize you."

She laughed. "No worries. I'll let Mr. Harms know you're here."

"Oh, can you tell him I found a job?" I said before she turned to walk away.

"Sure," she said, smiling. She walked through a door on the right that led to various offices.

A few minutes later, she returned with a piece of paper.

"He said that since you found a job, you can just fill out this form and have your boss sign it. Bring it back here and drop it off. Then you're all set."

I took the form and thanked her. I was relieved and looking forward to breakfast, so I darted out of the office.

I turned to the right and headed toward the front door. Something caught my eye. It was two people, standing very close to each other at the end of the hallway. I had already turned toward the door when I decided to look back. It was a guy and a girl kissing. They were about fifty feet away, and I couldn't quite make out who they were at first. Then I stopped and stared hard. Kate?

I walked in their direction, my footsteps echoing slightly in the empty hallway. After a few steps, they both looked in my direction. Jeremy and Kate?

I stopped. We stared at each other. They both wore stunned expressions.

Anger was not a strong enough word for how I felt at that moment. Infuriation was a little closer, but even that could not explain the rage that came over me. I wanted to attack them both and inflict pain. I wanted to yell and scream and cause a scene. I clenched my fists and bit my lip. I took one step toward them, and then I turned and marched toward the front door.

"Wait!" Kate called as she ran toward me.

I walked faster. With a fifty-foot head start, I could be out of the building before she caught up to me.

"Alex, please," she said, and I could tell that she was getting closer.

I crashed through the first of the two double doors, and she caught up to me just as I stepped outside the second set of doors.

She placed her right hand on my shoulder, and that made me even angrier.

"Don't touch me!" I yelled as I turned to face her.

She looked terrified.

"You and me—we're not friends anymore. I can't believe you!"

She opened her mouth to talk, but I interrupted her. "I don't care what your explanation is! As far as you're concerned, I died in that car accident!"

She was tearing up, but I didn't care. That was exactly the reaction I was going for. I couldn't believe what I had just seen, and the more hurt she was, the better.

I shook my head at her and clenched my teeth, giving her a grave look of disdain. She lifted both hands to her face and started crying uncontrollably. I just stared at her for a second, not saying anything.

"Goodbye," I said as I turned to walk away. Rick was parked far enough from the doors that he couldn't hear me, but he was close enough to see that she was crying.

I arrived at the car and got into the front passenger seat, not once making eye contact with Rick.

"You OK?" he asked.

I looked over at Kate, who was in Jeremy's arms. He'd come out to comfort her.

"Never been better," I said, still shaking with rage.

We drove in silence for a few miles. Then Rick got a call from work. I was relieved that he spent the rest of the drive talking on the phone. I just stared out at the passing scenery and kept seeing Kate and Jeremy kissing at the end of the hall.

We stopped at IHOP and got a table for two. I was immediately revisited by memories from my youth. My father and I used to go there often. We always left full and a little closer to each other than we had been when we went in. We mostly came after Bailey was born, when my mother was too busy with all the things that came with a new baby to make breakfast for us. I got the hint that my mother wanted us out just as much as we wanted to leave. My dad always said that women get crazy after they have a child, and it's best to just leave them alone.

I ordered a stack of classic pancakes, and Rick had an omelet. The server was an older woman; she had to be in her late fifties. She was heavyset and smiled as if she had just won the lottery while she took our orders.

"So you want to talk about anything?" Rick said after she brought our coffee.

I thought for a moment. At first, the thought of talking about Kate and Jeremy with Rick seemed awkward. Then I wondered who else I could talk to. Alicia was great, but she and I were not close—not like I was with Rick. The only other person I really had was Kate, but, of course, she was the star of this melodrama.

"Just one of my friends—or at least I thought she was my friend— did something I didn't like," I said.

"You mean Kate? She seems really nice," Rick said as he took a sip of his coffee.

I sighed. "She never called. She never visited me in the hospital, and then the first time I see her outside the hospital, she's kissing a guy I absolutely hate."

Rick shrugged slightly. "She did visit, you know; she took it pretty hard. I was there."

"Carl said she came," I said.

Rick shook his head. "I saw her many times, once with Carl. The first time, she was there with you by herself. It was right after the accident. I came to the door and heard someone crying, and when I walked in, she was at your bedside, sobbing her eyes out. She looked at me and then just got up and left, crying the whole way. Not sure you should write her off so quickly, Alex. People handle things differently. What happened to your family was not easy. We were all affected."

His words made me feel very bad for yelling at Kate. I guess I could understand why she went out with Jeremy—that jerk was a predator, and I bet when he caught wind of the accident, he ran to her side to "comfort" her. I knew his type, and Kate was the perfect prey. She always had a boyfriend because she had such a large emotional disconnect with her parents, especially her father. What I couldn't understand was why she had not been there for me the way Carl was. There was a withered bouquet of flowers from her among the lot that I'd taken home, but she was conspicuously gone from my life—so much so that at times I found myself forgetting all about her.

"Well, she still could have come to see me, you know, when I was awake. She didn't even call when I left the hospital," I said bitterly.

"Like I said, everyone has their way of handling things. Just give it time. Promise me, though, the next time you see her, you'll talk to her about all this."

"No way. That's in like two hours," I said, realizing that Kate and I had registered for all the same classes.

"Well then, at least promise that if she approaches you, you'll give her a chance to explain. You don't even need to say a word; trust me. This has happened to me, and I regret the day I lost a good friend because I couldn't at least hear him out, let alone forgive. Remember, Alex, what you've been through can be seen in two ways. Right now, it's by far the worst thing that has ever happened to you, but you just as easily could have died right there with the rest of your family. Even the doctors said your survival was a miracle. Don't waste the time you have now on anger. You should treat every day as if it is a gift from God and cherish every relationship."

I nodded. He was right. I was wrong. A few tears fell from my eyes.

"OK," I said, wiping them away with my sleeve. "I promise."

The heavyset server returned with our pancakes, still smiling. I was so hungry that I inhaled them in a matter of minutes—so fast that Rick was only halfway through his omelet when I finished. He smiled at the sight of me.

"You want seconds?" he asked as he poked his plate with his fork.

"No way," I said, patting my stomach. "Sorry I ate so fast, but it's been so long since I've had IHOP."

He shook his head and smiled. "I don't blame you. If it was me, I think I would have ordered and eaten the entire menu. I had the flu one time, and it lasted a week. I couldn't eat anything. The second I was better, your dad and I went out, and I ate seven double cheeseburgers. I was so full I wanted to puke."

"Seven?" I said, amazed.

He smiled and nodded as he chewed. "Well, I don't think I'll ever be able to do that again, no matter how hungry I am."

"How old were you?" I asked.

He thought for a minute, his eyes wandering. "Second year of college." Then I saw a flicker in his eyes, and he looked down at his plate. While I'd lost my mom and dad, he'd lost his sister and his best friend. I could tell it still hurt to talk about the past.

"Rick, can I tell you something?"

He looked up. "Sure. Anything."

"I had a dream about my parents and Bailey. We were in a restaurant or some kind of outdoor café, and we were right by the beach. I even heard the sounds of the waves. They were all wearing white, and I somehow knew that they were all dead. In the dream it felt right, you know? Like their dying was OK. They were even smiling, and I was smiling. So what I mean to say is that I think that they are all OK. It was like they came to visit me one more time before they went on. They all seemed so happy."

He nodded. As I was talking, I'd noticed that his eyes were beginning to water, and when I finished, a single tear fell from his right eye. As he wiped it away, he said, "I had a similar dream, except they came to my house. They told me to take care of you, that you'd make us all proud. I agreed to take care of you as if you were my own."

"Proud?" I asked. "My dad said the same thing to me in my dream. He said, 'We are proud of you,' and I wasn't sure what that meant. It's so weird that he would say something similar to you."

Rick shook his head and wiped more tears. "Sorry," he said.

"That's OK," I said.

"It's just...I didn't even tell Alicia about the dream. Actually, you're the first person I've told. And you're right—it felt so real. Come to think of it, I did know that they were dead, and I was OK with that, like it was no big deal."

I nodded, and a chill ran down my spine. "Wow."

Rick shrugged. "You know, I guess things aren't what they seem. All these things, they happen for a reason. Since the accident, I've been going to church every Sunday and Wednesday. You should come."

I nodded, but I disagreed. I had always believed in something—God or whatever you want to call him—but my dad taught me a lot about organized religion, and I'd grown to dislike it. My grandfather, my dad's father, was a pastor, and he had been very hard on my dad. He taught him a lot about faith, and the more my dad learned, the more he came to believe that if everyone just practiced his or her own religion at home, the world would be a better place. And now, even with something following me around and pulling souls out of people's bodies, I still believe the same thing.

"So do you think our dreams were real?" I asked.

Rick nodded. "No doubt. When my father died, he came to me in a dream, and it felt the same way. Since then, the only dreams I've had of him were like memories. Even my mother told me that months after he died, she had a dream that he came to visit her. These things are real, Alex. The fact that you lived through that horrific accident should tell you all you need to know."

I sipped my coffee and watched as the heavyset server wobbled her way around the dining room with a pair of dishes. She smiled as she placed them on a table occupied by an elderly couple. Her back was to me, and when she turned, she took notice of me looking at her. She wobbled back in my direction.

"Anything else I can get you, hon?" she said with a bright smile.

I couldn't help but smile back. "No."

"You ate those like you had never had pancakes before. You must have been really hungry," she said.

I nodded. "Yeah, it's been a while since I've had them. They were very good. Thanks."

She looked over at Rick and said, "Is this your daughter, sir?"

Rick shook his head. "Niece."

"My parents died in a car accident," I said.

She looked at me, and the smile left her face. "I'm sorry to hear that, dear. When was the accident?"

"A little over a month ago," I said. "It was my parents and my little sister."

She raised her eyebrows. "I heard about that accident. That was terrible. It's a blessing you survived, you know."

"That's what everyone keeps saying," I said.

Her face suddenly turned solemn. "My dear, when God blesses you, it's for a very good reason. You should pray every day and be thankful. God chooses to take whom he wants, and he leaves others be. You have a purpose, I assure you."

She seemed to make sense, but, just like my father, I didn't like being preached to. "Thanks," I said shortly, hoping that would end the conversation.

She tilted her head at me, noticing my evasiveness.

"You know why I smile all the time, dear?" she asked.

"Because you want good tips?" I said. I felt Rick lightly kick my shin under the table.

She laughed gently. "For three years, from age thirty-seven to forty, I was homeless. Slept under an overpass, pushed shopping carts around, the whole nine yards. The manager here, his name is James. He saw me outside one day in the parking lot. I was looking for cans. He told me he'd give me five dollars if I cleaned the parking lot. Well, I did it, and he gave me the money. I came back a few days later and did it again, and he paid me again. After two months, he offered me a job washing dishes. That's what I did before he made me a waitress. That was my first job in over ten years. A few weeks after that, I got my first paycheck, and for the first time in a long time, I smiled. I've been smiling ever since." She looked at me intently. I was moved by her story. "Every day is a blessing, my dear; don't you ever forget that."

I nodded, unable to respond.

She smiled, collected our dishes, and placed our check on the table. "I'll take that up when you're ready," she said to Rick.

"Thanks," Rick said.

She walked away.

"Some story, huh?" Rick said.

"Yeah."

We paid our bill and said our goodbyes to the waitress. She told us her name was Faith and she worked every weekday. We could come by anytime, and she'd take care us. I felt full and happy, so I decided that would be a pretty good idea—maybe even as soon as tomorrow.

We drove back toward the school, and the food I had just consumed started to do somersaults in my stomach. I looked at the clock; it was just before ten, and third period was about to start. I was less worried about the physics class than I was about seeing Kate. A part of me hoped she was so distraught by our altercation that she had just gone home, and I could put off seeing her until tomorrow.

Rick dropped me off and bid me a good day. I thanked him again for the job and gave him the document that the co-op coordinator wanted signed so that he could take it to work.

It was between periods as I walked into the school building. As soon as I was through the front doors, I encountered a rush of bodies walking in every direction.

I pulled out my schedule and looked up the classroom number. It was across the building in D hall. I started walking in that direction, and as I did, I was visited with a hundred different memories of the past three years. The building was a very large square, and it had a big courtyard in the middle. Freshman classes were located close to the front of the building, and classrooms for higher grades were located progressively farther from the main entrance.

Behind the main structure were the gymnasium and pool, and beyond them, in the outdoor area, was a park, a football field, and a baseball diamond.

Even with an entire year left before I would graduate, I was already beginning to miss the place. As I crossed the underclassmen's hallways, I recalled all the life changes that had occurred within these walls. I was saddened to think about how big a part Kate played in most of my memories.

I noticed a lot of students staring at me. Many of them said hello or gave me a nod and a smile. I returned their greetings in kind, and for the first time, I realized how many people knew who I was because of the accident. I was more popular than the star football player at this point. I was the girl who had cheated death. Little did they know that death seemed to be very displeased by that and had been following me around ever since.

I arrived at my locker and looked at my schedule, which had the combination to the lock. I opened it, and I was instantly shocked.

Every inch of the inside of my locker was covered with some sort of decoration. Flowers of all colors, pink and red streamers, and the little bows that you put on presents. On the door, a banner said, "Welcome back, Alex!" in big, pink block letters. Under that message, the paper was torn, and a piece of tape hung down. I thought about it, and only one explanation came to mind: Kate had put this whole thing together, and she had removed whatever she'd taped there after I had yelled at her.

My heart sank at the thought of her sobbing as she opened that locker and removed the proof that she was behind that extravagance.

"Hey, Alex!" Carl called from behind me.

I turned around, and he was standing right behind me. I smiled, and he leaned in to kiss me. I sidestepped his advance, and he almost fell into my open locker.

"Whoa, Carl. Sorry," I said, feeling kind of bad. "It's a reflex; I'm just not comfortable with that stuff in public."

He gave me a disappointed smile. "That stuff?"

"You know what I mean. Whatever. I think the rules of being boyfriend and girlfriend mean I should be mad at you right now anyway," I said, raising my eyebrow at the open locker full of decorations.

He looked at the locker and then back at me. "Yeah, I heard about what happened with you and Kate today. I'm sorry, but when you were in the hospital, Dr. Reynolds said not to tell you things that would get you mad, and well, I thought the thing with Kate and Jeremy would royally piss you off."

"Well, you could have said something yesterday or the day before. I had to find out by walking in on them kissing. I can't believe it. Then I yelled at Kate and made her cry. I don't know; I feel so bad now," I said.

Carl opened his mouth to speak but hesitated. It appeared that he was choosing his words carefully. "I think she was wrong not to visit you once you were awake, but I don't think her seeing Jeremy is a big deal," he said finally. The look on his face told me that he was bracing himself for what I was about to say.

I understood. He was right. Deep down, seeing Kate kissing Jeremy made me angry, but another emotion was also rooted down there: jealousy. Carl, as my boyfriend, had identified it. He was telling me that I had nothing to be jealous about. I had a boyfriend already, and Kate was free to date whomever she wanted.

"You're right," I told him. "It was just…I don't know. I should talk to her, shouldn't I?"

Carl nodded. "Third period is going to start soon. Maybe after that."

I smiled and squeezed his hand. "Thanks."

He smiled, and the bell rang right after that. I gave him an excited look. I wasn't used to hearing the bell go off six times a day, so it startled me. I lifted up on my tippy-toes and gave him a kiss on the cheek. He blushed, and we went off in different directions.

Physics was supposed to be one of the hardest courses for seniors. I thought chemistry had been especially difficult last year, and to hear that it only got harder was pretty daunting. Mr. Polderman was the teacher, and from what I knew, he was pretty eccentric. Carl had told me over the weekend that he had gotten divorced during summer break. He had dark-brown hair, stood about five and a half feet tall, and wore round-rimmed glasses. He was standing in front of the whiteboard when I walked into the classroom with all the other students.

"Well, hello Ms. Drummond. Welcome to physics," he said with a lisp that seemed to slither all the way across the room and tickle the inside of my ear.

I just smiled, embarrassed, as all the students stopped and looked at me.

"We are so glad that you could be here. Please have a seat in the front row," he said. "I will be cutting the lesson short today so that we can have a chance to talk."

I surveyed the front row, and there was a single desk chair open. There were four rows, all with single desk chairs lined up neatly. As I walked to the front of the room, I saw Kate out of the corner of my right eye. She was sitting in the second-to-last chair in the row closest to the door. I could clearly make out her flowing, sandy-blond hair and the pink shirt she'd had on earlier. I could feel her gaze on me. It was as if her eyes were emanating some sort of energy. I ignored it and sat in my seat.

Mr. Polderman smiled as he watched students take their seats. He walked over to my desk and crouched down in front of me like a baseball catcher. I found it a bit comical for a guy of his stature to feel as though he needed to make himself even shorter—his head barely showed over my desk.

"If you need to take a break, just let me know," he said quietly so that only he and I could hear.

I shook my head. "I'll be fine," I said.

He smiled and stood up, announcing to the class, "Very well, then. Let's learn some physics." His lisp twirled the word "physics" all around the room.

The class seemed to drag. All the while, I could feel Kate looking at me from the back of the room. I wondered what was going through her mind and whether she wanted to talk to me. I wondered if she'd be the one to initiate contact, or I would have to. I wondered if things would ever be the same between us. A part of me said that there was no way that could happen. Although I did not adhere to many of the current social ideals, I was pretty sure that girls dating guys who had tried to rape their best girlfriends was a big deal. I was certain she'd had sex with him too. I saw the way they had held each other; one of his hands had been between them, no doubt doing its patented move.

Kate was a dichotomy. One of the nicest girls in the world, but she craved the attention of men more than a homeless man craves a soft mattress and a hot meal. She was two people, indeed. Once, she'd tried to share some details of her sexual deviance, and although it was rather arousing, I told her to stop. It didn't feel right to hear about the Kate I didn't know, and it felt even worse seeing the Kate I *did* know swapping spit with the boy I hated. Carl had insinuated that I was jealous. I realized that he was right—but now that I think about it, I believe I was more jealous of Jeremy taking Kate away from me than the opposite of that.

The hour grew longer, and the lively discussion Mr. Polderman was having, seemingly with himself, neared its conclusion. I watched, uninterested, nodding when it appeared that he was making a point to give the impression that I was paying attention.

Fifteen minutes before the hour ended, Mr. Polderman stopped the lecture.

"OK, I want everyone to do the questions at the end of chapter four," Mr. Polderman said. "Please make sure they are completed by tomorrow and turned in at the beginning of the class. You can take the next fifteen minutes to begin working on them. At the bell, you are all excused."

I heard the sound of pages turning all around the room. Mr. Polderman looked at me and smiled. He gave me a nod in the direction of the door, and I understood.

"You can leave your bag, Alexandra," he said as I reached down for it.

I got up and followed him out. His tight khakis swished with every step he took.

I followed him across the hall to an empty classroom. He opened the door with his key and led me in.

"You can sit there," he said, pointing to a desk chair in front of the teacher's desk.

He pulled the teacher's chair over and sat facing me at an angle. "We—myself and your other teachers—wanted to talk to you on your first day back. Look at it as a welcome back. We just want to get an idea of how you're doing. We have not really dealt with a situation quite like yours and are concerned that it might cause...well, issues with your grades. We want to see to it that you graduate."

I nodded. "I want to see to that too. It was hard missing so much time, and honestly, I'm not really sure how I'm going to catch up. But I will study really hard."

He smiled. "That's good to hear. We want to make sure we do everything we can to help that along. We did some brainstorming, and we all agreed to personally tutor you so that you can catch up with the other students. We will rotate staying after school an hour a day for the next few weeks and go over the lessons with you. You have four core classes, so we can do one each day, with Fridays off. And it would only go on for as long as you need it."

I was taken aback. "Really? You guys all want to work more for me?"

He laughed. "We work as hard as we need to. We are all honored to help you back on your feet. From what we have heard, you are one brave woman."

I felt flattered. "Well, thanks, but...I mean, I feel bad to make you guys stay after school. One of my friends has helped me a lot, and he said he was going to continue to help."

He shook his head. "You are not making us do it; we are offering. In fact, we are insisting. Just try it out this week, and we'll take it from there. A daily one-hour session with the teacher from each one of your core classes should get you caught up in no time."

"OK, well, I guess that's fine. Where would I go?"

He looked around the room. "This classroom is as good as any. This is usually used for the bilingual classes, but they are being held only in the mornings this year. So you'll come here right after school, and one of us will be here to greet you. Ms. Walmers, your history teacher, said she would like to do Mondays, so you'll meet with her today."

"And you?"

"Thursday is our day."

"That's really very nice of you guys. I'm so thankful," I said.

"Let's make sure you kick the year off right and get caught up. That will be all the thanks we need," he said, standing up and putting his chair back behind the teacher's desk.

At that moment, I looked out the windows to my right. In the empty courtyard, I saw Azrael staring at me. I quickly looked away.

Mr. Polderman looked in the direction of the windows. "Something wrong?"

I shook my head and ran my hands through my hair. Terror was likely apparent on my face. "No, no. Can we skip today?" I asked, my voice cracking slightly.

"Of course. Are you sure you're OK?"

I nodded and said yes as I stood and headed for the door without looking back at the window.

"You sure you're all right?" Mr. Polderman said, meeting me in the hallway.

I breathed deeply. "Just some aftereffects of the accident," I said. "Sometimes I get some anxiety. My doctor said it's normal."

He mulled that over for a moment, nodding. "Well, let me know if there is anything I can do."

"Thanks," I said, smiling to mask my fear.

"You know, if you ever want to just come by my class after school and talk, that would be fine. Since my divorce, I spend the first few hours after school preparing my next day's classes and grading papers. You can come by anytime."

I pretended to be surprised by his reference to being divorced, even though I wasn't. The way he said it so nonchalantly, I bet it had been headline news at school for weeks.

"You're so nice. Thanks. I think I'll do that. It's been pretty tough."

He gave me a sincere smile. "It's life. When my mother died, I thought I would never recover. I did. When I went through a nasty divorce this past summer, I thought that was the end too, but it wasn't. Your brain is fully equipped to handle grief, especially when it has time to deal with it. I remember that talking to people always seemed to make me feel better, so feel free."

"Can I ask you a question?" I said.

"If you want, we can go back in the room—"

"No, no. Never mind. I'll just come see you tomorrow."

"Well, what about today? You can come by during lunch."

I hesitated. "I have to go see my doctor. It's probably better if I talk to him first."

Just then, the bell rang, and a flood of students entered the hallway from the various classrooms on either side.

"Thanks again," I said.

He smiled, and I smiled back.

I waited until all the students, including Kate, had walked out of class. Kate turned left, and I was standing on the other side of the hallway. With all the students between us, she didn't see me. I watched as she walked away with her head lowered. I knew she was thinking about me.

Once the classroom was empty, I went in and got my bag. I pulled out my cell phone and called Rick.

It rang three times, and then he picked up.

"Hello," he said loudly over the sounds of machines operating.

"Hey, Rick. Sorry to bother you, but is there any way you can pick me up?" I asked, already feeling bad for asking him.

"Hold on," he said in the same loud voice. I listened as the machine sounds slowly quieted down.

"What's up?" His voice was more normal, as the noise was farther away.

I hesitated. He hadn't heard me the first time, and I thought I could just take it back. Then I remembered Azrael in the courtyard, and I was filled with fear all over again.

"Would you be able to pick me up?" I asked reluctantly.

He sighed, and I expected the first thing out of his mouth to be a resounding "No way." But he said, "Sure. Is everything OK?"

"Yeah. I just want to see my doctor. I need to talk to him."

There was a pause, and I figured that Rick was thinking about what to say next. I jumped in before he could make any assumptions. "The pain in my ribs is coming back, and I'm having a problem sitting for a whole period. I wanted to see if he could take a look at it."

"OK," Rick said, sounding a bit relieved. "Go to the main office and let them know that I'll be there in about thirty minutes. Alicia will have to take you to the doctor."

"Oh, Alicia. How about if she just comes get me? I totally forgot. I should have just called her instead of bothering you at work."

"No, no. She would have a pretty hard time leaving the house with the twins on her own. This way, I can drop you off at home, and you can help her out. Don't worry; the boss here has been my best friend ever since the accident, and he understands."

"Thanks," I said, feeling relieved.

"No problem. I'll see you in thirty."

"OK. See you soon."

I hung up the phone and collected my things. Just as I was about to walk out, Mr. Polderman walked in. I smiled and walked briskly past him. I cringed, hoping he wouldn't say anything, as all I wanted to do was leave school. Thankfully, he let me pass.

As I walked down the hallway, I looked in either direction and did not see Kate. The last thing I wanted to do was see or talk to her. Even the thought of talking to Carl seemed like a chore. I just wanted to leave and get as far away from the school and that courtyard as possible. As much as I told myself that I wasn't afraid of Azrael, I was. It was a petrifying fear that I'd felt since the accident, when I thought I was going to die.

I checked into the office and was received without question. My request to leave was granted by the secretary at the front desk, and I took a seat. I pulled out my cell phone, dug through my bag, and found Dr. Khan's number. I put it in my phone. My fingers were shaking, but I decided that rather than call him, I'd send him a text message.

"Hey, this is Alexandra Drummond. Can I come see you today?" I texted.

I wrapped both hands around the phone, anxiously awaiting his response. After about five minutes, the phone vibrated.

"Sure, what time?" he responded.

"In about an hour and a half?" I texted back.

A minute passed. "Yes, at my office," he responded.

A sense of relief came over me. Although he was not a psychiatrist, he had made me feel so much better before, and I knew that seeing him that day would do the same.

"Thanks. See you then," I responded.

I put the phone back in my bag and took a deep breath. I told myself that everything was going to be fine and to calm down. Unfortunately, something deep within me told me otherwise.

12

I T WAS ABOUT ONE IN the afternoon when I arrived at Dr. Khan's office. I was greeted by an older receptionist, who told me to take a seat in the waiting area, and he'd be right out.

I sat down and pulled the top magazine from the coffee table. The name of the publication was *Hour,* a magazine I'd never heard of. I flipped through its large, colorful pages, not reading a single word, just looking at the pictures.

I had calmed down tremendously since seeing Azrael in the courtyard, but I still had a bad feeling about the whole thing. On the way to Dr. Khan's office, I kept asking myself why this thing was following me around, what he wanted, and how I could make him go away. The only answer I could give myself was that I was nearing the end of my life, and he was just hanging around to pull my soul from my body.

I thought about the last time I had seen Azrael, which was on the front lawn of Rick's neighbor's house. I had told myself maybe he was there to take the soul of the neighbor who was raking her leaves. I asked Alicia the next day, and she told me that she knew all the neighbors on the street, and they were all fine. That told me he had been there for me. And today in the courtyard, he most definitely was there for me as well.

Another thought occurred to me, although I pushed it back into my subconscious as soon as it surfaced: maybe I was crazy, and Azrael was just a hallucination. Maybe everything around me was a play, and the people in the play were all my friends and family in an effort to cure me. I remembered the way the kids had looked at me and how nice everyone was. Maybe they were all in on some kind of rehabilitation exercise in which I'd go back to living my day-to-day life, and they would pretend everything was OK so I would get better. Although it was hard to believe, it seemed plausible. Why else would everyone seem to be walking on eggshells when I was around?

The next thought that came to mind was stranger still. What if I was still unconscious and all this was just a dream? I mean, it felt real, and something told me that it wasn't a dream, but what if it was? What if my head injury was so severe that I was put into a long coma, and my mind was making me believe that all this was happening to me, when in reality, I was just lying motionless in a hospital bed with a catheter between my legs? This thought was actually somewhat comforting—the idea that none of this was real seemed like a better alternative than anything else I could imagine.

Dr. Khan walked into the lobby and gave me a smile. He was wearing a pair of khakis and a black, long-sleeved dress shirt that was tucked neatly into his pants.

"Alex, how are you?" he said as he approached.

I stood to greet him and gave him my best smile. "Good, I guess."

"Let's go back to my office and talk," he said, pointing down the hallway he had come from.

His office was pretty far down the hallway. We passed about six offices. The doors of three of them were open, and older white men were sitting at desks, staring at their computer screens.

"Here, to the right," he said as he stepped in front of me to open the door.

His room was small. Behind his desk a three-foot-wide window stretched from floor to ceiling, with a horizontal shade hanging from the top. His desk was small and cluttered with paper; only scattered spots of dark wood showed among the piles of documents.

Dr. Khan walked around the desk and sat down, his chair letting out a gasp of air as he settled in. I hesitantly sat down as well. I was suddenly very nervous. At first, it had seemed like a good idea to come and see him, but now I wasn't so sure. The times I had seen Azrael had been horrifying, but when they passed, I didn't want to think about them again. It was like waking from a bad dream—you don't spend the rest of the day thinking about it; you try your best to forget it ever happened.

He looked at me and smiled. "How can I help you?"

I paused for a second. Maybe I should just make something up, I thought—tell him my ribs still hurt or something like that. Then I thought how stupid he might think I was for insisting on an appointment today for something so benign. He probably was setting aside some important stuff so I could come in and tell him a ghost story.

With that thought in mind, I said, "I saw him again."

Dr. Khan gave a slight nod, and his expression grew tense. "Where?"

"Well, it was twice," I said, not looking directly at him.

"Twice?" He sounded alarmed.

"Yeah, last Friday and earlier today."

He was looking up at the ceiling, deep in thought. Tears began to form in my eyes.

"I'm scared," I said, beginning to cry.

He handed me a box of tissues. I pulled one out and dabbed my eyes with it. With everything I had, I took a deep breath and calmed myself down.

"Am I crazy?" I asked, staring into his eyes.

"No, no, Alex. You are nothing of the sort. You—"

"'Cause I saw a movie once where everyone around the main character was acting as though everything was OK just so the guy would get better and think he was leading a normal life. But the truth was that the guy was really crazy. Is everyone around me just acting, waiting for me to get better?"

Dr. Khan actually was holding back a smile, and I immediately knew that was not the case. "That would be a pretty elaborate stunt to pull," he said, "especially considering that you went back to school. How many students are in your school? A thousand or so? We would have spent months instructing every student how to react to you. Something like that would not even be possible."

He made sense, and I felt stupid, but at least I'd gotten the question off my chest. "Then why does he keep haunting me? How can I stop him?" I asked.

Dr. Khan sighed at this question. "Well, tell me about the encounters."

I told him every detail I remembered about Friday and this morning. He was most intrigued by how Azrael had seemed to hypnotize me. I didn't remember much about the trance, but I did remember that I had felt enchanted—as if I were being pulled in.

"And your uncle and Carl were with you in the car and saw the whole thing?" he asked.

"Yes, it was right before I went to visit my family's graves. They told me I was frozen for a minute and did not respond to them."

Dr. Khan shook his head and rubbed his chin. "Did Azrael look any different?"

I shook my head. "No, not at all. But he's mocking me. He knows what he's doing. Whenever I see him, I'm filled with so much fear that I can hardly breathe. It's like he has some kind of power."

Just then, the desk phone rang. Dr. Khan and I looked at it.

"Will you excuse me?" he asked.

"Sure. Do you want me to leave?"

"No, just hold on. If it's important, I'll take it in the hallway."

He picked up the phone. "Dr. Khan," he said.

I heard a muffled voice from the receiver, speaking in a loud tone. It sounded like a woman. Dr. Khan's eyes widened, and he clenched his teeth.

After about twenty seconds of the muffled voice yelling at him, he said, "Can I call you back? I'm in a meeting."

The voice on the other end of the line seemed to get louder, and I knew at once that the caller was his wife. I looked around the room. A console table to my right had a large picture of Dr. Khan's two girls. Next to it was a much smaller photo of him with a woman I took to be his wife. She was extremely pretty, and together they made a stunning couple.

"Please, Ramia, I have to go," he said calmly.

I looked at him. His eyes were wide, and I could see that he was getting flushed. He bowed his head and started to massage his forehead.

"I told you it's not what you think, and that's all. You just have to believe me," he said. It appeared that she had said something that finally got to him.

"I could go," I said, and then I wished I hadn't, because I heard the muffled voice get even louder.

"No!" he exclaimed. "No, this is a patient! I'm hanging up now!"

He slammed the receiver down and looked up at me apologetically. "I'm sorry. Go on."

I was frozen for a moment. I wasn't sure whether to continue or ask him if I should leave. "Are you sure?"

He gave me a forced smile and nodded. "Yes."

"OK, well, I was just saying I could almost feel his presence, and he seems to have some type of power over me. I really don't know what to do," I said.

"You might want to see Dr. Reynolds. This sounds a lot more serious than I first thought. If you are being put into trances, that could lead to all kinds of injuries. Maybe he could prescribe some medication or something that could help," Dr. Khan said.

"Medication?" I asked. "So you do think I'm crazy?"

He sat up in his chair. "No, but I think it's very possible that your visions of this Azrael could be prevented with drugs specific to treating these types of disorders. Personally, I believe you, but there is no other way to treat something like this."

I looked at him solemnly. Part of me felt betrayed. He had been so encouraging in the hospital, but now he was no different from anyone else. Even though I had my doubts, I was not going to take pills, because deep down, I knew that what I was seeing was real. Pills were for people who saw fake things.

"I don't want medication. Or should I say, I refuse it? Isn't that how you guys put it? I thought you believed me. I guess I was wrong."

He shook his head. "Alex, even so, how else do you propose I help you? If I had some magic way to make this guy disappear, I would do it. But for now, what am I to do?"

He was right, but I was still disappointed. Tears started to form in my eyes, and I took another tissue.

"I suggest you stay home for another week, just to see how things go. If you don't want the meds, that's fine. But get some more rest," he said.

I nodded. This sounded like the best idea. The last few nights at Rick's house, I'd had dreamless sleep. Azrael had not made any appearances within the home. Maybe a week away would do me good.

"OK," I said. "But no medication. I'm not hallucinating."

"Fair enough," he said as he pulled out a small pad of paper. "I will write you a note so you can be excused from school."

"And work," I added, remembering that Rick had just gotten me a job, and now I would have to miss the first week.

"And work," he said.

I sat in silence as he scribbled on the pad, ripped the page off, and then scribbled on a second page. He shuffled the two papers together and handed them to me.

"Thanks," I said.

He smiled. "Anytime. And feel free to come see me again if you need to."

As I started to get up, he said, "I'm sorry about the phone call, by the way. It was very unprofessional of me."

I didn't know what to say. For a split second, I wanted to ask him what it was about, but I thought better of it. "That's OK. If you ever need someone to talk to, let me know," I said playfully.

He smiled. "Thanks."

I left his office and said goodbye to the receptionist on the way out. I felt a little better, but I was still disappointed. As I made my way through the corridors of the hospital, my thoughts turned to the other demon in my life, Manuel Alderas. I had meant to ask Dr. Khan how he was doing. I had tried to keep homicidal thoughts out of my mind, but now that things seemed to have taken a turn for the worse, those thoughts came rushing back. I cursed him under my breath and wished he would live. He didn't deserve to die for what he had done to my family. He deserved to rot in a prison for the rest of his life. That, to me, was a far greater punishment.

When I reached the main lobby of the hospital, I turned and walked to the information desk.

"Ma'am," I said to the older woman sitting at the desk staring at her computer, "Do you know what room Manuel Alderas is in?"

"Sure, hold on," she said as she continued to stare at the screen.

A moment went by as she typed the name on her keyboard. "Alderas," she said.

"Yes."

She looked up from the screen. "I'm sorry. He is not to have any visitors. He's flagged. I can't give you that information."

"Is he still in intensive care?" I asked, fishing for a clue.

She smiled. "I can't say."

I sighed. "OK, thanks."

I walked away, but instead of heading outside, I went back into the hospital. He had to be in intensive care. Dr. Khan had told me he was in a deep coma not too long ago. One way or another, I decided, I was going to find a way to pay him a visit before I left.

I arrived at the intensive care unit after about a five-minute walk. There were locked double doors in my way. A button and speaker were on the wall to the right of the doors. I thought for a minute and then hit the button on the speaker.

A quiet buzz came from somewhere past the doors, and my nerves started to get the better of me. I decided to turn and walk away, but then the double doors swung open for an older woman who was wheeling out a basket filled with towels. What luck, I thought. I seized the opportunity and walked briskly ahead.

As I strode onward, I kept my eyes in front of me. Nurses and doctors walked by me, but I did not look them in the eye for fear they would somehow recognize me and banish me from the area. I turned a corner, and all the way down the hall, I saw a police officer sitting outside one of the rooms.

I walked faster, my heart rate increasing with every step. The officer looked up from the magazine he was reading once he realized I was heading his way.

"Hi," he said with a slight smile as I approached.

"Hello," I said. He was a young man. He had firm features, and even though he was sitting down, slouched over a magazine, I could tell he was very muscular.

"Can I help you?"

I took a deep breath. "Yes. I was wondering if I could visit Manuel," I said, half pointing at the door.

"And you are?"

I froze. If this officer had been on watch for more than a day, he probably would have met Manuel's whole family. Then again, maybe they didn't come to visit. Carl had told me that he was running from the police after stealing a car when the accident happened. Maybe this guy had nobody.

"His sister," I said with much hesitation.

The officer laughed lightly. "You?"

I looked at him, confused. I wasn't sure what he was getting at.

"He's like four feet tall and has dark skin, and you're almost six feet tall and whiter than a ghost. I can guarantee you and him did not come out of the same mother."

"Well, can I still see him anyway?" I asked.

"Who are you?"

I decided to tell him the truth. "Alexandra Drummond. I was in the accident that he caused," I said.

The officer sat up in his chair and closed his magazine. "Really? How did you get in here?"

I remained silent. I wasn't sure whether I had committed a crime or anything like that, but I was not about to admit it to a uniformed police officer.

"Look, I lost my whole family a month ago, and this guy caused the accident. I just want to see him. If that happened to you, wouldn't you want the same thing? I could show you my ID, if you want," I said.

He stood up, leaving the magazine on his chair. He towered over me as though I were four feet tall. "C'mon. I'll show you in, but don't try anything."

"Try anything?"

"I do this from time to time, and you would not be the first victim to try to come to the hospital and kill the guy," he said.

This caught me off guard. I had wanted to kill him. When I was in the hospital, I'd thought about it all the time. Of course, I didn't think I could ever do it.

As soon as the officer swung the door open, I heard a rhythmic beeping noise followed by air compressions. We walked into the room. He was lying on the bed with tubes in his mouth and wires coming from every direction. He was small, even smaller than I had imagined. His dark skin contrasted with the white of the bedsheets, and he lay perfectly still.

"He's not doing too good, from what I hear," the officer said as we looked at him.

I looked around the room and saw no flowers, no cards, and no sign that anyone had come to visit.

"Has he had any visitors?" I asked.

"Not a single one that I know of. I've been on this watch since he was put here. If he hadn't done such a terrible thing, I think I'd feel sorry for the guy. Sounds like he might not last very much longer."

I looked up at the screen. In my time at the hospital, I had learned how to read the monitors, and from the looks of it, he was barely hanging on. All his vitals were well below where they needed to be, and he looked terrible. He had nobody and nothing to live for, and he'd killed everyone in my immediate family. I wanted him to live. I wanted to see him stand trial and get sentenced to jail for the rest of his life. I wanted him to spend the next fifty years of his life remembering what he had done and suffer the same way I was suffering. Dying, for him, was not fair. It was too easy—too light a punishment for what he had done.

I stepped closer. From the corner of my eye, I saw the officer take a step in my direction. I was sure he was thinking I might do something, but his concern was wasted. That little boy looked as if he was going to die no matter what happened—either by my hand or when his body gave up on him in a few weeks.

I turned to the officer and gave him a faint smile. My eyes were watery, but I wasn't going to allow myself to cry. "I'll go now," I said.

"I'm sorry for your loss," he said. "I guess I should have told you that a second ago. Really, it was a terrible tragedy."

I nodded.

"Listen," he said in a hushed tone, taking a step toward me. "I overheard the doctors say that he has some type of laceration in his heart and that he'll die without a transplant. Also, I heard one of the doctors say he's got a rare blood type. I can guarantee you this guy is way down on the totem pole to get a new heart. So, you know, he'll get what's coming."

"I want him to live," I said. "He deserves to rot in a prison, not die in a comfortable bed."

The officer nodded slightly, as though he agreed. "He'll rot in hell. I think that's worse."

Maybe he was right. I'd never believed in it before, but Azrael had changed my perception altogether. Nonetheless, I wanted to live the rest of my life knowing for sure he was being punished for what he had done, and that could happen only if he lived.

"I guess," I said. "Anyway, thanks for letting me in. I'm sure you're not allowed to do that. I really appreciate it."

"No problem," he said as we started for the door. "I've got a kid myself, and I can't imagine that happening to me. It must have been hard just coming here."

We left the room, and I extended my hand to shake his. "Thanks, and what's your name?"

"Officer Brian Moran," he said with a smile as he shook my hand.

"Officer, can you call me and update me on his condition?"

"Sure," he said.

I pulled out a pen and a scrap of paper from my purse, wrote down my cell number, and gave it to him. "Thanks again," I said.

He took the paper and tucked it into his front shirt pocket. He gave me a half salute and bowed as I walked away.

I called Rick, and he picked me up at the front of the hospital to go home. I spent the rest of the afternoon and the next day in my room. Carl called a few times, and we talked. I told him that I didn't want to see anyone, but I assured him that I still liked him a lot. He tried to ask me about Azrael, and I stopped that conversation dead in its tracks. Mostly, I wanted to just sit around, read my books, and take short naps. My first try at getting back into civilization had been a failure, and I owed it all to Azrael. Every night, I went to bed anticipating that he would visit me, and every night I would wake up just fine. I had dreams, but not of him. It was as if Rick's house was a sanctuary from his presence—the one silver lining in a sky filled with dark clouds.

13

By Thursday evening of the same week, I was feeling a little better. Sitting alone in my room, I was able to get a lot of thinking done. I determined that I needed a plan to resolve this Azrael burden. I could not stay home in fear the rest of my life. I had to confront it head-on. I decided that the next time he popped into my life, I would face him and demand answers. I knew he could speak, and it was very apparent that he could see me, so I was sure we could have a conversation. My only fear was staring into his eyes, but I figured I could look past him or down at the floor. If that didn't work, I was going to fight his glare with everything I had. He was not going to win, even though he had thus far; I would not let this ruin my life.

When Rick came home around six in the evening, I was sitting on the couch, watching a movie with Alicia. The twins had finally fallen asleep, and we'd decided to take a break.

"Hey, girls," he said as he dropped a portfolio on the kitchen table.

"Hey, Rick," Alicia said, passing the bowl of popcorn to me. "We're watching a movie. Wanna join us?"

Rick smiled at me. "Sure. But first, I have a surprise for Alex."

"Really?" I said.

"I was able to get the day off tomorrow, and I thought you and I could go up to Silver Lake and camp for the weekend."

I immediately rose to my feet. "That would be awesome!"

Then I thought about Alicia and the twins and how she would be alone the whole weekend. I looked at her, and she was smiling enthusiastically. Then I realized that they must have decided on this already.

"Alicia is going to her mother's for the weekend, so she'll be OK," Rick said, and Alicia nodded. "We think you need some time away, and I remember how much you loved camping when you were younger. I think it would be perfect."

I was ecstatic. I gave Alicia a hug, skipped over to Rick, and hugged him too.

"You can pack after the movie," Alicia said, motioning for me to come back to the couch.

Rick joined us, and we watched the movie together. Throughout the movie, my mind wandered as I thought about our trip. My father and I used to go on these excursions. Those were good times. He taught me to fish, shoot a bow and arrow, and build a fire. Most of all, he taught me about life. We spent hours talking about his past and his experiences. He was not an old man, but he had a lot to share.

Rick had come with us a few times when I was very young—maybe six or seven. As I got older, it was just my father and me. I was happy to be going back.

Before the closing credits came up at the end of the movie, I jumped from my seat and ran upstairs to prepare my clothes. I heard Rick and Alicia laughing as I ascended the stairs.

Alicia lent me one of her suitcases, and just after midnight I was done packing. I tucked myself in and fell asleep instantly.

That night, I dreamed about my father. I was reliving one of our camping trips. He was roasting a marshmallow, and I was sitting idly by, watching. It was silent; as much as we talked, we had a lot of silent moments too, and I just watched as he turned the white marshmallow at the end of his stick ever so gently. He looked up and gave me a smile, and I smiled back.

In another dream, I was with Bailey. We were sitting in the living room of our old house. She was teaching me a poem she'd learned that required her to trace the lines of my palms. She finished the poem, and then we went out into the backyard and played handball.

I woke as the early-morning sun shone through my window. I looked at the clock; it was a quarter after seven in the morning. Rick had told me that we would leave at eight. Silver Lake was just a two-hour drive, so we would get there in plenty of time to set up our camp and get a good fire going to make lunch.

I used the bathroom and got dressed. I tied my hair back and put on a baseball cap. I dragged my suitcase with me as I went downstairs.

Rick was also prompt. He was rolling his suitcase through the living room on his way out the door.

"Get some breakfast. Alicia made egg sandwiches," he said as he walked past me.

I sat at the kitchen table, and Alicia served me two egg-and-cheese sandwiches on wheat toast, a glass of orange juice, and of course, a piping hot cup of coffee. I sipped the coffee eagerly. This was the earliest I had gotten up since my first day of school.

"I hope you guys have a good time," Alicia said, sitting down next to me.

"I hope so too. The weather is supposed to be perfect, and I'm hoping there aren't any mosquitoes," I said.

"Your school called this morning. They want to know if you're going to be able to come back on Monday," she said.

I thought about it. It had been five days since I had seen Azrael. I had spent the week mostly around the house, but I had gone out grocery shopping with Alicia, and one night we all went out to dinner. It was like a bad nightmare: I seemed to forget it as time passed, and I thought maybe after this weekend, I could move on.

"I think so," I said.

"Well, they did say if you wanted more time to take it."

"Maybe," I said. I didn't want to comment further, as another thought crossed my mind. I was so excited about going on this trip that I'd failed to realize that maybe this whole week, Azrael had been waiting for me to leave my house. I had always felt very safe here. I felt as if he could not get to me as long as I was at home, and now I would be exposing myself out in the wilderness. I started to worry, and I could tell Alicia took notice.

"You don't have to go back, you know; it's up to you," she said as she read my expression.

"That's not it. It's just…" I paused, thinking of the right thing to say. "I get anxiety once in a while. It's been since the accident. It comes and goes."

Alicia gave me a warm smile. "Well, if school makes you anxious, we can always arrange for you to finish your studies from home. That was a suggestion they had for us before you came out of the hospital."

I actually liked that idea very much. "Really?"

"Yeah. Just say the word, and we can make it happen. They said you would just have to go for exams, and we could have a tutor come here."

"A tutor? Would we have to pay him?"

She shook her head. "One of your teachers, Mr. Polderman, offered to tutor you for free. He said since you only had four core classes, it wouldn't take more than two hours a day. The administrators agreed to waive the elective class, and if you couldn't work, they would waive the co-op class as well so that you could graduate on time."

I was surprised she was telling me all this now. It sounded as if they had really thought it through. "Why did you wait to tell me?" I asked.

"They wanted to see how you would do before we presented this as an option. The principal thought that if we gave you the option right away, you would likely choose that route and never even give going back a shot. Sorry I kept it from you."

I was annoyed, but I understood her point. And the principal was right; I would have chosen that route rather than go back. What bothered me was that they all were in it together. My mind returned to what I had told Dr. Khan—that everyone around me could just be playing a role, like in a play. I had suspected it before, but now my suspicions were buttressed by credible evidence. I wondered how much of a role Dr. Khan played in all this. He had looked me square in the eye and assured me that there was nothing going on behind my back.

"Any other plans you guys have?" I asked.

Alicia sighed. "We aren't planning anything, honey. We just want to do whatever we can to help. One of your teachers is willing to come to your house—unpaid, mind you—and spend two hours of his time so that you can graduate on time. That's a lot from someone you barely know. You should be grateful."

Her words made me feel bad. "You're right. I'm sorry. I don't know. It's been really hard, you know."

"I know, and if there is anything we can do to help, we will." She placed her hand on my arm. "And if there is anything you ever want to talk about, let me know."

I looked at her and instantly felt better. "Thanks," I said.

"Now eat up. You guys have a long ride ahead of you," she said.

I finished my breakfast and walked outside, where Rick was packing the last of the supplies into the SUV.

"You ready to go?" he asked, slowly closing the back door of the SUV so as not to disrupt the tightly packed cargo in the back.

"I can't wait," I said. "I can't tell you how much I appreciate this. It was the best idea you guys could have come up with."

Rick smiled as he pushed one last time and the back door locked into place. "In that case, just remember it was my idea," he said jokingly.

I laughed. "OK, I'll give you the credit, but we have to stop at the ice cream place when we get there—just before we get to Silver Lake. Then it will be the best idea."

"Oh yeah," Rick said, his eyes wandering. "That was the place we took you when you were very young. What were you, like six?"

I nodded. "Yeah, and we went a few times after that. I still think about it all the time. Do you remember where it is?"

"Yup," Rick said. "Let me go say goodbye to Alicia, and we'll hit the road."

Having already said my goodbyes to Alicia, I walked over to the passenger side and got in. The car was parked in the same direction as when I'd seen Azrael the week before. I looked over to the spot where he had been, and it was empty. I wondered where he had gone and if he would pay me a visit on this trip. Lately, he had not been in my thoughts, but since I found out last night we were going on this trip, he had crawled back into my subconscious mind.

As my thoughts began to wander for the first time since I woke up that morning, I remembered the dreams I'd had the night before. I remembered feeling so good first thing when I opened my eyes and not knowing why. It was as if a warm blanket had been thrown over me on a cold winter's night. I had seen my father and Bailey in a few of my most treasured memories. I wondered if they were still around, still close, and if they watched over me. The words of my father still rang in my ears every time I thought about the dream by the beach. He was very proud of me. He'd told Rick the same thing in his dream. I still wondered what hidden meaning lay behind his choice of words.

Rick got into the car, interrupting my daydream. I was staring where I had seen Azrael that day, looking at nothing in particular.

"Alex?" he said, sounding alarmed.

I turned and smiled. "Not this time, Rick. Nothing there," I said, but I had slipped.

"Nothing there?" he asked suspiciously. "You never said there was something there."

I sighed. "There wasn't; did you see anything that day?"

He shook his head.

"Well, there you go. There was nothing there."

He looked forward and started the car. As he put the car into gear, he said, "You know, Alex, I don't think it would hurt if you opened up and told me what's on your mind. Of course, when you're ready, but I think it would help."

He was watching the road as he turned the car out of the driveway. I searched his face, and I could tell that what he'd just told me was a planned speech. Then I thought, maybe all this was planned. The whole trip—getting me out to the woods, earning my confidence, and getting me to admit my own insanity. Suddenly, I felt myself get warm and annoyed. Something just short of anger boiled up from within me.

"There's nothing to tell, Rick," I said. "I already told you, I had some anxiety, and I've been having a hard time with all this. That's all."

Rick was calm, and I could tell that he had expected my reaction. "When you're ready, Alex. When you're ready."

I bit my tongue. I wanted to respond, but I knew that by doing so, I would be admitting that he was right. I pulled out my headphones, put them over my ears, and turned on my music.

I calmed down after a few songs and decided to just try to have fun. No matter what Rick's plans were, he still just wanted to help me out; that, I knew for sure. So rather than ruin a good time, I decided I would just enjoy myself.

The best part of the drive up to Silver Lake was the last hour. We got off the main freeway and onto a country road. It meandered through cornfields and rolling, tree-covered hills. Every few miles, a stoplight turned red, but for the most part, we traveled at a constant speed. I rolled my window down and felt the warm air. For early October, the temperature was warm. It was approaching eighty degrees, which was an anomaly in Michigan. It caressed my skin like silk and sent a chill of excitement down my spine. I remembered the smell of the air very well; it was that of fresh country and open pastures. It was the air of my youth, a time when I was with my family, a time that I still had my daddy.

Some of the trees had already changed color, and the picturesque mixture of red, yellow, and orange left us breathless. I had listened to my music the whole way, but now I was lost in the beauty that surrounded me.

"Ice cream place is just up the road," Rick said, pointing ahead.

Warm memories came back to me of my father saying those same words. I felt as gleeful as I had back when I was ten years old. I was the happiest I'd been since the accident.

"Butter pecan cone," I said. "They have the best—"

I stopped short. Rick and I stared at the white building with the large ice-cream cone sign. All the windows were boarded up, and a big yellow sign in the front said For Sale/Lease. My heart sank. All those warm memories seemed to flutter away like pigeons in the park.

"What the heck," I said in disbelief.

"That's terrible," Rick said as we drove by. "That place has been open for decades."

"Maybe they moved," I said.

"Maybe, but my guess is that the economy has been so bad that people are not going on as many vacations, so there's less traffic for places like this. The businesses around Silver Lake can't survive on just the locals." Rick let out a sigh. "Man, I can't believe the economy is this bad. Thank God I still have my job."

I looked in my side-view mirror, and the white building and its ice-cream cone ornament slowly receded in the distance.

Rick must have taken notice of my depressed mood. "Well, we can always get some ice cream at the campsite. They have the general store, and from what I remember, they have a soft-serve station."

I nodded as I resumed looking ahead of us at the passing trees. I had no interest in soft serve from a general store. I wanted butter pecan from the place my daddy took me when I was younger. I began to cry.

Rick pulled over as my sobbing turned into a heavy cry. I heard the loud crunch of rocks as the SUV skidded to a halt on the shoulder of the two-lane highway.

"Alex, I'm sorry," Rick said. He put his arm on my shoulder as I buried my face in my hands.

"It's…it's not…it's not your fault," I said, my sobs making it hard to catch my breath and formulate a complete sentence.

"Is there anything I can do?" he said gently.

I sniffled and wiped my eyes. I lifted my T-shirt and dried my face. "No. Sorry, it's…" I sniffled and heaved some more. "I just wanted some butter pecan. I don't know why, but I just wanted some." Another round of tears poured from my eyes.

Rick pulled me into his chest and hugged me tightly. He smelled like my father had, sweet musk. His arms were strong and tight around my shoulders, and his heart pounded lightly as my head rested against his chest. He held me like that for a minute, and my tears stopped falling. I retracted, and he gave me a smile.

"This is going to be good for you, Alex," Rick said. "If you cry or find yourself sad, just remember that this is a good thing."

I nodded as I wiped my face again with my T-shirt.

We drove in silence the rest of the way; even the radio was off. We got to the campsite about forty-five minutes later. I pulled out my iPhone and checked my calls. I saw that Carl had tried to call a few times. I had the phone on silent, so I'd missed them. I sent him a text, telling him that we had arrived safely and that I would call him after we set up the camp.

Rick had found the site where my father and I often camped. There was a small creek about a quarter of a mile north, and Silver Lake was about a ten-minute walk in the opposite direction. There were many favorite things I liked to do when I went camping with my father, but the one that topped the list was sitting atop the hill that led to Silver Lake and watching the sun go down over the trees. Silver Lake itself was sunken in, and all around it was a sandy beach pitched toward the water at almost a forty-five-degree angle. The best place to sit was right where the beach started to slant downward. From there, you could see the whole lake.

We unloaded all our stuff and carried it to the site. Rick set up the tents and got kindling for the fire. I organized all the food and laid the blankets and pillows in the tents. I had not realized that Rick had brought two tents; my father and I used to sleep in the same tent. It felt a little awkward, but I didn't say anything.

"You want to go to the store?" he asked as he finished putting up the second tent.

"No. I think I'll stay back and get the fire started," I said.

"Are you sure?" he asked.

"Yeah. I'll be fine. Thanks."

"Did you want anything from the store?" Rick asked, a hint of caution in his voice.

"No, thanks. I'm over the ice cream. Maybe later on we can go together," I said with a smile.

He gave a little laugh. "OK, Alex. I'll be right back—ten minutes tops," he said.

"'Bye," I said, and he walked off toward the car.

I was a very good fire builder, and Rick knew that. I looked at the stone fire pit. It was circular and about three feet across. There was a dirty metal grate, used for cooking, on top. The fire pit was only about two feet high, but it had four little openings at its base. It was just enough room to insert a blower to get a fire going more easily.

I stacked some leaves and a whole bunch of twigs in the middle and lit them. The leaves crackled beneath the twigs, and as the fire grew larger, I added more and more twigs. I went on adding larger and larger pieces of wood until the blaze was tall and hot. I was so entranced by the process that I failed to realize that almost thirty minutes had gone by since Rick had left for the store.

I dialed his number, and the phone rang a few times. Then I heard ringing coming from one of the bags on the ground, and I knew right away that he had forgotten his phone. I started to worry; my stomach turned with anxiety.

I looked around the clearing. Maybe I could jog to the store. From what I remembered, it was only about two miles away. It would take at least twenty minutes. Then I thought about Rick coming back and not finding me. That would make things worse. I looked at my phone again and tried to make sure I was not just imagining that thirty minutes had gone by. I looked at the message I'd sent Carl; that was almost an hour ago.

I called Carl. His phone rang a few times, and then he picked up.

"Hello," he said.

"Hey," I said. "I have a bit of a problem. Rick left for the store, and he's been gone for a while, and he forgot his phone."

"What?" Carl sounded worried. "Where are you now?"

"I'm at the campsite."

"Do you want me to come? I can get my dad's car and be there as soon as possible," he said.

"Carl, that's sweet, but it's like two hours away. Maybe we can just talk. I'm just worried, and I think he'll be back."

"Maybe he had car trouble. How long has he been gone, exactly?"

"Maybe thirty minutes," I said.

"Well, that's OK; that's not that long. It's no big deal. Nothing to worry about."

His words made me feel better. I went over to the folding chair that I had set up next to the fire and sat down. The fire warmed me, and having Carl on the phone made me feel secure.

"How was your drive?" he asked.

"Nice, I guess," I said as I looked past the fire at the place in the woods where Rick would be coming from. "The ice cream place by Silver Lake is closed down."

"No way," Carl said.

"Yeah, I really wanted a cone, but I guess it wasn't meant to be."

"I'm sorry, baby." Carl said the word "baby" very awkwardly, as if he'd been waiting for the right time to lay it into a sentence.

"Baby," I said, smiling. "That's cute."

He laughed, and even though he was not right in front of me, I knew he was blushing.

"What am I going to call you?" I asked playfully.

"Daddy," he replied, and we both laughed.

Suddenly, a figure appeared in the woods past the clearing.

"Carl, I think Rick is back," I said as I stood up and started walking in his direction.

As I got closer, I realized that it wasn't Rick at all. It was Azrael.

I froze. He kept his gaze on mine, and he walked slowly toward me. He was among the trees, and I could see his dark eyes glaring at me.

"Alex," Carl said on the phone, "Is it him?"

"Yes," I replied distantly.

Azrael crept past the trees and into the clearing. He was only about twenty yards away, and our eyes were locked. I felt my entire body going numb as he approached. My breathing tightened, and my heart slowed. I felt myself get weak, so weak that the phone fell from my hand.

"Girl," he hissed, "how do you see me?"

His dark eyes penetrated me, and I could feel him pulling me in. Without instruction, my body started to walk toward him. I was no longer in control.

"How?" he hissed louder, and his voice sent shock waves of fear through me. I felt the hairs on my neck stand on end, and my entire body trembled in fear.

"I command you to answer, girl."

I came to a complete stop only a few feet from him. I was still unable to control my body, but I could speak. "I...I don't know," I said, my voice trembling.

He snarled. His pointed teeth showed between his lips. I could tell he was not happy with that answer.

He raised his hand perpendicular to his body, and with four fingers he motioned at me as if he were telling me to get up. I felt myself rise above the ground. I tried to turn my head, but I was paralyzed.

"I will raise you as high as the tallest tree and let you fall to your death. Now, tell me. How do you see me?" His voice was powerful and commanding.

I was at least three feet above the ground and shaking uncontrollably. "I don't know!" I said as loud as I could.

He left me suspended for a long moment, seemingly waiting for me to say something else. Then he let his hand down, and I fell to the ground. I came down with a thud, landing on my back, flat against the ground. Then the feeling came back to my arms and legs, and I was able to move again. I immediately sat up and looked at the spot where Azrael had stood. He was gone. I was shaking as if I were wearing a bathing suit in February. I looked around the clearing. Nobody was there.

I stumbled to my feet and turned in every direction. Nothing. I listened for him, but all I heard were birds chirping and the gentle rustle of leaves as the wind passed through the trees. I let myself fall to the ground, trembling, and I began to cry.

I cried for what seemed like an hour until I heard Rick's car pull up past the trees. The car came to a halt, and the car door slammed.

"Alex," he called.

I couldn't respond to him. My crying had subsided, but I was still trembling on the ground.

I heard him jogging toward me. "Alex," he called out again.

"Here," I replied faintly. I was weak and terrified.

He broke through the tree line, rushed to my side, and knelt down on one knee.

"What happened? Are you OK?"

I shook my head, and another round of tears started pouring from my eyes.

"I'm so sorry. I got a flat on the way to the store. I tried to call, but I left the phone—"

"He was here," I said breathlessly between sobs.

"Who! Who was here?" he said, alarmed.

I looked up and stared him right in the eye. "Azrael," I said.

14

W<small>E DIDN'T SPEAK FOR AN</small> hour. Rick had not questioned me when I told him that Azrael had been there. After I had a chance to collect my thoughts, I realized that he must have known the entire time. We sat staring at the fire, and finally, I broke the silence.

"So you knew?" I asked, my eyes still on the fire.

"Carl told me," he said softly.

"When?"

"After that episode by the house. I insisted that he tell me what was going on. I know you wanted to keep it a secret, but, Alex, we're worried."

"We?"

He paused. "I told Alicia too. Please don't take it the wrong way."

I was suddenly filled with anger. "What's the wrong way, Rick? That I'm some kind of psycho?"

"Alex," he said pleadingly, "we want to help you."

"Help me?" I yelled. I was on the verge of tears. "How can you help me? You guys think I'm crazy, but I'm not! He's real, and he wants to kill me!"

"Calm down, please," he said in a monotone voice.

"I can't be calm. Some scary thing is after me, and I don't know what to do."

"Nobody is after you, Alex."

"Nobody? Are you serious? I was just lifted off the ground and dropped on my back. Who did that? You think that was nobody?"

"Lifted off the ground?" he asked, eyebrows raised.

I shook my head. I still didn't want to tell him everything, and I wished I hadn't told him that.

"Listen," he said. "You're just having a hard time with all this. These things happen. Dr. Reynolds told us you just need time."

This worried me. "Dr. Reynolds? What did you tell him? Please don't tell me he knows about this."

Rick sighed. "He just knows you've been having some hallucinations. I told him you haven't had them for a while, and he suggested I take you somewhere that reminded you of the past. He said that would help you with the posttraumatic stress."

"They're not hallucinations," I said curtly. "Whatever this thing is, it's real. How else do I know his name? Carl looked it up; he's the angel of death."

Rick shook his head. "I should take you home," he said. "Maybe you just need some more time to rest."

"No," I said. "I want to stay. I'm not afraid of him anymore. He can't hurt me; I know it now."

Rick looked confused. "What do you mean?"

I paused for a moment. At first, I thought about not responding, but I felt as if a great weight was pushing down on my chest.

I took a deep breath. "When he came today, he asked me how I could see him. I told him I didn't know. Then he lifted me off the ground and threatened to kill me. I was so scared. I insisted I had no idea how or why I could see him. Then he let me drop to the ground and disappeared. If he could kill me, he would have; but he didn't. He seemed to be more concerned with why I could see him than anything else. I think he's just as worried about me as I am about him."

Rick looked at me in shock. "Carl told me he wears a suit or something like that?"

I nodded. "A black pinstripe suit, and he has a gold watch. What else did Carl tell you? Did he tell you how I saw him take my family? Or did he tell you how I saw him take the lady in the hospital too? I had no idea she was dying, Rick. She was stable and everything, then he just walked into the room, and all the alarms went off. She died, and I saw him pull her soul right out of her body. That was real—as real as I'm talking to you right now. I see him the same way I see anyone else."

Rick was wide-eyed. "That's unbelievable."

"I know, and now I'm starting to think he's worried about me. Why else would he be coming after me to demand that I tell him how I see him?"

Rick had no reply to that, and we stayed silent for a while. The fire crackled, and a warm, gentle breeze whistled through the leaves above.

"Have you tried to confront him?"

I looked at Rick, wondering whether he really believed me or was just playing along. "Why? Do you believe me?"

He looked uncertain. "Well, I don't think you're crazy, if that's what you mean. And if I don't think you're crazy, then what you're saying must be true."

I looked back at the fire. "No. I tried to, but every time I stare into his eyes, I'm frozen with fear; it's like he has some sort of mind control over me."

Rick took a small branch and threw it into the fire. We both watched for a moment as the bark started to burn and the fire grew higher.

"You sure you want to stay here? We could just go home, you know," Rick said.

I looked around. The trees surrounded us like a fortress, and past them, the shadows of the forest stared back at me. I was still scared. Perhaps I would not sleep a second that night, knowing that he could be out there, watching me. My mind told me just to go, but something else was telling me to stay. I opened my mouth to speak, but I could not say the words.

"It would not be a big deal. You've been doing just fine at home. Maybe you just need some more time—"

"No," I said. "I want to stay all weekend like we planned, and I want to go back to school on Monday. Enough is enough. This thing is not going to control me."

Rick nodded. "OK," he said, trying to sound cheery, "then let's eat."

He turned to the bag he had brought back with him and pulled out a package of hot dogs. He smiled. I tried, but I could not smile back.

"Alex," he said, his eyes unblinking, "whoever he is, if he comes back, you let me know. I will take care of him. Or he can join us for s'mores after we eat the hot dogs."

That made me smile. "I don't think he eats s'mores."

Rick shrugged. "His loss. Anyway, put it out of your mind, and let's have some fun. We can eat, and then we'll go to the lake. Forget any of this ever happened."

I nodded at him confidently. He was right. I would forget, at least for today. But after this weekend, I would find a solution to this. I had a new piece of information, and I would have to find the strength to fight back. He was not going to win, not by a long shot.

***

We spent the afternoon at the lake. Rick wanted to go fishing, so he rented a boat. I just stayed on the shore and watched. He tried to get me to go out on the water, but I just wanted to bask in the sun and think for a while. Somewhere around midafternoon, I fell asleep. I woke to the sound of children yelling. I looked up and saw two boys, about five or six, fighting over a kite. I smiled as I watched them in a tug-of-war over the kite string.

I sat up and looked out at the lake. Rick was not alone, as he had been when he first went out. Some pedal boats were circling him, and swimmers of all ages cavorted in the shallows. Seeing this made me excited, and I leaped up to my feet and ran down the steep beach to the waterfront. It was much warmer than it had been earlier, well above eighty.

I jumped into the water, shorts and all, and immediately felt the cold chill of the lake engulf my entire body. I let my head go under the water and then, after a few seconds, I came up with a gasp. It felt so good, and I bobbed down again as I swam toward the deeper water.

I called out to Rick, who looked up. As soon as he saw me, he started the boat in my direction. After a few moments, he was next to me.

"Having a good time?" he said loudly over the small boat's engine.

"Yeah. How about you? Catch any fish?"

He smiled as he positioned the boat so that I could get in. With his head, he motioned at some ropes going over the edge of the boat, and I could tell there were at least four or five fish tied to them under the water.

"Wow!" I exclaimed.

"Yeah, they're biting pretty good today. I've been throwing them back for the past hour."

I climbed into the boat carefully as Rick held his weight on the other side so that it wouldn't tip.

"You want to try catching one?" he asked.

"Sure," I said as I sat on the middle thwart and picked up one of the fishing poles.

Rick turned the boat around and took me to the spot he had been in when I first saw him. I smiled at a cute boy who passed us in a pedal boat.

"Can you bait it?" he asked.

I nodded, and without hesitation I dug my hand into the container of worms and pulled out a big, slimy night crawler. As my dad had taught me, I pinched the worm right in the middle and cut him in half. Then I placed one of the halves back in the container and slid the other half onto the hook, careful not to expose any of the metal. I looked up at Rick, who was smiling. I could tell he was impressed.

He pointed out to a spot on the water. "That's been a pretty good spot for carp. Toss it out there."

I did as he said, and my lure fell into the general area he had pointed to. I settled in my seat and set the pole on the edge of the boat. I turned to the cooler and pulled out a can of soda.

"So you're doing better?" he asked, sipping on his own diet soda.

"I took a nap," I said, looking out over the water. "I think I'm going to be just fine."

"Being out here reminds me so much of your dad, you know," he said solemnly.

"Yeah, so many memories in this place," I said.

"Remember when you were like six—we came out here, and your dad forgot his swim shorts, so he swam in the cargo shorts he had on?" Rick said.

I smiled. "Yeah. He forgot his wallet in his pocket, and all his money got wet. I remember that because the whole ride home, he had all the money spread out on the dashboard so it could dry."

"You remember what happened next?" Rick asked.

I burst into laughter and said, "Yeah, he got pulled over, and the cop was like, 'Sir, why is all that money on your dashboard?'"

Rick was laughing along with me. "Yeah, the cop thought it was so funny when Victor told him the story that he didn't even give us a ticket."

Just as I was about to tell Rick another story, I saw the end of the fishing pole move.

"Rick," I said, "I think I got a bite."

"Go get it, then," he said, motioning for me to get up.

I picked up the pole, pulled back on it, and then wound it up. Whatever it was, it was big.

"Wow, looks like it's got some fight," Rick said as he watched the end of my pole bend almost forty-five degrees toward the water.

I wound it up some more and pulled back. The fish fought the line, and I could see its tail flap up above the surface. Even from about twenty feet away, I could tell it was a really big fish, much bigger than the ones Rick had caught.

"Wow!" Rick said at the sight of the tail splashing about. "That's a huge one! You need help?"

"No, I got it," I said with determination. I wanted to do this myself, and as strong as this fish was, I was going to be stronger. "Get the net ready. I'll pull it in, and you net it."

Rick turned and picked up the net as I struggled to pull the fish closer. I was met with fierce resistance with each new attempt to bring it in. At one point, I was afraid that the fishing pole would just snap in half, it was being bent at such an angle.

I got the sense that everyone around us was watching, and when I looked up, I was right. The fish was so big and was splashing about so hard that everyone within a fifty-foot radius took notice.

"He won't quit," I said as I pulled again.

"Don't keep pulling. By the looks of it, you're gonna snap the line. Let me try to edge the boat closer. Make sure to wind it as we approach," Rick said.

Rick started the motor, and I started winding the reel as we approached. The fish likely took notice of our advance. It started to swim in the other direction. Fortunately, the distance between us closed significantly even with the fish swimming away, and now it was only about five feet from the boat. As it swam to the surface, we could tell it was enormous.

"Wow! That's a largemouth bass! It has to be two feet long!" Rick exclaimed at the sight of the fish.

I pulled it closer, and Rick readied the net over the edge of the boat. Only a few feet away now, all I needed was one more tug, and it would be within range for Rick to scoop it out of the water. I gave it a little slack, wound it, and then tugged back with all my might. The line snapped, and I tumbled backward in the boat. My sudden movement caused the boat to rock, and as I lost my balance, I fell backward over the edge.

My back hit the water first, and then I was fully submerged. I faintly heard Rick yell my name as I went under. I'd instinctively taken a deep breath before falling in and immediately turned my body around so that my back faced the surface of the water. The cool lake chilled me immediately, and the waters below were dark and murky.

Just before I swam up, I noticed something floating about ten feet below me. As I focused through the murky water, I immediately realized what it was: a body.

Filled with fear, I burst up to the water's surface. Rick was readying himself to jump in after me, even though he knew I was a great swimmer.

"Are you OK?" Rick asked urgently.

I nodded. "I have to go back down. I saw something."

Rick looked confused. "Saw what?"

"I'll be right back," I said as I took another deep breath.

Rick yelled my name, but by that time, I was already below the surface.

I looked back at the spot and saw the body floating facedown. It was dressed in all white clothing. I turned and started descending toward it. As I approached, I could make out light-brown hair flowing in the water. The body was slender and lanky, and I guessed it was a female.

I reached out and turned the body toward me. To my surprise, the body felt warm, and as it slowly turned, the face was revealed. The skin was as white as a porcelain doll's. The eyes were closed. The face was familiar, but I couldn't quite place who she was. Suddenly, her eyes opened, revealing nothing but pale white eyeballs matching the pale skin. The sight was terrifying. I recoiled and screamed under the water, knowing that the only person who could hear me was myself. I turned for the surface, but right before I swam up, I took one unbelieving glance backward. This time, nothing was there.

I broke through the surface with a gasp, spitting out some of the water that had made it into my mouth when I screamed.

"What happened?" Rick exclaimed in a panicked tone.

I wiped my eyes and looked up. I decided not to tell him. It had just been a hallucination that I had no business seeing—unless I was, in fact, crazy.

"I thought I saw something like a body, but it turned out it was just a tree branch," I said, making the explanation up as I spoke.

Rick's forehead crinkled in confusion. "Tree branch?"

"Yeah, it had branches that looked like arms. I thought it might be somebody—you know, a dead body."

Rick reached out and took my hand to pull me closer to the boat. Then he went to the other side to balance it while I climbed in.

"Good thing it wasn't a body, then," he said.

I got into the boat dripping wet. I felt my body shaking and realized that I was in shock at what I had seen.

"I'm really cold," I said quickly, before Rick could notice my shaking.

He turned and pulled a towel from under one of the thwarts and gave it to me. I wrapped myself in it.

"Let's go cook up some of these fish," he said.

I nodded in agreement as I buried my head in the towel. I sat at the very front of the boat, and Rick went to the back to operate the engine. As the boat motored along, I faced away from him, looking forward at the approaching beach.

With everything I had, I pushed back the image of the woman underwater. I pretended it hadn't even happened, and surprisingly, it worked. I figured that because I'd seen so many things that nobody else had seen, my mind had learned how to forget quickly. I told myself I would think about this later, after we ate, after we built another fire, maybe even after we got back home.

My shaking subsided, and we got to the beach. Rick dropped me off and said he'd return the boat and meet me at the campsite. I gave him the most genuine smile I could muster, and he seemed to accept it without hesitation.

WE SPENT THE REST OF the day at the campsite and decided to save the fish for the next day and eat what we had packed for dinner. I barely slept that night. The image of the pale white face of the woman was embedded on my retinas when I closed my eyes. Every hour at night, I sat up in my tent, unzipped it, and looked out at the dark forest. Once dawn broke, I finally fell asleep. Rick let me sleep in until I woke sometime before eleven in the morning.

We went for a nature walk and then went to the general store to get some spices for cooking the fish. As Rick had promised, they did have soft-serve ice cream, which I helped myself to.

It was around two in the afternoon by the time we got back to the campsite. Rick did all the work. He gutted the fish, cleaned them, and cooked them. He told me to build the fire and just sit back and relax. I pretended to read my book, sitting on one of the folding chairs, but I really was thinking about the woman's body underwater. The one thing that kept eating away at me was how real she had looked and felt. Her body had been warm. I couldn't believe a hallucination could be so real.

We ate our meal and talked about the past. Rick told me stories about myself when I was only three. He made me laugh so hard I almost choked on a piece of fish. Once we finished dinner, he asked if I wanted to go home. I thought about it for a minute and decided that would be the best idea.

We packed up and loaded the car. Once we got in, I called Carl on his cell.

"Hey," I said. "Rick and I are coming back a day early, so maybe we can hang out tonight." I impressed myself with how natural my voice sounded.

Carl must have gleaned the same impression, because he paused for a second. "OK," he said. "You sure? 'Cause we can—"

"No, I'm sure. We should be back by eight. I need to take a shower and stuff, so come over at nine thirty," I said.

"OK," he said.

"I'll call you when I get home," I said.

Rick listened to the radio most of the ride home. He attempted to engage me in conversation, but after I gave him numerous one-word answers, he just turned up the radio, and we drove on, listening to the newest pop songs.

I spent the ride thinking about everything that had happened since the accident. I walked through every step in my head, searching every memory I had, and by the time we arrived at the house, I had made up my mind about Azrael.

Carl's car was already in the driveway. I smiled, shaking my head. He was so anxious to see me he couldn't even wait another few hours.

"Just go in and see your boyfriend. I'll get the stuff out of the car," Rick said as we pulled up to the house.

I gave him a smile and a hug. "Thanks," I said. "This trip was fun, and you've been so understanding. I know it must be hard having to deal with me."

He shook his head. "You'll be fine. Just make sure you let me know the next time you see this Azrael guy, and I'll take care of him."

I smirked at his comment, if he only knew, I thought.

"I'm not afraid of him," I said. "See you inside." I left the car.

I felt better being home, and I was telling Rick the truth about not being afraid of Azrael. After all the thinking I'd done on the ride home, I was sure that he couldn't hurt me even if he tried. It made perfect sense. If he was, in fact, the angel of death, I had seen that much with my own eyes. He had no power to kill. He was more concerned about me and how I could see him.

The way he followed me around, the way he had looked at me when I first saw him before he took the souls of my family—he was concerned. The one thing I didn't understand was why he was so concerned. This, I hoped, Carl could help me out with.

Carl was sitting on the couch in the living room when I got into the house. By the sound of it, Alicia was downstairs doing laundry. He sprang off the couch, and we embraced in the kitchen. I kissed him gently on the lips. We walked over to the living room, hands clenched. His clammy palm gripped my hand tightly.

"How are you?" he said as we sat on the couch.

"Much better, but we have to talk. Let's go up to my room," I said.

"OK," he said.

Carl sat on the bed, and I pulled my computer chair over. I told him in detail what had happened. He hung on every word, seemingly not blinking through the whole story. He was immediately mad at me for not telling him earlier. I explained that I didn't want to worry him and that it was actually a good thing that it had happened, as it made me feel better about the whole situation.

"I don't get it," he said. "After that, how can you be better?"

I straightened my posture and lifted my chin up. I wanted him to see I was confident in my resolution. "I'm not afraid of him because I know he can't hurt me. As long as I know that, I couldn't care less what he does or where he pops up."

Carl looked confused. "How do you know he can't hurt you? Didn't you just say he lifted you off the ground and dropped you?"

"Yes, but he threatened to kill me first, and he didn't even come close. If he had the power to do anything like that, he would have done it. Carl, I think he's concerned, and now it makes sense why he's been following me around. He's not haunting me; he's trying to figure out how I can see him. The only part I can't figure out is why he's so concerned."

Carl shook his head, and he appeared in deep thought as he stared at a spot on the floor.

"I thought about it the whole way here," I said. "Every time we saw each other, he just looked at me, and now I realize that he was just as confused as I am. He has no idea what's going on, either, you see? This is some kind of messed-up thing, and somehow the accident—you know, my head injury—has allowed me to see him." I trailed off when I saw Carl's face. It was painted with concern.

"Why are you looking at me like that?" I said. "You don't believe me?"

"Alex, I really don't know," he said. "I don't think you should take this thing so lightly."

"Lightly? What do you mean, lightly? This *thing* is following me around everywhere I go, and I have to figure out why."

"I'm just saying that anything that has the power to pick you up off the ground and drop you has the power to hurt you. What if he picked you up and dropped you off a cliff or a building? I mean, this is scary."

"I'm done being scared, Carl. It's a month and a half since the accident, and I'm ready to move on. You need to help me out on this. I need to figure out why he cares so much about me seeing him. If I figure that out, maybe I can fix this. Maybe I can—I don't know—reason with him," I said.

"Reason with the angel of death?" Carl said. "How do you reason with a thing that takes people's souls?"

"There's gotta be a way. He was the one to open the dialogue. Maybe next time we meet, I can talk to him, figure this out. He might even tell me why he's so concerned about me. Aside from that, you have to see things from my perspective. I know now he's not just trying to haunt me. I thought that was what he was doing the entire time. Truth is, he's just like me: confused. Maybe he's scared too."

Carl fell back on the bed and ran his hands through his hair. He was facing the ceiling as he said, "Maybe he's just waiting for the right time to hurt you, Alex. I don't know about this theory. It doesn't add up."

I stood up, stepped over to the bed, and sat next to Carl, who was still lying down. He propped himself up on his side with his elbow.

"I thought of that too, Carl. The right time to hurt me would've been out in the woods, where we were all alone. He's not going to hurt me; I can feel it."

"OK, so what now? What do you do?"

I thought for a minute, and then I said, "I think I'll go see Dr. Khan on Monday. Maybe he can help me sort this out."

"Why don't you try him tomorrow?" Carl said.

"Sunday? He wouldn't be working."

Carl shook his head. "He was in on a lot of Sundays when you were in the hospital. I bet he's working. I'll call him."

"You gonna come with me?" I asked.

"Of course," Carl said and smiled.

We stared at each other for a long moment, and for the first time since we had become girlfriend and boyfriend, he initiated a kiss.

We went on kissing for a while on the bed, not getting too close. I thought about kissing Jeremy and how I'd lost control. With Carl, I wasn't like that. He was gentle and proper and never made any move past kissing and rubbing my shoulders. He made me feel so safe and happy.

We spent the next few hours just talking about school and other things. Carl was so sweet. He had gathered all my assignments for each of my classes for the past week and sorted them in a binder. He said he would bring it to me the next day. We kissed again briefly, and then he left.

I went to bed as soon as he left. Just before I fell asleep, I thought about the woman with the white face again and seeing her seemingly life-filled body at the bottom of Silver Lake. The image of her had gone as fast as it had come. I hadn't told Carl about it. I was sure he wouldn't believe me, and frankly, I hadn't let myself believe that it was real, either.

16

Islept until eleven in the morning. I woke once, to the sound of the
car starting around eight—no doubt it was Rick going to church. I had
a pang of guilt because I wasn't going with him, but once he was gone, I fell
back to sleep.

When I rose again, I lay in bed for a while, staring at the ceiling. The image of the woman at the bottom of the lake once again surfaced in my mind. I
wondered if it had any meaning, or I was just imagining it. I wished now that
I hadn't panicked. Maybe it was my panic that had caused her to disappear. I
couldn't get the sight of those white eyeballs out of my mind. They were just
as chilling as Azrael's pitch-black eyes were. I shook away the image and sat
up in my bed. I looked out the window, where the sun shone brightly.

I stepped out of bed, unplugged my phone, and looked at the missed-call
log. Carl had called twice before ten in the morning. I smirked; he had a lot
to learn about his new squeeze. Ten in the morning might as well be four
in the morning for me, especially on a Sunday.

I dialed his number. It rang twice, and then he picked up.

"Hey," he said.

"'Morning," I said.

"Sorry if my calls woke you—"

"No," I said. "My phone was on silent."

"Oh, that's good. Then I don't feel so bad."

"Even if you did, don't feel bad. I need someone to wake me up early. I always sleep late on the weekends," I said. I was lying, though. The truth was that I never wanted to have to be up earlier than eleven on weekends, but a new boyfriend didn't need to know that.

"OK, well, I set us up to see Dr. Khan. He said to come by at two. He said he's happy to see you, even on a Sunday."

"That's really nice of him," I said.

"Yeah, he really seems to care. I like him," Carl said. "I'm gonna come by in twenty minutes. You want something to eat?"

"No, thanks. Alicia will probably have breakfast made already. Poor lady, she works so hard with the twins. The least I could do is eat the food."

"OK. See you soon," he said.

I said goodbye and hung up. I went downstairs to the kitchen, and as expected, Alicia had already made coffee and was beating some eggs.

"Heard you talking on the phone. Thought I'd start breakfast. Hope omelets are OK," she said as she continued to swirl the eggbeater around in the glass bowl.

"You really don't have to do this every morning. I'm the one who should be doing this for you. You guys have been too nice to me," I said.

She smiled. "Alex, if I wanted you to cook, I might as well take us all out to eat. Your mom, God rest her soul, told me you didn't know a ladle from a soup spoon."

I laughed. She was right; I didn't. "Whatever. I'm good at other stuff. Cooking isn't my strong suit."

Alicia, still smiling, said, "You are. Anyway, I love cooking for you and Rick," she said as she poured the eggs into the frying pan, which let out a hot sizzle. Just then a cry came from the babies' room.

"I gotta go give them a bottle. This omelet will be fine on low heat until I get back. Just watch it for a minute," she said as she turned down the flame under the pan.

I nodded, poured myself a cup of coffee, and sat at the kitchen table. When she got back, she served me the omelet, and we had breakfast together. When we finished, I helped her with the dishes.

Carl arrived right after we finished the dishes. He knocked on the front door, and I went to greet him.

"Hey," I said.

"Hi. How you feeling?" he said as he walked in.

"Good. We were just having some breakfast. You want some?"

He smiled. "Sure. I'm starving. I ran out of the house without eating anything. Guess I couldn't wait to see you."

I smiled, and I was pretty sure I blushed too. I gave him a quick kiss on the lips to show my thanks. Then he blushed.

"C'mon in. Alicia said she'd make you an omelet while I get ready," I said, showing him into the kitchen.

He sat down at the kitchen table, and I went up to my room to get ready.

I put on a pair of jeans and a T-shirt. It was a shirt Carl brought me the day they picked me up from the hospital. It had a little *M* for Michigan on it. I thought about my father when I wore the shirt. He was the biggest Michigan sports fan I had ever met. I felt a flutter of pain in my stomach as his image came to mind. I quickly looked away from the mirror. The pain of dealing with death was just a prelude. It seemed to fade, and in its stead was the missing. The missing never really faded, and frankly, I never thought it would go away. I would learn much later that it didn't go away; it just got easier.

I ran downstairs. Carl was done with his breakfast, and he took my hand as we walked out. Alicia wished us luck and said we should be back by four for dinner.

Carl was driving his mother's minivan. It looked similar to the one we had, although I wasn't much of an expert on cars, so it could have been totally different.

We drove to Dr. Khan's office, listening to the latest pop hits on the radio. I was amazed at how many new songs had come out since I had been in the hospital. Many of them were not that good, but they all had one thing in common: a catchy hook that induced rhythmic head bobbing.

We arrived at Dr. Khan's office. The parking lot was empty except for a few cars.

"Are you sure he's here?" I asked, wondering if there was anyone in the building other than the cleaning crew.

"For sure. I called him just before I picked you up. He said to ring the bell at the front of the building, and he'd come and get us."

We arrived at the front of the building, and sure enough, there was a small, black panel with a white button right next to the door. Carl rang it, and within minutes, I saw Dr. Khan walking through the double doors.

"Hello," he said, half smiling as he opened one of the doors.

"Hey, Doctor," I said.

"Come in. It's just us today," he said as he held the door open for Carl and me to walk through.

The building was semidark, as most of the lights were turned off.

"You know, I really feel bad for bringing you in here on a Sunday," I said apologetically.

Dr. Khan smiled. "Anything for you, Alex. Plus, my wife took our daughters to New York for the weekend to visit her parents. I don't watch football; so frankly, I have nothing better to do."

"Now, that's hard to believe," Carl said.

"What? That I don't watch football or that I have nothing better to do?" Dr. Khan asked.

"I guess both," Carl said.

Dr. Khan let out a little laugh. "Let's meet in my office. I made a fresh pot of coffee."

We walked through the dark, narrow hallways of the medical building and arrived at Dr. Khan's office. I took a cup of coffee, and we sat down.

"So what can I help you with?" Dr. Khan said as he sat down.

I explained the last encounter with Azrael, and his eyes widened when I told the part about being levitated and dropped to the ground. Then, before I realized what I was doing, I blurted out the part about the woman in the lake. In my head, I'd played the scene in the lake a million times, and even though I didn't want to say it, it just came out.

Carl turned to me in surprise. "You never told me that," he said.

"Well, I didn't believe it was real at first, but I can't stop thinking about it. I don't know; it was so scary at the time, but I wish I could go back and see if it was real. You know, maybe if I shook her or something, maybe—"

"That can't be real," Carl said. "Are you sure you didn't dream it?"

I opened my mouth to speak, but Dr. Khan interrupted. "From what I know about posttraumatic stress, it is very common to mistake other things for people. The fact that the image disappeared as soon as it came tells me that it was probably just a hallucination," he said.

"It was so real, though," I said, thinking of the woman under the water.

"I'm more concerned with the levitation. Now, are you sure that's exactly how it happened?" Dr. Khan asked.

"Yes," I said, not appreciating the skepticism. "He lifted me up off the ground and dropped me. He was concerned with figuring out how or why I could see him. I've decided that he is just as concerned about me as I am about him. I'm not afraid anymore."

Dr. Khan seemed to survey my expression. I could tell he was sizing up my last statements. "Then what is it that you'd like me to do? It sounds like you've got things figured out."

Carl said, "While we know that he is concerned about Alex and how she can see him, we are not sure why he cares so much. I mean, he's been following her around everywhere, and now he's lifting her up in the air and stuff like that. Why is he doing this? What does it matter?"

Dr. Khan sat back in his chair and nodded. He was contemplating the questions. "Maybe he's never been seen. That's very possible."

"How's that possible?" I asked. "Aren't there stories about the angel of death or whatever you want to call him? A lot of people have claimed to see him."

Dr. Khan raised his eyebrows. "Claimed," he said. "You, my dear, have proof that you've seen him. And frankly, I believe your story over all the others. Think about it. Every other account of this being, so to speak, is of a tall skeleton with a black cloak and a large cane. Either that or some variation. You've described this guy as though he were right here next to us, and frankly, it makes sense to me."

"But why does that bother him enough to haunt her?" Carl asked.

Dr. Khan thought for another moment. This seemed to stump him. Then he said, "Maybe he's afraid you might do something to get in his way. Remember what you told me about the woman in the hospital? I've thought about that a lot and how certain you were that he arrived right before the alarms went off—before she died. Now it makes a little sense. Look at it from his perspective. You see him, and then someone dies. What if you decided that you would step in the second you saw him—as he was waiting for a death to occur—and you saved the person's life?"

Now I sat back in my chair. This made perfect sense to me. I remembered how he'd stared so intently as he dragged the woman's soul out of the hospital room. His eyes had pierced through mine, but now I knew that he was questioning my gaze. If he had a brain in that scary head of his, I bet it was thinking what Dr. Khan had just told us. "You're right," I said.

Carl turned to me and nodded. He seemed to agree. "Then, maybe the next time you see him…I don't know…you can tell him that."

"Tell him what?" I asked.

"Tell him that you know why he's concerned and that you won't get in the way of his business," Carl said.

I smiled, mostly to myself. It was as if we were talking about a guy on the street. "Carl, I can't talk to him. He has some power. He can freeze me. How am I supposed to talk to him?"

Carl shrugged. "Close your eyes. Or turn around. Something like that. Maybe it'll give you just enough time to say a few words."

I looked at Dr. Khan. His face told me that he agreed. "Makes sense," he said. "You stated that he communicated to you. Now you can communicate to him. Just do it before he puts that trance on you, and maybe that'll send him on his way."

I sighed. It all sounded a lot easier than it would be in practice. But I agreed it was worth a shot.

We went on to talk about my injuries and how well I was healing. Close to the end of our conversation, I said, "Thanks for meeting me today, Doctor. I feel better now."

He smiled. "Anytime." Then he looked at Carl. "Carl, would you give me a second to talk to Alex?"

"Sure." Carl nodded, stood up, and walked out of the office.

Once the door was closed, Dr. Khan said, "Alex, I'm worried about you." I sighed. "I am too."

"I'm not saying that I think you're crazy—you are very convincing. I'm worried that whatever this thing is, maybe it will cause you to hurt yourself. We also can't rule out the chance that you are in fact hallucinating. I just don't want you to get hurt."

"I know I saw it, and I know this happened," I said. "But…I don't know…maybe I'm seeing things."

He sat back in his chair. "Last time I asked you to contact Dr. Reynolds, and it doesn't sound like you've done that. I strongly suggest you go to him. Or, how about an inpatient rehab unit?"

I shook my head vigorously. "I'm not going to another hospital, let alone a crazy one. Maybe I should go see Dr. Reynolds."

He nodded. "I think it's a good idea that you have regular sessions with him. I think it would help you out a lot."

Although I didn't like the idea, I reluctantly agreed. "OK," I said. "I still have his card. I'll call him and set something up."

"Sounds good. I'll talk to him today or tomorrow and let him know you'll be calling."

I looked over to his credenza, where his pictures were displayed. I noticed that the one with his wife was gone.

"Looks like you lost a picture," I said.

He looked uncomfortable. "We're getting divorced," he said.

I was shocked and felt bad for even bringing it up. "I'm so sorry. I didn't mean to pry," I said.

He leaned forward on the desk, folding his arms on it. "No, it was my fault. I crossed the line."

I didn't really want to pry, but his cryptic response piqued my interest. "Crossed the line?"

"I...well...you know...I shouldn't tell you." He looked at me with sad eyes. Then, after a moment, he said, "I cheated on her with my old girlfriend. Two weeks ago, when I was at a convention in Vegas. I don't know what got into me. We just met for a casual dinner after I saw her on the first day of the convention, and then things just got out of hand. I guess I still love her. Since the convention, we've kept in touch on a daily basis—phone calls and text messages. Well, I was sure my wife knew, so two days ago, I just told her. And she stormed out. Went to New York with the girls to stay with her parents."

"I'm sorry," I said, not really knowing what else to say.

"No, I'm sorry for saying anything. It's just that I haven't told anyone, not even the other woman. She still thinks I'm with my wife. I'm in the middle, not knowing what to do, so I've just been working every day."

I couldn't believe what I was hearing. Dr. Khan didn't seem like the type of person who would ever cheat on his wife. We sat there in silence for a long while. I could tell he was thinking about whether he should tell me more.

I broke the silence. "My best friend started screwing a guy who tried to rape me the night before the accident. I stopped talking to her. I felt really bad, and...well, I don't know...I really haven't gotten over it yet. I think that in time, I will. Maybe your wife feels the same way. Maybe if you just let time pass and try to win her back, she'll get over it too."

He shrugged. "Yeah, maybe you're right, but I don't know. This other woman—she's…"

When his voice trailed off, I said, "You still love her."

He nodded.

"That's tough," I said.

He nodded in agreement and then stood up and extended his right hand to shake mine. "Don't forget to call Dr. Reynolds," he said, giving me his best smile.

"And don't forget to get some rest. You can't work every day," I said.

He nodded. "I'm going straight home. Sorry for telling you all that really—"

"No apology needed," I said. "You sit here on a Sunday afternoon, listening to my crazy ghost stories. It's the least I can do."

He smiled. "Thank you. I don't have very many people to talk to. I guess I've been bottling this in for too long. Please, don't hesitate to call me. I'll do everything I can to fix this for you."

I nodded. "So you say I should try to talk to Azrael?"

"I can't think of anything else. If this thing is as real as you say it is, what else are you going to do?"

He opened the door, and I stood in the doorway, extending my hand again to shake his. I gave him a smile. "I think we're both going to be OK," I said.

He returned the smile. "I hope so."

I left his office and found Carl sitting in the dark waiting room, playing on his phone.

"Everything OK?" he asked as he hopped out of his chair.

"Yeah. He went over some clinical stuff about the surgery," I said, trying to sound convincing. I felt uncomfortable lying to Carl, but I was certain that Dr. Khan didn't want me to talk about his marital problems with anyone else.

"OK, well, so what's next?" Carl asked as we headed for the exit.

I thought about that for a second. It was actually a pretty tough question to answer. What was next? I mean, I couldn't summon Azrael and talk to him. Normally, when he popped up, it was a complete surprise.

"I really don't know," I said.

We walked outside and started toward the car. We were about ten feet from the car when Carl stopped dead, and his face lit up. He seemed to be hit with some revelation.

"This might sound crazy—"

"It probably is," I said. "Most 'this sounds crazy' ideas usually are."

He smiled. "No, really. Think about it. What's the biggest problem we have?"

"That I can't simply go to Azrael's house, knock on his front door, and say, 'Hey there, guy who takes people's souls, can we talk?'" I said.

"Exactly," Carl said. "But what if you hang out where he would most likely be spotted?"

"Like where?"

"A hospital, a cemetery, a morgue—I don't know, places where there are a lot of dead people," he said.

I thought this over. He was right.

"OK, well, what do you think is the best place?" I asked.

"The hospital," Carl said immediately. "I mean, where else do people die all the time? He has to be there like twenty hours a day."

"OK, that's probably true, but how do we just hang around the hospital without having security breathing down our necks?"

Carl appeared to be stumped, but it lasted only a moment. Then he smiled. "I know exactly how we do it," he said. "C'mon. Hop in. I'll tell you on the way home."

We got into the car, and he did tell me. As it turned it out, it was one hell of a good idea.

17

PART OF CARL'S PLAN INVOLVED me going back to school, which threw the whole idea of finishing my classwork at home out the window. I figured that no matter what, I would've chosen to go back to school anyway. I already felt like such a burden on everyone, but to have Mr. Polderman at my house almost every day tutoring me definitely crossed the line.

Another part of his plan involved telling Rick that I could not work at the construction site. I told Rick over Sunday dinner. He didn't seem too bothered by my revelation, and who could blame him? I hadn't really shown myself to be a very stable person over the past few weeks, and I imagined he was worried that I might not do too well at his job.

The following day was Monday. Carl and I woke up really early to go to the school's main office. When he picked me up, he had a hot cup of coffee in the cupholder on my side of the center console. I immediately took it and sipped with the same passion I imagined most cocaine addicts exhibited when they were getting a fix. The first sip instantly brought me out of my semicomatose state, and the world around me resumed traveling at regular speed.

"You really love that stuff," Carl said, smiling. While sipping my coffee, I hadn't realized that he was still parked and watching me drink.

"Well, yeah, it's seven in the morning. Who the heck can function at that hour?" Then I realized that he didn't have a cup of coffee in his hand. "Don't you drink coffee?"

He put the car in gear and merged onto the street. "No," he said as he checked his side-view mirror. "I can't have caffeine. It gives me jitters and anxiety attacks."

"What? Really?" I asked. "Then how do you wake up so early all the time?"

Carl smiled. "I open my eyes," he said playfully.

"You know what I mean," I said. "Seriously, if it wasn't for coffee, I would have failed every class I've ever had that started before eleven in the morning."

"Don't know," he said. "I do just fine without it. You know, there was a time when people didn't have coffee to wake them up in the morning."

I took another sip. The coffee had cooled. It didn't burn my tongue to take a bigger gulp, but it was still warm enough that I felt it going all the way down my esophagus.

"I really feel bad for those people," I said. "I bet they were late for a lot of early-morning appointments."

"Well, I'm never late, and I don't drink coffee," Carl said.

"That's 'cause you're a nerd, Carl," I said, giving him little punch on the shoulder as he stopped at a traffic light.

He turned to me and smiled. I smiled back. His dark-brown eyes seemed to sparkle even though the sun was barely peeking above the horizon. I had never known what people meant by feeling butterflies in the stomach, but just then, I felt one of my own flap its wings, just a little. Embarrassed and likely blushing, I looked away, and Carl refocused on the road ahead.

We arrived at school just before seven thirty. Carl parked in the student parking lot. I felt a little bit awkward as his car came to a stop. For most seniors, arriving at school with a boyfriend or girlfriend was pretty customary. Actually, it was the cool thing to do. Most of the other kids who didn't have to take the bus just rode with their friends. But the cool kids—they all came in pairs, male and female. They were the envy of the rest. However, that was not what was making things awkward. Another aspect of arriving at school with a significant other was the early morning make-out session. It was very common to see cars parked in odd places in the thirty minutes to an hour before school started, and of course, everyone envied those in the parked cars.

We sat in silence for a moment, parked in the student parking lot. All the cars around us were empty, and there was no sign of any new ones pulling in. He didn't leave the car. In fact, he left the engine running so the heater would keep the car warm. I didn't so much as motion for the door handle. In fact, I placed the cup of coffee in the cupholder on the car door, not the one between us. Then it just happened.

Every other time I'd ever kissed Carl, it had been...well, it had been nice. I was mildly aroused and always knew when it was time to stop. This time, it was different. It had been a few days since we'd made out, and since then, I'd found myself thinking about him more. I would smile to myself in the dark right before bed as I thought about a joke he'd told. That morning, I even caught myself spending a few extra minutes in front of the mirror, adjusting my hair and even putting on some cover-up.

I kissed him with the same passion I had felt that one night with Jeremy. He pulled me closer, and half my body was over the center console. I felt the gearshift lightly jab into my hip as I rested my mouth firmly on his. I took his right hand, which was neutrally placed on the small of my back, pulled it around and held it to my breast. He gave me a squeeze, and I felt a small jolt of electricity flow through me.

I reached down and felt between his legs. I caressed him gently, and he let out a moan of pleasure as our lips came apart. Feeling wild, I looked around to make sure nobody was looking, and then I unzipped his pants. He was staring at me in shock.

Not really knowing what to do, I just started rubbing him and watched for a reaction. He seemed to enjoy it, and so I continued, all the while looking around for any onlookers.

"Don't worry; I'll keep an eye out," I said, as I noticed that he too was looking around.

He tilted his head back in pleasure and closed his eyes. I kept on going until he convulsed and let it out. He smiled with satisfaction and breathed deeply.

"Wow," he said, looking at me.

I smiled. "Wow, indeed." I was a little bit shocked by the brevity of the whole thing.

He smirked. "Well, my underwear is soaked."

I laughed. "Oops. Maybe we should go home and get you a new pair."

He smiled. "No biggie. I have a gym bag in the trunk. I have an extra pair."

I gave him a kiss, and after he zipped up, we both got out of the car. He went around to the trunk and got his bag. I just looked at him. While he was the one who'd had most of the fun, something about pleasing him gave me a deep sense of satisfaction. I thought about all the times I had looked at the parked cars in the student lot and told myself I would never be one of those girls. Now that I was, though, it wasn't so bad. At only eighteen, I learned there are two types of envious people in this world: those who want, and those who act as if they don't want. I had always been one of the actors, but deep down, I had wanted.

We walked to the school, hands locked. Carl walked funny from the uncomfortable wet mess between his legs. We went to the locker room first, and he changed; then we went to the cafeteria and had breakfast. We joked and laughed over cinnamon rolls and eggs. Carl told me what he had done over the weekend while I was with Rick at Silver Lake. Then he recounted a few scenes from his favorite sitcom, which had aired over the weekend. He did such a good job telling the jokes that I almost choked on my food.

Once done, we headed to the office to finalize Carl's master plan. The school had a co-op placement at Crescent City Hospital for kids who couldn't find jobs. We needed to spend time at the hospital without raising suspicion. Working there was the best plan of action. Although Carl was already working at Macy's, he agreed that he'd work fewer shifts at his job to make time to work with me at the hospital.

The transition was painless. The girl I had run into the first time was there, and she seemed excited that we wanted to work at the hospital. Of course, it would not be until much later that I learned why she was so excited. In any event, all we had to do was fill out one form to cancel our current co-ops and an application to work at the hospital. It took about ten minutes, and as we were about to leave, the girl told us to report to the hospital first thing after school that day.

"Wow, they pay ten dollars an hour," Carl said as we walked out of the office. I knew he was only getting eight fifty at Macy's.

"Yeah, but it was way too easy to get in. I bet there's some kind of catch," I said wearily.

"You're probably right. I told my manager at Macy's yesterday that I would just work two shifts at the hospital for a couple weeks, just in case."

I nodded. "Well, if this plan works, maybe we'll need only a few days."

Just as we arrived at our lockers, the first bell rang, which meant it was twenty minutes until first period. Since Carl and I didn't have first- or second-period classes due to our co-ops, he agreed he'd spend the first few hours of the day tutoring me at the library.

When I opened my locker, I gasped in surprise.

"What? What is it?" Carl said, sounding concerned.

In the bottom of the locker was small glass vase that held some flowers. The bouquet was so large that it barely fit in the locker and was pressed up against the walls on either side. A card sat at the top.

"Did you do this?" I asked.

He shook his head.

I bent over and got the card. Reading the first word, I instantly knew that it was from Kate.

> *Allie,*
>
> *I've rewritten this message in my journal maybe a thousand times, trying to get it right, and it's because there is so much I want to tell you. I know it must have been hard seeing me and Jeremy, but I wish I could have had a chance to explain. One thing I am so sorry for was not coming to see you once you got better. I have no excuse for that. It was just that when I saw you in the hospital with those tubes and wires, I almost died. I was so scared, and I think I cried every night for two weeks. I couldn't see you like that, and the more I didn't come, the more my pain seemed to go away. I know that sounds selfish, but I don't know what else to say. Then, the one time I came to see you, when they said you came to, you somehow knew about me and Jeremy, and you kept swearing and saying terrible things. I know now that wasn't you, but you have to see it from my perspective. I was so hurt. Please forgive me. I don't want to lose my best friend.*
>
> *Kate*

I had tears in my eyes as I finished reading the card. I looked at Carl, and I could tell he knew who it was from.

"Did you talk to her?" I said, sniffling.

"No. This is a complete surprise to me too," he said.

I handed him the card, and he read it.

Once done, he said, "You should talk to her. It's time."

I nodded. He was right. Third period, I was going to pull her aside and put this behind us. I agreed with Kate; I didn't want to lose my best friend, either, even though, arguably, Carl had filled that role already. But still, this was Kate. She was the first one I called whenever I had good news, bad news, or if I just felt bored. She was the most popular girl in school, and I was not even on the C-list, yet we hung out on a regular basis. She had loved Bailey, and she was always at my house. Ever since middle school, we'd been like sisters. I couldn't just throw that away. Plus, while I was sure that I'd pleased Carl in the parking lot earlier, I was surer that I had no idea what the heck I was doing, and Kate was the right person to ask. There was a special bond between girlfriends, and while easily broken, it was also easy to mend.

I spent the next few hours in the library with Carl, going over the notes from the last two weeks of class. All the while, my mind never left Kate. She must have known that I was coming back to school that day, and the likely leaker of that information was Alicia. My stomach turned as I thought about what she might have been going through all these weeks. She said she cried every night for two weeks, which sounded almost impossible. But knowing Kate, that was a probability. She always did things with passion, and she took everything to the extreme. If she drank, she got drunk. When she was throwing a party, it was an extravaganza. When she decided to spend a lazy day at home, she dressed like a hobo and never left the couch.

We finished our studies, and when the librarian went to the back room—and since we were the only ones in the library at such an early hour—we sneaked in another quick make-out session. Carl seemed very pleased about my enthusiasm, and frankly, I was just feeling…I don't know… frisky. Something about him today was different, and I think I owed it all to my weekend altercation with Azrael. I had been so scared when I was suspended in midair, and it was Carl whom I thought about first. It was not because I was talking with him on the phone; it was because I was afraid I wouldn't see him again. Deep down inside, I think I loved him.

At the third-period bell, Carl and I left the library. He walked me to my locker and then kissed me goodbye as he left for his class. I was headed for physics, my first class of the day with Kate. I decided that I would be very bold, and I would just sit right next to her and apologize. I rushed to the class as fast as I could, hoping that I would have at least a minute to talk before the second bell rang, signifying the beginning of third period.

I arrived at Mr. Polderman's classroom just two minutes before third period was about to start. As soon as I walked in, I looked at the back of the classroom and locked eyes with Kate. She was sitting in the same chair she had sat in before. She gave me a faint smile, and I returned it in kind.

I walked slowly toward her. At first, she seemed to hesitate, but then she rushed to her feet and embraced me.

"I'm so sorry," she bellowed as she hugged me and started crying.

"Me too," I said and started crying too. We stood there in each other's arms sobbing. The third-period bell rang, but neither of us noticed. It was not until Mr. Polderman approached us that we even realized that the entire class had filed in and everyone was staring at us.

"Ladies," Mr. Polderman said as he gently placed his hands on our adjoining shoulders, "Are you going to be OK?"

Kate and I broke apart, our sobs subsided, and I looked at her. She nodded with that same faint smile on her face. "Yeah, we're good," she said.

As soon as she spoke those words, a few of our classmates erupted in applause. Then the rest of the class joined in. I couldn't help but smile, and Kate smiled back as we took our seats.

"All right, all right," Mr. Polderman said. "Let's get into today's lesson." His lisp was in full force that day, making me smile.

I looked at Kate, and she was smiling gently.

That afternoon, I sat with Kate in the cafeteria. We skipped our fifth-period class (seniors got away with murder at Crescent City High School) and just talked. She acted totally shocked when I told her about Azrael, but I saw through that right away.

"So Carl has told you everything," I said.

She shrugged. "Well, yeah. I was worried, and I demanded it. It wasn't hard."

I smiled. "You always get what you want."

She gave me a wink.

"Did he tell you about our plan?" I asked.

She nodded. "Yeah, last night he called me."

"So you're having late-night chats with my boyfriend?"

She smiled. "It was like six o'clock, and we talked for five minutes. Anyway, I already have a boyfriend."

An awkward silence followed. We hadn't discussed Jeremy at all. I had sent a text to Carl asking him to leave us alone at lunch, and I was sure she had done the same with Jeremy.

"Yeah, he's a real winner," I said.

She sighed. I wished I hadn't said that, but it had slipped. One thing I didn't regret was smashing Jeremy's face with the glass bottle; that, I wished I could do one more time.

"I understand you're still mad. I would be too. But if this thing is serious, and we're going to be friends forever, you need to accept him. I mean, your kids might one day call him uncle."

I laughed. This was the part of Kate that I found the most comical. Every new boyfriend was "the one," and they always broke up with her after a few months of getting the milk for free.

"What's so funny?" she demanded.

"Kate, I love you; you know that. But you said the same thing about Steve, and he dumped you junior year. You can't expect me to take you seriously," I said.

"Well, Jeremy is different. I had sex with Steve."

I was shocked. "So you and Jeremy never…" I finished my sentence by twirling my index finger in a circle.

She shook her head with a look of confidence. "No," she said. "And you and Carl have gone further around the bases than Jeremy and I have."

I recoiled. "What? What did he tell you?"

She laughed and slouched toward me. "Allie, someone saw you guys in the parking lot this morning. Everyone knows."

Now I was in total shock. "How? There was no…" Then I thought about the red Chevy truck that had been parked on the other side of the lot.

"Wait," I said. "What does 'everyone' know?"

She smiled but looked a bit bemused. "You guys did it in his car."

"Oh my God!" I exclaimed. "How the hell can you mistake a hand job for sex?"

Kate burst into laughter, and we both immediately looked around the cafeteria. We were the only ones in there, but I was so loud that my words had echoed, and anyone within the vicinity could easily have heard me.

"My sweet Allie finally rubbed one out for a guy. I'm so proud," she said once her laughter subsided.

"Whatever. I still want to know how someone thought we had sex."

She shook her head and shrugged. "You guys got out of a car that likely had steamed-up windows. You were parked for a while, I'm sure. Keep in mind that sex is not the only thing that goes on in the student lot before school. A lot of these kids are dumb enough to smoke pot there. Some kids were probably smoking, and they saw you guys."

The mention of pot made me think of Jeremy. "Was Jeremy there?" I said mockingly. "You know, smoking pot?"

She dismissed my comment. "No. He doesn't smoke anymore," she said.

I was surprised. From my vague recollection, he was something of a marijuana connoisseur. "Wow," I said. "You've got him pretty whipped."

She gave me a sly smile. "I've learned from my mistakes," she said thoughtfully.

I nodded. "You know what, Kate? I'm sorry. I assumed he'd been to the promised land more times than Moses with you. I was wrong to think that."

She smiled with satisfaction. I could tell this was a point of pride for her. But I knew Kate, and I knew that as proud as she was, it was ridiculously hard for her to abstain from sex. She may have been an addict, maybe not, but she was definitely experienced—and from what I gathered, never satisfied.

"Thank you," she said. "Now tell me more about your plan with this thing that follows you around. Allie, I looked it up, and he's nobody to mess with."

"Yeah, well I've seen that firsthand. The problem is that I keep seeing him. Ever since the accident, he's been following me around. Like I told you earlier, he seems to be very concerned with how I can see him. This got me thinking that maybe I just need to confront him and tell him to leave me alone or something like that. Maybe he'll hear me out."

Kate sighed and shook her head. "But what if he hurts you?"

"He already has, at least mentally. Kate, I can't sleep right. Every few nights I have dreams, and he's in them chasing me. Every dream I have ends the same way: he catches me, and I wake up. I was so scared at first. Now I think I'm just crazy. I want to move on with my life, and I want this thing out of it."

Kate just looked at me, concern painted all over her face. I had a feeling she wasn't completely convinced that what I was saying was real. I was OK with that. I didn't blame her; I would be skeptical myself.

"It's at least worth a shot," I said. "After school, Carl and I are going to go to the hospital and start working. I'm almost guaranteed to see him there. Someone must die at least once a day."

"Oh," Kate said sympathetically, "that's so sad."

"Well, it's true. I'm tired, Kate. I hate him so much."

Just then, the sixth-period bell rang. Kate and I had precalculus, which was a class we had to attend. We packed up our stuff and dumped all our trash in a nearby can.

"Allie," Kate said as we started walking toward class and the halls slowly filled with students, "I really missed you."

I smiled and looked at her fondly. "I missed you too."

With that, we went to class. Best friends once again.

18

AFTER SCHOOL, CARL AND I went straight to the hospital and reported to the human resources department. We were greeted by a young receptionist. Carl seemed to like her; I could tell because he stuttered when he talked. She gave us some forms to fill out and told us that we would follow Dan around. He would show us what we would be doing. We walked to an adjoining waiting room and sat down to fill out our paperwork.

Once done with our forms, we turned them in to the receptionist. A few minutes later, a tall black man approached us. He looked to be in his forties, but he had a youthful pep in his step.

"Hello," he said. "You guys the new students?"

We smiled and nodded. Carl stood up to shake the man's hand. "Yes, sir. I'm Carl."

The man smiled and shook Carl's hand. I followed suit.

"I'm Dan," he said as he took my hand.

"Alex," I said with a smile.

"Great. Now that we're friends, let's show you guys around. Either of you ever been here?" Greg asked.

I looked at Carl. He gave me a faint smile. "She stayed here after her accident," Carl said. "I used to visit her all the time."

Greg turned and looked at me. "Accident?"

"Yeah, I was in a car accident at the end of August. I lost my parents and my little sister," I said.

He nodded solemnly. "I remember you," he said. "Yeah, you were the talk of the hospital for a few weeks. You're lucky to be alive."

Yeah, "lucky," I thought. Here I was, working in a hospital so I could confront some demon that was haunting me not two months after losing my entire family. I was pretty lucky.

"Thanks," I said.

"OK, well, today I'm gonna show you guys around. HR will be getting you badges, and next time you come in, you'll be on your own. Don't worry, though; it's not a tough job. All you gotta know is where to go and where not to go. And of course, how to run the washing machines."

I looked at him quizzically. "Washing machines?"

Dan smiled. "Yeah. How else you going to wash the sheets?"

I looked at Greg and then at Carl. It suddenly occurred to me that I had no idea what job we'd just signed up for. I was so focused on finding Azrael that I hadn't bothered to ask.

"You did read the job description at the school, right? It was right on the form you filled out," Dan said.

I shook my head no.

Dan laughed. "Oh man, this is going to be fun. Sorry, little lady, but you're in for a real shock. No way can I sugarcoat it. C'mon now; we got some work to do. Talking ain't gonna get us anywhere."

Dan motioned for us to follow him, and we did.

I quickly learned why it had been so easy for us to get jobs in the hospital. Even with Michigan's failing economy and high unemployment rate, there were some things people just did not want to do. Collecting and washing laundry from sick or dying patients at the city's biggest hospital was one of those things.

Now, it was not so much the constant smell that followed us around as we went from bedside to bedside, filling Dan's cart. It wasn't even the constant standing around, waiting for rooms to be cleared of doctors and other hospital staff so we could go in and collect the dirty sheets and towels. Actually, who am I kidding? It was all those things, and most of all it was seeing sick people tied to tubes and wires. That brought back bad memories of my time there.

After we filled our cart, Dan showed us to the laundry room. He gave us a half-hour tutorial on how to operate the machines and how to properly fold the sheets and towels when dry.

By the end of the two-hour training session, I was ready to tell Dan and Carl that I wanted to quit. Judging by the look on Carl's face, I imagined that he was thinking the same thing. They took our pictures before we left. I wondered if that was their standard procedure—waiting until after the orientation to officially coin their new hires. I imagined many new prospects ran out the door as soon as they saw what would be before them.

The receptionist we had met earlier gave us a couple of folders and told us to read the safety information by Friday, which would be our first official day. Carl and I walked out together, both silent until we got into the car.

"I guess it's not so bad," Carl said as he started his car.

I held back my true feelings. It was horrible. But Carl was doing me a big favor, and ultimately, this job would be a means to an end. "Yeah," I said.

"So I'm sure you would have told me, but did you see anything?" he asked.

"No," I said. "But it will happen, for sure. Either that, or he'll wait until you're gone and come to me. Actually, now that I think about it, today is Monday, and I haven't seen him since Saturday. I haven't had any bad dreams, either."

"That's good," Carl said. "But didn't you say you didn't see him the whole week before you went to Silver Lake?"

"Yeah," I said. "You know, Carl, it might be a coincidence, but I never see him in Rick's house. You think that means something?"

Carl shrugged. "Maybe he's like a vampire—he can't come into your house without an invitation."

"That's not funny," I said, a little annoyed.

"It's not meant to be funny." He looked at me as we arrived at a stoplight. "Alex, I completely believe you, and that's got me thinking. What else is out there like this? You know, maybe some of these myths are real."

"Maybe," I said.

Carl drove on as I stared out the car window in silence. He was out there waiting for me, I thought. If our plan worked, he wouldn't have to wait very long.

19

I SPENT MOST OF THAT EVENING in my room with Carl. As our passion for each other strengthened, so did our willingness to explore our desires. What I was feeling for Carl was new and exciting. I felt myself floating around most days just thinking about him and the time we spent together.

The week went by almost without a hitch. I started to get into the routine of it all, which went something like this: I barely made it to my first class; I was half-asleep during the boring sessions; and in true senior fashion, I skipped all the unimportant ones. Without any Azrael sightings for a few days, things seemed to be taking a turn for the better.

As Mr. Polderman promised, I was tutored for one hour after school each day by my core-class teachers. I felt bad, though; they all likely had families and were taking an hour away from them to help me. By Friday of the first week, I decided that I would only do one more session with each teacher and then let them know that I would be fine continuing on my own.

I also finished reading *Bag of Bones*, the book I had been reading before the accident. One of the things I used to do was summarize the book to Bailey during our little camping sessions in the backyard, modifying it, of course, so that it would be G rated. I found myself crying my eyes out when I was done. It wasn't the story so much; it was knowing that that was the last thing I'd shared with my baby sister.

It was Friday afternoon, and I was done with my after-school tutor session with the math teacher. I sent Carl a message, asking him to meet me at
my locker. It would be our first full day of work at the hospital, and we both
dreaded the prospect. He met me by my locker, having already packed his
book bag with books. I greeted him with a kiss, and he held my hand as we
walked toward the student parking lot.

"So what's the plan?" he said, once we got into his car.

I shrugged. "I guess we just do our job and let the rest take care of itself.
We're going to be all over the hospital collecting towels and sheets; someone
has to die sometime."

Carl nodded. "And you are going to call me once you see him, right?"

"Of course," I said.

"OK, well, let's go get our hands dirty," Carl said.

He drove off.

Our first day was actually worse than expected. I didn't see Azrael,
but the job was even harder than Dan had made it look. The smells were
atrocious. I found myself gagging when I removed sheets from my basket
to put them in the washer. Carl didn't seem to handle it well, either. He
held his nose with his left hand and moved the sheets into the washer with
his right.

We went on like that for about four hours. We visited every part of the
hospital, and at no point did I see Azrael.

We left that evening tired and disappointed. Carl dropped me off without coming in, and I crashed as soon as I fell into bed. Saturday would be
worse; we had an eight-hour day ahead of us. Sunday, I would work four
hours by myself while Carl put in time at Macy's.

The workdays came and went as another week passed; still no luck seeing Azrael. A large part of me wondered if he had ever been there to begin
with. This was the longest I had gone without seeing him. Maybe it was an
illusion after all.

Rick picked me up from work on a Sunday. It was midafternoon on a
mid-November day that was cold even though the sun was shining brightly.

As soon as I hopped into the car, I knew something was wrong. Rick
often wore his feelings on his face, and I could tell that he had something
to tell me.

"Hey," I said. "Everything OK?"

He nodded. "I think so," he said. "I just got a call from Dr. Khan on the way to pick you up. He says that Manuel died last night."

I was shocked. I immediately remembered the image of Manuel in the bed, how he looked so sickly and small. I had had a feeling then that he wouldn't make it, but hearing it aloud was still surprising.

I was not happy with the news. I wanted him to live and stand trial for what he'd done. I wanted to look him in the face and tell him how badly he had ruined my life. His selfish and illegal acts should not go unpunished.

"I'm sorry, Alex," Rick said. "His punishment is with God now."

I didn't say anything in response, and he drove off.

That night, I had so many mixed emotions as I lay in bed, waiting to go to sleep. Carl and I had spoken on the phone after he got off his shift at Macy's. I told him that I wanted to go to Manuel's funeral, which Dr. Khan had told Rick would take place on Wednesday around noon. I wasn't sure if survivors of accident victims did that, but I wanted to be there to watch them lower him into the ground. Something deep down told me that it would make me feel better. Even if it didn't, maybe I could use it as motivation to find closure in this whole thing.

I woke up early that Wednesday morning, even though I didn't have to. I had put in a shift at the hospital the evening before, and I was feeling a little sore. I lay in bed for a while just thinking about the past few weeks. I smiled when I thought about Carl and how we had become so close. He said he would go with me to the funeral, and we could take the day off from school and hang out.

I got out of bed around ten and checked my phone. Carl had left a good-morning message, time stamped promptly at eight, with a heart emoji. I rolled my eyes and smiled as I made my way to the bathroom to get ready.

Rick had gone to work, but Alicia was busy in the kitchen. She began making breakfast for me the second she heard the shower go on in the bathroom. They both refused to go to the funeral, not really giving any reason why, but I couldn't say that I blamed them.

I ate my eggs and toast and called Carl, who came and picked me up.

Carl had a coffee waiting for me in my cupholder, now a time-honored morning ritual of ours. I gave him a generous kiss hello. I knew he probably thought I was crazy to want to do this, and I appreciated all his support.

"You going to be OK?" he asked as we drove off.

I nodded. "Yeah, this is actually a good thing. It's closure for me. It feels right, you know?"

Carl nodded slowly. "I guess I can see that."

As we drove past the hospital, I looked over at Carl and said, "I think we should quit the hospital."

He seemed to perk up but then caught himself. "Are you sure?"

"I am. I've been thinking, Carl. It's not good for me to dwell on the past. I need to move on. I haven't seen Azrael since that day in the woods, and I think he might just be gone from my life. If he pops up again, then so be it. But for now, I just need to live my life."

As we idled at a stoplight, Carl turned to look at me. "I think that's a good idea. I mean, not that looking for him was a bad idea, but it's a good idea to just move on."

"I think so too. Maybe things were just meant to happen this way."

"Maybe—"

"You got a green light," I said, pointing forward. He turned and started moving.

"You were saying?" I said.

"Yeah, I was saying this might end up being a good thing. Maybe—"

"Carl, stop!" I screamed. As we passed an intersection, I saw the woman with the white face standing on the corner looking out at me. I was stunned.

Carl slammed on the brakes. We screeched to a stop just past the intersection, and the woman was out of sight. Without thinking, I opened my door, jumped out of the car, and ran toward the spot where I'd seen her standing. I heard Carl screaming my name from behind me, but his words failed to register.

I ran to the corner I had seen her on, and there she was, about two blocks from me. She stood staring at me with her arms extended, as if she was summoning me to come to her. I ran in her direction. No matter how fast I ran, she never appeared to get any closer. It was as if she was floating backward on some invisible cloud.

A few blocks into my pursuit, I heard a scream. I was at an intersection, and as I looked to my right, I saw Azrael standing in the middle of the street across from me, staring into his gold pocket watch.

Directly in front of Azrael, a little boy was about to cross the street just as a car came speeding toward him. Behind the little boy, the woman who was the source of the scream fell to the ground. It all happened in slow motion.

I ran in the direction of the boy, who was not reacting to his mother's screams or to mine. I looked at the driver of the car. He appeared to have his eyes on his cell phone. I screamed at the top of my lungs, but he didn't look up, nor did the little boy stop.

Just as the boy stepped in front of the car, I reached him and pushed him out of the way. In the next instant, the car struck me head-on. I was tossed up in the air and crashed back first against the windshield as the car came to a screeching halt. I let out a scream of pain as I felt my hip and back crack beneath me. I rolled over the top of the car and fell flat on my face in the street. Eyes still open, I stared at the empty street in front of me. Azrael stood there, his eyes wide and dark like two bottomless pits, his lips curled over his pointed teeth, and his mouth hanging open. Just before I blacked out, I read his expression; it was shock.

Sometime after that, I wasn't sure how long, I woke up in the hospital.

The room was spinning as I opened my eyes. Just as I focused, a nurse came in to greet me.

"Good morning," she said with a gentle smile. "How are you feeling?"

My head hurt, and the left side of my body was numb. I could barely speak, but I said, "OK."

"Do you know who I am?" she asked.

I looked at her intently. I did not know.

"No," I said.

She smiled. "My name is Kiley; I'm your nurse." Then she asked, "Do you know where you are?"

I let out a deep breath. My head was throbbing now as I tried to form thoughts. "No."

"You are at Crescent City Hospital." Then she asked, "Do you know what day it is?"

Again, I tried to think. Information seemed to be tucked away in some locked safe in my brain, and I had lost the key. "No."

"Today is Monday, September ninth," she said, smiling.

Although I had no idea why, hearing the date troubled me. It sent a shiver through my body, starting with my toes and ending at the nape of my neck. Then, all at once, I fainted.

I T WAS A FEW DAYS before I came to again. It was at night, and I was alone in the hospital room. The analog clock on the wall didn't work; its hands were frozen on twelve thirty. Underneath the broken clock was a dry-erase board on which the date, September 12, had been written.

I closed my eyes and held in a deep breath. A shiver ran through me as I read the date, but I did not know why. It was as though I had something very important to do, and I knew that I had to do it very soon, but I couldn't remember what it was. I opened my eyes and read the date again.

I looked around the room. Even in the darkness, there was something very familiar about it. To my right was a window, and immediately beneath the window was a bench with a cushion on it. It appeared to be a spot for a visitor to sleep or sit. To my left was a wingback chair with a white blanket folded on the seat. In front of me was the door to the bathroom, and on the wall to the left of the door were the broken clock and dry-erase board. Under the date, some information was written. My nurse's name was Kiley. My doctor's name was John Cooper.

On the windowsill, I noticed, was a book. The moon's light was shining on it. I could not read the title on the spine of the book, for it was too far away.

"Nurse?" I called not too loudly but not quite whispering. "Kiley?"

I heard footsteps coming in my direction, and at the door appeared the young blonde I had seen before.

"Hello," she said, coming to my bedside.

"Hi," I said, looking at her badge. It read Kiley Steele.

I studied the badge intently.

"Have we met?" I asked.

She nodded. "I've been your night nurse about six times in the past few weeks. But you were not awake most of times I've been here, except for a few days ago."

I nodded, unable to call up any memories of her.

"Your memory has been affected," she said. "You suffered a closed-head injury. If you don't mind, can I ask you a few questions?"

I nodded.

"Do you know where you are?" she asked.

I looked around, and it seemed pretty obvious. "At the hospital," I said.

"Good. Do you know which hospital?"

That was actually a tough question. I thought for a second, and then suddenly the name surfaced like a message that comes up when one shakes a Magic 8 Ball.

"Crescent City," I said.

She seemed very pleased and walked to the foot of my bed. She pulled the clipboard from the foot of the bed and held it just out of sight from where I lay. A pen was tethered to it with a short string.

She wrote something down and then looked up at me. "Do you know what day it is?"

Of course, I thought; it's right in front of me. "Yes, it's September twelfth," I said. Saying the date aloud gave me chills far greater than simply reading it had.

She nodded and wrote something else down. "OK. Before we can go on, I need to call the doctor. He's on call this evening, so he should be here in less than a half hour. Is that OK?"

I nodded. "Yes." Then a thought occurred to me. It was so obvious, I was shocked that I hadn't thought about it sooner. "Do you know what happened to me?" I asked.

She placed her gentle hand on my shoulder. "Dr. Cooper will talk to you. I'm not supposed to say anything."

I was confused. As hard as I tried, I couldn't remember anything about the past. Aside from knowing my own name and a few other pieces of information, I had no idea what was going on.

I sighed. "OK," I said. "But can you tell me if I'm going to be OK? You know, like, am I going to die?"

She smiled. "I think you're going to be OK. I will say that the fact you are talking to me right now is nothing short of a miracle. You're very lucky."

"Thanks," I said, feeling a little better.

Nothing short of a miracle. The words swirled around in my subconscious as I lay back in my bed and Kiley left the room.

I stared up at the ceiling blankly. In the dim light of the room, it was barely visible. As I stared outward into the emptiness, I saw a face floating above as if it were painted on the ceiling. It was very faint at first, and I could barely make it out. I looked closer and saw the outline of two dark eyes and a nose. Then the mouth seemed to open, revealing pointed teeth so sharp they looked like the ends of giant needles. My breathing slowed, and my gaze was fixed on those dark eyes. In the background, I heard the siren of the computer that was right next to me. I tried to move, but I couldn't. I tried to scream, but I had no voice. I felt myself go numb, and then everything went dark.

T HE NEXT WEEK OF MY life was nothing short of torture. I felt as if I were awake, but, as I would learn later, I was in a deep coma. It had been triggered by a sudden spike in blood pressure that occurred the night I saw the face on the ceiling.

For six long days, I was lost in a maze of dreams both vivid and barely memorable. The one that occurred most often was that of a man in a black pinstripe suit.

The dream always started the same way. The man in the suit would be walking down a street. I was standing across the street. He would see me and then give chase. The first thing I would do was try to open the front door of a house close to me; it was locked. I would run to the backyard, all the while knowing that the man was just steps behind me. Somehow, I would reach an empty field, where I would stop and look behind me. The house and the man would be nowhere in sight.

A voice would call to me—a female voice, one I knew very well. I would turn in the direction of the voice and see her standing across the field, dressed in white. I would run toward her, but she never got any closer. She stood with her arms extended to me, her face white as a ghost. The expression on her face was that of emptiness, her mouth hung half-open, and her eyelids were low.

The man in the black pinstripe suit would then suddenly reappear. He came at me from the left as I ran across the field. I turned to run away from him, and that was when I would fall. Seconds later, I'd feel a cold hand on my shoulder, and I'd struggle to get away. I would scream, and then the dream would be over.

I had no good dreams the whole time I was in the coma—at least none that I could remember. When I finally woke up, it was September 18. It was early afternoon, and the sun was shining brightly.

When I woke up, a nurse named Brenda greeted me. She explained that I had been in a coma for six days, something that seemed impossible. She also explained that Dr. Cooper would come to see me soon, and he would talk to me. She did some tests, asked me some questions, and left me alone.

A few hours passed, time I spent staring at the wall and thinking. I was starting to recall some events of the past, but much of it did not make sense. I knew that I'd been in a car accident; that much, I was sure about. I knew that something terrible had happened. The problem was that I felt as if the accident had been months ago, but in fact the nurse had told me it had happened just weeks ago.

My memories seemed to be clouded, and there were large gaps. I remembered no names or people, just events. I remembered the man with the black pinstripe suit. I had seen him many times over the past few months; that, I knew. Who he was, I had no idea.

At about three in the afternoon, a tall, older man in a white coat walked in. He greeted me with a smile. "Hello, Ms. Drummond. I'm Dr. Cooper," he said.

"Hi," I said.

"Do you mind if I take a seat? We have a lot to talk about," he said, motioning to the wingback chair to the left of the bed.

I smiled, finding it awkward that he felt the need to ask. "Sure."

He sat down and folded his right leg over his left. He opened a folder that he had tucked under his right arm and placed it on his thigh. He pulled out a pen and looked up at me with a smile.

"OK, well, I am very glad you came out of your coma. We've been closely monitoring you for some time now. Tell me first, how do you feel?"

"I guess OK. My head hurts, and my left side feels really numb. Underneath the bandages, I'm itchy. I can't really remember very much, but I know I was in an accident. The nurse told me you could tell me about it. Do you know exactly what happened to me?"

He nodded. "I do. But first, do you mind if I ask you some questions?"

"I guess not."

"OK. Can you tell me what you remember about the accident?"

I took a deep breath. "Well, I don't remember very much about the accident itself. I remember seeing a man dressed in a black pinstripe suit. I've had dreams about him—almost every night, it seems. There is a woman in my dreams too. She's faceless, kinda like a porcelain doll. I think she's trying to help me."

Dr. Cooper just looked at me blankly. I could tell he wasn't sure how to respond.

Now I was confused. "Why? Was there more? He was here," I said, pointing up at the ceiling. "He was floating right above me."

"I think you may be experiencing some hallucinations due to your closed-head injury," he said. "I am going to refer you to therapy."

I nodded, now feeling a little worried. "Am I going to be OK?"

"I think so. Your vitals are looking good, and you came back from the coma much quicker than we expected. What you are going through is normal. I've seen it many times. You are a very strong young woman to have survived such an accident. Not many people would have."

His words gave me great comfort.

"What about the past?" he said. "Do you remember anything from the distant past?"

I thought for a second, but as hard as I tried, I couldn't remember a single thing. "No, nothing," I said.

"That's OK. I have some exercises for you to do. Eventually, you will start to regain the memories. The brain is very complicated, but it is capable of amazing things. From what I have seen of you so far, I have no doubt you'll get your memory back very soon."

He then walked me through some mental exercises he wanted me to do to help with my memory loss. After he was done, I asked, "Was there anyone in the accident with me?"

He closed the folder he was holding and sat up. "You lost your family. Your young sister, Bailey; your father, Victor; and your mother, Patricia."

I was shocked to hear this, but without any memories of them, it was as though he were telling me about something he had heard on the news.

"You have some family here for you, and they are very excited to see you. I am going to let them introduce themselves. The more interaction you have with people from the past, the better it is going to be for you."

"OK, thank you," I said.

He wrapped up by asking me different questions about the pain level associated with the various injuries I had, and then he left, promising to return very soon.

I lay in my room for a long while, just thinking. I looked over at the windowsill; that book was still there. I squinted, trying to read the spine but was unable to.

I rang the buzzer for the nurse.

"Yes?" a disembodied voice called from the speaker on the buzzer.

"Hi. Can I have some juice, please?" I asked. I planned to ask whoever delivered my juice to get the book for me, and I didn't want the nurses to think that I was wasting their time, getting me a book from the windowsill.

"Sure. Apple OK?" the voice asked.

"Yes, please," I said.

A few moments later, an older woman walked in holding my juice and a Styrofoam cup filled with ice. I hadn't seen her before.

"Hello, my name is Stacey. I'm taking over for Brenda. Her shift just ended. Here's your juice," she said, placing it on the tray table next to me. "Brenda tells me you're doing a lot better."

I nodded. "Yes, thanks. I feel better too. The pain is not as bad as it was before. I hope I get my memory back soon."

She nodded as she looked up at the screen to check my vitals. "It takes time. Maybe all at once, you'll get it back, or maybe it will come in small increments. That happened to my father," she said, now looking down at me. "He lost his memory when he was in an accident. He didn't remember any of us for about two weeks. Then, all of a sudden, it all came back. He said it was my mother who did it. She told him a story about their past that he remembered, and within seconds, all his memories came rushing back."

"I hope that happens to me," I said.

She gave me a warm smile. "I know it will," she said. "Anything else I can get you for now?"

Speaking about memory, I'd almost forgotten the reason I'd summoned her in the first place. "Yeah. Can you get me that book that's on the windowsill?" I asked, pointing.

She walked over to the windowsill and picked up the book. She looked at the cover and read the title aloud. "*Bag of Bones*," she said.

She handed me the book, and I looked at the cover. It depicted a little girl submerged in water. The author was Stephen King. Something about the cover looked eerily familiar.

"Good book," she said.

I looked at her. "I think I've read this before, but I really can't remember what happens."

She smiled. "Well, maybe you should read it again. It could help bring back your memory. Also, the doctor has cleared you to have visitors. One of them is waiting in the lobby, if you want me to let him in. Interacting with people also helps with the memory loss."

I was excited to hear this. Having no distinct recollection of the people in my past had left me in a state of bewilderment. "I would like that," I said. "Who is it?"

"How about I let him in and he'll introduce himself," the nurse said.

I agreed, and she walked out. A few minutes later, a boy appeared in the doorway and walked hesitantly into the room. He had dark-brown eyes and light-brown hair, and he was holding a manila envelope. He gave me a smile. "Alex, hello. I'm Carl," he said.

He extended his hand, and I shook it. "Hi," I said.

He looked at me in silence, and I surveyed his face. He indeed looked familiar; however, I could not formulate a single memory with him in it.

"I know you probably don't remember me, but we're friends from school. We have had a lot of the same classes together, and we've known each other for many years," he said. He spoke slowly, as if I wouldn't understand him if he talked too fast.

"It's nice of you to come and visit, Carl. You're right; I don't remember much," I said.

He sat down next to my bed. "I wanna show you some things," he said, opening the envelope he was holding.

I watched as he pulled out a small pile of pictures. He shuffled through them. I could only see the backs of them.

"Dr. Cooper said it would be helpful if you looked at some pictures first. He told me to show them to you one at a time and just let you look at them. See if you remember anything."

I nodded, thinking this sounded like a pretty good idea.

Carl handed me the first picture. It was of a house. It was a Cape Cod with red shutters. The front door, right in the center, was red as well.

"Is this my house?" I asked.

Carl nodded. "Yes. Do you remember it?"

I shook my head. "No, but it's nice."

He waited a second as I looked at the picture and then handed me another. It was of me and some people who I assumed to be my family. We were huddled around the fireplace, all dressed up. It looked like Christmas.

I sighed. Knowing that I was staring at a picture of my dead family was unsettling.

"That's my family," I said solemnly.

Carl stayed silent as I studied the photograph. I looked at the little girl; she was under my left arm, smiling. She had pretty blue eyes, just like my mother did in the picture. I had taken after my father, with brown eyes.

The little girl was wearing a cute red dress that had straps over the shoulders. Under the straps was a white dress shirt that had lace on the sleeves. Something about it did start to look familiar. I tried to rack my memory, but nothing surfaced.

"Anything?" Carl asked.

I shook my head. "No, but maybe it would help if you told me about my family."

"Well, you guys were very happy," he said. "Bailey was so cute, and your parents were the perfect couple."

He paused. I could tell it was difficult for him to talk about them.

"That's OK," I said. "Let me see another picture."

He handed me another photo. It was of me and a small group of teenagers. It appeared that we were at school, and I looked younger, maybe by two or three years. Still, I drew a blank.

We went on like that for about a half hour. Carl showed me two dozen photos, and none of them jarred any new memories. After we looked at the pictures, he told me stories about my past. He told me about my family, the kind of girl I was in school, and my friends—namely, a girl named Kate who was coming to see me later in the day.

Even after a long talk, I still didn't remember a single thing about Carl or any of the photos he'd shown me. I was very disappointed, and noticeably, he was too.

"Well, maybe it will happen soon," he said. "After all of this has set in."

"Yeah, I guess," I said.

"How about I get you something to eat? You used to like Mitchell's; it's a burger place. Dr. Cooper said that should help as well."

I smiled. This sounded like a great idea. "I would love that. The food here isn't exactly gourmet."

He gave me smile and a nod. "Be right back. I'll call Kate and let her know to come by. Your aunt and uncle want to visit too. They'll likely come this afternoon." He looked down at my copy of *Bag of Bones*, which was on the tray next to me. "By the way, I borrowed that from you. I hope that was OK. I read it when I hung out here after school."

"Hung out?" I asked.

"Yeah, Kate and me. Rick, your uncle, he would come too after work. They let us in only two at a time, but we were here a lot. It's kinda funny; today was the first day we all took a break, and you happened to wake up. Everyone is really happy to see that you're gonna be all right."

Hearing this made me feel bad. All these people I couldn't remember had set their lives aside for me.

"Thanks," I said appreciatively.

"Anyway, you should finish reading it," he said, pointing at the book. "It's pretty good."

"I will," I said. "And really, I can't wait to remember everything, 'cause it sounds like you're a pretty great guy. You and everyone else, of course."

He smiled and blushed. "Thanks. Give me like an hour, and I'll come back with Kate and the burgers."

We said our goodbyes, and he walked out of the room.

Taking his advice, I decided that I would read the book. I picked it up and opened it to the first page. Only a few pages into it, I had the sensation of déjà vu. I kept reading. Sooner or later, I would remember everything, I thought. It was only a matter of time.

CARL CAME BACK ABOUT A half hour later than he'd promised to. I barely noticed, as I had been reading the entire time. He stood at the doorway and gave my door a few knocks.

I looked up. "Come in, Carl," I said.

He walked in with a pretty blond girl, who gave me a hesitant smile. I smiled back.

"Hey, Alex, this is Kate," he said awkwardly.

"Hey, Allie," she said in a hushed tone; she looked as if she wanted to cry.

"Hi," I said.

I stared at her for a long while; she looked just like her pictures. I wanted so badly to remember her, but I couldn't. The safe in my subconscious was locked shut, and there was still no key in sight.

Carl placed two greasy brown paper bags on the small tray table next to me.

"Well, how about we eat first, and then we can talk?" he said, looking back and forth between us.

"Sounds good to me," I said as the aroma of the bag finally reached me.

Carl ripped open one of the bags and produced three burgers wrapped in wax paper. The second bag was full of french fries. We ate in silence for a few minutes. Kate and I exchanged glances. It was almost as though she wasn't sure what to say to me, and since I had no recollection of her, the feeling was mutual.

Carl finally broke the ice. "So, Kate, Dr. Cooper said it would be a good idea if you told Alex some stories about the past."

Kate nodded and put down her half-eaten burger.

"There're so many," she said, looking up as she thought. "Oh, I have a perfect one. One summer—it was after our sophomore year, you and I 'borrowed' my parents' car and went to the mall," she said, using air quotes for the word *borrowed*. "You drove, 'cause you had your learner's permit. We shopped, and you complained 'cause you hated shopping. Then we went to the movies. Everything was going so good until we got back to the car and realized that you had left the keys in the ignition, and the car was locked." We each let out a little laugh as she continued the story.

"That's not even the funny part. So I was so scared to call my parents 'cause they were out of town and weren't due to come back till the next day. And of course, we couldn't call the cops, 'cause we didn't even have licenses. So you came up with a great idea. You said that once your dad was at a car wash and locked his keys in the car, and one of the guys had a really long metal thing and opened the car door really easily. There happened to be a car wash just outside the mall, and it was still in the middle of the day, so we walked over there. We got to the car wash and told the manager our problem, and being that we were two cute, little teenagers, he believed us and agreed to help us out.

"So we hopped into the car-wash guy's car and led him back to my mom's car. We sat back as he tried to unlock it. A few minutes passed, and the guy was having a hell of a time, trying to get it open, and then a cop car pulled up. The cop shined his light, and we were all like, What the heck is going on? So the officer jumped out of the car and grabbed the guy from the car wash, threw him on the hood, and started to cuff him. You and I were yelling at the officer that it was our car, and he was yelling at us to get on the ground. So we did, and he put those zip-tie things around our wrists and put us on the ground next to the car-wash guy's car.

"So we were sitting there, crying like bitches, and the car-wash guy was in the back seat of the police car, when this old lady came up to us with one of the workers from Macy's. She pulled out a set of car keys, and she clicked the fob, and the lights for the car we were trying to get into turned on. Little did we realize that we had convinced this poor car-wash guy to break into some old lady's car, thinking it was ours, when ours—the same exact kind of car—was parked two lanes away."

"Oh my God!" I gasped, and then we all burst out in laughter.

"What happened after that?" Carl asked.

Kate, still giggling, said, "Well, the cop called my parents, and they got all mad. Your mom came and took us home, and the cop didn't give us a ticket, even though he said he should have. The car-wash guy was so nice, though. He was laughing about the whole thing."

Carl and Kate both looked at me. I think they thought that this story would stir up some memories. Unfortunately, it didn't.

"That was a great story. I guess I can't wait to remember it," I said, smiling.

Kate went on, telling more stories. Of course, none was as amusing as that one, but they were fun to listen to anyway. We joked and laughed for a few hours, and even without having any coherent recollections of them, I quickly figured out why they were my friends: we fit together perfectly likes pieces of a jigsaw puzzle.

Since the rules in the intensive care unit allowed only two visitors at a time, Carl and Kate left so that Alicia and Rick could come in.

Rick was a tall man. He too looked just like his photo. Alicia was a short, pudgy blonde.

Rick told me stories about the past and about my parents. Alicia chimed in once in a while with tidbits that she recalled. They both teared up when we talked about my family, and I found myself crying too.

"I really hope you get your memory back soon," Alicia said, wiping the tears from her eyes.

"I hope so too," I said. "It's so weird, you know? It's like my brain is not working in certain parts. I keep trying, but the memories just won't come."

"Well, maybe you need to stop trying. Maybe that's the key. Dr. Cooper said sometimes people remember everything all at once, and it comes without any notice," Rick said.

"Yeah, I think that might be the best thing to do. It's really frustrating me, not remembering," I said.

Rick smiled and looked at his watch. "Well, Alex, they said we had to be out by seven thirty, and it's seven forty-five now. How about tomorrow we come back and do this again? You have no idea how excited we are to finally see you up and about."

"Thanks, guys," I said. "I think I want those burgers again tomorrow too."

"Of course," Rick said, getting up and giving me a kiss on the forehead. "I'll come by right after work. We'll have a good time."

Alicia gave me a hug, and we said our goodbyes. Once again, I was left to myself. I picked up my book and started reading. A few hours later, I fell asleep with the book resting in my lap. Just before I drifted off, a thought surfaced in my mind. It was an isolated thought, one that seemed to just hang in the air right above my head. It told me one thing and one thing only: the mother dies. Those words swirled around my head as I fell asleep. The mother dies, the mother dies, the mother dies.

My dreams that night were numerous. The man in the black pinstripe suit visited me again. I woke up in the middle of the night, the room dark and silent around me. I checked the time on my cell phone, which read 3:35 a.m. I closed my eyes and instantly fell back asleep.

I found myself in another dream. I was standing outside the Cape Cod–style house with the red shutters that I had seen in the pictures. I was on the sidewalk right in front of the house, and as far as I could tell, the day was warm and bright. I watched as two adults walked out of the front door with a little girl. They were smiling and laughing and paid no attention to me. The little girl ran over to her bike, which was sitting in the driveway, and jumped on. The man and woman sat down on a bench that was on a small patio in front of the house. I watched as the man reached over and put his arm around the woman. They and I looked on as the little girl rode her bike up and down the driveway. She bobbed from right to left as her training wheels buttressed her. I got the feeling that they couldn't see me, and instead of approaching them, I just stayed put. The thought that had occurred to me before I fell asleep came again. The mother dies. I looked at the woman sitting on the bench, but something told me that I already knew that she died. The mother dies. The thought came again.

I looked at the girl, who was still cheerfully riding her bike up and down the driveway. Suddenly, she stopped and looked at me, and her expression immediately changed to one of emptiness, the smile wiped clean from her face. I looked over at the man and woman on the bench. They too were staring at me blankly. Their unblinking faces sent a shock wave of fear through my body. I wanted to turn and run away; however, as I tried to turn, I felt as though I was planted firmly in the ground. My feet refused to move an inch. I stumbled and fell. I struggled to get up, but some invisible force was holding me down. The little girl, the man, and the woman all spoke at the same time, their voices a loud, uniform, monotone chant.

"The mother dies," they said over and over again. Each time, their voices got louder and louder. I covered my ears and screamed, but I couldn't drown out the chants.

I woke up breathing hard and shaking in fear. The image of the dream lingered in my mind and then slowly faded away. I looked around the room. It was still silent and dark. I lay back in my bed and stared up at the ceiling as my breathing slowed and I calmed myself. Then a thought occurred to me that jolted me upright. All of a sudden, it was as if a cork had been removed in my brain, and all my memories came rushing back. By some kind of miracle, the locked safe was flung open, and everything came pouring out.

I immediately grabbed the phone and dialed Carl's number. A faint voice answered.

"Hello," Carl said.

"Carl, I need you to come here right away," I said urgently. "I remember everything, and it doesn't make sense."

I heard a rustling on the other end of the line. After a moment, he said, "What? Really? Oh my God, that's amazing. But it's like five in the morning. I don't think they'll let us in."

"OK, well, as soon as you can, please come. I need to talk to you," I said. "I—"

The sound of a female voice in the background made me stop. "Who's that?" I asked.

"Oh, it's Kate," he said awkwardly.

"Kate?" I asked, confused.

"Ah, yeah. She wants to talk to you," he said.

"Hello," Kate said.

"Hello," I said, very unsure of what to say. Why was she with Carl at five in the morning within earshot of the telephone? Had they been sleeping together?

"Allie, are you OK?" she asked.

I didn't respond for a moment. Then I said, "No, I don't think so."

She spoke, but I didn't hear a word she said. I was in a silent state of shock. I stared up at the dry-erase board, my eyes fixed on the date. I hung up the phone without saying another word.

THE INTENSIVE CARE UNIT WOULD open its doors for visitors at 8:00 a.m. Dawn was breaking, and about an hour had passed since I had called Carl. Since then, my mind had been racing, and my stomach was doing somersaults. Nothing—not one bit of it—made any sense.

There I was, in the hospital for the second time after an accident that happened months earlier, as far as I was concerned. The dry-erase board in front of me said September 20, even though that date had passed almost two months before.

My last memory before I found myself in that place was of an accident that almost claimed the life of a little boy. I had saved him, and after that, I found myself in Crescent City Hospital almost two months earlier. How could that be?

I had questioned my own recollection at first. Of course, any sane person would. I had thought that maybe it was all a dream, and I was really waking up from the coma just then. But my mind refused to accept that as the truth. The events were too real, too vivid. Plus, when you woke up from a dream, you knew that what you were remembering was a dream. In this case, I did not have that feeling. I was certain, with the obvious hesitations, that those things had happened and were in fact very real.

I stared, fixated, on the date, still not believing what I was reading. I had even called the nurse and asked her, and she had given me the same date. When I asked if she was sure it wasn't November, she paused for a second and then affirmed that it wasn't. I imagined that she was taken aback by the question; I certainly would have been.

As visiting hours approached, I made one resolution with myself. I was not going to tell anyone about this. I was going to pretend that everything was OK until I had things figured out. I had lived in a time when everyone around me thought I was a nutjob for seeing this thing in a pinstripe suit walking around with a rope, pulling souls out of people's bodies. I loathed the thought of going through therapy again and having to pretend I was getting better even though I wasn't.

It also sounded like Kate and Carl had gotten together. This one was for the record book. As hurt as I was at the thought of her touching the boy I loved, I couldn't say a word. I would have to bite my tongue and accept it, as everyone else did. A part of me wanted to believe that maybe they were just sleeping next to each other, something very innocent. I mean, where could they be, anyway? Kate and Carl both lived with their parents. How could they be doing anything at either home? Maybe Kate had visited Carl's house, and they had both fallen asleep on the couch watching TV, I thought, my hopes slowly rising. It was perfectly reasonable that Carl's parents could have called Kate's parents, and they had decided to let their children be for the night.

What nagged at me was the way Carl's voice had changed when he knew I had heard Kate's voice. He sounded guilty. Then I was struck with a thought: Carl was a virgin. He had told me right before any of this happened. Was he still a virgin? I couldn't bear the thought.

I wished that whatever mechanism I had triggered that made time change the way it had would cause time to stop right now. I knew for a fact that Kate and Carl would be there at 8:00 a.m. when the doors opened, and I wanted some more time to myself.

I looked at my cell phone, which had rung a few times after I hung up on Kate. Undoubtedly, Kate or Carl had been trying to call me. Maybe I should call them and be very brief. I could tell them that everything was fine, that I just wanted some time to myself, and that they should just go to school and come by tomorrow or the next day. Of course, I thought, that could arouse suspicion in them. Anyone who woke up from a coma and just got back her memory would likely want nothing more than to see the people whom she loved most.

They would arrive in less than two hours. I laid my head down and thought of a new idea. I would fall asleep, and hopefully stay asleep for a long time. Like an ostrich with its head in the sand, I would lie there until I had the courage to face the world. Who knows, maybe I'd wake up and realize that everything was a dream.

I fell asleep and woke up a few hours later, unsure of the time. I heard Kate's and Carl's hushed voices talking to each other, so I kept my eyes closed. I wasn't ready to face them—not yet. I decided that I would pretend to be asleep for a while in hopes they would just leave.

As it worked out, I fell asleep after about twenty minutes with my eyes closed. I felt as though a few hours had passed the next time I woke up. I kept my eyes closed and listened intently. I heard no voices in my room. I slowly raised my head from the pillow and took a peek around. I was on my left side, so all I saw was the wingback chair to my left and the open door. Nobody was there. I turned my head to my right to see if anyone was sitting on the bench under the window. Sure enough, Carl was there, looking right at me. I was startled to see him. Kate was lying on her side next to him with her head resting on his lap. Any hope that they were just having an innocent platonic relationship evaporated in a flash.

"Hey," he said in a hushed voice.

"Hey," I replied, giving him the best smile I could muster.

We looked at each other silently for a minute, and then he said, "So you're back?"

"Yeah, I'm back," I said.

"Thank God," he said. "We were so scared."

I looked down at Kate, sleeping soundly, her head nestled on his thigh. He followed my gaze.

"So...you and Kate?" I said.

He shifted uncomfortably and didn't make eye contact. "Yeah, it kinda happened after the accident," he said. "Sorry I didn't tell you, but the doctor said to not throw too much at you all at once."

I sighed. Things just seemed to get more and more confusing. I was not sure whether to be mad or happy. "What about Jeremy?"

Carl looked at me, confused. "Who?"

My stomach started to do those somersaults again. "The new kid. You know, the guy that lives down the street from you."

Perplexed, Carl just shook his head. "No, I don't know him," he said. "Why? What about him?"

"I, um…" I had no idea what to say. "Well, maybe I'm confused about something else. Never mind."

Kate began to move about, and Carl and I both watched as she opened her eyes. She propped herself up with Carl's help and looked at me, smiling brightly.

"Allie, how are you?" she said.

"Good, I guess," I said.

She got up, walked over to me, and gave me a hug. "Oh my God, it's so good you're gonna be OK. We were all so scared."

I didn't say anything. I just hugged her for a long while. I have to admit that even with all the confusion, that did make me feel better.

She retracted and asked, "So how did it happen? You know—how did you get your memory back?"

"No clue. It just happened," I said. "Early this morning, when I called you guys…" I trailed off, unable to finish my sentence.

Kate looked at me and then at Carl. "Did you tell her?" she asked Carl. Carl nodded.

Kate returned her attention to me. "Sorry we didn't tell you, but Carl and I have been together pretty much since the accident."

I smiled as best as I could. "I'm really happy for you guys."

"Thanks," Kate said. "Carl's been so sweet, and you know this has been tough on all of us."

I nodded. "Yeah."

We were all silent for a moment, and then Carl said, "So you want something to eat? It's almost twelve, and if you ask me, I'm starving."

"Sure, that sounds good," I said.

"Oh, Allie, Dr. Cooper said he wanted to talk to you as soon as you woke up. How about if Carl and I go grab some food, and I'll tell the nurse you're up," Kate said.

I nodded. "Sure." But the truth was, I wasn't really ready to talk to Dr. Cooper. My thoughts turned to Dr. Khan, who was conspicuously missing—if he'd ever been there to begin with.

They each gave me a hug and left the room. I decided that I would just play it cool and not divulge any details about anything until I was sure that what had happened to me was real. When I first woke up that morning, I was sure the past two months were real; now, not so much. Aside from the whole Carl and Kate thing, how was it that Carl didn't know who Jeremy was? How could I have imagined the whole thing? It made no sense. As I lay in my bed waiting for Dr. Cooper, a little voice in my head kept saying, "You're crazy, Alex. Just admit it; you're crazy." I was starting to think that maybe the voice was on to something.

Dr. Cooper came to see me twenty minutes after Kate and Carl left. He went through his checklist of questions, and I did nothing to reveal the seemingly alternative existence I'd come from.

Kate and Carl came back, and as promised, we had lunch together. Most of our conversation was of the "remember when" variety. A thick air of discomfort hung in the room. I knew they felt it too. I still couldn't believe they had gotten together, and I was working hard to hold back my questions. Sometime after Kate reminisced about our last trip to the movies together and before she started on a new story, my curiosity got the better of me.

"So how did it happen?" I said, looking at Kate. "You and Carl—how did you guys hook up?"

Kate looked uncomfortable. I looked at Carl, and he started to blush.

"I don't know, a few days after the accident," Kate said as she tucked her hair behind her right ear.

"How?" I asked, insisting.

"Allie, I don't know. You want every detail? I mean, things have been so hard on us, and Carl has been so great. We just kinda fell into each other's arms, I guess," Kate said.

"I'm sorry if it bothers you, Alex. Really, we didn't mean it to, you know," Carl said, his words attracting a look from Kate.

"Why would it bother her?" Kate asked Carl.

"It doesn't bother me," I lied. "It just came out of the blue, you know? We have all known one another so long that I never thought one of us would hook up with the other."

"Well, I did ask you out last year, so I thought maybe it would be kinda weird," Carl said.

"It's not weird," I said.

"You know, you never told me why you never asked me out first," Kate said to Carl.

Carl shifted in his chair uncomfortably. Kate sounded serious, but I knew better. She was messing with him, for sure.

"Well, you were dating that guy, and…I don't know. I figured you'd say no anyway," Carl said.

"And you figured I'd say yes?" I said, acting indignant.

"Well, no," Carl said. "Well, yes. I don't know. I mean, Kate was—"

"Too pretty for you, right?" I said.

Kate looked at me and smiled, holding back her laughter; Carl was situated behind her, so he couldn't see her face.

"No. You guys are both pretty, but Kate had a boyfriend, and you were single," Carl said, sounding as if he was choosing his words very carefully.

"So I was the leftovers 'cause the real prize was taken?" I said.

Kate burst into laughter, which in turn made me laugh.

"You guys are messed up," Carl said, but he looked relieved.

All three of us laughed for a while, and as much as it bothered me to see them together, I knew that I had a lot of things to figure out. Maybe it would be better for now, but watching them still made my stomach turn.

Rick and Alicia came by around six in the afternoon, and we had dinner together. It was nice. They told me that I could come live with them. That got me thinking about the room they had made up for me before, and once again, I found myself thinking about the past.

They left at the prescribed hour, and as the clock approached nine in the evening, I was alone again. I decided to put off thinking about things just a bit longer and picked up my book to read.

I hadn't read more than three sentences when the thought struck me so hard that I felt faint. "The mother dies," I said quietly to myself.

Before the accident with the little boy, I had finished that book, and in the book, the little girl's mother dies. I knew that just as well as I knew the sky was blue. I turned the pages and was able to locate the exact page when it happened, and there it was, clear as day. The character was shot, and she died.

I closed the book and placed it on the tray table next to me. All day, I had been filled with self-doubt because nothing I remembered was the same. There was no Jeremy, Kate had been visiting me the whole time, Kate and Carl were together, and even my nurse and doctor were different. My nurse, I thought. Kiley Steele—that was her name—she was the first nurse I remembered. She was Jeremy's cousin.

My mind started working a mile a minute. So many things were different, but maybe just as many—if not more—things were the same. There was one way I could find out for sure.

I pressed the nurse call button, and after a few seconds, a female voice said, "Yes? Can I help you?"

"Yeah, I know you guys are pretty busy, but could I talk to Kiley Steele if she's here?" I said.

"Hold on. Let me check," the woman said.

After about a minute, she came back. "Actually, she was just about to leave. I told her to stop by your room."

"Thank you," I said.

I waited about five minutes, and then Kiley appeared at my door. She smiled at me as she walked in. "Hello. Can I help you?" she asked.

"Hi. Yeah, I was wondering, do you have a cousin named Jeremy?" I said.

She nodded. "I do. He lives in Lansing. Why?"

"And does he have a brother named Albert? Who is, you know, a bigger guy?"

She nodded again. "Yeah."

"Sorry. I met them before, and they told me they had a cousin named Kiley Steele, so I guess you're the same person," I said.

She looked confused. "OK. That's right. Small world, I guess. Did you want to know something about them?"

I shook my head. "No, I was just checking."

She looked perplexed. "OK. Well, I gotta go now, but I'll be back in this unit tomorrow. I was filling in on another unit across the hall. My friend told me that you're doing really well."

"Yeah, I have my memory back, and I guess I'm excited because I'm remembering all these things, and I like verifying that they're true."

"That's really good. I'm so happy for you. I bet you would make a great news story."

"What do you mean?" I said.

"Well, I always wanted to be a journalist, and sometimes I write human interest stories for some of the local papers. I haven't been published yet, but maybe if you wanted to tell your story, they would publish it," she said.

I hesitated for a second, unsure how to respond.

"Sorry. Forget I even asked. I'm sure you're going through a lot right now," she said, looking ashamed.

"No, no, it's OK. I just don't really want to talk about it yet, you know? It's hard," I said.

She nodded with a smile. "I understand, and I really hope you make a full recovery. I'm so happy you have your memory back."

"Thanks," I said.

Before she left, she sent a text message to my phone so that I would have her cell number and told me to call her anytime.

I lay back in my bed, wondering what other things were the same in the reality that I had just been in and this one. There was a pen on my tray table and some white napkins. I folded a napkin in half and placed it on top of my book to make it easier to write. I started a list of all the things I remembered happening before.

Almost two hours went by, and I had almost five napkins filled with local, national, and international events that had occurred between late September and the day I saved the little boy in November. If even half these events happened, it would be proof that I wasn't crazy. I had the Red Sox winning the championship, some crazy things happening in Syria, and Apple announcing a new product called the iPad Air.

Something kept nagging at me the whole time. My mind kept returning to the night before the accident, when I went to a party at Jeremy's house. That was why I'd overslept the next morning. But if Jeremy wasn't even in town this time around, then what had happened that night? I tried to remember, but I couldn't. It was as if the night was blacked out of my memory.

I decided to pick up the phone and call Kate and see if she knew something.

Her phone rang a few times, and then she picked up.

"Hey, Allie," she said.

"Hey, Kate, can I ask you something?"

"What's up?"

"You know the night before the accident? I can't remember what happened. Do you remember?"

She was silent for a second, and then she said, "Yeah, we went to a party."

"Which party?"

Another silence, and then she said, "You really don't remember?"

"No, not at all."

"It was Morgan's party. You didn't want to go, and I convinced you. We ended up leaving early. It was pretty boring."

I thought for a minute. Then I remembered that there was supposed to be a party at Morgan's house that night. The more I thought about it, the more it didn't make sense. If I had left early, then I would have gone to bed early. The entire time, I had blamed the accident on the fact that I had overslept. Now I wasn't so sure.

"The guy who hit us—his name was Manuel something, right?" I said. "He was running away from the cops, stole a car."

"Who told you?" She sounded surprised.

I almost said that nobody had told me. But I didn't want to arouse any suspicions that I was mentally unstable, so I lied. "I overheard a nurse and doctor talking. They thought I was asleep."

"Sorry, babe. We wanted to wait a little longer to tell you that it was that damn criminal. Worst part is, he's still alive. I bet he doesn't even have insurance. My dad said that he's getting medical treatment, and our taxes are paying for it," she said. I'd never heard Kate talk so morbidly.

He would die soon, I thought. But, of course, I kept that to myself. "I've had a long time to think about it, and I guess there's nothing we can do now," I said. "Wishing the past would change doesn't help things get better."

Kate was silent for another second, and based on what she said next, I understood she was choosing her words very wisely. "Allie, you really seem to be taking this very well. I mean, if it were me, I don't know if I could be as strong as you."

She was right. I was taking it very well, but that was because I had already grieved for over two months before something or somebody hit the reset button on my life. Thinking quickly, I said, "Kate, I cried so much to myself that I don't have any more tears to shed. I had a dream," I went on, recalling the first time this had happened, "that I was with my family in a café by a beach. They were all dressed in white, and they seemed so happy. They told me that everything was going to be fine and that they were so proud of me. Every time I'm sad, I remember that dream, and it cheers me up. Wherever they are, they seemed happy."

"Wow. When was that?" Kate asked.

"Well, it was sometime after the accident. I don't remember because of the coma. But the dream was so vivid, and I was so sure it was real. You know, I've read that when you are visited by the recent dead in your dreams, they're coming back to say goodbye before they move on."

"I believe that too," Kate said. "My mom told me that when my grandma died, she came back and visited her. She said it was so real, and they talked for a long time."

"Did she visit you?" I asked, knowing that Kate's grandma had just passed away a few years earlier.

"No, not that I remember," Kate said.

"She probably didn't like you," I said.

"Whatever, Allie. I was her favorite," she said. "She called me Cutie Katy."

I smiled. One thing was for sure: I was glad that this time around, Kate and I remained friends.

"Oh, Allie," Kate said.

"Yeah?"

"You're OK with me and Carl, right?" she said. "I know it's kinda weird. He was your friend and all, and he asked you out. It's just that, well—"

"He was there when you needed him. I understand. Carl's a great guy, maybe the best I know. Just make sure you don't break his heart."

"Oh no, I would never do anything like that. He is so much nicer than all the other boys I have ever been with, and I don't know…I think we have something special."

Her words sent flutters of anxiety through me. He was *my* boyfriend, I thought. He was my "special" guy. I had to act as if it didn't bother me, though. I knew that much.

"I'm very happy for you." No, I'm not, I thought. "Maybe he'll be the one for you." I really hoped not.

"That's so sweet," she said. "I'm doing things differently this time around. He's not the typical guy I usually go out with, but it seems like it's working out pretty well. He is so nice, and he does all kinds of things to make me happy. I can tell he's not just after…well, you know."

"The milk," I said, laughing to myself.

"Yeah, yeah, I'm a slut. Not anymore, Allie. This one is different."

I sighed. I really wanted to remind her of the numerous "this one is different" conversations we'd had in the past, but it was getting late, and I had much greater worries on my mind.

"Well, I'm beat. I'm going to sleep," I said.

"OK, hon. You get some rest. Tomorrow is Saturday, and Carl and I intend on hanging out with you all day long. It'll be fun."

"I look forward to it," I said.

We said our goodbyes, and I hung up. Kate and Carl together. I had never thought that would happen, not in a million—actually, more like ten million—years.

I looked over the list I'd written down. One of the events was coming up. It was a national event, something to do with Syria. I remembered people talking about it right after I woke up from my coma. While I didn't remember the date, I knew it had happened in late September.

I perused my list and wondered how many of the things I'd noted would actually happen. I thought back to the accident with the little boy. I had saved his life. The next thing I knew, I was waking up almost two months in the past. My head hurt just thinking about it.

Then I thought about the look on Azrael's face. He had looked shocked. He knew something; I could feel it. I had done something that I wasn't supposed to do—that was what that look told me. But the idea that it could take me back in time, somehow rewind my life—that, I couldn't understand.

I laid my head on the pillow and looked up at the ceiling. The room was dark and silent. I wondered if Azrael was going to haunt me again. In a way, I wished he would. The next chance I got, I would confront him. He would do his eye-hypnosis thing, but he knew something, and I had to find out what it was. With that thought in mind, I fell asleep.

24

I WOKE UP EARLY ON SATURDAY. The early-morning sun was beaming through the windows in the hospital room. I felt warm and uncomfortable. As I moved my head on the pillow, it felt damp. I'd been sweating in my sleep.

I sat up, and the room spun around me as if I were on a merry-go-round. My stomach turned with nausea, and I immediately lay down on the pillow. I rang the buzzer for the nurse, and a minute later, Kiley appeared at the door.

"Hi," she said.

"Hi, Kiley. Sorry to bother you, but I'm not feeling well," I said.

She walked over to my bedside. "What's wrong?"

Then, before I answered, she got a concerned look on her face and said, "Oh my, you've been sweating up a storm." She put her hand to my head. "You're burning up."

"And I feel nauseous. When I tried to sit up, the room was spinning," I said.

"You've got a fever. I have to call Dr. Cooper right away," she said. "Can you hang tight for just a minute? He's in the hospital this morning."

I nodded. She rushed out of the room.

A few minutes later, Dr. Cooper arrived, with Kiley following him.

"Ms. Drummond, good morning," he said.

"Not so good for me," I said hoarsely.

"Well, let's see if we can do something about that. Kiley tells me you're running a fever. You might not remember—actually, I'm sure you don't—but you had quite a fever when you first came to us. Can I take your temperature?"

I nodded.

He pulled out a thermometer and motioned for me to open my mouth. I did, and he placed it under my tongue. I held it there for a minute. He looked alarmed when he read it.

"Oh my, you are at 103. We need to get you some meds right away." He looked over to Kiley. "Give her alternating Motrin and Tylenol," he said.

Kiley nodded and left the room.

The doctor looked back at me. "When did you first notice this?"

"Just a few minutes ago, when I woke up. Am I going to be OK?"

He nodded confidently. "You'll be fine with meds. Fevers can spring up as you heal. You had a serious head injury, and you lost a lot of blood. I'd say for now, consider yourself lucky that we are not dealing with something much more serious."

There was that word again—lucky, I thought. If everyone just knew half the things I'd gone through, nobody would ever call me lucky again.

He gave me some instructions, mostly to drink as much as I could, even though the nausea was going to make it difficult. He said he'd come back and check on me later.

He left the room, and Kiley came back a few minutes later with a small bottle in her hand. It was glass and had a metal cap. She walked over to the set of drawers next to the computer. She pulled out a syringe and uncapped it. I cringed at the sight of the needle.

She smiled. "Don't worry. I'm going to feed it through your IV; you won't feel a thing."

I was relieved to hear that. She withdrew some medicine from the bottle by sticking the syringe through the top and then injected it into my IV.

"I'm going to run and get you some water. Just sit back and try to relax." She started to walk out and stopped. "Oh, and I'll get you a new pillow too," she said, smiling at me and winking.

As soon as she left the room, I passed out.

I woke up in my recurring dream in which Azrael chases me to the open field. Only this time, I stopped before I reached the field, and I turned to face him. He was coming at me fast, but his legs didn't move. It was as if he were floating just inches above the ground.

"Stop!" I screamed at him.

He did stop, just a few feet in front of me. He had a sly smile, and his black eyes glared at me.

"You cannot win, girl," he hissed in his deathly voice.

"Why are you doing this to me? Why are you chasing me?" I demanded.

His smile grew larger, and his dark lips parted, revealing his pointed teeth.

"I have done nothing," he said. "You have dug your grave, girl. I shall make sure you're buried in it very soon."

"Tell me what you know. Tell me what happened to me," I said, my voice starting to shake with fear.

He kept smiling and stepped toward me. I tried to move, but I was planted firmly in place. Our eyes locked, and as he walked past me, I couldn't shake his gaze. My head turned slowly, following his eyes.

He stood perpendicular to my left shoulder. My entire body was frozen, except for my head, which had followed him. He dropped his head down toward me so that our noses almost touched. He smelled terrible, like old rotting garbage. He had no breath. Droplets of saliva dripped from his sharp, pointed teeth.

"You will be mine," he said, his voice now deep and powerful. "I let you get away once, but only once. This time, I will have your soul. You grave is waiting. Your hour draws near."

I was shaking, but my body was frozen in place. I wanted to scream but found that I could not.

"Very soon, I will have you," he snarled.

His mouth opened far wider than the size of my head. I looked deep into his mouth, and all I saw was darkness. I felt myself being sucked into the bottomless abyss as he moved closer, and his pointed teeth surrounded my head.

I woke up screaming and immediately sat up in the bed. The smell, that rancid rotting smell, was still at the tip of my nose. Reactively, I started wiping my nose, trying to remove the putrid stench. I was breathing so hard that one would think I'd just finished running a marathon. A few seconds later, I realized that it was all a dream, but it had felt so real, smelled so real. It was all a dream, I told myself.

Kiley ran in and came to my bedside. "Are you OK?" she said, looking alarmed.

I didn't answer right away. I had to catch my breath.

She put her hand on my shoulder. "Alex, are you OK?"

I nodded as my breathing leveled off. "Yes. Bad, bad dream."

She sighed with relief. "Oh, man, it must have been. You screamed so loud, I think they heard you downstairs."

I nodded again, although I was really not sure why I was nodding. Truth was, I was terrified. Even with my eyes open, I still saw his mouth opening wide, and those teeth. And that smell; it was the smell of death. I had never experienced anything like it—not even the times I had encountered him before, never like that. I told myself it was just a dream, told myself it wasn't real. A part of me said I was lying to myself; it felt as real as anything else. I started crying.

Kiley pulled me into her chest, and I cried uncontrollably. She kept rubbing my back and telling me that everything was going to be OK. I didn't believe a word of it. Nothing was going to be OK. Nothing. My worst fear was realized. He was after me; he had said so himself. "Your hour draws near," he had said. Those words swirled around my head as tears continued to pour from my eyes.

As my sobbing lightened a few moments later, I noticed that Kiley and I were not alone in the room. Standing at the doorway were a few of the hospital staff, all with solemn looks on their faces. I wondered how long they had been standing there. I figured they all had probably come running when they heard my scream. This thought made me feel uncomfortable. Crying in the presence of one person was not so bad, but in front of a group of people, it was quite the opposite.

I looked away from them, pretending they were not there. Kiley still had her right arm around my shoulder. She gave me a hesitant smile.

"Can I get you anything?" she said.

I shook my head.

"Well, the good news is that the fever is down. It went down as soon as I pushed the meds," she said.

"Thanks," I said.

I looked back at the doorway, and the assembly of hospital staff was starting to disperse. I felt like some kind of zoo animal, one that had acted out of turn and had to be tamed by its master. I wanted nothing more than to tell them all the truth, tell them about this lunatic demon that had been following me around. Tell them about how I had somehow traveled back in time, only to find out that half the things that had happened to me before were different. If they knew what I'd been through, if they themselves were put to the same test, they would realize how difficult it had been for me.

"How about something to eat, huh?" Kiley asked.

I nodded.

She left the room, and I sat back in bed. I kept thinking about the dream, about what Azrael had said. My body kept shaking, as his image seemed to linger on the edges of my retinas. Every time I blinked, I saw his mouth and those sharp, jagged teeth.

It was about three in the afternoon. Kate and Carl must have come by when I was sleeping. I wanted them to come back; I didn't want to be alone. In fact, I needed them to come back. I couldn't do this myself, not by a long shot. I would tell them everything, even about the time travel. I would prove to them I was not lying by telling them things that would happen in the future that I had experienced before, like the Syria thing—that would happen soon. I would have to convince them. I needed them on my side. I couldn't face Azrael alone. If he was going to kill me, then I would put up a fight. I couldn't let him win.

I remembered the day I had saved the little boy. The look on Azrael's face—it was pure shock. Dr. Khan had been on to something. Azrael was afraid of me seeing him because of what had happened with the little boy. I'd saved his life; maybe he was supposed to die. Somehow, that was related to what happened after. Somehow, I traveled back to the point of the accident with my family. I knew these things were related; they had to be.

I picked up the phone and dialed Kate. She sounded happy to hear that I was awake and stated that she and Carl were at the hospital, on their way up to my room.

I hung up the phone and took out the napkins, the ones on which I had written the list of things that would happen in the future from my old past. I studied it, trying to remember the thing that would happen closest to the current date. It had to be a national event, something that could not possibly have changed.

Then it came to me. It was not on the list, but I remembered it, and it would happen that day—Saturday, September 21. Even better, it was so unpredictable that nobody could ever have seen it coming. That way, my story had to be true. In fact, I needed it to happen not just to convince Kate and Carl, but myself as well. While everything told me that I hadn't gone insane, I still had my doubts.

Kate and Carl walked in, followed by Kiley, who had a tray of food.

Kiley placed the tray on the tray table next to me and asked if I needed anything else. I shook my head and thanked her.

"How you feeling?" Kate said, giving me a hug.

"Better," I said.

Kate felt my head. "Wow, the fever is way done." She smiled.

"Hey, Alex," Carl said, standing at the foot of my bed.

"Hey, you too," I said, trying my best to sound cheery. "Guys, I really need to tell you something, and it's going to sound really crazy. But I need you to listen, 'cause it's real important." I looked at Carl and then at the door. "You might want to close the door."

Carl closed the door. I instructed Kate to sit on the wingback chair to my left, and Carl sat at the foot of my bed.

I started off by explaining the accident and everything that had happened, even the part about Azrael. They listened wide-eyed as I told them about Azrael and what he had done to my family.

I went through the entire chronology of events that had led to the accident with the little boy. I made it a point to leave out the part about Carl and me. It just didn't feel right. Then I told them about the time travel. This brought very confused expressions to their faces. Kate tried to say something, but I hushed her with an extended palm. I couldn't stop talking. I felt as though I were purging some sort of disease, and I could not stop until it was all gone.

I got up to the present day, and then I said, "I understand that all this is probably impossible to believe, but I have real proof. The first proof I have is going to happen today. And I have more." I held up the napkins. "I'm willing to bet that all these things will happen over the next month or so."

Kate looked at Carl, and then they both looked at me. Carl said, "Alex, this is nuts. You mean to tell me you traveled back in time?"

I nodded. "I am certain of it."

"And you're sure none of this was a dream?" Kate asked.

"I've asked myself the same question, and things keep happening that tell me that's not possible. For example, Kiley. She's my nurse, but before, she lived in Lansing. Her cousin is Jeremy, the guy Kate dated before. I asked her if she has a cousin named Jeremy and if he has a brother named Albert, and she said yes. How could I have known that?"

Kate and Carl both looked stumped. Then Kate said, "So what is this thing that's going to happen?"

I rummaged through the bedsheets and found my remote control. Carl got up from his seat at the foot of the bed and turned to face the TV. We all looked at the television as I turned it on and changed the channel to ABC.

Michigan Wolverines vs. Connecticut Huskies, College Football, the broadcast summary stated on the television screen.

"Football?" Kate said.

"Yes," I said.

"Yeah, Michigan is going to kill them. Connecticut is horrible in football," Carl said.

"No, not even close. Michigan wins—but just barely. In fact, they don't win the game until the end. They get a last-minute touchdown that saves the day. The final score is going to be twenty-four to twenty-one."

Carl looked at me. "That's crazy," he said.

"It is," I said. "But if it happens, wouldn't you say my story is true?"

"Allie, honey, we believe you," Kate said.

"I appreciate that, Kate, but the truth is, I'm not sure that *I* believe me," I said. "Everything has been so confusing. I'm filled with all this doubt, but things keep happening that tell me it was all real."

The broadcast returned to the pregame show after a commercial. The game hadn't started yet, and some of the commentators were talking.

"So who is Jeremy?" Kate asked as we all made ourselves comfortable to watch the game. "You said that Kiley had a cousin I dated."

"Oh, yeah. He was some boy who lived here last time. You knew him before the time travel. I really don't know much more about him."

Kate nodded but looked confused. I chose not to elaborate any further, and she didn't ask any follow-up questions. Of everything that had happened to me in the past, Jeremy was the one person I was glad to forget.

The game began a few minutes later. Carl had gone to the vending machines and gotten snacks. I had a Snickers bar and two bags of barbecue chips, both of which are at the top of my personal food pyramid, right next to coffee and cherry slushies—all part of an eighteen-year-old girl's balanced diet.

During the first half of the game, we mostly talked about Azrael. I told them most of my experiences but left out the really scary stuff, especially the dream I'd just had. As I expected, Carl pulled out his phone to run a Google search on Azrael. Before he even started typing, I told him what he would find. They both wore expressions of spooked amazement. I wondered how much of what I said they believed. I tried to put myself in their shoes and pictured someone telling me what I was saying. Would I believe it? I didn't know if I could.

As the first half of the game ended with a close score, Carl looked at me in amazement. "Man, we could have made so much money if we'd bet on this thing. Seriously, nobody in America would have thought Connecticut was going to give Michigan a game."

Kate slapped him on the arm. "Carl, don't be an ass. Didn't you hear what she's been through? All you can think about is making money?"

Carl had a sorry expression on his face and turned to me. But before he could apologize, I said, "That's OK. He's right. Too bad. We could have at least gotten something out of this whole mess."

Kate rolled her eyes. "You act like you have money to bet anyway."

"You do," Carl said to Kate. This made me smile. Kate's family was pretty well off.

"You think my dad would give me money to gamble?" Kate said.

"No, but you could tell him it's for school—like you need to take a college course so you can get a head start," Carl said. He actually sounded pretty serious about the idea.

"Carl, you're crazy. I'm not going to lie to my dad, and I'm definitely not going to waste his money gambling," Kate said.

"How is it wasting? You'd give it right back as soon as we win the first game. Look at this, Kate; Alex already knows what's going to happen. That's almost too good to be true. Do you realize we could be rich with this information?" Carl said.

By the look on her face, Kate seemed to be getting pretty angry with him. Before she could respond, I jumped in and said, "Well, Carl, truthfully, this is about the only game I remember. After I left the hospital, things were so crazy that following sports was the last thing on my mind."

Kate looked at me with a satisfied expression. "See? She doesn't even remember any of it, so just drop it already."

Carl looked defeated as he picked a chip from the bag and gave it a crunch. "I was just saying," he said under his breath as he turned and faced the TV.

We watched on, and eventually, the game ended just as I had predicted. A last-minute touchdown by a Michigan player saved the day. Kate and Carl turned to me, amazed at the result.

"So what happens next?" Kate asked. "Like, what do we do about this thing that follows you around? Is there any way to stop it?"

"I don't think so," I said. "I think he's royally pissed and will do anything to get me."

"Get you?" Carl asked.

"Kill me," I said. "I think he wants to kill me."

Kate and Carl looked at me, shocked. "Are you serious?" Kate said. "Allie, we can't let that happen. We have to do something."

I shrugged. "I don't know what to do. What, do you want me to call the police and say, 'Hey, there is this weird demon in a three-piece suit that wants to kill me. Oh, and by the way, I'm the only one who can see him.' It's nuts. I have no idea how to stop him."

"Allie, you can't be serious. It sounds like you've accepted this. I can't believe you would talk like this," Kate said.

"Kate, if you went through what I've been through, nothing would seem the same anymore. The only thing I have working for me is that I think that he himself cannot kill me. If he could, he would have by now."

"Well, that doesn't make me feel any better," Carl said. "I mean, this has to stop somehow. There has to be a way we can get to him."

I looked over at Carl. I found myself staring at his lips as he spoke. I remembered the gentle kisses we had shared, and goose bumps ran down my spine. Like before, he would help me. I also knew that he, like before, loved me. This time around, right from the start, I loved him too.

"That's so sweet, Carl; but like I told you, we tried last time, and nothing worked," I said. "I think for now I just need to work on getting out of this place and see how things go."

"Alex, I'm scared that he's going to hurt you. I want to act before something happens. I mean, there has to be something we can do," Carl said.

I shook my head. "Carl, there's nothing we can do right now. I promise I won't let him hurt me."

"Allie, do you want me to sleep here?" Kate asked.

"Thanks, but that's OK. You don't have to. I know how uncomfortable it is," I said. "And seriously, you guys don't need to worry about me. I'll be fine."

"I really hope so," Kate said.

"I guarantee it, Cutie Katy," I said.

Kate smiled and rolled her eyes. Then she gave me a hug and kissed me on the cheek.

"We'll be here bright and early tomorrow. It'll be Sunday, so we can have breakfast together," she said.

"Pancakes," I said.

"Pancakes, it is," she said.

Carl gave me an awkward hug. Even though I wanted to pull him closer, I didn't. After that, they both left. I watched through the doorway, and as they walked away, Kate reached out and held Carl's hand. A flutter of jealousy passed through me. I turned over on my side and stared out the window.

I LAY AWAKE FOR A WHILE, fell asleep around four in the morning, and slept for eight dreamless hours. I woke up a little bit after noon to see Kate sitting next to me in the wingback chair, reading a book. She looked up immediately when she saw me rise.

"Morning, Allie," she said.

"Hey," I said.

"I gotta get out of here," I said to her. "I thought about it last night. Remember that boy I told you about? I have to go see if he's still alive."

Kate shook her head vigorously. "Allie, you can't. They said you need a few more days before they can let you go. Your wounds need to heal."

I looked at her sternly. "No. I leave today. And you and Carl are going to help."

"Allie—"

"I said no! Kate, you are my best friend, and I know you want what's best for me, but I can't stay here anymore. I have to find out if the boy is alive."

"What's that going to prove?" she said. "You said you didn't save him until a month and a half from now. If he gets hit by the car, it hasn't happened yet."

"I need to know that he's real. Kate, something tells me that I did not just change a few things; I changed a lot. If that's the case, the boy might

190

still die, but from something else. I swear I will come right back. I just have to go see for myself. Please, Kate; please. You're my only hope."

I shifted my legs off the bed. I knew I was able to walk, although the pain in my side still stabbed me from time to time. I stood up, much to Kate's dismay.

"See?" I said. "I can walk just fine."

"Even if you wanted to leave, you know they won't let you go," she said.

"Who says I'm going to ask their permission?"

"What? You can't sneak out; they'll see you."

"Not if I'm wearing a disguise. You have to go back to your house and get me some clothes."

She shook her head. "I can't."

"You will," I said as I walked over to the bathroom, dragging my IV stand with me.

I heard her sigh, and as I entered the bathroom, she walked out.

About a half hour later, she was back with a small shopping bag filled with clothes. I smiled when I saw her walk in.

"I knew you would do it," I said.

"One hour. That's all. Carl is outside. He thinks you're crazy too, but he's willing to help."

She pulled out a hoodie, a pair of jeans, and a brunette wig.

"Why the wig?" I asked.

"Allie, do you seriously think you can be gone for an entire hour, and not one nurse is going to walk in? Plus, your machines have to be hooked up to someone. If the heartbeat stops, they'll think you died."

I smiled. "So you're gonna take my place?"

"That's the plan," she said as she walked over and closed the door.

I carefully took off the monitor the nurse had attached to my finger. She had shown me how to remove it when I needed to go to the bathroom. I attached it to Kate's finger, and she put on the wig. Then I removed the IV insert from my hand. I had seen it done a hundred times, and it was a lot less painful than I had thought it would be.

I put on the clothes that Kate brought, and she jumped into the bed with the wig on. I drew the hoodie over my head, found a pair of sunglasses in her purse, and put them on.

"Kate, this really means a lot to me," I said.

Alan Baker

She smiled. "You're crazy, but I love you. Please be back soon."

I gave her a hug and then went to the door. I stopped with my hand on the knob. I wondered if I would even get past the threshold. Then I heard a siren.

I looked over at Kate, who nearly jumped out of bed. I motioned for her to get back in bed. She looked alarmed. I motioned again for her to return, and she did. I remembered this siren. It was the one that had gone off when the old woman died next to me. I had a feeling the siren was not for me. With that, I opened the door and saw hospital staff rushing past me. I was right; it was coming from another room.

I took one look back at Kate and gave her a hopeful nod. Then I exited.

I walked quickly past the staff, and nobody even gave me a second look. Whatever the siren was for, it had sent everyone around me into a panic.

I made it to the main hallway and walked briskly to the exit. Pain kept jabbing me in the side as I walked, but I ignored it.

Carl was sitting in his car just past the main entrance. I got into the passenger seat.

"Hey, Alex," he said.

"Hey, yourself. And thanks," I said.

"It's cool. Let's be quick."

"Yeah, it's pretty close to here. It won't take long at all," I said.

I directed him to exit the same way he had come in. He turned onto the main road, and we reached the stoplight that we had stopped at last time. Once we passed the stoplight, I had him drive slowly in the right lane as I surveyed the residential streets that we passed. Then I saw it. He drove past it and turned onto the next street, and then he turned back toward the street that I had run down to save the little boy. Marcel Street. He made a right and then a left. We drove one block to the intersection where I had saved the little boy.

"Here it is," I said as he stopped at the stop sign. I pointed at the street that ran perpendicular to Marcel. "The boy was crossing there, and the car was coming from the right. I remember that the driver was not paying attention to the road, and the boy was coming out from behind those bushes."

Carl looked where I was pointing.

"I ran across the street and pushed the boy out of the way, and that was when the car hit me. There was a woman maybe twenty feet behind the boy

192

on the sidewalk. She had fallen. My guess was she was chasing after the boy when she tripped."

"That was really brave of you. You could have killed yourself," Carl said, his eyes still on the street corner.

"Maybe, but I think I was not supposed to be here in the first place. You see, all these things changed when I saved that boy. I don't know…maybe it would have been better…"

"Better?" Carl said, turning to look at me. "That a little boy could've gotten hit by a car? How's that better?"

"Carl, so many other things are not the same anymore. Plus, I think I really pissed off this Azrael monster."

Carl shook his head. "That can't be, Alex. I won't accept that. You were meant to save that boy, and you risked your life doing it. It was supposed to happen that way. Maybe that was the reason you could see these things in the first place."

"It's just so hard to understand why these things happened. Maybe I'm just crazy."

Carl just shook his head. He seemed to ignore the last thing I said. He was such an idealist; that had not changed one bit.

We sat there in silence for about ten minutes. No little boy with blond hair was to be seen the entire time. In fact, the entire neighborhood was still—not one person or car passed us.

"Do you think we should knock on some of these doors? Maybe the neighbors know of a little boy who lives on the street," Carl said, breaking the silence.

"What's the excuse? Why would we say we're looking for him? Sounds creepy, if you ask me," I said.

Carl smirked. I could tell that he hadn't thought about it that way. "Yeah, you're right," he said. "Well then, what do we do? You can't be gone forever. You'll be in big trouble."

"I know, I know. Just another ten minutes," I said, trying to urge him on.

He nodded silently, and we sat there awhile longer.

It ended up being about twenty minutes, as the clock hit three in the afternoon, and another nonstop pop hour started on the radio, helping us to pass the time. A few cars had gone by, but there was still no boy.

"Let's get back," I said.

"OK," Carl said. Without hesitation, he started the car.

I was in big trouble when I got back. Of course, the nurse had been alerted once I removed the heart-rate monitor, and unbeknownst to me, it was standard protocol to check the patient when something like that happened. Carl had gotten twenty missed calls and maybe fifteen text messages from Kate. He had ignored all of them so that he could give me the time I wanted, waiting for the boy. As angry as Kate was that she was being ignored, my stomach fluttered at his gesture.

My excuse was that I had just wanted some fresh air. Of course, that was not well received. Dr. Cooper told me I'd put myself at great risk, and my injuries were too severe to be out and about, and on and on. I didn't care. They had no idea what I'd been through, and a short drive down the street was nothing compared with the harm that followed me around everywhere I went and even haunted my dreams.

Carl promised that he would go back to the spot where we'd parked every day after school and see if he could spot the kid. And he did that for a week straight, at least. After that, I told him to give it up. Maybe one of the other things that had changed was that the kid didn't live in Crescent City anymore. Maybe he hadn't even lived there in the first place. He could have been visiting family. Either way, I figured that road was a dead end. I would have to look for answers elsewhere.

A few days later, on a Thursday, they moved me up to the room I had stayed in before. As soon as they rolled me in, I remembered the scene with Azrael and the old lady who had died. The bed was empty when we entered the room; last time, the old lady was there before I was.

It was room 233; I remembered that too. But this time, I was alone. I tried to remember the woman's name, but the thought would not surface in my mind. Then, just before I fell asleep for a nap, it hit me: Isabelle Nelson.

I rummaged around in the nightstand next to me, and in the top drawer, I found a phone book. I flipped through the Ns and found Nelson. I went down with my index finger and found Isabelle. There were four of them. I picked up the phone and started dialing the first number, and then I stopped. What would I say? "Hey, are you the Isabelle Nelson who used to be in the hospital, back in my alternative reality?"

I thought about it but could not come up with anything. I put the phone down and just stared at the names for a second. Then I called Carl.

"Hey," he said, picking up after the first ring.

"Hey. Can you do me a favor?"

"Sure."

"I'm gonna give you four numbers. Can you look them up online and get an address for each of them on the reverse phone lookup website?"

"OK. Did you find the boy?"

"No, but back when I was here before, I remembered that there was an old lady who died right next to me. Her name was Isabelle Nelson; I want to see if she's still around. Based on what I remember, she died about now, but when they wheeled me into the room, she wasn't here."

"OK. What are the numbers?"

I gave them to him. He said he'd look them up and call me back. He did. One of the addresses was on the same street where I had saved the little boy. Carl said he'd looked it up on Google maps, and it was in fact three houses down from the corner where the boy almost got hit. We decided we would go to visit as soon as I was discharged. I put the phone down and stared at the empty bed next to me for a long while.

I WAS SCHEDULED TO LEAVE THE hospital a few days later. The entire time leading up to that I spent thinking about Isabelle Nelson and the address near the corner where I'd saved the boy. I went through every scenario in my mind, thinking through all the possibilities. I could not believe that Isabelle and the boy were somehow related. Of course, considering all the things that had happened to me in the past few months, it seemed as plausible as any other scenario.

Rick was waiting outside my room as I changed into a fresh set of clothes that he had brought. I knew he was ready with the wheelchair that he would eventually cart me out with. I hadn't told Rick anything about any of the crazy things that had happened to me, and I'd sworn Carl and Kate to secrecy. He had found out about my transgression of leaving the hospital, and he more or less believed that all I'd wanted to do was smell some fresh air.

"All done," I called out, and on cue, Rick opened the door, pulling the wheelchair behind him.

"You know I can walk, right?" I said.

"It's hospital rules," he said.

I rolled my eyes. I had heard that before.

I sat down in the chair, and Rick collected my bag.

"I'll come back up for the flowers once you're in the car," Rick said.

"Sure," I said.

He wheeled me out the open door and onto the elevator.

Kate and Carl were at school. They'd be getting out in a few hours. We had a plan to go over to Isabelle's house, and Kate had come up with a pretty brilliant idea on how we could talk to her without looking like buffoons.

We exited through the hospital's main doors. The air outside was warm, and an overcast sky hung above us. I got into the passenger seat, and Rick went back in to get the rest of my things.

He loaded up the SUV—the same SUV he had before the time travel—and got in.

As before, we talked about visiting my family's grave site, and he asked again if I wanted to go. I told him that I wanted to wait a little longer, and he seemed to understand.

We got back to Rick's house and found that Alicia had prepared us some lunch. The twins were fast asleep, and we sat at the kitchen table and ate.

Once again, I felt safe. I knew the surprise that awaited me upstairs with my room and started preparing myself to act as if I didn't know what was coming.

After lunch, they took me upstairs, and I did my best acting job. It was much easier than I thought it would be. Tears still fell from my eyes as I read the card they had set on the nightstand. This time around, Kate had signed it.

"Kate and Carl are coming by after school, and they're taking me out," I said once we got back downstairs.

"Are you sure you don't want to rest a little?" Alicia said.

"I've been resting for the better part of a month. I really just wanna get out," I said.

"Where you guys going?" Rick asked.

"They said it was a surprise. I bet it's the movies," I said.

I felt bad lying to them, but I really had no other choice.

We sat at the dining room table, drank coffee, and ate snacks until Kate and Carl arrived. I quickly rose to my feet when I heard their car in the driveway.

"You should invite them in for coffee," Alicia said as I reached for my purse.

"No, that's OK. I'm really anxious to go out. Being in a hospital room for a month does that," I said. That part was mostly true. I really did want to go out, no matter the destination.

I stepped out on the stoop and immediately spotted Kate and Carl exchanging some light kisses over the center console of the car. Jealousy boiled up in me again, but what was I going to say? I bit my lip and slowly walked over to them, pretending not to notice and hoping they'd stop.

They did stop, but not until I actually entered the car. A brief moment of awkward silence ensued, as it was obvious they'd both been oblivious to the outside world until they heard the car open. I remembered when Carl and I had been like that together; it seemed so long ago.

"Hey, Allie," Kate said as she fixed her hair and lipstick in her vanity mirror.

"Hey, guys," I said.

"Hey," Carl said hoarsely as he put the car in gear.

I looked over at the seat next to me and saw a large encyclopedia. "So you think this is going to work?" I asked Kate as she continued to freshen up.

"It will at least give us a reason to go over there without being arrested," Kate said.

"I don't know, Kate. Who buys encyclopedias these days? Everything is on the Internet," I said.

"Old ladies who don't know how to use the Internet," she said. "My dad got suckered into buying that one, having never heard of *Wikipedia*. When I showed him the website, he was amazed by how much stuff was on it."

It all seemed pretty logical. She was right; it might get us a few seconds of face time with Isabelle.

As we drove, my mind wandered back to the day that Isabelle Nelson had died next to me in the hospital room. I remembered seeing her young body being pulled out of her. I remembered the alarms blaring as her heart suddenly came to a rest. Most of all, I remembered the cold, unnerving stare of Azrael as he walked by me dragging his latest victim behind him.

We reached the house and parked right in front of it. It was one of many condos crammed together along the street, all with red wooden doors. As instructed by Kate, I was wearing the "cutest" outfit I had available. Against her instructions, I had refused to put on makeup. I figured that would just tip off Rick and Alicia that something was up, as they knew I never wore any, and prompt them to ask more probing questions.

Carl was going to stay in the car and wait for us. We figured that having a guy with us would throw things off, and of course, what was more disarming than two cute high school girls selling something?

Kate and I stepped out of the car and walked up the porch steps. I checked the address twice as we approached. I had written it on a small sticky note, which I put in my pocket once we reached the door. Kate knocked three times lightly, and we looked at each other in nervous anticipation.

As we waited, no sound came from inside the home. Kate knocked again. We waited for a response and heard nothing. No floorboards squeaking, no yells of "I'll be right there" from the occupant inside. Nothing.

Dejected, I looked at Kate. She matched my look with her own.

We turned and were starting to walk down the steps when we heard the front door open behind us. The hinges let out a painful creak.

"Can I help you?" I heard an old woman say.

We turned around in unison. The front door was half-open, and a delicate old woman stood there.

"Yes, hello," Kate said, letting a big saleswoman smile spread across her face as she walked up the steps again. "We're selling encyclopedias for a fund raiser at our high school," she said. "We would love the chance to come in and show you what we have to offer, if you're interested."

The old woman looked at her blankly. Then she looked at me. I couldn't tell if she was the same Isabelle Nelson who'd been in the hospital bed next to me. This woman looked thinner and lighter skinned. Of course, it was possible that she was not even Isabelle Nelson. The phone directory gets updated only once a year, and this was the end of the year. Isabelle Nelson could have moved months ago.

"I'm not interested," the old woman said.

"Well, I'm sorry to hear that," Kate said. "But I'm sure you might reconsider once you've had a chance to see what this book has to offer. It goes over all the major subjects taught in school today. It's the perfect gift for—"

The old woman waved us away. "Thank you, but really, I'm not interested." She started to close the door.

"Please," I said. "We just need a minute of your time. It's really important."

Only half of the woman's face was visible through the crack remaining. "And why is that?" she asked.

"You're Isabelle Nelson, right?" I said, half expecting her to slam the door shut as soon as she heard the question.

Out of the corner of my eye, I saw Kate's head turn quickly toward me. That was not part of the script, of course, but considering that the door was closing anyway, I figured it was worth a shot.

The old woman was silent for a second, as if she didn't know how to answer. Then she said, "And if I am, what's it to you?"

"My name is Alexandra Drummond, and this is Kate Thompson. I was in a terrible accident about a month ago that claimed the lives of my family. Let's just say that a lot of strange things have happened to me since then, and a woman named Isabelle Nelson was a part of those strange things. I'm just trying to figure things out."

The old woman opened the door a little more. I could see her whole face, and she looked at me appraisingly for a second.

After a moment of silence, she said, "Come in," and opened the door all the way.

As we walked into her home, we were immediately struck by a thick cloud of warm, humid air. The temperature outside was in the midseventies, but in the old woman's house, it had to be pushing ninety degrees. The next thing I noticed was how dark it was. Immediately to the left of the front door was a small living area with old flower-patterned furniture. The drapes were drawn shut, and the old TV situated in front of the couch was off. To the right was a door that led to a dining area, and past it, I could see a cluttered kitchen. All the drapes were drawn shut in those rooms as well.

She motioned for us to sit. There was one sofa, a love seat, and a single armchair. We chose to sit side by side on the sofa. The old woman closed the door and locked both the bottom and top latches.

"I'll make some tea," she said as she started in the direction of the kitchen. Her walk was more of a slow shuffle; she barely lifted her feet off the floor.

"That's OK," I started to say, but the old woman ignored me and kept walking. I immediately got the feeling that tea consumption was compulsory in her home.

Kate and I sat awkwardly as we heard tea-making noises coming from the kitchen. From where we sat, she was not in sight, but based on the noises, we could tell what she was doing. We exchanged nervous smiles as the old woman labored on.

"Do you think she's crazy?" Kate whispered to me.

"No, I think we are the crazy ones," I said.

Kate found that funny, and she covered her mouth as she laughed.

"What are you going to tell her?" she asked.

"I don't know. The truth, I guess," I said.

"You can't," Kate said, shaking her head.

"What else am I supposed to say?"

Kate just looked at me, and before she could answer, the old woman appeared in the doorway, carrying a tray with a teapot and some mugs.

I darted to my feet to help her, but she refused. "Just have a seat, dear. I can handle it," she said as she shuffled toward the coffee table.

I did as I was told. Kate and I waited as she made her way toward us and finally placed the tray on the table. She did it with such precision that it barely made a sound. I figured she must spend a lot of time drinking tea and watching her old television set.

She descended ever so carefully into the well-worn armchair. "Please help yourselves," she said, "and pour me a cup too."

I hunched over the coffee table and poured three cups of tea. There was no sugar, and the tea was dark and rich in color.

"That's a chia I picked up at the grocery store," the old woman said. "It's strong, but it arouses the senses. Very important these days, you know."

I nodded and smiled and handed her a cup. Then I put a cup in front of Kate.

We all took sips and sat back in our seats. The warm air, already thick with humidity, was filled with an even thicker awkward silence.

"So you are Ms. Drummond," the old woman said.

I nodded. "Yes. Did you see the story about the accident in the paper?"

She nodded. "Yes, the paper. That's where I've seen you. I'm very sorry about what happened to you."

"Thank you," I said. "And I'm really sorry about barging in like this, but like I told you, things have not been the same since the accident."

She nodded almost as though she understood. "And you've come to find something out from me?" she asked.

"Well, if you are Isabelle Nelson," I said.

She smiled. "I am."

"Well, I really don't know why I came, exactly. Let's just say there was, or possibly there is going to be, an accident on the corner, right here by your house. And you and I...we met before. Of course, you don't remember, but it was in the hospital. Anyway, I found out that you lived here, and it's right by the accident, and...well, I don't know...I guess I think maybe the things are connected."

As I spoke, Isabelle just sipped her tea and nodded. She did not appear to be surprised or confused by my cryptic explanation. In fact, she seemed to understand me completely.

"So we met before, you say," she said after a moment. "In the hospital?"

I nodded.

She looked up above me, as if she were thinking. "Yes, I remember. I was in the hospital a month ago, right around the time they brought you in. I saw you. I was in my bed in the hallway, and they were moving you. We came within inches of each other. You were not awake, though."

I was surprised to hear this. I hadn't seen her my entire time in the ICU. In fact, my only memory of Isabelle was when she died next to me, before I traveled back in time.

"I dreamed about you that night, you know," she said. "Very vivid dream, in fact. You don't know this, but you are part of the reason I decided to leave the hospital. You and that wonderful nurse, Ms. Steele."

I was shocked at the revelation of her dream and by her reference to Kiley Steele. "I don't understand," I said.

The old woman smiled and took another sip. Then she said, "Oh, I'm willing to bet you do understand a little."

I looked over at Kate, who was speechless, her eyes unblinking and wide.

"I'm in my last stage of cancer," Isabelle said. "And Ms. Steele convinced me that it is probably better to stay home and spend my last days in my house with my family. My daughter, she comes by every weekend, and I get to see my grandson. He's three. His name is Peter. He's an adorable little guy, but he's a handful because he's deaf."

As she was describing her grandson, the image of the little boy crossing the street flashed before me. I recalled how my yelling had not fazed him. He was deaf; that explained it.

"He's involved in the accident," I blurted.

The old woman smiled and shook her head. "No, you saved him," she said.

I looked at her, shocked. "I don't get it."

She placed her cup down on the coffee table and leaned back in her chair. "My dream—the one about you. I was home, and you came knocking on that door there," she said, pointing at the front door. "When I opened it up, you stood there with Peter, and you guided him into the house. He gave me a great big hug, like he missed me or something. We said nothing to each other. You smiled, and then the dream was over."

I saw tears forming in her eyes, and as she continued the story, they started to fall.

"I didn't know what it meant. Maybe nothing. Maybe I dreamed about you just because I had seen you the same day, before I fell asleep. Anyway, the very next day, my doctor wanted to start me on chemotherapy. I had the choice to decline and just go home, being that I had very little chance of making it anyway. That nurse, Steele, she told me like it was—what the chemo was going to do and that it would likely not work. Her words, along with the vivid dream I had of you the night before, made me come home.

"Now, I see Peter almost every day. I swear that's the best medicine. You see, I keep the house really warm too—I'm sure you've noticed it by now. That stops tumors from growing."

For a moment, her words just hung in the air as Kate and I nervously sipped our tea. We had no idea how to react to any of this. It felt so eerie, and a numbing feeling came over me, as if someone had just told a spooky ghost story.

I was digesting what she was saying, and it started to make sense to me. The Isabelle Nelson of old had stayed in the hospital because she probably never saw me, and she definitely never ran into Kiley Steele. The Isabelle Nelson of now—she was right here, alive and breathing a week after she was supposed to die. Sure, she lived in an oven, but I think that given the choice, she'd prefer this over the other thing.

I turned to Kate and gave her a nod. She mistook this as an indication that I wanted to leave, but that was not my intention.

"Well, OK, Mrs. Nelson, it was really nice talking to you," she said as she started to get up.

I stayed put, and when she stood up, I looked up and said, "Give me one minute. I want to ask her a few more questions."

Kate gave me a stare. I knew right away what she was thinking. The whole time we had spent planning this little escapade, she had reiterated over and over again that I was not to disclose the weird occurrences that had happened to me recently. I had reiterated to her over and over again that if I had to, I would. I needed answers. She was afraid that I would be jailed or thrown in the loony bin for knocking on a stranger's door and telling her some long tale about death and time travel.

But Isabelle Nelson was not a stranger. I knew that now. She was connected to all of this, and I had been guided to this very spot for a reason. Somehow, I knew that as well.

Kate smiled rigidly and turned for the door. As soon as she was out, I looked over to Isabelle. And like a geyser unable to hold back the rising water pressure, the short story of my recent past erupted out of me. I did not stop talking, and Isabelle did not stop listening, until I had told her every last detail.

"You've been blessed," she said without hesitation at the end of my story.

I looked at her, bemused. "How? My family is gone, and I have this thing following me around everywhere, trying to kill me."

"Well, you're still alive, and if this thing had the power to kill you, I think it would have done so by now," she said. "But look what seeing that thing enabled you to do. You saved my little grandson, and it appears that you have delayed my death as well."

The numbness I'd felt before came back in full force. She was right; I had never thought about it that way.

"You have to understand something," she said. "I know my days are numbered, and frankly, I've known it for quite some time now, even before the diagnosis. But I have no regrets, dear. I've lived my entire life just the way God intended. I had a happy marriage. I have a wonderful daughter and a lovely grandson. If that thing you are talking about were to walk in that door right now, I would shake his hand and ask him to point me in whatever direction I need to go. As my grandmother used to say, those who have faith accept death, but those who are truly enlightened by faith embrace it."

I nodded. A single tear fell from my right eye as she finished speaking.

"Thank you," I said.

"No," she said, shaking her head vigorously. "You deserve all the thanks."

She extended her arms to me, and I got up from the couch and gave her a hug. A few more tears fell from my eyes.

"What about Peter?" I asked after our embrace.

She gave me a coy smile. "If anything is going to happen to that boy, it'll have to be over my dead body."

I smiled. She gave me another hug.

I left Isabelle Nelson's house watery-eyed but feeling much better about myself. As we said our goodbyes, I was standing on her stoop. Something told me that this would be the last time I would see her. As it would turn out, I was right. I also felt that Peter would be safe and sound and never cross paths with that speeding car. I was right about that too. Because, I would later learn, before Isabelle Nelson died, she would spend three more months on this earth than she had spent before. And instead of dying alone in a hospital bed, she would pass peacefully in the night in the home in which she had lived for the majority of her adult life. As for Peter, he would be sleeping soundly in his own bed, having escaped any chance of being hit by a car, and on his way to living a long and prosperous life.

I WENT BACK TO SCHOOL THE following Monday. As before, I walked the halls feeling the eyes of the entire student body upon me. My class schedule was exactly as I remembered it. I had co-op the first two hours of the day, which meant that my first class started at third period. Unlike before, Kate was with me as I entered Mr. Polderman's classroom.

I had inquired about Mr. Polderman and his marital status, and Kate confirmed that he was in fact recently divorced. He was also sporting the infamous lisp that I vividly recalled.

The last few nights before I went back to school were filled with bad dreams, and Azrael was in all of them. I had the recurring dream that he was chasing me to the open field a few times, but a new one was thrown into the mix. In the new dream, I was lying on a table, unable to move an inch, and Azrael was standing over me with a devilish smile on his face. Then Azrael wheeled me around as though I were on a hospital bed, except I wasn't in a hospital. We were on a sidewalk right in the middle of Crescent City. The dream would go on like that for a while, and then I would wake up.

I tried really hard to put the dreams behind me and block them out of my mind. It was very difficult to do so, and I often found myself lost in a trance in the middle of class as the dreams replayed in my head.

Although the visit to Isabelle Nelson's house had made me feel better at the time, in retrospect it raised a lot more questions than it answered. I pondered them mightily, trying to understand the chain of events that had led me to the spot I was in. The biggest question was why so many of the details had stayed the same but others had changed. Mainly, I had seemingly changed the fate of a little boy and an old woman.

Fifteen minutes before Mr. Polderman's class ended, he announced that the rest of the class would work on the assignment for the day, and he motioned for me to leave the classroom with him.

We went across the hall to the empty classroom, and just as I entered it, I froze with fear. My first sight was of the courtyard outside the windows of the classroom, and I remembered Azrael standing there. He was not there now, but my eyes were still fixed on the very spot where he had once stood.

"Everything OK?" Mr. Polderman asked as he walked past me to the teacher's desk at the front of the classroom.

"Yes," I said, shaking off the memory.

I sat down in the same chair I had occupied before, and he pulled the teacher's chair over to me and sat down as he had before.

"We are very happy to have you back in class, Alex," he said. "That was a terrible thing that happened, and we want to do everything we can to help you out."

"Thank you," I said, nodding and smiling.

Then he told me about their plans to tutor me after school, all things I already knew, but I pretended to be surprised and smiled and nodded as he spoke.

"Your aunt and uncle tell me you're taking this very well and that your recovery was good," he said.

This was new. I wondered what Rick and Alicia had told him before— probably that I was a basket case and needed to be handled with kid gloves.

"Well, it's been hard, but I'm doing my best to look forward to the future. I wish it hadn't happened, but there isn't much I can do now," I said.

"That's very true. Tragedy is a double-edged sword, sorrow and regret. We often ask ourselves what if, or we say if this had happened, then maybe things would be different. Thoughts like that, although natural, make recovery much harder—"

His words turned on a light in my head. "Mr. Polderman," I said, interrupting whatever else he was about to say, "Can I ask you a question, like a science question?"

His face lit up. "Sure."

"Is it possible—you know, scientifically—to change the past? I've seen stuff on the Discovery Channel about the possibility of time travel and all that, but could someone change the past?"

"Through time travel?" he asked.

"No, like something that I do now—could it change what happened in the past? Like, for example, if I save someone's life now, do other things change?"

"I don't think I understand," he said.

For a second, I almost digressed, but then I trudged on. "Like, let's say someone stopped something from happening that was supposed to happen; is it possible that the past could change?"

He pondered this for a moment as he rubbed his chin. "Well, if you mean is it possible for a person to alter a past event by altering the future, the answer to that is probably not. Now, I say 'probably not' because there is one theory—actually, it's more of a thought exercise."

He walked around the desk to the dry-erase board and took a red marker from the ledge.

"It's called Newcomb's paradox." He drew a line across the board.

"The paradox itself assumes, though, that the person who is changing the future event actually knows what's going to happen in the future. This person is called the predictor. Of course, he has to always be right, and in a variation of the paradox, the predictor is able to actually change the future, not just predict it, as the name implies."

He looked at me and saw confusion painted all over my face.

"Let me try to explain it." He wrote a capital letter *A* at the right end of the line and put a vertical slash under it that crossed the first line he had drawn.

He pointed at the letter and said, "Let's say that this is the grade you're going to get on an exam, and let's assume that this exam is sometime in the future. For instance, two weeks from now." He wrote "two weeks" under the vertical line. "Now that A is not obtained through luck; events have to occur to lead you to get a good exam score."

He added three more vertical lines across the horizontal line to the left of the *A*. He wrote "study," "do homework," and "maintain health" above the lines.

"Now let's assume that there is a predictor who not only knows that you will get an A on this exam but also has the power to change that score. So let's say that the predictor decided that you will get an F on the exam instead of an A." He crossed out the *A* and put a capital letter *F* above it.

"If this predictor had the power to change this score, then what do you think would happen?"

"The things in the past would change," I said without hesitation.

A large smile appeared on this face. "Exactly. You see, if the predictor could simply alter the future event somehow, then events leading up to the test would have to be different. Something along this line would have to change so that it could yield the result of an F on the exam. So either you would not study or do your homework, or you would get sick the day of the exam and do very poorly."

"Well, what about if the person taking the test studied really hard and did everything she could to prepare?"

"In that case, then something else would have to happen to cause the test taker to bomb the exam. Maybe the test taker wakes up with a really bad headache the morning of and is unable to focus. Maybe her nerves get the better of her, and she draws a blank on the exam. Basically, any number of things could happen."

I mulled this over for a moment then said, "So you're saying it's possible for a future event to change the past?"

"Well, in this hypothetical it is. In real life, I don't see how it's physically possible."

"What if the predictor, in real life, knew some information about what should happen that she was not supposed to know? You know, like she could tell the future, and she decided to alter the future event?"

He looked at me and nodded. "I guess that could work. But how would anyone know the future?"

"Well, let's say that the predictor knew that someone was going to die, and she saved that person's life. Would that work? Would it change the events that led to the person's death?"

Mr. Polderman rubbed his chin. "Well, if you're saying that the predictor saves the life of someone who was supposed to die, then I guess that could fit into the hypothetical. Theoretically, events that led up to the person's death would have to be altered so that the person does not die. That would only work, of course, if we are talking in absolutes. You see, the hypothetical assumes that the predictor can change that future event, and no matter what happens, that future event must occur the way the predictor wants it to. In theory, I guess it might work."

My heart was racing as I started putting together the pieces of the puzzle. "So this could be true. In real life, I mean."

He gave me a bemused smile. "Well, Alex, the idea of a predictor who knows how the future will turn out is not a real possibility."

I didn't respond because I knew that he was wrong. I just nodded my assent.

"You seem intrigued by this. You know, physics is arguably the most interesting science. It's filled with what-ifs and unexplained phenomena just like this."

I smiled. "It's very interesting."

He wiped the dry-erase board, came back around the desk, and sat in his chair. He continued to tell me about the teachers' plans and how the year had gone thus far. I was lost in a daze, thinking about the discussion we had just had and its application to my current situation.

I thought about the boy, the travel back in time, and the look on Azrael's face. Azrael had known something would happen when I saved the boy. I had changed an event that was supposed to happen—that little boy was supposed to die. When he didn't die, all the things that had happened that led to that point changed as well. Kiley Steele being in Crescent City instead of Jeremy. Kate had told me before the time travel that between Kiley's father and Jeremy's father, it was almost a toss-up who would get the job at Ford and move to Crescent City. Last time, it had been Jeremy; and Isabelle Nelson never met Kiley. But this time around, it was Kiley's family that came to Crescent City, and she treated Isabelle. Isabelle said it was Kiley who persuaded her to go home instead of staying in the hospital, where she had died before. And because Isabelle was home, she would live on and watch over Peter, who would not get hit by the car.

All of this was initiated because I had some unexplained ability to see Azrael. If it wasn't for that, I would not have saved the boy. I was the predictor, the one who had the power to change the future—and with that, change the past.

"Mr. Polderman," I said, interrupting something he was telling me about my class schedule.

"Yes?" he replied politely, but I could tell that he noticed that I had been in a daze the whole time he was talking.

I turned and looked at the spot in the courtyard where Azrael had stood before. Nobody was there. I turned back to Mr. Polderman and asked, "What if I knew that someone was about to die, and that someone else was dying because of something he did. If I saved him, would that change what he did?"

Perplexed, Mr. Polderman cocked his head to the right. "Like what? What did he do?"

I chose my words carefully. "Let's say he was in an accident, and because of that accident, he was about to die. What if I saved his life? Would that change the accident?"

"Well, that's a bit vague. How would you know this person was about to die?"

"Say I knew the exact day and time. If I saved his life, and he lived past that time, would that change the past? Could it?"

"Alex, we are still talking in hypotheticals here, aren't we?"

I nodded, but it was rather unconvincing.

He said, "Assuming you knew the exact day and time, and assuming that person was supposed to die, then I guess, yes, the theory would hold that whatever accident you refer to might not happen, considering that it was the thing that eventually caused the death."

I looked back over to the courtyard, and this time, I saw Azrael standing there. I wasn't the least bit startled or scared. I had known he would come. And I knew he was somehow listening to this conversation and knew that I had just figured out a way to beat him.

I looked back at Mr. Polderman, who was following my eyes. He peered quickly at the courtyard. "Is there something you are looking at out there?"

I shook my head and smiled, and then I looked back at Azrael and stared him right in those dark eyes, knowing he could hear me. "No," I said. "Nothing at all. I was just remembering when I was younger, how certain things used to scare me. This courtyard reminds me of that."

"That's odd," Mr. Polderman said. "What kind of things does this courtyard remind you of?"

"Wild animals, spiders, large beasts," I replied, keeping my gaze fixed on Azrael.

Mr. Polderman got up from his chair and took a few steps toward the window. We both stared into the courtyard. "It does have lots of trees. So these things—they don't scare you anymore?" he asked.

I shook my head. "No. I learned one thing that got me over the fear."

Out of the corner of my eye, I could see Mr. Polderman turn and look at me. "Yeah? What's that?" he asked.

"I learned that they're more afraid of me than I am of them."

28

KATE WAS WAITING FOR ME outside the classroom when I finished with Mr. Polderman.

"Have fun in there?" she asked as I approached.

"Lots. I figured something out that could help," I said.

She looked at me, confused. "Figured what out?"

"Let's find Carl, and I'll tell you both."

We walked down the senior hallway and then through the underclassman hallways. I was getting occasional stares from other students. They didn't faze me, though; I was focused, and my mind was racing as I considered the possible implications of Newcomb's paradox on my current situation.

Carl had gym third hour, and the gymnasium was on the opposite side of the school. It was our lunch hour now, so we would have plenty of time to talk.

We met Carl about halfway through the school, in the sophomore hallway. He had a bright smile, and his cheeks were a little red from gym class. His hair still was damp from his shower.

"Hey," he said to me, and then he turned to Kate.

I watched as Kate leaned in and gave him a peck on the mouth. I thought about the time he tried to kiss me in the hallway when we had first gotten together. I had immediately thwarted his efforts and likely embarrassed him in front of whoever was watching. If only I hadn't, I would have had one more kiss from him.

"We need to talk," I said. "Hurry up and get your lunches and meet me in the cafeteria."

"What about you?" Kate said. "Aren't you going to get lunch?"

I shook my head. "No, I can't eat right now."

"I'll get you a sandwich," Carl said.

"You don't have to, really," I said.

"Allie, you have to eat. C'mon. We can stand in the lunch line together," Kate said.

I reluctantly followed them to the lunchroom.

It seemed that no matter how early we got to the lunch line, we were always the last ones to arrive. The double line was already pouring out of the lunchroom's two double doors.

There were two lunch counters, each with identical food laid out under warmers. We preferred the left line because it was closer to the kitchen, and the food always seemed to be fresher. Past the warmers was a refrigerated pit containing all kinds of cold sandwiches. They had bologna and cheese, peanut butter and jelly, and egg salad. On days that I didn't like the warm offering, I chose the egg salad.

We stood in line together, Kate and Carl comfortably cuddled close to each other with Carl's hand gently resting around the small of Kate's back and me playing the third wheel, standing behind them. After a few uncomfortable minutes, we finally reached the food warmers. Today's choices were cheese or pepperoni pizza. I promptly pulled a slice of pepperoni and placed it on my tray.

Carl took two slices of cheese, and Kate, passing on the pizza, took an egg-salad sandwich. Carl insisted on paying for all our lunches, and while I wanted to object, I didn't. I just smiled. He was dating the best-looking girl in school, and with that came some high expectations. Since I'd known Kate, I don't think she had ever paid for her own lunch, even at times when she didn't have a boyfriend. There was always a boy or two who pined for her, and that usually resulted in them picking up the tab in the lunch line.

We found our seats. It was a round table for six, and we spread out so that nobody would sit next to us.

As we slowly chewed our food, I told them about my conversation with

Mr. Polderman and the revelation I'd had. They remained silent as I gave them every detail I understood about Newcomb's paradox and said that that was exactly what had happened to me the first time I saved the boy. I did my best to explain things the way Mr. Polderman had explained them to me, but I was sure I got some of it wrong.

"So you're saying that when you saved the boy, you reset time and changed the past?" Carl asked.

"Yes, and that's why I think Azrael has been stalking me this entire time," I said. "I think he knows about this whole thing and what would happen if I ever got in the way of him taking someone's soul. So when I saved the boy, which I had no business doing, everything changed so that the boy wouldn't die. That's exactly what happened to me. It's the reason I traveled back in time."

"This is crazy," Kate said.

I nodded in agreement. "Yeah, but it's the only explanation for all this, and actually, it seems to work. Everything that's happened to me in the past few months has been crazy, and until today, I didn't understand why it happened the way it did. Now I do."

Kate and Carl spent a silent moment thinking it through as I took a bite of my pizza and a sip of soda.

"So what now?" Carl asked.

"I have to save Manuel, the guy who hit us," I said.

"What?" Kate said in disbelief. "You can't do that. That bastard killed your entire family."

"No, don't you see? Right before I saved the little boy, Manuel died. It was in the second week of November. That's over a month from now. Even though so many things have been different since last time around, the only real changes came because I saved the boy. Steele, the nurse, being at Crescent City Hospital and convincing Isabelle to stay home instead of undergoing chemo. All the other things too."

"No way," Kate said, "You don't know that. You said it yourself: Isabelle's grandson dies in November too. How do you know that the accident doesn't happen anyway?"

I shook my head vigorously. "It doesn't. I know it doesn't. Something is telling me that it won't."

"How could you even save Manuel? You're not a doctor," Kate said.

"Yeah, but I know a doctor who can help us out. His name is Dr. Khan. He was my doctor before the time travel instead of Dr. Cooper. And last time, before I saved the boy, I went to visit Manuel. The officer who let me in told me that Manuel needed a heart transplant but that he was unlikely to get it because he was really low on the list, and he had a really rare blood type. If I can convince Dr. Khan about all this, maybe he can move him up on the list so he can get a transplant, and maybe he won't die."

"This is crazy," Kate said again.

"OK, let me get this right," Carl said. "You think that if you save this guy's life, somehow time will change again, and your accident will never happen?"

I nodded.

"What if he just lives, and nothing changes? What then?" Carl asked.

I shook my head. "I'm sure that things will change. There's a reason that Azrael keeps haunting me. When I was talking to Mr. Polderman, he was standing in the courtyard, and I knew he was listening."

"Who, Azrael?" Kate asked, her eyes wide.

"Yes, he was there, and I knew he would come. He was looking at me, and for the first time, I was not afraid of him. I have it figured out. This is the reason he's been after me all along. He was shocked the first time he realized that I could see him, and he's been trying to scare me away ever since. When I saved that boy, I saw the look on his face. He was shocked. You see, he's afraid too, and he knows now that I know how to stop him."

"This is crazy." Carl said it this time.

"It is, but really, it's my only hope. I have one chance to make things right. I have to try," I said.

"So what do you want us to do?" Carl asked.

"Are you saying you guys want to help me?" I asked.

They both nodded, and Kate said, "Allie, as crazy as this is, we are still your friends. Maybe you're right, but we won't know unless we try."

I smiled. "Good. First thing I need to do is get ahold of Dr. Khan."

"How are you planning to approach him?" Carl asked.

"Well, I have some inside information, and I did him a favor, so I think he'll help me out. But it'll have to wait until next week," I said.

"Next week? What's going on next week?" Kate asked.

"He's coming back from a convention in Vegas, and something is happening at that convention that is going to change his life," I said.

A week passed. I continued to go to school as usual. Azrael was conspicuously missing—both from my dreams and when I was awake. I took this as a good sign. Perhaps he didn't want to reinforce what I had figured out. I guessed he thought that if he haunted me more often, I would know for sure that I was right about what I needed to do. Nonetheless, I welcomed our next encounter. After a week, the idea of saving Manuel took root, and I was not going to let anyone, especially Azrael, get in my way.

Kate and I arrived in front of Dr. Khan's office at nine in the morning. We didn't have to be at school until ten, but if our meeting ran long, we would have no problem skipping our first class. My decision to bring Kate was based on that whole "disarming teenage girl" theory; it had kind of worked on Isabelle Nelson.

Kate parked in the lot; there were only a few cars around us. I had never taken notice of Dr. Khan's car, so I wasn't sure if it was among them. I was pretty sure he was inside, though, as I had called ahead and determined that he had an appointment at nine. We waited for a minute, neither of us saying a word.

"Ready," I finally said.

"What if they call the cops on us or something?" Kate replied.

"We're just here to talk. Besides, it wouldn't be the first time someone called the cops," I said.

She breathed out slowly. Kate was deathly afraid of altercations. I credit this to her growing up in a house in which her parents fought all the time. It didn't matter, though; there would be very little of that, I guessed.

Almost in unison, we stepped out of the car. The October air was cool and damp. It was easily my favorite morning air. It felt so fresh as I breathed it in.

We walked slowly to the front of the building. The large glass entrance revealed just one old man standing in the foyer, reading the directory. I bet myself that he was Dr. Khan's first appointment. Then again, the building housed many medical offices, so he could be there to see anybody.

We walked in, and from memory, I led Kate to Dr. Kahn's office. We stepped into the small waiting area. A nurse was behind the sliding-glass window, and she gave us a blank stare.

"Hi," I said as we approached the window. "We're here to see Dr. Khan."

The nurse, who had light-brown hair and looked to be in her late forties, just gave us a funny look and said nothing.

"We don't have an appointment. We just want to talk to him for a quick second," Kate said in a sweet, charming tone.

"Well, the doctor sees people by appointment only, so I don't think I can have you see him," she said.

"But it would be only for a second—we swear. It's a matter of life and death," I said, hoping the drama would sway her opinion.

It did not. In fact, she raised her eyebrows and gave me a look as if I were crazy. "Life or death doesn't get you in here without an appointment. If you'd like, I can set you up, but I can tell you right now, it may be next week before you can see him."

This was the same thing I had been told when I'd called to schedule an appointment over the phone. We were getting nowhere, so I changed gears. "OK, well, can you pass along a message to him? Can you tell him that Alexandra Drummond is here to see him? Maybe that will help."

"Help who? You? 'Cause it sure as hell isn't going to help me," the nurse said sarcastically.

"Please," I begged.

The nurse rolled her eyes and slowly got up from her chair. We stood in silence in the waiting area for a few seconds. The old man who had been at the directory walked in, and we exchanged smiles.

To our right was a door that I remembered led to the screening rooms and offices. It opened. Dr. Khan popped out; he looked at me dead-on.

"Alexandra?" he said.

"Yes," I said.

"C'mon back," he said.

I followed him in, and Kate started to tag along. Dr. Khan turned and said to Kate, "Please, just Alexandra."

Kate smiled and turned back toward the waiting room.

We walked down the hallway. The forty-something nurse gave me an irritated look when we passed her.

Dr. Khan led me in to his office, and I took a seat in front of his desk. He walked around his desk and sat down in his chair. I saw the letter I had sent him resting on top of his desk.

"Thank you," he said.

"For what?" I said.

"For saving my marriage," he said.

"You're welcome," I said, very satisfied that things had worked out the way I'd planned. "So the delivery guy found you in time?"

"Yes. Just as I was sitting down to have dinner, he gave me your letter. All the things you wrote came true. She was there, and she approached me. We talked for a while, and things got intimate. But as they did, I kept remembering your letter and what you said would happen if I slept with her. Before it went any further, I stopped our little date and immediately ran back to my room and called my wife. We talked for hours about nothing, but it made me forget about the other woman."

I was just nodding. Aside from telling Dr. Khan about his potential infidelity, I had also detailed everything that had happened to me since the first accident, including the time travel, Azrael, and my encounters with him. It took seven typed pages to fit all the details in, and it appeared that Dr. Khan believed all of it.

"So you believe me?" I asked.

"I have thought about that for an entire week, and although it's hard to believe, I don't see how else you could have known all the things you knew. I mean, you detailed conversations that you and I had and told me things about myself that almost nobody knows. Not to mention you predicted that my old girlfriend would be at the convention, and that was something I did not even know. There is no plausible way you could have had access to this information unless we had talked about it."

Step one of the plan was complete. "So if I ask for your help on something, would you give it?"

"Depends on what it is," he said.

I reached into my jeans pocket and pulled out a piece of paper. On it, I had written all the information about Manuel that I could remember. I handed it to him.

"On November thirteenth, a little over a month from now, Manuel, the guy who hit my family, dies. He needs a heart transplant to survive. You need to find him a donor," I said.

Dr. Khan just looked at me, bemused.

"I told you in the letter that when I saved the little boy's life, everything changed. Well, there's more to it. I believe that if I save Manuel's life, everything will change again, and this time, the accident that claimed my family won't happen."

"How can you be so sure about this?" Dr. Khan asked.

I was prepared for this question.

"Because the things that changed since I saved the little boy were things that caused him to be on that road to begin with. You see, before the time travel, his grandmother Isabelle died well before he got hit by the car. She died because she stayed in the hospital and received chemo treatment for her cancer. I was right next to her when she died. This time around, she was at home. She said that a nurse, Kiley Steele, convinced her to stay home. That nurse was not working in Crescent City Hospital before the time travel; she was working in Lansing. The reason she was in Lansing was that her father did not get a promotion and did not move to Crescent City. But this time, he did."

I paused for a second to let him digest this.

"You see, because I saved that little boy, all the things that led to his death had to change, and that's what happened. You and I met before. You don't remember that, but all the things I put in the letter—they were true about you."

"When did you figure all this out?" he asked.

"Last week, my physics teacher called it Newcomb's paradox. Obviously, I didn't tell him about any of this."

Dr. Khan seemed to be deep in thought, and then he said, "Well, this letter is postmarked almost two weeks ago. How did you know I could help you then?"

I leaned forward in my chair and stared into his eyes. "That's something else I can't explain, Dr. Khan. Originally, I was only doing it so that I could help you, because deep down inside, I felt that I needed to do it. It was not until after I sent that letter that I figured any of this out. Somehow, I know this is what I have to do."

"Well, you saved my marriage, and frankly, my life," he said.

"So are you going to help me?" I asked.

"You have to understand something. Getting a heart donor is a near impossibility. If you think about it, it's a very random process. Another person has to die from an accident for you to have a viable heart. Even then, the success of a transplant depends on many factors. If it's true that he has a rare blood type, then it could be impossible—not to mention the fact that I have no control over who gets a heart and who doesn't."

I sighed. "Well, there has to be something you can do to help me. Can't you look for a heart or call some people to get him moved up on the list? He has to live."

He shrugged. "I can try, but don't get your hopes up. One thing I can do for you right now is check on his status. He may be past the point that a transplant will even save him. Of course, I wouldn't be able to disclose that information to you unless you were his next of kin. Do you know if he has any family?"

I shook my head. "I visited him before the time travel. The officer who let me in said nobody had come to see him. So I don't think so."

"Well, how about you try to find a family member and have him call me. I will call his doctor and get his status. I know most of the surgeons at Crescent City pretty well, so I should have no problem getting the information."

"Well, what if I can't find someone?"

He gave me a coy smile as he handed me one of his business cards. "I'm sure you'll find someone. Just have him call me Friday, and I will update him."

I understood.

"Thank you so much," I said.

"No, thank you. Really, Alexandra, I owe you a lot. I'll do whatever I can to help you out," he said.

"So you believe me—you know, about everything?"

"I guess I do. Nothing you've said thus far has been false, and I can't explain how else you could have known any of this. I've thought about it a lot, and really, I guess I have to believe what you're saying."

I smiled. It made me feel really good to hear him say that. "Thanks," I said.

Dr. Khan walked me to the waiting room, where Kate was sitting. We said our goodbyes again, and he apologized for not letting Kate in. Kate returned a kind smile and accepted his apology, but I imagined she was relieved that she had not had to be part of our little meeting.

Once we left the building, Kate asked, "So what happened?"

"He's going to help us out," I said.

"Really?" she said.

"Sounds like it, but I'm going to need you to do something for me," I said.

Kate looked at me anxiously as we got into her car. "What?"

"You have to play Manuel's sister—just over the phone."

She turned the key and put the car in gear. We drove out of the parking lot and onto the street before she responded.

"OK, so let me get this straight. You've already had me impersonate you—which, by the way, my parents are still very mad at me for. Now you want me to impersonate someone I don't even know?"

I nodded matter-of-factly. "Sounds right."

She sighed. "One phone call."

I smiled, turned to her, and kissed her on the cheek. "You're the best," I said.

She was just shaking her head and smiling as we headed toward Crescent City High School.

Azrael did not show himself for the rest of the week. I settled into school, and as the newness of it faded, the mundane day-to-day repetition of classwork and homework dragged on. I grew more and more anxious as Friday approached, hopeful that Dr. Khan would give me good news.

I spent most of my time in class thinking about everything that had happened thus far and wondering how all of it had come to be. I still questioned the legitimacy of it all and my own sanity. But this time around, unlike before, I had some hard evidence to prove that what I had gone through had actually happened.

I also thought about Bailey and my parents a lot. Even though it had been what amounted to three and a half months since the accident, I still missed them terribly. Coming home to Rick, Alicia, and the twins just didn't feel right. I felt like an outsider intruding on their personal space. A few nights earlier, I'd had a hard time sleeping, so I got out of bed to use the bathroom downstairs. I was surprised to see Rick in his underwear, eating a bowl of cereal at the kitchen table. I pretended I didn't see him and walked quickly past the doorway and into the bathroom.

I heard his footsteps go toward his bedroom and then back to the kitchen. When I walked by again, he was back to eating his cereal, but this time, he was wearing a pair of sweats. We talked for a few minutes. In the end, though, I just felt bad for encroaching on his personal space.

I thought about moving out, maybe getting a real job and paying my own way. But after some quick arithmetic concerning the amount of money I would need for my own place and the possible jobs I could get, I figured that moving out really wasn't an option. I had no skills to speak of and had never really had a job in my life. I had no experience, either.

I kept coming back to my plan and how saving Manuel's life would solve all my problems. If I was right, Manuel would live, and he would never cause the accident to begin with. Things would change—they would have to— and our paths would never cross. Still, I was filled with all kinds of doubt. Maybe I was just making myself believe that this would happen because it was the only thing that would save my family, or maybe saving the little boy's life was different than saving Manuel's life would be.

I kept thinking about the accident with my family, and how changing any one of so many things could have prevented it altogether. We could have left the freeway a few seconds earlier or later or even not at all. My dad could have followed the other cars that appeared to be going in the other direction instead of insisting that he knew the way. I could have awakened earlier that day, and we would never have been on that road. We would have gone in the opposite direction, heading to the wave pool. Any one of those things—along with a thousand other things—could change if I saved Manuel's life. If Newcomb's paradox and all that stuff were real, then I was the predictor with the power to change the future. And by doing so, I could change the past.

I woke up Friday at seven in the morning. Truth is, I had barely slept. I kept thinking about what Dr. Khan would have to say. Kate decided she would skip her first two periods so we could call Dr. Khan together. I didn't have any classes until after ten, due to co-op. Unfortunately, I still didn't have a job, but apparently, the co-op administrator didn't care.

Kate and I met for coffee around eight at the IHOP Rick had taken me to. I saw the heavyset server, and as before, she walked around smiling brightly to each person she encountered. She didn't wait on us, though. A middle-aged woman who wore glasses and looked as though she weighed seventy pounds did. She had a thick, raspy voice, no doubt from years of smoking.

"What can I get you girls?" she asked just seconds after we sat down in a booth.

"I think we're just having coffee," Kate said.

The server looked annoyed. I understood why; these days, there was a coffee shop on almost every corner that accommodated those "just getting coffee." I felt bad for her.

"I'm going to eat," I said as she was about to walk away.

She gave me a halfhearted smile and said, "Do you know what you want?"

"Stack of the regular pancakes," I said.

She jotted it on her notepad.

"So you ready?" I said, turning to Kate.

She shrugged nervously. "I guess."

"Remember; you are his sister, and you are from out of town and just heard about the accident. I think Dr. Khan knows that we're going to be impersonating her, so don't be nervous."

"I just never did anything like this before—you know, lying like this. It feels wrong," she said.

I rolled my eyes. "You've never lied?"

"I have, but not to a doctor about something this serious," she said.

"How about this?" I said. "Just pretend Dr. Khan is your dad, and he's asking you if you're still a virgin."

"Oh my God!" she exclaimed. "Allie, that was uncalled for."

I laughed, and she smiled and shook her head.

"Whatever," she said. "Like I said, just one call. That's it."

The server brought the coffee and after that, my stack of pancakes. I ate as Kate was texting Carl on her phone.

"Carl says hi," she said.

I smiled. He had wanted to be in on the scheme, but we had decided that a female calling would be better received.

I finished eating and left the server a sizeable tip, considering the balance of the bill. We left the restaurant and drove to a park about ten minutes away. The air was calm; the sky, overcast; and the temperature, a comfortable sixty-five. We lowered the windows as we parked in the lot adjacent to the park. We faced a playground and watched two little boys who were swinging side by side on the swing set, each trying to outdo the other.

"OK, it's nine," I said. "You're up."

I handed her Dr. Khan's business card, which I had been holding on to all morning. She took it and dialed his number.

She held the phone to her ear. I could hear the muffled ringing on the other end. Then a woman answered, but I couldn't make out what she was saying.

"Yes, can I speak to Dr. Khan?" Kate said.

The muffled female voice spoke again.

"This is Maria Alderas; I am the sister to Manuel Alderas, one of Dr. Khan's patients. He told me to call today about Manuel's condition," Kate said.

A silence ensued, and then I heard another muffled voice come on. This time, it was a male voice.

"Hello, Doctor, this is Maria Alderas. I was calling you about my brother, Manuel Alderas. Sorry, but this is the first I've heard about what happened to him. I live in Minnesota," Kate said.

I heard Dr. Khan talking on the other end, and he continued to talk for about a minute.

"So there is nothing you can do?" Kate said.

Hearing that made me slump in my seat.

"Wow, that little? You say six percent?" Kate said.

On the other end of the call, Dr. Khan continued to speak for another thirty seconds.

Kate thanked him and hung up. I had heard everything I needed to hear, so my guess was that she had nothing but bad news for me.

"So?" I said after she hung up.

"Not good," she said.

"How not good?" I asked.

"He said that Manuel's blood type is very rare—only six percent of people have it, and it is very unlikely that he will get a donor," she said.

I sighed. "What is it—the blood type?"

"I think he said O negative," she said.

Hearing this made my insides turn. It started with my stomach, and then it felt as if my entire abdomen was twisted in six different directions. I felt faint. My heart started to race.

"What's wrong?" Kate asked, seeing my expression.

"I'm O negative," I said.

"So?" she said, sounding baffled.

I didn't respond. Instead, I looked above the dashboard at the swing set where the boys were playing. Directly behind them and about fifty yards from where we were parked stood Azrael. He was standing upright, his greased hair flowing gently in the breeze and a devilish smile on his face.

"Allie, are you OK?" Kate asked, but I didn't react. Instead, I stared at Azrael's smiling face, and anger started to boil up deep within me.

He had known all along. He knew that Manuel's blood type would match mine; he knew that I would eventually discover that; and ultimately, he knew that if I wanted to save Manuel's life, the only heart that would be available to him would be my own.

My anger turned to blind rage. My heart was pounding deep within my chest, and I lost all control. I burst from the car and dashed toward Azrael, screaming obscenities as I ran. Kate was screaming at me, but I didn't hear a word she said.

I darted past the boys playing on the swing set. I could see out of the corner of my eye that they stopped swinging, and their gazes followed me.

Azrael didn't move an inch. He remained smiling, and as I approached him, he extended his right arm parallel to the ground.

I was suddenly jerked to a halt. His black eyes narrowed, and his smile turned into a sneer. I felt a paralysis come over my entire body; I was unable to move an inch. Even the muscles in my face felt as if they had been numbed by a powerful sedative.

"I told you that you'd be mine, girl," he hissed.

I tried to respond to him, but my body would not react to my brain's commands.

"You thought you were outsmarting me. You thought you had things figured out. You were wrong," he said. "Your soul should have been mine the day I took the rest of your family. You've been lucky, overstayed your welcome. Now you have no choice. You will be mine at last."

I felt my face loosen up, as if he were allowing me to talk.

"Why are you doing this?" I asked. "What have I done to you?"

His smile returned. "Nobody escapes death. Not a single soul. Especially not some little girl."

"Will things change if I give him my heart? Like before, will they change?"

He kept on smiling. He raised his hand slightly, and I felt my body rise off the ground. He left me suspended in the air. "These are mysteries you cannot understand. But no matter what you do, little girl, I will have your soul eventually. And as long as you walk this earth, you will have to face me. You cannot cheat me and live in peace."

I struggled to free myself of his grasp, but I couldn't. My gaze was fixed on his. His black eyes drew me in, held me still. They stopped my struggling, made my body limp, and set my thoughts adrift. Staring into his eyes, I saw it all. I saw Bailey and my parents. I saw my house on Eagle Street, my room, our little camping site in the backyard by the old oak. Then I saw the accident, the bloodied bodies of my family sprawled about in the mangled car. I saw myself lying motionless in a casket. My eyes were closed, my skin was pale white, and Azrael was standing over me with a satisfied smile. The image, the thought of it, shook me to my core. Then I blacked out.

30

I WOKE UP IN KATE'S ARMS. She was propping me up with her left hand and gently tapping my face with her right.

"Allie," she said, "Are you OK? I called nine one one."

I just looked at her.

"Allie? Can you hear me?"

I nodded and then slowly sat up. She moved away from me slightly to give me room to sit. All I saw in her face was fear.

"What happened?" I asked.

"I don't know," she said. "I was so afraid. I still am. That couldn't have been real."

"What couldn't have been real?"

Her eyes started to water. I could tell she was desperately trying to hold back her tears.

"It was so scary," she said.

"Tell me," I said.

But it was too much for her. Kate started crying harder than I'd ever seen anyone cry before. She fell onto my shoulder, and I felt my shirt dampen with her tears.

"I don't remember anything; just that I saw Azrael. He was here," I said.

She collected herself and pulled back. "That's why you jumped out of the car?"

I nodded.

"What happened when you saw him? What did he do to you?" she asked.

I shook my head. "I don't remember after that. I remember running to him, yelling at him, but after that, I don't remember a thing."

"Allie, you were floating," she said.

"Really?" I said, acting as if it were the first time something like that had happened. The difference this time was I didn't remember anything about the incident.

Before Kate could respond, sirens blared behind us. An ambulance and a fire truck barreled down the road and pulled into the parking lot where we had left our car.

"I fainted, that's all," I told her, looking her dead in the eyes.

She nodded.

I looked over to the ambulance. Two medics got out, and two firefighters got out of the fire truck. As I turned back to face Kate, I noticed that the boys who were playing on the swing set were staring at me with blank faces.

"Hello. Are you OK?" the first medic asked as he knelt down beside Kate and me.

"I'm fine," I said. "I fainted. I think maybe I was dehydrated."

He looked at me appraisingly. He was a younger man, maybe in his late twenties or early thirties.

"I'm going to check some of your vitals," he said. "Miss, would you give us some space?" he said to Kate.

The medic went through his routine checks, and then he walked me over to the ambulance. The fire truck drove away.

I sat down on the back of the ambulance, the doors open on either side of me. The second medic was talking to the little boys. I watched the expression on his face as the boys spoke. He looked more and more confused as the conversation went on.

Kate was standing next to me as the first medic hooked me up to an IV. I cringed when he stuck me with the needle.

The second medic walked toward us, and when he was about fifteen feet away, he called, "Sam, can I talk to you for a second?"

Sam, who was attending to my IV, didn't turn. "Hold on. I'm getting her hooked up."

"You're going to want to hear this," the second medic said.

Sam finished what he was doing and walked over to his partner.

I looked at Kate, who looked concerned. She was about to speak to me, but I gave her a quick shake of the head. I didn't want the medics seeing us talking. I didn't want them thinking that anything had gone wrong other than me simply fainting.

I watched as the medics spoke in hushed tones. Sam looked confused. After about a minute of conversation, Sam walked over to the kids, who were still on the swings. He spoke to them, no doubt confirming what his partner had just told him.

Sam finished talking to the boys, and both medics walked back in our direction. As Sam approached, he was rubbing the back of his neck with his right hand and looking confused. "Are you sure that's all that happened? You just fainted?" he asked.

I nodded. "As far as I can remember."

"Did you run out of the car, screaming and cursing?" Sam asked.

"I ran. I don't remember the screaming and cursing part, though," I said.

"Why did you jump out of the car?" Sam asked.

"Exercise," I said.

Sam looked over to the second medic, who just gave him a shrug.

Sam looked back at me and then at Kate. "Those boys said they saw you floating in midair."

I laughed. "Really?"

Sam looked at Kate. "What about you? What did you see?"

Kate looked hesitant. My stomach turned; she was not very good under pressure.

"Well," she said, "like Alex said, she jumped out of the car to get some exercise, and when she got to the spot where you found us, she just fell down."

Sam looked back at me and said, "Shouldn't you girls be in school?"

I nodded. "Yes, but we both are part of the co-op program, which means we don't start until after ten." This was a lie too; only I was in co-op.

Sam mulled this over for a second, and then he said, "Well, I have to take you in because we gave you the IV, but I'm sure they'll discharge you as soon as you get there. I have to write up an incident report. I think I'll leave out the part about you floating in the air."

I smiled, but it was more out of relief than in acknowledgment of his joke. "That would make some story, though," I said.

"Yeah, I guess it would," he said.

They loaded me into the ambulance. Kate gave me a hug goodbye and said she would meet me at the hospital.

They placed me in the emergency wing, and I immediately demanded to see Dr. Khan. As I waited for him, Kate walked in.

"Allie, we gotta talk," she said.

As in most emergency rooms, we had only a curtain separating us from other patients.

"Well, this is probably not the place," I said in a hushed tone.

"I have to tell you this. We can whisper," she said.

"OK, but be quiet. If someone walks in behind you, I'll tap your arm, and you immediately have to stop talking."

"Well, what the boys said was true," she said. I could see that this was very difficult for her.

"But there was more that they didn't see," she said. "When you went up into the air, I ran and stood in front of you. I was screaming and trying to reach for your legs, but you went up too high. Then I saw your face. Allie, your eyes. They were completely black."

"What?" I said a little louder than I should have.

Kate took a quick look around and then continued. "There's more. You were saying words that I didn't understand. It didn't even sound like your voice. It was like a hissing sound. Then"—she paused, collecting herself—"then, black tears started falling from your eyes. Your face turned white." Her own tears started to fall. "I thought you died."

I couldn't believe what she was saying. I still didn't remember anything that had happened. Black eyes? Azrael had black eyes. How had that happened to me?

"What did I say? Do you remember any of the words?"

She wiped the tears from her eyes and stared past me in deep thought.

"Adesse or Adey. Something like that. You kept repeating it," she said.

"Give me your phone," I said, and she handed it to me.

I brought up Google and started searching the word. The first query came up with no results, and then I typed it in using a different spelling. *Adesse* was a word. It was Latin, and it meant impending doom.

I froze for a second, staring at the screen. Something jogged my memory, and an image flashed before my eyes. I was lying in a coffin with Azrael standing over me. I started to tremble, but I held my composure.

"What?" Kate asked.

I looked up at her and said, "I need your help."

"What is it?"

I swallowed hard. "Manuel needs a heart, and I have one to give. I'm going to need your help."

Kate recoiled, and she almost screamed, "Are you crazy?"

I shushed her and pulled her close to me. "Kate, you have to trust me. I mean, you believe everything I've said so far—about Azrael and about the time travel and the little boy. He's trying to scare me away. He thinks that if he shows me images of my own death, I won't do it."

"Do what? What are you saying?" Kate said, still speaking loudly.

I shushed her again.

"I can save my family; I know I can. I know what he's trying to do. If Manuel lives—if I give him my heart—then the past will change again, and the accident will never happen. Don't you see?"

She shook her head and ran both hands through her hair.

"You saw what happened today. That was real. He's after me no matter what I do. If I don't do this now, he's just going to haunt me for the rest of my life."

"What if it doesn't work? What if Manuel dies anyway or nothing changes?" she said.

"It has to work," I said.

"Allie, this is crazy—"

"Crazy is a girl being suspended in midair and saying words she didn't even know existed. Crazy is saving a little boy who was supposed to die and somehow falling in some sort of time warp. These things all happened to me for a reason, and this is just the last chapter, the final thing that has to happen. I'm not afraid of dying, and I'm not afraid of Azrael."

Kate sat down on a chair next to my bed. She looked down at the floor in apparent shock.

Just as I was about to offer some words of encouragement, Dr. Khan walked in.

"Hello," he said politely as he stepped through the curtains. He looked at me solemnly.

"Everything OK?" Dr. Khan asked.

I nodded and sat up in the bed. "Fine."

Kate said nothing.

"Well, I looked through everything. Looks like you'll be OK. There was something I wanted to talk to you about," Dr. Khan said.

Kate looked up, and Dr. Khan gave her a smile. She did not return the smile. Instead, she got up and walked through the drawn curtains.

Dr. Khan came close to my bedside and said in a low voice, "I've been standing outside this curtain for a few minutes. I heard what you and Kate were talking about."

I recoiled. I hadn't expected this. "What did you hear?" I asked.

"That you want to kill yourself," he said.

I looked down at my lap and fiddled with my fingers. I thought about responding, but I had nothing to say.

"You know, Alex, this is a very common thing. Posttraumatic stress. People go through this all the time after a bad accident," he said.

I looked up and stared him in the eyes. "Get me the medic who came to the park," I said.

He looked confused.

"Go get him now, before he goes somewhere else. His name is Sam," I said.

"What does that have to do with anything?"

"It has to do with everything," I insisted. "Go."

Dr. Khan went to the phone on the nightstand next to me. He picked up the receiver and dialed a few numbers.

"Yes, is Sam still in?" he said.

A second went by, and then Dr. Khan said, "Hey, Sam. Do you have a second to come by bed seventeen in emergency?"

Another second passed. "OK, thanks." Dr. Khan hung up.

"He said he'll be here in five minutes. Now, would you care to tell me what's going on?"

"I saw Azrael again," I said. "I lost control. I ran toward him, but he froze me. He lifted me up in the air and suspended me. I don't remember much, but I remember seeing myself in a coffin."

Dr. Khan looked concerned.

"I think he's trying to scare me. I think he knows that if I prevent Manuel from dying, that will save my family, just as I told you. Just like with the boy, if Manuel lives, everything will change."

"Hello," a voice said outside the curtain. It was Sam.

"Come in," Dr. Khan said.

"Hello again," Sam said, giving me a smile. "Doctor."

Dr. Khan looked at me. "So?"

"Hey, Sam," I said. "Sorry to bother you, but the doctor and I need something cleared up. I was telling him that crazy story those boys told you at the park. Can you tell him what they said?"

Sam shrugged. "Sure, uh, yeah. They said they saw you floating in midair. I didn't tell you this, but one of them said he heard you saying some really freaky things. Then they saw you drop to the ground. I think they said you were about ten feet off the ground. Pretty wild stuff."

I looked at Dr. Khan. "See? I told you. Crazy kids think of the craziest stories."

Sam said, "Yeah, it's a crazy story, all right. But those kids didn't seem like they were lying. But what am I to do? I can't write up something like that. Everyone would think I was crazy—or stupid for believing a couple little kids."

Dr. Khan was speechless.

"Thanks, Sam. Sorry to bother you. I just wanted to make sure we had that right," I said.

Sam gave both of us a nod. "OK, guys. Gotta get back out there. Hope you feel better now," he said as he turned and walked through the curtains.

Dr. Khan refocused on me. "So this really happened," he said.

"Get Kate," I said. "She saw everything."

Dr. Khan nodded slowly and walked through the curtains. He returned with Kate.

"He knows," I said to her as soon as she passed through the curtains.

She looked up at Dr. Khan. "Really?"

"Yes, I told him. He heard what we were talking about. I had to explain it," I said.

Dr. Khan looked at Kate. "What did you see?"

Hesitantly, Kate recounted the events. I watched Dr. Khan the whole time; he was captivated.

"I just can't believe this continues to happen to you, Alex," Dr. Khan said after Kate finished the story.

"The only way to stop it is to give Manuel my heart," I said.

Dr. Khan shook his head. "You can't know whether that would work. Now, I believe you; I told you that last time. You saved me from doing a very bad thing. But that was based on things you already knew. This is different. How do you know things are going to change again?"

"I just know," I said. "And if you're not going to help us, that's fine."

"Us?" Dr. Khan said, looking over at Kate. "Are you going to help her?"

Kate looked at me and then back at Dr. Khan, but she didn't respond.

"If not," I said, "I will do it by myself."

"Alex, I can't let that happen. You know I am required to report you if I think you can be a harm to others or yourself. If you walk out of here…" Dr. Khan paused and poked his head between the curtains and then returned and spoke in a hushed tone. "If you walk out of here and commit suicide, I could lose my license."

Unperturbed by his words, I just looked at him expressionlessly. "OK. Then I'm not going to do it."

Dr. Khan rolled his eyes. "Alex, please—"

"I said I wouldn't do anything," I said. "And if there is nothing wrong with me, can I go now? I have to get to class."

Dr. Khan took a deep breath. He seemed to be deep in thought for a moment. "You're fine." He jotted something on the chart and hung it up at the end of the bed. He looked at Kate and then looked at me.

"Just think about it, please. Call me," he said.

I nodded.

"Take care, girls," he said and walked out.

I was discharged from the hospital, and Kate and I went to class. The note I received from the nurse said that I could be excused from class for the day, but I was reluctant to go home. Plus, I needed to talk to Kate.

Although I had decided that taking my own life was the only way to change the past, the thought still terrified me. Kate and Dr. Khan were right. What if it didn't work and all I accomplished was killing myself? But then again, dying was not so bad. Azrael was going to haunt me forever. Who would want to live a life filled with horror? Not to mention the fact that I felt that this was, in fact, the path I needed to follow. Something in the pit of my stomach that I could not explain told me that everything that had happened to me thus far was leading up to this—that it all had happened for a reason. Death was terrifying, sure, but the regret I would feel knowing that I'd had a chance to save my family and did not take it would be unbearable.

By the end of the school day, I was exhausted. Right before our last class, Kate and I decided that we had to tell Carl. She sent him a text, telling him to meet us at the park after class—the same park where I'd seen Azrael.

Kate and I arrived before Carl did. The park was empty. We got out of the car and walked over to the spot where I had levitated and inspected the ground.

"I still can't believe it happened," Kate said, looking up in the air where I'd floated.

"It was not the first time," I said. "And if I don't do something, it won't be the last."

Kate sighed. I could tell she was very shaken up about everything. I could also tell her thoughts were torn between helping me and forcing me to stop. Upon further reflection, I was happy that the episode this morning had occurred. Without it, I didn't know if she would ever believe me.

"So how are you going to tell Carl?" Kate asked as we watched him pull into the parking lot.

"Well, we have to start with telling him everything that happened today and all the stuff we did with Dr. Khan about figuring out what Manuel's blood type is and how it matches mine," I said.

We watched in silence as Carl parked and got out of his car. He was smiling as he walked toward us. Just before he was within earshot, I said, "Just let me tell him. All I need you to do is confirm the story from this morning."

"Hey," he said.

"Hey," Kate said as she leaned in and gave him a kiss on the cheek. As always, Carl blushed.

"Hey, Alex," he said.

"Hey, yourself," I said, smiling as if nothing were wrong.

"So what's up? You said we needed to talk," he said to Kate.

Kate looked at me.

"Yeah," I said. "Let's go sit down on that bench." I pointed to a bench at the edge of the playground, no doubt meant for parents to sit on while they watched their kids play.

We sat side by side, Carl between Kate and me. I was to his left. He leaned forward, putting both elbows on his knees, and looked at me.

"So what's up?" he asked.

I told him everything that had happened. Then I told him about Azrael and what he had done to me. Kate stepped in and gave her account of the event, including the details about my sudden ability to speak Latin and my blackened eyes. About halfway through our recitation, he stood up and started pacing in front of us. He was looking down at the ground and rubbing the back of his neck with his right hand.

"This is unbelievable," he kept saying.

Then I dropped the bomb. "And I have to give Manuel my heart. We have the same blood type, and I am the only donor available. He died last time around. If he lives, everything will be different, and maybe the accident will never happen," I said.

He stopped pacing and looked at me. "What! Are you crazy?"

"And I need your help," I said.

Carl stared into my eyes and then knelt beside me. "Alex, you can't be serious."

"Carl, I am serious," I said.

"Well, I can't let you do it," he said, sounding as though he might start yelling.

"Carl, what if you lost your family, and something deep down inside you told you that you had a chance to save them? What if you didn't listen to that feeling and some demon was chasing you around? Could you live with yourself?"

"Alex, I can't believe that he is going to chase you around all your life. He's tricking you. You said it yourself; he wants you dead."

"He's not the reason I want to do this, Carl," I said. "Something is telling me that this is the right thing to do. Something is telling me that I have to do this."

"What? Kill yourself?"

I kept my calm. Something about his reaction made me feel good. I saw love in his eyes, deep down. He had hidden it since I woke up after saving the little boy. But now, it was pouring out of him like water breaking through a dam.

I reached out and took his hands. "Carl, please. You have to believe me. Last time—you know, before the time travel. You were the only one I had on my side." I looked over to Kate, who was watching us with a blank stare. I looked back at Carl. "And something I didn't tell you guys was that we were in love, you and I. I still love you now, and I always will, and I know you love me too."

Carl couldn't hold my gaze. He looked down at the ground. I wondered what Kate was thinking, but it was more important that I convinced Carl to agree with me, so I plowed on. "Everything I have told you so far has been real. You heard from Kate what she saw this morning. You know how I knew all those things about the future. That little boy was supposed to die, and because I was able to see Azrael, I saved him. Manuel is supposed to die too. If I save him, give him my heart, everything will change. I know it will."

Carl let go of my hands and stood up. He turned around and looked out at the park, with his back to me. I looked at Kate. She had tears in her eyes.

"So what do we do?" he said, his back still facing me.

"I don't know," I said. "But whatever it is, we need to do it quickly."

31

THAT NIGHT, I DID NOT sleep. I stayed up all night on the Internet, researching ways to commit suicide without damaging vital organs. I couldn't believe how much information was out there on that subject. I decided that the best way would be to inject myself with a sedative and dip myself in an ice-water bath. Then Carl would have to inject a dose of some powerful drugs to slowly stop my heart. I thought maybe Dr. Khan would help, and he could be the one to do it, but knowing him I doubted he would jeopardize his career like that.

I also decided that I would prepare a will or something like that. I read online that I could write one in my own handwriting and have two people witness it, and it would be as good as if a lawyer had done it. I would make only one request, and that would be that upon my death, Manuel would get my heart.

I plotted and prepared for most of the night. I tried to think of ways of how I could persuade Dr. Khan to help us. I knew he would lose everything if it got out that he tried to assist in a suicide. Then again, if he was forced to do it, he would have a very good excuse. The thought came to me that perhaps the only way this was going to happen was if, at the very least, we made it appear that Dr. Khan was being forced to help me at gunpoint. It would be even better if we could make it appear that they all were forced to help me—even Carl and Kate. If it failed, so be it; I would be the one holding the gun, and they could all call me crazy. I thought of my father's handgun, still tucked away among the boxes in Rick's basement.

I went back to my computer and started looking up criminal penalties for people who force others to do things at gunpoint. I remembered from movies that there were defenses if the perpetrator was crazy. That would be my way out, if this plan failed. I would tell whatever doctor treats me all about Azrael and my time travel. That doctor would inevitably determine that I was crazy, and the police would not charge me with a crime. Sure, I would be locked up in a loony bin for a decade or something like that, but for the opportunity to save my family, it would be worth it.

I turned off the computer and lay on my bed. I looked at the clock on my nightstand; it read 3:37 a.m. I stared up at the ceiling. Since I'd turned off the computer, the only light in the room came from the window behind me, on the left side of the room. I looked over at the window and was startled. In the corner, to the right of the window, was a dark figure.

I was frozen for a second. I could only make out a silhouette. It was so dark that I could not see whether the figure was facing me or facing the corner of the room. It did not move. I got up slowly and walked toward it. As I approached, the features defined themselves, and I saw that it was the woman with the white face—the one I had seen at the bottom of the lake and who'd led me to the accident with the little boy. She was facing the corner of the room. I reached out to touch her on her shoulder.

"Hey," I said softly, my hand coming to rest on her right shoulder.

Instantly, she disappeared. It was as if nothing had been there to begin with. I looked around the room, and I saw her again. She was across the room, facing the door. I walked toward her, and halfway there, I blinked. She disappeared again, reappearing at the end of the hall, at the top of the stairs. This time she was staring at me, not more than ten feet away. She was expressionless, her skin white. She had no eyes, just bumps of pale skin where her eyeballs should have been. The sight of her was terrifying.

I was frozen for a second. We stared at each other, my heart pounding uncontrollably in my chest. I took one hesitant step toward her, and then another and another. With each step, her blank gaze remained fixed on me. When I was about halfway to her, she disappeared, and when I looked down at the bottom of the stairs, there she was, staring up at me.

I wondered if Azrael had anything to do with this. The woman had appeared to me only twice before, and Azrael had been involved in both of those encounters.

I stared down at her at the bottom of the stairs. She did not move. She just stared back at me. I slowly descended the stairs. By the time I reached the bottom, she was gone. The staircase opened up to the dining room, and I looked around the dark room. She was not in sight. I walked around the first floor of the house slowly, trying to avoid the squeaky sections of the hardwood floors. I went through the kitchen, the family room, the living room, and even the bathroom. She was gone.

In the bathroom, I stopped and looked at myself in the mirror for a second. *Am I cracking up?* I thought. She had been right there in front of me, and now she was gone. Or maybe she was still there, and I just had to find her. The thought that this was all Azrael's doing stayed in the forefront of my mind.

I walked over to the bedrooms; there were two of them, side by side. The twins slept in one, and Rick and Alicia in the other. I tried Rick and Alicia's door first. I started to open it, but then I stopped. The hallway light was on, and I turned it off so that light wouldn't wash into the room when I opened the door. The hinges let out a faint creak as I slowly pushed the door open with my index finger. I poked my head in and looked around the dark bedroom. Nothing but the oversized bedroom set and two lumps on the bed, breathing heavily and sleeping soundly. I slowly closed the door and turned my attention to the twins' room. Their door was already open. I poked my head in and looked around. Two cribs separated by a changing table sat against the far wall. The twins slept soundly, and the room was otherwise empty.

There was only one more place to search in this home, and that was the basement. I had butterflies at the thought of it. I had been to the basement a few times to help Alicia with the laundry, and it creeped me out. It was always dark. The ceiling was low and unfinished, revealing all types of pipes and wires. There was also a distinct musty odor throughout the entire space. I walked slowly toward the door that led to the basement. I took a deep breath and opened it.

There were three steps down, then the staircase turned sharply to the right, and another ten or so steps led to the bottom. I descended the first three steps and stopped at the top of the remaining stairs, staring down into the basement. Panic filled me when I realized that a light was coming from the basement. It was not the regular ceiling light. No, this was just a light, more like a faint glow, almost bluish, and it was coming from the far end of the basement. As I stared at it, I noticed that it was pulsating ever so slightly. It would get a bit fainter, grow brighter, and then get faint again.

I reached for the light switch and flipped it. Nothing happened. I flipped it up and down a few times, but the faint blue light was the only illumination in the dark basement.

For a second, I hesitated. I thought about closing the door, walking back up to my room, and closing my eyes tightly. Whether or not I went to sleep, I would not open them until morning. But I couldn't do it. Whatever was down there had come for me, and it had come for a reason. I wanted to know what the reason was.

So I took the first step down. The steps squeaked as I descended. I still could not see the source of the light. I moved slowly, stopping after each step to listen for any noise. When I heard nothing, I took another hesitant step.

At the bottom of the stairs, I looked in the direction of the light. It was very small, and it was coming from the floor in the far-right corner. It was too dark, and I was too far away to identify its source.

I tried the light switch, and not surprisingly, it didn't work, either. I took a deep breath and started walking in the direction of the light on the floor. The basement was cold, and the musty smell seemed to increase in intensity with every step I took.

Halfway to the light, I made out what it was: my iPod. I couldn't believe it. I had lost that device in the accident and hadn't even thought about it since. But here it was, in the basement and turned on. I hustled over to it and picked it up. The headphones were still connected to it, and music was playing. I read the display. It was the same song I was listening to when the accident occurred. Suddenly, I was very scared. I felt as if something was around me, close to me, breathing on my neck. I turned quickly and lashed out with my right hand. I hit nothing but cold, empty air. I used the iPod's light to shine in front of me and see what it was.

"Who are you?" I said faintly, wondering if it was the woman.

No reply, but I still felt the presence next to me. Every time I turned in its direction, it would disappear, and the feeling would come from the opposite angle. I turned to run for the stairs, but they had disappeared—they'd been swallowed up by the darkness.

"Hello," I said, this time a bit louder. "Who are you?"

The presence was behind me. I felt fingers graze the small of my back. I screamed and darted away, only to run into one of the walls. My breaths were short and rapid, my heart rate was ramped, and all around me was perfect darkness—except for the light from the iPod. I felt my way along the wall until I found a corner. I crouched down with my back to the corner and stared out at the darkness. Whatever it was, it would now have to come at me from the front.

I pointed the iPod screen away from myself and just waited. For a long while, nothing happened. Then, all at once, the thing came rushing toward me. I heard its steps start from the far end of the basement, and it trotted in my direction. Whatever it was, it sounded as though it had four legs. As it came closer to me, I was too scared to hold my ground. I quickly rose to my feet and ran to the left, along the wall.

The thing homed in on my location, and I could hear it charging for me. The laundry room, I thought. Along one of these walls was a door that separated the rest of the basement from the laundry room. Using my left hand, I felt for the door. I could hear the thing's footsteps coming closer and closer. I felt its presence right behind me as I finally found the door, jumped inside, and slammed it shut. There was a loud thud against the door as the thing ran into it. Whatever it was behind the door, it was very large.

With every ounce of strength I had, I pushed against the door and locked the latch.

"He won't come in here," said a female voice behind me.

I jumped and turned in the direction of the voice.

This room was totally dark, just as the adjoining basement was. I saw nothing.

"Who are you?" I asked, lifting the iPod up in front of me.

There was no reply as I slowly searched the laundry room with the light of the iPod.

"Please tell me what's going on," I said to the dark as I searched.

"Here." The voice was to my right.

I turned quickly and shone the light in the direction from which the voice had come. Nothing.

"Help me," I said.

I jumped as another loud thud came from the other side of the door. That thing was trying to get in. "Please," I said to the darkness.

"He's trying to fool you," the voice said.

"Who?" I asked. "Azrael?"

When I said his name, I heard the thing on the other side of the door growl deeply, sounding like a thousand wolves right before they attacked. Terrified, I fell backward and pressed up against the first wall I could find.

"Yes," the voice said.

"So what do I do? Please help me," I said, but my voice was losing strength, and the thing on the other side of the door was pounding on it so hard that I was amazed it hadn't shattered into pieces.

"Trust yourself," the voice said. "Be strong."

As the pounding at the door continued, I slowly rose to my feet and turned to face the door.

"Are you going to help me?" I asked.

"Always," the voice said.

I took a deep breath, and in one motion, I lunged at the door, unlocked the latch, and braced myself. The thing fell through the doorway, and I fell backward, hitting my head against the wall behind me. A bright light shone over me, and once I refocused my eyes, I saw the thing for what it was.

"Rick?" I said in utter shock.

"What the hell is wrong with you?" he said. "I've been knocking at the door like a maniac. What are you doing down here?"

I felt the back of my head. There was a bump.

"Did you hurt yourself?" he asked as he helped me to my feet.

I shook my head.

"What are you doing down here?" he repeated.

"I…" I started to reply, but I realized that I had no explanation. I looked down at the iPod in my hand, but it was not an iPod at all. I couldn't believe my eyes.

"What is that?" Rick asked, looking down at my hand.

"It's a bracelet," I said.

I looked up at Rick, who stared at me with wondering eyes. Past him, I saw Alicia in her nightgown, standing just outside the door to the laundry room.

"Alex, are you OK?" Rick asked.

I nodded. "Just looking for this." I held up the bracelet. "And it looks like I found it."

"It's four in the morning. Why are you down here now?" Rick said.

"Couldn't sleep," I said, looking at the bracelet.

"C'mon, let me make you some warm milk," Alicia said from behind Rick.

"Hold on," Rick said to Alicia. "Why didn't you answer me? I was pounding at this door like a madman."

I looked at his concerned gaze. The answer was not something he needed to hear, and a reasonable alternative explanation was not something I could muster up, so I just said, "I don't know."

We walked up to the first floor. Alicia made me some warm milk, and she and Rick sat with me at the dining room table as I drank it.

"You couldn't sleep, so you decided to go on a scavenger hunt in a dark basement?" Alicia asked.

"I wanted to find this bracelet. The lights were on when I went down," I said.

"They were off when we walked down," Rick said.

I took a large sip of warm milk, using the time to think up a more believable story.

"I don't know. I've been so stressed lately with school and everything. Just felt like rummaging through my old stuff," I said.

"What is it, anyway?" Rick asked.

I showed it to him. He took it in his hand, slowly turning it in the light from the chandelier above us. He read the two names aloud. "Bailey & Alex," Rick said.

"You know what?" he said, looking at Alicia. "Bailey had one of these on when we buried her, remember?"

Alicia nodded.

"That one's mine," I said. But that was a lie. My bracelet was upstairs in the top drawer of my night stand. Alex & Bailey, it read. This bracelet was the very one that Bailey was buried with, and it was now in Rick's hand.

"We made two the week before the accident. I couldn't sleep, so I decided to go looking for mine. You guys said all my stuff was downstairs in the laundry room, and I decided I would find it," I said, sounding much more convincing, I thought.

Rick nodded slowly. He was still looking at me with an appraising stare. He handed me the bracelet.

"I still don't understand, Alex," Rick said. "We're really worried about you."

"I'm fine," I said. "In fact, I've never been better."

"I find that very hard to believe," Alicia said.

"Well, it's true. At least since the accident, I've never been better. I have clarity now that I didn't have before. I understand a lot more, and things seem to make more sense," I said.

"Yeah? Like what?" Rick asked.

"Like life in general and everything that has happened. It was so hard to deal with, and I thought I would never get over losing my family, but I feel like they are still with me, with us."

Rick nodded. "That's true."

"And, well, I couldn't sleep, and all I thought about was Bailey and how we made this bracelet together before the accident. I thought that if I found it, I would feel better. And now that I have it," I said, turning the bracelet in my hand, "I feel great."

We sat in silence for a moment. I sipped my milk.

The silence was broken when one of the twins cried out from the bedroom.

"Excuse me, guys. If I don't stop her soon, she'll wake up her sister, and then none of us will get back to sleep," Alicia said as she rose from her chair. "Have a good night, Alex. Feel free to sleep in. Tomorrow is Saturday." She gave me a kiss on the top of my head and then walked toward the bedroom.

Rick watched her leave, and then he turned to me. "So you wanna tell me what's really going on?"

"I did," I said.

"I didn't want to scare Alicia, but before you opened the laundry door, I heard you talking to someone. Who were you talking to?"

I looked at Rick. His concern was apparent, and for a second in the dim light of the dining room, he looked just like my father.

"A woman. I don't know who she is," I said.

He raised his eyebrows. "Really?"

"Yeah, she's the one that led me down there. She wanted me to find this," I said, holding up the bracelet.

"Led you down there?"

I nodded. "Is that so hard to believe? You go to church. Don't you believe in ghosts and stuff like that?"

He mulled this over for a second. "Yeah, I guess," he said, but he still looked worried.

"Well, anyway, she just was telling me that she wants me to be strong and that she will always be with me. And it's not a coincidence that I found this bracelet, either. I feel better now. I'm not scared anymore. I'm not scared of anything."

"Scared? What do you mean scared?" Rick said.

I hesitated. Of course, that didn't make sense to him; this Rick (unlike the pre–time travel Rick) had no idea about my encounters with Azrael.

"In general, you know. Scared of moving on, scared of not having my family with me. I'm not going to let that bother me anymore."

"That's a very good outlook. But I don't know that I want you wandering around in the dark by yourself. That scares me," he said.

"Don't worry. I think it's over. I can feel it. Everything is going to be better now."

"You sure about that?"

I nodded. "Damn sure."

He smiled. "OK, well, let's talk more about this tomorrow. Right now, I want to get a few more hours of sleep. And don't forget church this Sunday. You and me."

I nodded. "Sounds good to me."

We got up from the table, and he gave me a hug and a kiss on the forehead.

"What did she look like?" he said, once he let me go. "The woman."

I looked at him and thought for a second. The truth was that she had looked very scary to me. But he didn't need to know that.

"Peaceful," I said.

With that, he wished me good night, and I walked up to my room. As I lay in bed, I clenched the bracelet tightly against my chest. I looked over to the corner of the room where I had first spotted the woman with the white face. I was startled, but only for a second. The thing that had chased me around in the basement was perched upright in the corner, staring at me with red eyes like lasers. It was an overgrown wolf with black fur and a mouth filled with jagged teeth. I could hear it breathing heavily.

I just stared at its red eyes for a long while, and it stared right back at me. For the first time since the accident, I wasn't afraid. I could tell the beast knew that. I blinked, and it disappeared. I turned over in my bed, thinking one thing and one thing only. Tomorrow would be the day I killed myself. It had to be done.

32

I WOKE UP JUST BEFORE TEN in the morning. The sun was shining brightly through my window, and my room felt warm. My pillow was damp from sweat. While I had slept soundly for a few hours, my body was filled with anxiety. In the last few minutes before I fell asleep, I had decided on my course of action. It would be difficult and possibly get me arrested, but I had to try.

After using the bathroom, I called Carl. He answered on the first ring.

"Hello," he said.

"Hey, Carl, we need to talk."

"You want me to come over?"

"Pick me up."

Alicia made breakfast for Rick and me, and we talked about school and Rick's job. He'd been called into work, so he rushed through his breakfast and left.

I told Alicia that Carl was on his way over to pick me up, and he and I would be going to the mall with Kate. It was a lie, and I felt bad, but I had discovered that I was very good at lying.

Carl came in the through the side door. It reminded me of the time he had come as my boyfriend, before the time travel. He looked worried, and Alicia took notice of this right away.

"Hey, Carl. You doing OK?" she asked as he sat next to us at the dining room table.

He looked at me. "Yeah, just got a lot of stuff on my mind."

"Well, you're dating Kate. I'm sure that can't be easy," I said, trying to lighten the mood.

"She's fine," he said shortly.

"How about some eggs and coffee?" Alicia asked.

"He doesn't drink coffee," I said.

He looked at me quizzically, and I remembered that he had told me that before the time travel. After a second, he seemed to understand how I knew this about him.

"Yeah, no coffee, but I'll have some orange juice, if you have it," he said.

Carl and I watched as Alicia walked into the kitchen, pulled out a skillet, and got an egg carton from the refrigerator. Once she was fully entrenched in making Carl's breakfast, he turned to me.

"You can't do this," he said quietly, so that Alicia would not hear.

"I have to," I replied in a low voice.

"I thought about it all night, and I don't think you're right about everything. I think he wants you to do this. I think he thinks that you should have died in the accident, and he's trying to trick you so he can get your soul."

I shook my head. "No. I'm very sure. We'll talk about it when we leave. More stuff happened."

Alicia came back with a plate of eggs. "So you guys going to the mall?" she asked as she placed the eggs and juice in front of him.

He looked at me. "Yeah," he said faintly.

Carl finished his breakfast, and we said goodbye to Alicia. I wondered if this would be the last time I would see Alicia, Rick, or the twins, for that matter. Not wanting to arouse any suspicion, I acted no differently than I would normally act. I took no chances.

As soon as we walked out of the house, Carl said, "I'm not going to let you do this."

"Carl, I don't need this right now."

We got into his car.

"It doesn't add up," he said.

"It does, and some more stuff happened last night that we need to talk about."

Carl put the car into gear. "Where are we going?"

"Go to the cemetery," I said.

"Why?" Then he put it together. "OK. That's fine. But I have to make a stop at the hospital."

"The hospital? Why?"

"My grandmother was admitted last night. I haven't gone to see her yet. You can come in with me," he said.

"Really? That's horrible. Is she OK?"

"Yeah. They're running tests," he said.

I'd only met Carl's grandmother one time, and that had been at our middle school graduation. She was, by all accounts, the quintessential granny—silver hair, skinny build, wrinkled face, and a pleasant smile. I hoped she was OK.

"OK, but can we go to the cemetery first?" I asked.

"It won't be long. We can go after," he said.

"OK, then let me tell you what happened," I said. I recounted the events of last night. I told him every detail I could remember. Oddly, he did not seem to be taken aback by any of it. It wasn't like before, when every one of my stories had captivated Kate and him.

"So what do you think now?" I asked when I was done.

"I think you are being fooled," he said.

"But what about what the woman with the white face told me?"

"How do you know it wasn't a trick? How do you know that anything that happened was not just this Azrael guy trying to fool you?"

"I can feel it," I said. "I know it's not a trick."

"Alex, are you saying that you are willing to risk your life over a feeling? Listen to yourself. This is crazy."

"Feelings are all we have, Carl. I know that now. And I'm not just risking my life; I'm saving my family's lives. I thought you were going to help me. If you've changed your mind, let me know now."

He was silent as we made our way down Michigan Avenue.

"I want to help," he said. "But what if it goes wrong? What if you're wrong? I wouldn't be able to live with myself. Not to mention that I'd probably go to jail for helping you."

"No. I came up with an idea that is going to fix all that," I said. "And it has to be done today."

"I'd love to hear it, but let's wait until after the hospital," he said.

That was the second time he'd said that. I found it odd. For that matter, his tone this morning was odd. He barely looked me in the eye. Admittedly, that was par for the course on most days, but that day, he was especially evasive.

"Carl, what's wrong with your grandmother?" I asked.

He kept his eyes on the road. "I told you I don't know. They're running tests."

"Did she at least tell you what the symptoms are?"

He shrugged, not saying anything.

"It's weird, but last time—you know, before the time travel—nothing was wrong with her," I said.

He shrugged again. "You said it yourself. Things changed."

"Yeah, but this is..." I trailed off as we pulled into the hospital's large circular driveway in front of the main entrance. I looked closely at the lobby. A small group of people stood just past the glass doors. The glare from the late-morning sun prevented me from seeing who was standing there. Then I looked at the parking lot adjacent to the circular driveway and saw a black Ford Explorer—one that looked just liked Rick's. Upon further inspection, I knew it was his. It had had the *M* for Michigan etched in the leather headrest.

This is a trap, I thought. They had decided that I was crazy, and now they were taking me in. I had to think fast. Too much was riding on this.

"Stop the car!" I yelled. We were about halfway up the circular drive.

"Alex, please. You have to—"

I jumped out of the car.

I heard Carl's tires screech to a halt as I fell out and rolled. I looked back at the hospital and saw a group of men running out of the front door. Rick was among them.

"Alex, please!" Carl yelled as he stepped out of the car. I ignored him and did the only thing I could do. I ran.

I ran down the slanted, grassy knoll, along the fence that separated it from the parking lot, and spun left onto the street we had used to enter the hospital driveway. At the end of the street was Michigan Avenue, a busy, six-lane highway.

I was halfway down the street when I felt a hand grab my right shoulder and spin me around.

"Let me go!" I yelled as Carl pulled on my shirt almost to the point of tearing it. Behind him, Rick and the others were quickly approaching.

"Alex, please! You have to let us help you!" Carl said, still holding on to my shirt as I thrashed at him with both hands.

"Let go!" I yelled again.

My shirt tore apart, and Carl then grabbed me around the waist. Hysterical, I started punching him on the back and yelling profanities. He was too strong; I could not break his grip.

"I love you! I don't want to see you kill yourself!" he said.

Love was the last thing on my mind. All I could do was scream. An instant later, Rick and others had reached us. One of the men had a syringe in his hand. Another came around me and held my arms behind my back.

"Don't hurt her!" Rick yelled. But he was too late. I was already hurt. Hurt that my own family and friends would do this to me. Hurt that the man I loved was in on the whole thing and Kate, my best friend, had done nothing to stop it. Most of all, I was hurt that I was losing my one chance to save my family. They'd be dead forever, I thought, and it was because I had failed.

I felt the needle enter my neck. I was staring at Rick, who was speechless, and just past him I saw Azrael, who was smiling. Then I blacked out.

33

I WOKE UP STARING AT STAINED white ceiling tiles. My thoughts were adrift, and a headache was pounding away between my ears. I felt faint. For a moment, I wasn't sure where I was or why.

Then, all of a sudden, I jolted awake from my daze. Sharp pains shot from my wrists and shins. I was tied down to the bed. I lifted my head, chin to chest, and surveyed my surroundings. Other than my bed, a metal sink and mirror, and a small television in one corner near the ceiling, there was nothing in the room. The walls were pale beige, and the door was closed—undoubtedly, it was steel or something along those lines.

I wanted to scream, but I thought better of it. They thought I was crazy, and a crazy person would scream in this instance, attempting to proclaim her sanity. Of course, maybe even a sane person would do the same, but either way, that was what they expected. I would not give them that. More importantly, I needed to find a way out of there.

I took a few deep breaths and stared at the ceiling. I cleared my mind for an instant and thought about my possible options. The first thought that came to mind was to just act nice, play nice, and pretend to be fine. That had worked well enough for me up until that point. Maybe they'd just keep me there for a day or two and then cut me loose. Then again, they might keep me longer, which could prove to be a problem.

I tried to formulate a plan in my mind, and then slowly I fell asleep.

The next time I opened my eyes, it felt as though many hours had passed. There was no window in the room, so I didn't know whether it was light or dark outside. I was still restrained, so I just looked over at the large steel door.

"Hello!" I yelled as loud as I could.

There was no answer.

"Hello!" I yelled again.

A moment later, I heard some noise from the other side, and the door started to creak open. In came an older woman wearing a light-blue nurse's outfit.

"Why, hello," she said happily as she made her way to my bedside.

"Can I be let out of these restraints?" I asked. "I think the steel door is enough, don't you?"

She gave me a smile that looked out of place, considering the circumstances. "Not until you've seen the doctor, dear. He'll let us know what to do."

I sighed but held my composure. "Well, what about my family? Can I see them?"

She gave me that smile again and said, "Not right this instant but very soon, dear. I think they're all as anxious to see you as you are to see them."

"Are they here?"

She nodded. "Oh yes, in the lobby. They've been here all day."

"All day? What time is it?"

"Just after eight in the evening," she said.

I let out another sigh. Ten hours had passed. Ten hours closer to when Manuel would be dead, and ten fewer hours that I had to work with.

"OK, well, can I see the doctor soon, then?" I said.

She smiled. "Yes. I've already paged him. He'll be here in just a few minutes."

"Can you at least loosen my straps?"

She looked at me hesitantly.

"I know you probably hear this a lot, but I'm not crazy; it's a misunderstanding," I said.

She smiled again, but this time it appeared to be forced. "OK, but just a little," she said. She loosened each of the straps around my wrists and ankles.

She left the room, and I rested my head back on my pillow. I heard the door close tightly as she exited.

I thought about Carl and couldn't believe that he had put me through this. I knew it must have been hard for him, but just the same, he was the one person I thought I could rely on. I guess killing myself wasn't going to be as easy as I thought.

A few minutes passed, and the door creaked open again. I lifted my head off the pillow. An older white man wearing glasses walked in.

"Hello," he said cheerily.

"Hi," I said, looking him over. He wasn't dressed like a doctor. He wore khaki pants and a flannel shirt. He wore a badge clipped to his waist. It was bouncing around as he moved, so I couldn't read it.

"I'm Dr. Greg. How are you doing, Alexandra?" He wore the same fake smile I had seen on the nurse.

"Considering the circumstances, I think I'm pretty good," I said.

He let out a little laugh, also fake. I'm sure he heard that line at least twenty times a day.

"Well," he said, "you know why we have you here, don't you?"

I nodded. "Yes. I threatened to kill myself."

"Yes, that's what your family says. But is that the truth?"

I was ready for this line of questions, and I quickly replied, "Yes, I did. I haven't been myself since the accident."

He nodded, looking solemn. "You've been through a lot, and we just want to make sure nothing bad happens. What you're going through is not uncommon, you know. Many people that have been through this type of trauma contemplate suicide."

I just nodded.

"Your family tells me that you initially didn't show that much grief after coming out of your coma," he said. "They said you seemed to handle it very well. But shortly thereafter, you started talking about seeing a man who was following you around. They say you thought he was some type of demon or something like that. Is that true?"

I nodded. "Yes, but I haven't seen him for a long time," I lied. Carl had spilled the beans about Azrael. This, I was not expecting.

"Well, they are saying that you think that if you killed yourself, you'd undo the accident somehow. Is that true?"

I nodded. At this point, lying would only put me further behind the eight ball. "Well, yes, that was something I was thinking about."

"Well, we see this very frequently, Alexandra. People that have suffered great loss, as you have, go through a great range of emotions. One of those is to think they could have changed things. They blame themselves, and often-times that leads to suicide. Not exhibiting the type of grief one would expect after such a loss could mean that you've bottled up all those emotions, and when they are finally released, they cause you to make rash decisions."

I said nothing in response; I just nodded.

"The post-traumatic stress that you're experiencing can be medicated. We have a wide range of medicine that can help you through this."

I took a deep breath and said, "How long do I have to stay here?"

"As long as you need. We want to see to it that you make a full recovery. I'm a therapist, and many others work in this hospital. We can help you work through your grief and help you make a full recovery."

"I'm not crazy," I said.

"I know you're not, and we don't have any crazy people here. You see, illness is not just relegated to the body; it afflicts the mind as well. If you have a bad fall and break your arm, you wear a cast and give it time to heal. The same goes if you experience a great deal of loss all at once. The mind needs to heal too. You can't blame yourself for what happened. That is one of the first steps to recovery."

My eyes started to water, but I held back the tears. I did blame myself, and I did have a way to change things. I knew this to be true; it had to be.

"Now, one of the things we would like to do is talk about the accident and how it has affected you," he said. "Of course, we can do that as soon as you are ready. I reviewed your chart, and it appears that you refused psychiatric treatment. That's OK. I'm not blaming you, but we think it's necessary at this point."

I looked around the room and then back at Dr. Greg. "Well, is it possible I can leave and just come back for sessions? Honestly, I don't see how anyone can get better locked up in a room like this."

Dr. Greg smiled slightly. "Well, that depends on your progress. You see, the reason you are in here is that we believe you pose a risk to yourself. We need to establish that will no longer be the case before we release you."

I sighed. "Well, can you at least untie me?"

He nodded. "Yes, we can do that. This is protocol, and we like to talk to our newly admitted patients before doing so. Normally, when people wake up after being admitted, they are much more…well, let's say more animated." He said the word *animated* slowly, pronouncing each syllable. I know he wanted to call them crazy, but based on what I could tell, that was a bad word around that place.

"Well, I'm not animated, and I don't think I need to be here very long," I said.

With his right hand, he pulled a little black book from his shirt pocket and flipped through it. "Tomorrow, I can see you at ten in the morning. That will be our first session. Is that OK with you?"

I looked around the room again. "So you're saying I'm going to stay here for a while?"

"No, I'm not saying that. All I'm saying is that we need to begin your treatment and then see how it goes."

I let out another sigh. That didn't sound good. I was going to be there for weeks; I knew it. By then, Manuel would be dead, and any chance I had of saving my family would die along with him.

"Well, what about visitors? Who am I allowed to see?"

He looked up from his little black book and said, "Anyone, really, during visiting hours, of course. Only medical professionals are allowed after hours. We have separate visiting rooms at the front of the facility."

His response gave me an idea. "Well, can I see my doctor? His name is Ameer Khan. He's been helping me a lot."

Dr. Greg nodded. "Sure. That's fine. Keep in mind he's a medical doctor, so we would not really require his expertise."

"Well, he's more than a medical doctor to me; he's been a good friend, and I think he can help me out," I said.

"Sure. I'll make a note to let him know. So would ten in the morning be OK for you tomorrow?"

I looked around the room again, this time half smiling. "Well, I don't know. It looks like my schedule is pretty wide open—unless you want to let me out."

He shook his head and smiled back. "No, but I will untie you, and I will see you tomorrow at ten."

He jotted down the appointment and then put the book back in his pocket. Then he came around my bed and untied me slowly. I could see that he was watching me the whole time, watching my hands and my feet, waiting for me to do something. I wondered how many people attacked him when he let them loose at this point in the meeting. I bet a lot did.

Once loose, I sat up on the bed. I looked down at my clothes. I had on the same outfit from this morning, and my shirt was torn. "Will I get to change my clothes?"

He nodded. "Yes, your family brought you a suitcase of clothes. We have them. A nurse will come by after I leave and get you a change of clothes."

"Is my family still here?" I asked.

He looked at his watch. "I'm not sure, but visiting hours ended at eight, so you will have to wait until tomorrow to see them."

I felt angry at first, but then relief came over me. Truth was, I didn't want to see anybody. I needed time to think of a plan. Time was running short, and I had no idea how long I would be there.

"I guess that's OK," I said.

He looked at me carefully, as if he were trying to read my mind. "You know," he said, "You shouldn't be upset with them. They are only looking for your best interest. They love you very much."

I sighed a little. "Maybe you're right."

He smiled again. "Well, I feel like we are going to help you a great deal. You just have to trust us and trust the treatment. It's going to be hard at first, but I assure you, this will all be for the best."

I just nodded and looked past him at the steel door. What I would give to be on the other side of it right now, I thought. This wasn't going to be easy, and maybe I wouldn't make it at all. Maybe I would be here for the next month, and by then, Manuel would be dead. I started to cry.

He came over and sat next to me on the bed. My crying grew stronger, and I buried my head in my hands.

"I promise you that things are going to get better," he said softly.

I went on crying for a minute or so, and all the while, he sat next to me. He didn't say anything else.

After I calmed down, I turned to him and said, "Dr. Greg, how long do you think I will be here?"

He shrugged. "Can't tell. You know, it's all about your progress."

"What's normal? A few days? A few weeks?" I asked.

He mulled this over as I wiped the tears from my eyes. "Well, normally, it's just a few days, until we determine that you're stable enough to handle whatever it is that's bothering you. Our meetings are going to help you identify that issue. It's very important that we find the cause and address it head-on. Some patients are able to understand and identify the cause very quickly; others, not so quickly. So we'll just see."

I sighed. This was not the answer I wanted to hear. Somehow, I had to find another way out if they kept me there too long. I wished I could tell myself I had a plan, but I didn't.

"I can prescribe some medication that can help you relax," he said, no doubt seeing the worried look on my face. "It will be a small dose, but it should help you get some sleep. What do you think?"

I nodded. "OK, I guess."

He put one hand on my shoulder and looked me in the eyes. With a warm smile, he said, "There are a lot of people that care about you, Alexandra. Don't forget that."

I nodded but didn't say anything.

He stood up and looked down at me. "So I'll see you tomorrow?"

I nodded again.

He walked over to the large steel door. I watched as he looked through the door's small glass window and nodded to somebody on the other side. A moment later, the door opened with a creak, and he was gone.

Once the door closed, I buried my face in the pillow. I cried some more, but the tears didn't help. When I looked up from the pillow, I saw Azrael. He was standing in a corner, staring at me. He was smiling. I wanted to yell at him, throw things, and rip that smile off his face. But I knew they'd be watching me. They'd see me trying to hurt something that wasn't there.

"Leave me alone," I said, barely moving my lips.

His smile grew larger.

Anger boiled up in me. "Get out of here," I said, this time a little bit louder.

"They think you're crazy," he hissed through his overgrown smile. "Look at you, locked up in this place. You're a crazy, confused little girl."

I closed my eyes, holding back my rage, and turned to face the other direction. When I opened my eyes again, he was right in front of me. This time, he was almost right next to me. He was so close that if I reached out, I could touch him. I closed my eyes tightly, wishing him away, wishing he would just disappear.

"You've lost," he said with a sinister whisper. "I know your plan. I know what you want to do. It was I who put you in here. You've lost, girl."

His words felt like daggers passing through my soul, each one piercing me in a different spot.

"No," I said. "I can still save them."

He laughed. It was a strong, deep laugh.

"Silly little girl," he said.

I kept my eyes closed and breathed deeply, trying to calm myself down.

"You will never see them again," he said. "And I shall haunt you for the rest of your days until I have your soul as well."

I bit my lip and clenched the bedsheets tightly in my hands. He was trying to elicit a reaction from me; I knew it. He wanted me to lash out at him—put on a nice show for the hospital staff, so they would know I was a nutjob.

"I especially like the little one," he said. "What's her name? Bridgette?"

"Bailey," I blurted. "She's not yours, you animal."

He let out another laugh.

"You are a confused little girl, and you are playing with things you do not understand. Once I have taken a soul, there is no return. It is mine forever."

I opened my eyes and looked up at him. "Oh yeah? What about the little boy? Or Isabelle Nelson? I took them from you. They're still alive."

His smile weakened, and he stared down at me with his dark eyes. He didn't reply.

"Leave me alone. I know what you're trying to do, and it won't work," I said.

He held my gaze, and I felt myself starting to slip. As before, he was pulling me in with his eyes. I looked away.

He laughed again, this time harder and deeper. "You are a silly little girl," he said. "You do not know what you are doing. No one can escape death—not a single soul."

I flipped over in the bed and faced the other side of the room. I wished him away, wished I could escape that place and leave it all behind. I closed my eyes and rested my head on the pillow, and for the first time in a long time, I prayed.

After a long while, I opened my eyes and looked around the room. He was gone.

34

I HAD TOSSED AND TURNED ALL night, trying to think of a way out of there. I came to the conclusion that the only way out was to convince them that I was sane. It wouldn't be difficult because I knew that I was. All that had happened to me in the past few months might sound crazy to an average person, but I knew it was real. People would believe me if they had seen Azrael as I had or traveled back in time as I had.

My concern was that this plan would keep me there too long. I had just a few weeks left before Manuel would be dead and my opportunity to save my family would be gone.

I sat up on the bed and looked up at the little camera in the top corner of the room. I had noticed it shortly after Azrael disappeared. I wondered if they were watching. I pictured an overweight guy in a security outfit, half-asleep and hovering over a bunch of monitors. Or maybe Dr. Greg was watching. Observing me as if I were an animal in a test lab. My stomach turned at the thought.

Dr. Greg had said he'd be there at ten. I figured that was a few hours away. One of the night nurses had told me visiting hours started at eight in the morning. I wondered if my entire family would come back after having waited all day yesterday without seeing me.

I got up from the bed and walked around the small room. There was just enough room for me to walk in a small circle between the door and my bed. I decided that a little exercise would be good, so I walked around and around until I was dizzy. After my walk, I did some stretching, trying to loosen my muscles after sleeping on a hard mattress all night. When I was done, I sat down on the bed. Now I wanted coffee.

I walked up to the door and looked through the small square window. Outside was a large desk that had many computers side by side on it. There was a nurse at one of the computers. I waved at her, but she seemed deeply engaged in something on her computer screen and did not look up. I tapped the glass with my fingernail, making a faint sound, and she looked up. She gave me a halfhearted smile, got up from her chair, and walked toward me.

Instead of opening the door, she slid a small slot open just under the window. I hadn't even noticed it was there.

"Good morning. Can I help you?" she said.

At first, I was taken aback by the fact that she didn't even open the door to talk to me. Now I felt like a real prisoner.

"Ah, yeah, can I have some coffee?" I said awkwardly through the slot.

"Yes, I will ask your doctor," she said. "And in the future, if you need anything, use the call button at the head of your bed."

I looked over to the bed. I didn't see a call button. I turned back to her. "Why do you need to ask my doctor?" I asked.

"Well, caffeine can interfere with the medication you will be receiving, and we want to make sure it's OK before we let you have some. If you'd like, I can get you some juice for now, until he comes in," she said.

I shook my head in disbelief. "I guess I'll take some juice. By the way, what time is it?"

I heard a jingle from her wrist as she looked down at her watch. "Ten after eight. Anything else?" she said, sounding annoyed.

"No," I said quietly and walked back to my bed.

I rummaged around the head of the bed and found the call button. It was tightly lodged between the mattress and the headboard. It had a remote control for the television, and I turned it on. I flipped through the channels one by one. It was basic cable, and the stations had mostly news. I left it on CNN and put down the remote.

I lay down on my bed and stared up at the ceiling. This wasn't going to be easy, I thought. I had two hours until my first visit with Dr. Greg. I had to come up with a story. There was no telling what my friends and family had shared with the doctor, and I had to be prepared. Every question was going to be important; I had to put on a good show.

After a minute, the nurse brought in the juice and left it on the night-stand next to me. She asked if I needed anything else, and I just shook my head, not looking at her.

She left quickly, someone else opening the door for her as she walked out. For the next two hours, I sipped my juice and thought hard about how I would handle the meeting with Dr. Greg.

By the time Dr. Greg arrived, I knew it was well after ten in the morning. He was dressed in similar fashion as yesterday—khakis and a dark, long-sleeve, button-up shirt tucked into his pants. Unlike yesterday, he had a rather heavy-looking black briefcase in his right hand when he walked in.

I used the television programming to tell the time. The morning news had finished at nine, and that had been more than three half-hour shows earlier. My guess was that it was at least ten forty-five.

"Sorry I'm late," he said.

"That's OK," I said, smiling. I decided to appear calm and levelheaded.

Upon his entry, one of the nurses had rolled in a computer chair from the hallway. He positioned it so that it faced me, and I sat on the edge of my bed. He sat down and placed his briefcase on his lap. He opened the brief-case and pulled out a file folder and a notepad. I analyzed the folder; it was a plain manila folder with a small stack of loose-leaf papers in it. I guessed that written on those papers was all the dirt on Alexandra Drummond—from suicide talk to accounts of run-ins with invisible beings. He saw that I was staring at the folder and smiled politely.

"So how was your night?" Dr. Greg asked in a cheery tone.

"Good," I said, nodding and giving him my best fake smile.

"That's good. Some of our patients say they have trouble sleeping through the first few nights they are here. I always tell them it's the change of environment—like when you go to sleep at a hotel, it could cause insomnia."

I nodded, pretending to agree, but I didn't; hotels didn't have guards who stood by while a nurse was serving a carton of juice.

"You know, I was wondering if I can get some coffee," I said.

He smiled but shook his head. "Not until we've had a chance to talk.

We may decide to start you on some medication that could be affected if you have coffee."

I sighed but showed little of my frustration.

"I understand," I said, clenching my teeth.

"OK, well, let's talk about some of the things we do here and what we'd like to get accomplished."

I nodded, not saying anything.

"I've had a chance to speak with your family, and they have told me a little about you. Now I want to hear it from you."

"What do you wanna hear?"

"Let's start with your childhood. Tell me about that."

"Well, I was an only child for a while. My parents tried to have another kid for twelve years, but they couldn't. Then Bailey was born. She was six at the time of the accident. I guess my childhood was pretty good—no bad stuff happened. We were a loving family, and my dad and I were close."

"You say 'no bad stuff happened.' What do you mean by that?"

"You know, like I wasn't abused or anything like that. It was a good life. We weren't rich, but we had each other. My parents had a really good relationship, so it made things easy."

He nodded and jotted something down on his notepad, which he had placed on top of the closed manila folder. He then pulled the manila folder from under the notepad, placed it on top, and opened it with one fluid movement.

"It appears the accident was at the end of August. Correct?" he said.

"Yes," I said.

"It also appears that you refused therapy at that time."

"Yes."

"Tell me about that. Why didn't you want to talk to anyone?"

That was the question I had prepared for all morning. I said, "I was in shock, and even though the accident had just happened, I wasn't feeling the way I thought I would be feeling after losing my family. I didn't cry as much as I thought I would, and you know, in general, it was as if it didn't happen. So at that time, it was like, why go through therapy?"

He nodded slowly as I spoke and jotted some things on his notepad.

"Tell me more about these feelings," he said.

I thought for a minute, which was part of the act—pretending as if I hadn't rehearsed this entire conversation ten times in the last few hours.

"Well, it was weird, like I couldn't believe that something like this would happen, and even though they were gone, it was like they were still here. I tried to feel the pain, but I couldn't. You know, I had that amnesia for a while. Well, I got back all my memories and stuff, but it was like I forgot how to feel."

He nodded a little more vigorously this time as he jotted something else on his notepad.

"Forgot how to feel. Is that what you think happened?" he said.

He was buying my story. A flutter of excitement erupted in my stomach, but I suppressed all emotion.

"I don't know, Doctor; I really don't," I said, acting confused. "I mean, I still feel, but as for the accident, I'm just having trouble dealing with it and believing it happened."

"What about the visions?" he asked.

I nodded and looked away, trying to appear ashamed. I stayed silent for a long moment.

"It's OK, Alexandra," he said. "Take your time."

I looked back at Dr. Greg—this time, with watery eyes. "He follows me everywhere, telling me I have to kill myself. He won't go away."

"Was he here last night?" he asked cautiously.

He had reviewed the tape, and I was sure he had seen me staring at something and maybe even moving my lips, talking to someone.

"Yes," I said.

"What does he look like?"

"He has long black hair, black eyes, and wears a three-piece, black pin-stripe suit," I said all in one breath.

He looked down at his legal pad and likely wrote down everything I was saying.

"How many times have you seen him?"

I went on to tell him a few of the encounters. I left out the one in the park, when he lifted me up into the air. I wondered how much Carl and Kate had told him.

"Alexandra, your friends tell me that you believe you have to kill yourself before the person who caused your family's accident dies," he said.

I froze. I hadn't prepared for this question. I didn't know why—it was so basic—but I hadn't. "Not necessarily," I said, a bit choked up.

"Did they misunderstand?"

I thought quickly. "Well, first of all, I have no idea when he is going to die, so I don't see how I could even do that."

"Well, they say that you think you are able to see the future. They said it was pretty convincing. You were able to predict the ending of a very unpredictable football game and some other things about the news."

I bit my lip. Anger was starting to boil up inside me. Kate and Carl had told him a lot. They really thought I was crazy.

"What else, Doctor? What else did they tell you?" I asked.

"Well, Alexandra—"

"Call me Alex. Only my mother called me Alexandra. So what else did they say?"

"I see that you are getting upset. You have to understand that everything they told me was in an effort to help you get better."

"Did they tell you how I was lifted ten feet off the ground? Right in the middle of the park in broad daylight? Two boys watched the whole thing happen. How about how I was able to locate a lady I had never met before, and I knew her name and that she was sick. That's because at one time, I watched her die. And this thing that follows me around—he spoke her name. And that was how I knew how to find her—"

"Alex, please. I am only trying—"

"Listen, Doctor. I know you went to school and everything, but you know there are a lot of things your books can't explain. Well, guess what? Those things are happening to me. So if you think I'm crazy, give me a couple of pills and let me go home. Don't sit here and act like you know what I'm going through."

He didn't respond, and we were silent for a long moment. My words seemed to hang in the air.

"You said you watched her die, the woman. How does that relate to you finding her?" he asked.

I didn't respond for a second. I had let that one slip. To admit that I was seeing a demon was one thing, but to admit that I had traveled back in time was something else altogether.

"In my dreams," I said. "Every night, I dream about him, and one night,

I had a dream that he took this lady's soul and said her name out loud. Then, I went looking for her, and it turned out she had cancer. I was right."

He nodded slowly and then looked down at his notepad and jotted some notes. As far as I could tell, he didn't know that I was lying. Maybe Carl and Kate had stopped short of telling him about the time travel. At least that meant I had one thing going for me.

"So every night you dream about him. How about his appearance in person? How often does that happen?" he asked.

His tone and demeanor were calm and his eyes, gentle. He seemed unfazed by my previous outburst. I was sure that I was not the first patient to lash out, and he seemed to handle it quite well.

"Once in a while; not every day," I said.

"And how many times has he lifted you off the ground?"

"Just the one time," I said. Truth was, he'd done it twice, but the other time was before the time travel.

He nodded, scratching under his chin.

"If you're thinking I'm crazy, then you need to stop," I said. "He's real. I have information to prove it. Did my friends tell you how I was able to predict things and how I knew the ending of a book I'd never read? That didn't come from just anywhere. That came from him."

"So he tells you these things?"

"Yes. In my dreams," I said as quickly and confidently as I could.

He nodded, seeming to be in deep thought. "And he tells you to kill yourself in your dreams too?"

"Yes. And in person."

"Now, Alex, my concern—or should I say *our* concern, including your family and friends—is that you agree with this demon that you have to kill yourself. Based on what your friends say, that seems to be the case. Can you understand that?"

I nodded slowly but didn't respond verbally.

"So you see our issue here. We have to address the core of the problem and understand where these thoughts originated. Only then can we understand how to resolve them."

"So what you're saying is that I'm going to be here awhile?"

He looked at me solemnly. "They told me you think the person that caused the accident will die soon, and you need to take your own life before then. I consulted with his doctor, and even though he could not tell me much, he did say that the patient is in pretty bad shape. So we've decided that we will keep you here at least a few weeks. Until we can get rid of these visions and suicidal thoughts."

At that moment, I wanted to punch a hole in the wall. I shook my head. "You can't do this to me. You don't understand," I said. "Please."

"It's for your own good, I promise," he said.

Now I wanted to punch him in the face. Instead, I folded my arms, clenched my teeth, and balled my hands into tight fists.

"You have to trust us," he said.

I looked up at him. "Tell my family and friends I don't want to see them," I said through clenched teeth.

He nodded slowly. "I'm going to prescribe some medication. It's going to help you a lot, especially with your visions. The nurse will be by after lunch."

I turned and looked away, not wanting to hear any more. He had told me the one thing that I didn't want to hear. Now I would lose any chance I had of saving my family.

"I know this is hard for you," he said to my back. "But please, you have to trust us."

I didn't reply. I just stared at the wall in front of me.

I heard his steps as he walked way. After a moment, the door squeaked open and shut.

The anger and the frustration almost consumed me. How could they keep me here that long? I had rights too! They couldn't just lock me up like an animal. I was most angry with Carl; he was the one who had driven me there and dropped me off. He could have taken me anywhere else and warned me about what was about to happen. At least, that was what I thought he would have done.

Unfortunately, this wasn't the same Carl, and this wasn't the situation I thought I'd be in. If I was going to save my family, I needed to find a way out of there. I refocused and thought hard. I wasn't going to let Azrael win, not while Manuel was still alive.

35

I WAS LET OUT OF MY room for lunch. The Crescent Woods Rehabilitation Center wasn't as bad as I had thought it would be. The lunch was actually pretty tasty, and the common area, where I was allowed to roam free, was much nicer than the ones I had seen on TV shows that depicted places like that. In one room, dark-brown leather couches were arranged around flat-screen TVs. Patients could play foosball and air hockey, and a pool table was in another room. The tables and chairs in the cafeteria looked new, and in one corner, a sofa and love seat were arranged around a coffee table.

The most surprising part of all was that the patients actually didn't seem that crazy. In fact, they seemed downright sane to me. They all dressed similarly, in jeans and a sweater or T-shirt, not in those ugly gowns used on TV.

The cafeteria had five rows of tables and chairs; each row was composed of four long tables, each with three chairs on each side. Large windows overlooked a courtyard. I noticed a few people out there at one of the picnic tables. I remembered that it had been pretty cold the day before—the day I was brought in—and wondered how they could bear it. They seemed pretty comfortable, from where I was standing.

During lunch, I decided to sit alone and located myself as far as I could from the other patients. Many sat in groups, and like me, a few others sat alone. All of them looked perfectly sane, but of course I hadn't really talked to any of them.

I had a tuna fish sandwich and french fries. Both were freshly made as I watched, and both tasted as good as a tuna fish sandwich and french fries could taste. I was sipping my juice after finishing my lunch when a young woman came over and sat across from me. She had a half-eaten cheese-burger and some fries on her tray.

"Can I sit here?" she asked, smiling. She sat down before I answered her question.

"Yeah, that's fine," I said.

"Those pigs are talking about some dirty things, and I don't wanna hear that stuff while I'm eating," she said, motioning in the direction of a group of guys.

I noticed her eyes; they were dark, matching her hair. But something was different about them. They were big. They reminded me of Azrael's dark eyes. For a very brief moment, I was scared. Then it passed.

"Sorry to hear that," I said, not making eye contact.

"That's OK. You know how men are; get three of them together in the same place, and all they talk about is sex. They think I wanna join them," she said, inching her head close to mine and whispering. "Like, you know, with all three of them at the same time."

"Wow," I said, nodding but still trying to avoid her eyes.

"What's your name?" she asked. "My name is Cindy."

"Alexandra," I said. "But I prefer if you call me Alex."

"Alexandra. I like that name. Wow, I wish I had your name. Cindy is so plain, you know? Your name sounds like you're like some kind of important person. Alexandra."

I nodded, staring down at my empty tray.

She took a bite of her burger and then asked with a half-full mouth, "So why they got you here?"

"I'd rather not talk about it," I said, hoping to end the conversation and get up and walk away.

"Yeah, I was like that when I came, but I got used to it. I like it here. Since I've been here, I stopped seeing the men that followed me around all the time. I think they're scared to come in here."

I nodded and looked at her face briefly. She seemed pretty serious, so I was sure it wasn't a joke.

"What men?" I asked.

She sipped her pop through the straw. "It was four men, sometimes five; they'd be together or sometimes separate. They would just follow me around everywhere, but they wouldn't say nothing. They'd just stare at me."

The thought sent chills through me.

"What did they look like, if you don't mind me asking?"

"Well, their faces were blurry. I could never see what they looked like. Plus, most times I would be too scared to even look at them. You know, I would just close my eyes and pretend they weren't there."

She was silent for a moment as she took a big bite of her burger and sipped some of her pop, and then she asked again with a mouthful of food, "What about you? What are you in here for? You can tell me, I ain't gonna tell anyone."

I hesitated for a moment. I wasn't really sure I wanted to share my experiences with someone I had just met. I decided to play things safe.

"Anxiety," I said shortly.

She looked confused. "That's it?"

"Well, there's other stuff, but that's the main cause. They said I just need medication and some time alone, and I'll be OK. I lost my parents and sister in a bad car accident, and I've never been the same since," I said.

"That's terrible," she said, shaking her head.

"Yeah, but I think they're overreacting by keeping me here," I said.

"I think it's nice," she said. "I didn't have much of a home—you know, family always fighting, and my mother always being with a new guy, like, every other week and stuff. It wasn't fun. At least here I got some peace and quiet."

"Well, you can't stay here forever. What happens when you have to leave?"

"Oh, I ain't going back home no more. No way. Dr. Greg said he's gonna find me a long-term placement so I don't have to go back. He said my family ain't fit to take care of me, and I agree with him."

I nodded, feeling really bad for her. I really didn't know what was worse, losing a family or having one as bad as Cindy's.

"I just wish I could get out of here," I said.

She seemed to ignore my last comment and looked over at the group of guys, then back at me. None of the guys were looking at us.

"Why are you so concerned with those guys?" I asked.

"They're a bunch of pervs. They all want me to do it with them at the same time," she said.

I looked over at them. They seemed to be three normal guys having a normal conversation. None of them even looked in our direction.

"They don't seem to be looking at us," I said.

"They're trying to play it off like nothing happened so they won't get in trouble," she said with her head turned toward them.

I reached out and clenched her forearm. Under her shirt, her arm was surprisingly thin. I felt as if my hand could wrap twice around it.

"Please," I said to her as she turned to face me. "Do you know if there is a way out of here?"

She smiled and with her other hand took a bite of her burger and a sip of pop. "I've tried, and all I can say is there is only one way."

"How?"

"Well, you need some kind of medical excuse, like your ass not working right or something like that. You know, it's gotta be something they can't take care of here. Then they'll let you leave to go to the ass doctor and come back. They send someone with you to make sure you don't escape, but I bet if you tried, you could do it."

I pondered this for a moment and then asked, "Have you tried this yourself?"

She smiled and took another large sip from her pop. "Hell yeah. I tried, and I almost did it too. See, one day I had some pains—you know, down there," she said, pointing down between her legs. "They looked at it over here and couldn't find nothing. So after a few days, they had to move me 'cause the pains didn't go away. They said I needed some kind of scan that can only be done in the hospital. Well, anyway, the whole time I was with one of the nurses from here, but, you know, she's gotta take a piss once in a while, right?"

I nodded.

"Yeah, so she goes and takes a piss, and I was alone in the doctor's room. So I just left the room and got lost in the hallway. By the time I found the front, they had already caught up to me."

"So you really didn't intend to escape? It just happened?"

"Yeah, you could say that. But I figured that's the best way to do it, if you tried. So what, you gonna bust outta here?"

"I don't know," I said, looking around and hoping nobody had heard her.

"Well, if you do, I won't tell. I might like it here, but I don't really trust any of these doctors or nurses."

"I appreciate that," I said as she took another large bite of her sandwich.

We were silent for a while as I pondered this vital piece of information. I had no time to waste, and my next steps would be crucial.

"Thank you," I said to Cindy as I rose from the table.

"Wait, wait," Cindy said, holding out her arm to stop me. "You wanna meet the boys?"

I stuttered for a second, not really sure how to respond.

"C'mon. It'll be fun," she said, putting down her burger and taking me by the hand.

Reluctantly, I let her lead me over to the three guys, who all turned to look at us as we approached.

Cindy spoke first. "Hey, guys, I want you to meet my new friend," she said, showing me off as if I were an award she had received at school.

They each gave me a cautious smile and a nod. They all seemed pretty sane looking. One was an older man, very skinny with deep-set eyes. The other two looked to be in their thirties. Both wore glasses.

The guy with the deep-set eyes said, "Nice to meet you. What's your name?"

"Alex," I said, a bit embarrassed at all the attention.

"Isn't she pretty?" Cindy asked.

One of the guys with glasses rolled his eyes and shook his head. The other one said, "Cindy, you really got issues."

"I got issues?" Cindy said indignantly. "You're the one that uses needles to get high."

"Not anymore," glasses guy said. "Anyway, you just met her. I'm sure she's not too keen on you parading her around like she's some kind of show puppy."

"All I asked is if you guys think she's pretty. You know, maybe she wants to have some fun," Cindy said.

Shocked, I immediately looked at Cindy. "I'm...I'm not—"

"You really gotta stop with all that talk, Cindy," deep-set eyes said. "Why don't you let her go back to her room, and you go take one of your pills."

Cindy seemed to get angry. I watched as her face turned bright red. "You're an asshole, Dan!" she screamed, and then she stormed away.

A bit shocked, I just stood there as Cindy left the cafeteria.

"Don't worry 'bout her," Dan said. "She had a pretty rough childhood."

I just nodded. The two guys with glasses resumed eating, but Dan was still looking at me.

"I'm Dan, as you heard. This is Ray and Mike," he said, pointing at the two glasses guys, who barely looked up from their meals.

Another moment of awkward silence passed. Then I said, "She says you guys wanted to do something with her."

They all burst out in laughter, Mike almost choking on the food he had in his mouth.

"As you also heard," Dan said, "she's always the one that is making proposals to us. She's not right in that department. Heard she was molested by both her parents when she was little."

I cringed at his words and immediately felt bad for Cindy.

"That's too bad," I said.

"Yeah, but she's a nice gal when she's not angry," Dan said.

I nodded and decided it was time for me to go. "Well, it was nice meeting you guys."

"Nice meeting you," Dan said. Ray and Mike nodded and smiled.

I walked briskly to my room, and once inside, I fell on the bed. Finally, I had an idea. I had racked my brain, trying to figure out how to get out of there, and I finally got it.

A few minutes later, the nurse came in and gave me my medicine. She handed me a small white pill. I placed it in my mouth and washed it down with a gulp of water she served in a Dixie cup. I wasn't sure what the medication was supposed to do for me, but I figured that in a few minutes, I would find out. She told me that my family and friends were outside, waiting to see me, and as before, I said I didn't want to see anyone.

After the nurse left, I lay on the bed, staring up at the ceiling. After a few minutes, I felt a tingle go down my spine. It came like a shiver on a cold winter's night and filled my entire body. It was the drugs. My body went numb, and I fell asleep.

IT WAS JUST AFTER THREE in the afternoon when I woke up. I felt well rested and calm. But it was not a normal calm. A part of me knew the drugs were in charge, but another part just didn't care. I remembered the time I smoked marijuana with Jeremy. It was like that, but much more controlled. I found myself not wanting to get out of bed. I felt like just sitting there and vegetating for a while. But something deep within me was calling out, telling me to get up, telling me that time was running out.

I sat up in bed and looked around the room. I couldn't help but notice how good the feeling was. I was calm and relaxed, as though I were on vacation, sitting on a beach. Everything just seemed so great.

I shook my head vigorously. I had to stay focused—not just for me but for my family. I had to save them.

I lay back and looked up at the ceiling. The calm returned, and I found myself smiling. In my mind, I was at Silver Lake, lying on a blanket. The sun was warm and covered every inch of my body. I could hear the splashing of water at the shore as children played the way I used to play when I was young. When I was with my father.

My father! I said to myself, suddenly alarmed. I jumped to my feet and started to pace the room. The drug was some kind of sedative. It was getting me to think about other things, trying to distract me. I wiped my face with my hands as if it were covered with water and continued to pace the room. I tried to focus, but it was difficult.

I thought about what I needed to do. I had to act as though the drug was working, which, technically, it was; but they had to really know that. If they thought I was resisting, they might give me something stronger, something I couldn't resist. Then it would all be over. Manuel would die, and I would never save my family.

I sat down on the bed. The calm came over me again. For the time being, I had to let it take over, but just temporarily.

A knock came at my door, and then it opened, and Dr. Greg appeared. He walked in and sat in the chair he had been in before.

"Hello," he said.

"Hi," I said, smiling.

"How do you feel?" he asked cheerfully.

"Really good," I said.

"So the drugs helped a little?"

"Oh, yeah. I actually feel better than I have in a long time." That was both a lie and the truth. I really did feel great.

"OK, perfect. We gave you a medium dose, nothing too strong. It should calm your nerves and release serotonin into your bloodstream. The side effects are not too bad, but you might find yourself wandering off, thinking about different things. This will pass as your body accepts the treatment. Then you will just be calm and relaxed most of the time. My estimation is that you will not have any more visions."

"And if I do?" I asked.

"Then we will have to try something else."

"Have you ever treated someone and their visions never went away?"

He mulled this over for a bit. "Yes, but it is usually because they are not taking their medication regularly. We have a very high success rate."

"So what is it that you think I have? You know, like, what is my diagnosis?"

"Well, it's hard to say. You are definitely suffering from posttraumatic stress. We believe you may have been experiencing stress-induced persecutory delusions. I think that developed after the accident and as a result of you bottling up your emotions. I think a big part of you might be blaming yourself for the accident, so in a way, your mind is punishing itself. This is not uncommon."

I did blame myself. He was right about that. But I was not imagining anything. I had proof that was undeniable. But I played along.

"You're right. It was my fault," I said. Saying those words brought tears to my eyes. "I overslept. I caused us to be late. All because I wanted to go to a party. If we'd left early, we would have gone somewhere else and never been on that road."

He nodded, seeming pleased at my admission of guilt.

"Now I think about it every day," I said. "All the things I could have done differently, all the things that would have changed. I want to fix it."

"This is good," he said. "You have to face this guilt head-on. It wasn't your fault. You can't blame yourself. And thinking you can fix it doesn't help. You are just punishing yourself for something you didn't do. The sooner you see that, the sooner you will recover."

I took a deep breath. If it weren't for the drugs, I think I would have yelled at him—let him know that he and his science books about brains and feelings meant nothing to me. I had traveled back in time and seen a demon who took souls, and I was going to fix things. He had to believe that I was getting better, though, so I continued to play along.

"You're right," I said. "I have blamed myself since day one, and maybe that's why I keep seeing Azrael. Maybe this will help."

He smiled. "We talked a little bit about Azrael at our session in the morning. You seemed pretty upset when I left you. How do you feel now?"

I paused for a moment, remembering the morning, and then said, "Better."

"And how was your lunch?"

"Good."

"Good, good. I really want you to know that you can relax here. A major part of what we do is help to calm our guests. Make you feel at home. This is very important to the recovery."

I nodded, agreeing.

"Let me ask you, Alex: How frequently have you seen Azrael in the past few weeks?"

I thought for a moment. "Actually, not so much. Just a few times."

"OK, well, this is an important exercise," he said, reaching into his briefcase and pulling out a notebook. "I want you to think back to the last three times you've seen him. I want you to write down what he said, what you said, and where you were at the time. I also want you to tell me what happened immediately before and after you saw him. This is probably the most important part. I want you to be as detailed as possible."

I nodded, taking the notebook from him.

"When do I have to do this?" I asked.

"Well, our next session is going to be tomorrow morning. I was hoping you could have it done by then."

I looked down at the notebook and then back at him. "I guess it's not like I have anything else to do," I said and actually let out a real smile.

He smiled back. "OK, great," he said. "Let's make it ten in the morning tomorrow. I will bring some bagels and cream cheese. You like that?"

I nodded. "Yes."

"OK. Well, for now, I suggest you see your family and friends. I know you're mad, but they've been waiting a long time. Trust me—and I've told them this—you are not the first guest here to resent your family or friends. It's actually very common."

I nodded. "OK," I said, but I still had not decided whether I would see them. Even with the drugs, I was very mad at them.

"Do you have any questions for me?" he asked.

For a second, I almost said no. Then a thought came to me. Before they gave me the drug, I had had a plan. But I had totally forgotten about it.

"Yes. I've been having pains in my head for the past week, but I haven't said anything, 'cause I figured they would go away. They haven't."

He nodded and wrote on his notepad. "What kind of pains?"

"Don't know. Like a headache that just keeps coming back. It is on the side of my head that was hit when I had the accident. It's hurting me right now, actually."

He stared at me for a moment, and I didn't flinch. He seemed to believe me. But, of course, I couldn't be sure. He returned to writing on his notepad.

"I'll bring this up to your primary care doctor. Is that Dr. Khan?"

I nodded. "Yes."

I held back a smile. It had worked; he hadn't questioned it. Now all I had to do was talk to Dr. Khan, and I was sure I could persuade him to let me out of there for some type of exam or something like that. Then I would have a chance to make my escape.

Dr. Greg said goodbye and left. I sat down on my bed, thinking about my next moves. After about an hour of working it through in my head, I had another idea—one that would ensure my escape. Or at least I hoped it would.

Using the call button, I called the nurse. It beeped once, and then a disembodied, cheery voice said, "Yes? How can I help you?"

"Hi. It's Alex. I was wondering if Carl Landley is waiting for me in the front. I wanted to see him. Dr. Greg said I should see my visitors."

"Hold on," she said. There was a brief pause, and then she came back on and said, "Yes, dear. Actually, you have quite a few visitors. We have visiting rooms. Only two visitors per room."

"I just want to see Carl for now. Tell the others I'll see them tomorrow and not to worry about me."

Another brief pause, and then she said, "OK. I'll have an orderly come get you in a few minutes. Was there anything else, dear?"

"No, thank you."

I got up from my bed, walked over to the sink, and checked myself in the metal mirror above it. I straightened my clothes and combed my hair with my fingers as best I could. After a few moments the door creaked open, and a tall, muscular, older black man entered.

"Hello, miss," he said. "My name is Red, and I'll be your escort this afternoon."

He had a deep, soothing voice, and he smiled kindly.

"Thanks," I said awkwardly, walking out the door as he held it open.

He directed me past the nurses' station and down a hallway that had a series of offices on either side. We arrived at a large double door, and he slid a badge tied to his waist through a card reader on the wall. The door swung open, and for a moment, I thought about running through it. I guessed I would not be the first person to try that, and I bet that Red was well equipped to stymie any escape attempt.

After another turn, we arrived at another long hallway, this one with doors and adjacent viewing windows, like the type in hospitals that let people look in on baby incubators.

We walked past a few empty rooms and then reached the one that Carl was in. He was sitting in a chair, facing the doorway. There was a large brown table in front of him, and a few other chairs were scattered around the table.

He smiled and stood up as soon as I walked in. I smiled back, but it felt awkward.

"I'll be right outside," Red said and proceeded to close the door.

Carl and I stood there, just looking at each other for a second. We were both at a loss for words. I knew that he knew I was still mad at him. But I also knew that he had done what he had done because he didn't completely believe me. Before I left this room, I had to make him a believer.

"So how you doing?" he said slowly.

Without responding, I reached out, embraced him, and hugged him tight. We hugged for what felt like thirty minutes, and then I let him go.

"Let's sit," he said in his nervous voice. I knew it so well. I was a bit flattered that even after spending time with Kate, the prettiest girl we knew, I still had an effect on him.

He sat down, and I sat across from him.

Before he could say anything, I said, "I love you, Carl."

He looked shocked for a moment.

"I love you, and you love me," I said. "I told you that, and I meant it."

He nodded. "I do," he said.

I shook my head. "No, listen to me," I said, leaning in. "You and I are in love. You loved me from the first moment you saw me. I told you; before the time travel, we were together. I know you probably don't believe me, but Kate wasn't your girlfriend; I was."

He didn't look at me.

I plowed forward with my well-rehearsed lines. "OK, I'll prove it to you. I was reluctant at first. But after the accident, you stood by me and took care of me. You showed me what a great guy you are, and I fell deeply in love with you. I still love you. Seeing you with Kate breaks my heart."

"W-why are you telling me…" He stopped for a moment and seemed to be thinking. "You said things changed after the time travel. Were we one of the things that changed?"

I nodded.

"So we were really together?"

"Yes, and I can prove it. I remember in great detail everything you ever told me about yourself—not as friends, but when we were together. You told me that you fell in love with me the first time you saw me. You said it was in sixth grade, when I stood up to give a presentation in class. I was wearing a Daffy Duck shirt. You thought it was cool that I'd do that 'cause most kids in our grade would say that that was for kids. You said you liked how I didn't really wear makeup and how I always smiled."

He looked stunned. He was speechless.

"You told me that you're a virgin, and you're waiting until you get married. You said that even though you went out with a few other girls, you always thought about me—the same way you think about me now, even though you're with Kate."

"Why didn't you tell me this before?" he asked.

"Because I didn't want to get in the way between you and Kate," I said.

"Alex, don't be mad that we did this to you, please," he said. "You're right. I did this because I do love you. I've always loved you, and I wanted to protect you."

I looked him squarely in the eye. "If you want to protect me, then you need to help me."

He looked around, seemingly shocked. "What do you mean?"

"In a few days, or maybe even tomorrow, I am going to be moved to a hospital to have some tests. I need you to find out when that's going to be, and I need your help."

"Alex, that's crazy," he said, trying to appear calm, but I could see the worry in his eyes.

"Carl, I love you, but I love my family too. You put me here, and if you don't help me get out, I will never speak to you again."

I took a deep breath and paused for a moment. I was about to move forward when he said, "I saw a woman in a dream."

Shocked and immediately thinking of the woman with the white face, I said, "Really? When?"

"Last night. She was leading me somewhere and telling me things, but I don't remember what she said."

"She was telling you to help me. What did she look like?" I said.

"I don't know. It was just a dream," Carl said.

"Carl, she's been helping me. I've seen her clear as day. She spoke to me, told me she'd help me. Carl, I know it's hard, but you have to believe. I never thought any of this would be possible, but I've seen it all happen right in front of my eyes."

His eyes wandered as I spoke.

"There's something else, if you want proof," I said.

He refocused on me. "What?"

"Two things, actually. Did you see what Bailey was wearing when she was buried?"

"What does that have to do with anything?"

"Not her clothes. I mean on her wrist. Did you notice anything there?"

He nodded solemnly, his head turned slightly to the right. "A bracelet with your name and her name on it. I remember because…well, because I cried when I saw it."

"That's the one," I said. "And if you go into my room at Rick's house, you will find two of those bracelets in my night stand. We made them the week before the accident. One is going to read 'Alex & Bailey' and the other 'Bailey & Alex,' which Bailey was buried with. The woman in your dream gave that bracelet back to me the night before I was put here."

He looked at me, stunned. "Gave it to you?"

"Yes. She came to my house," I said. "At first, I thought it was my iPod or something like that. Then I saw that it was the bracelet."

He looked thoroughly confused, so I said, "OK, forget the iPod part. But you have to go look. There are two, and one of them is hers. There is something else there too." I swallowed hard. "That same night I got the bracelet, I decided that the next day, I would commit suicide. I wrote goodbye letters to all you guys. Yours was the longest one, something like fifteen pages. I detailed every moment we ever shared together before the time travel. It was one of the best times in my life, and I hated that you didn't remember any of it. I wanted you to know how much it meant to me and how much I love you. If, after reading that, you don't believe me, then you are not the guy I fell in love with."

He glanced over at Red and looked back at me. "Listen, Alex, I believe you and all, but I don't—"

I slammed the table with my hand, startling him. "If you believe me, then you need to help me!"

The door opened, and Red poked his head in. "Y'all OK in here?"

Carl looked over and said, "Yes. Sorry."

"Miss Drummond, you OK?"

I nodded and smiled. "Sorry."

Red closed the door and resumed his post.

I looked back at Carl, who at that point looked nervous.

"Sorry," I said. "It's just been so frustrating, and I need your help, Carl.

I know everything sounds crazy, and I understand why you helped them bring me here. I don't blame you for what you did, even though I was very angry when you did it."

He smiled slightly at this comment.

"But this is my only chance to fix things," I said. "I know I'm doing the right thing. Carl, imagine you lost your family like I did. And you went through the things I've been through. Wouldn't you be willing to risk your life to save them?"

He nodded hesitantly. "Yeah."

"Well, that's what I'm trying to do. Knowing what I know now, I would not want to live with myself if I didn't try to save them."

"But killing yourself, Alex?" he whispered.

I looked him squarely in the eye, unblinking and stern. "Carl, to save my parents and my baby sister, I would kill myself a thousand times. Now, are you going to help me or what?"

He shifted in his chair, and for a moment, he didn't answer.

"Carl, I love you. You have to help me. Read the letter, please. And get hold of Dr. Khan. Kate has his information. Convince him to get me out of here," I said.

He nodded reluctantly. "OK, I'll read the letter, and if it's as convincing as you say it is, I guess I'll help you."

I smiled and wanted to give him a kiss, but I held myself back.

I spent the next few minutes outlining the plan I had worked out. When I was done, we just stared deeply into each other's eyes, and for a brief moment, I was sure he would help me.

We spent the rest of the time talking about Rick, Alicia, and Kate. He told me that they'd spent the whole day yesterday waiting to see me. I felt bad, but I didn't have time for any more hurt feelings. The day Manuel died was quickly approaching, and I needed to be focused. We decided that he would call Dr. Khan and figure out when I would be moved, and then he would come back with everyone else so we could visit one more time. One more time, I thought. It was so ominous sounding. A shadow of doubt enveloped me, and I quickly pushed it away. I had to do this, and I had to be successful.

Just before Carl left, when we stood to embrace, I gave him a long, passionate kiss. He pulled back at first, but then he was helpless. As far as he was concerned, it was our first kiss. I just hoped it wouldn't be our last.

The Final Chapter

IT WAS LATER THAT NIGHT. It started at three fifteen in the morning. Looking back, I still have no idea how I'm so certain what time it was when I woke up lying on a bed of snakes, but I am sure. They slithered up my legs and around my body; one of them was wrapping itself around my ankles. It was as if my bed had been replaced by nothing but snakes. Slippery, slithering, disgustingly terrifying snakes. Worst part was, I couldn't scream or move.

My first thought as I lay there paralyzed, the snakes crawling in and out of my field of vision, was that I had died. This was hell, I told myself. Somehow, Azrael had won, and I was in hell. He'd appear any second to begin an eternal marathon of torment. My next thought was that if I wasn't dead, then this was surely a dream—just one of those dreams that felt real, like so many I had had with Azrael.

My last thought ended up being the truth: it was neither death nor a dream; it was real. I had awakened to the snakes. I was paralyzed, mute, and on the verge of fainting from fear.

Then I heard his voice.

"You think you're so smart," he said.

It came from my right. It was Azrael. His tone was unmistakable. I knew it was he.

"You think you can cheat me," he purred in his deep voice. "You are just a little girl, and I am tired of your silly games."

I tried to speak but couldn't. I tried to move my head to see him, but that didn't work, either.

"You will find that cheating me comes with many consequences, and those who try always lose." He laughed. "And you, a stupid little girl, think you are smart enough to beat me. Such silly thoughts," he hissed.

Suddenly, my head was jarred loose as if released from a vise. I immediately turned in the direction of the voice, and there Azrael stood, right in front of the door leading out to the hallway.

Deep inside, I felt an eruption of terror as I looked at him standing there in the dark. From that, a scream began in my throat. Then it stopped. I stopped.

The snakes seemed to sense my sudden calm, and they slithered more vigorously, some crawling up to my face and hissing at me with wide-open, venomous mouths. But still I did not react. I saw the look on Azrael's face change from sly arrogance to something far less confident. He continued to look at me that way as I calmly sat up in bed with the snakes wrapping themselves all around me. I stood up calmly. Snakes fell from my body to the floor as I walked intently toward him. All the while, I kept his gaze, holding him as he had held me so many times before. I never looked away, and his expression turned to one of utter shock as he watched me sidestep him and calmly turn on the water in the sink with snakes still slithering at my feet and crawling up my thighs. I cupped both hands under the faucet and lifted water to my face. The water dripped down my shirt and down my neck. The snakes felt as real as the water did, and I believed that on some level, they were real.

I dried my hands and walked back to my bed of snakes. I lay down, adjusted my pillow, and rested my head, facing Azrael. I gave him a slight smile and closed my eyes, going back to sleep.

When I opened my eyes again, it was morning. I was filled with exuberance at that moment.

Azrael had come to scare me out of my pants—not because he just felt like scaring me, but because he wanted to prevent me from leaving the complex. If the staff had seen and heard me screaming at the top of my lungs, fighting off invisible snakes, I most certainly would have been committed to stay there so they could observe me further, and I would not get my chance to leave. I was betting that that would be the day I would be taken to the hospital. I soon learned that was the case.

A knock came at my door, and then it opened slowly. It was Dr. Greg.

"Good morning," he said with a smile.

"Good morning," I said.

"Dr. Khan called me, and we have your exam scheduled at twelve at Crescent City Hospital." He looked at his watch. "That gives us about a half hour, and then you can visit with your family for about an hour. They are here already and excited to see you."

I feigned a smile as my stomach did a somersault. In a way, Azrael's failed effort to stop me that morning had given me even more confidence in my plan. But the fact remained that in a few short hours, I would be attempting suicide. I could be wrong, and that would be the last time I saw *anyone*, let alone what remained of my family.

As promised Dr. Greg brought bagels, we ate together then went through our routine. I finished the assignment he had given me, and we went over it. He went on to ask questions about what was going through my mind. I lied about how everything was getting better and how I had stopped blaming myself for my family's death.

We finished promptly at ten thirty. He walked out, giving me a few minutes to change my clothes. Then Red led me to the visiting rooms. I sat down and waited as Rick and Alicia were brought in.

They walked in as though they were entering the cage of a lion. I smiled intently and burst to my feet, hugging Rick first and then pulling Alicia in.

"I'm so sorry," I said with tears falling from my eyes. "Don't be mad at me, please."

Rick smiled his warm, genuine smile. "We're not mad, honey," he said.

"We were never mad," Alicia said.

After our embrace, we sat down at the table, Rick and Alicia on one side and me on the other.

"So how have you been?" Rick asked.

"OK," I said, nodding.

"We miss you," Rick said. "I know it's only been a few days, but we kinda like having you around."

"I've miss you guys too. I can't wait to come home," I said.

"They said you're doing great. Dr. Greg has told us that you really seem to be coming around."

I nodded and smiled my fake smile.

"How do you feel?" Alicia asked.

"Well, it's been different. Honestly, I had feared being put in one of these places since I started to have the hallucinations, and I mean, now I see it's not so bad." It's terrible, I thought. Then I said, "And everyone is pretty nice and stuff, so it's really easy to get better."

"Well, we're going to be here for you every day, if that's what it takes," Rick said, putting his hand over mine. "We want to make sure you're well taken care of."

"I will be," I said. And so will my family, I thought.

Rick went on to tell me the latest and greatest from his new construction job. Alicia went on about the twins and happenings around the neighborhood. It was a pleasant talk, and if it was to be our last, I think it was just fine.

Next up were Kate and Carl. Carl and I exchanged awkward glances as he and Kate walked in. Kate ran up to me and hugged me tighter than I had ever been hugged before.

"Allie, honey, I miss you so much," she said. "I swear I had no idea this was happening until after they put you in here."

"Hey, Alex," Carl said, and he gave me an awkward I'm-hugging-my-grandmother embrace.

We sat down together, and I could tell right away that Kate had no idea what Carl and I had planned. I gave him a big smile, and he smiled back.

"So they're saying that you're doing really well," Kate said.

I nodded. "Much better now."

"Are they giving you any drugs?" she asked.

"Yeah, something that calms me down. I take it twice a day. It's not bad," I said. What she didn't know was that I'd fake swallowed this morning's prescription. It was surprisingly easy, and I assumed that my good behavior had something to do with it.

"How does your head feel?" she asked.

I shot a quick look over at Carl, who looked the other way. "Still hurts."

"Well, I bet it's nothing. They'll check you out, and I'm sure you'll be all right," Kate said, sounding as if she were trying to convince herself.

"How's school?" I asked, trying to deflect the attention away from myself.

Kate shrugged. "Not the same without you."

"Any new Kate gossip?" I asked, poking fun at her.

"Whatever. You act like all I do is gossip," she said, rolling her eyes. Kate went on to tell me about the classes we had together and some of the stuff that had happened while I was away.

After she was done, I looked over at Carl. "You're quiet," I said.

He gave me a half smile. "Sorry. Had a rough night. Barely slept."

I immediately felt bad. I'd never really stopped and considered how this might be affecting him. I was sure it couldn't be easy to find the strength to go through with this. I wanted to give him a hug and a kiss, but I couldn't with Kate there.

"Sorry to hear that," I said.

We spent another twenty minutes talking about all sorts of high school happenings. Kate seemed to have my entire first week planned once I left that place. I just smiled and listened, enjoying every minute. If this was to be our last conversation, it too was just fine.

We all hugged and then they left, Carl's eyes locked on mine the whole time. I was trying to send him telepathic messages to be strong and trust me. He looked worried, and I didn't blame him. I was worried too. In less than an hour, I would be taken to Crescent City Hospital, and not too long after that, I would be taking my own life. I pushed back the doubt and followed Red back to my room.

"You OK?" Red asked as he held my room door open for me.

"Yes." I nodded and gave him a half smile.

"Well, for what it's worth, I think you and that boy make a better couple than she does with him," he said.

I gave him a real smile. I forgot that he had most likely seen us kissing the day before, and then he saw Carl walking in with Kate.

"Thanks," I said. "You're right."

He let out a little laugh. "Confidence. Now, that's what I like to hear. I'll be back in a few minutes to escort you to the hospital."

I looked at him, confused. "All the way to the hospital?"

He nodded. "Yeah, I know. Sorry, but it's the rules. Gotta keep you safe."

I was dumbstruck. I had anticipated some sort of escort, but not this guy. He was so big and strong. I never imagined they would let him leave the complex just to escort me.

"But won't they miss you over here?"

He shrugged. "I guess," he said. "Honestly, I like the fresh air. Plus, you're a nice girl."

As he left, closing the door, I gave him a smile, pretending that everything was OK, but it wasn't. Things had just gotten very difficult. I had to call Carl.

I waited a few minutes, and then I rang the call button and asked if I could use the phone. A few minutes later, my door opened, and a nurse I had not seen before stepped in with a black cordless phone.

As soon as she was gone, I dialed Carl's number.

He picked up on the first ring.

"Hey, just wanted to let you know they'll be taking me to the hospital, and Red is going to be my escort," I said. One component of my plan was that if there was a change of plans, I would call Carl before I was scheduled to leave. Another component was that we would talk in code and pretend that we were just having a normal conversation.

"OK," he said faintly. "What time are you leaving?"

Just from his tone, I could tell he was worried. "I'm supposed to be there at twelve, so I think pretty soon. Don't worry; I'll be OK. I'll call you once I get there," I said.

There was a brief pause. I knew that Carl was worried, so I added, "It's only a test, Carl. I cheated death, remember. This is nothing compared with that."

I'm not sure whether he got the point, but he said, "I know, I know," and we said our goodbyes.

The ball that had started to form in my stomach was bigger now, more pronounced. I looked at my hands, and they were shaking. My body knew what my mind had decided to do, and it was terrified. I have to stay strong, I told myself. I have to give the impression that I'm not nervous at all.

Red seemed to be a smart guy, and I was sure that I was not the first person he'd escorted out of the complex. Although she seemed to imply otherwise, maybe he was the one who'd escorted Cindy when she left the hospital. She'd tried to escape, and he would've been the one who stopped her. I bet they had seen me talking to her. Maybe they were worried that I'd try to escape too.

I was so confused that I started to get dizzy. I lay on my bed and stared at the ceiling. Worrying was not going to get me anywhere. I had to stay calm and focused. What I had told Carl was the truth; I had cheated death. I'd stared Azrael right in the eye, and I'd seen fear. Red was nothing more than a man. Big as he was, he was no demon, and he definitely couldn't pull souls out of people's bodies. I could beat him if I had to; I knew I could.

I stood up and started to focus. The fate of my family and me hung on the events of the next few hours. I had to be ready.

Red came and got me a few minutes later.

"Ready to roll?" he said with a smile as he stood in the doorway, propping the door open with his back.

I shrugged. "Sure."

I walked past him to the nurses' station. I handed the phone to the nurse and waited as Red filled out something on a clipboard. Once he was done, he looked up at me and tipped his head toward a hallway opposite where we stood.

"We're going that way," he said. "That's the back exit."

I nodded.

We walked along in silence for a bit as we made our way through a security door and into a long, narrow hallway. We walked by what looked like offices, and I figured that must be the administrative area.

"There's an ambulance waiting for us out back," Red said.

"I figured you'd be driving me," I said.

He laughed. "Oh no. Hospital rules. All patients transported by ambulance only. Just in case we get in an accident or something like that."

I nodded. "How long do you think this is going to take?" I asked. I really didn't care, but I figured that talking to Red would help throw him off my trail.

He shrugged. "Not sure, but they say they're giving you priority, which means you won't have to wait too long."

"Well, sorry in advance if it takes a long time," I said.

He gave me another little laugh. "My dear, anything to get out of the hospital is fine by me. Not to mention, I'm getting paid on this little trip. Makes it even better."

We arrived at a door with a sign that read Exit Adjunct Garage. Red stopped short of it and turned to me.

"Oh, and one last thing before we go," he said, a grim look on his face.

This was it, I thought. He's on to me, for sure. I clenched my teeth, trying not to look him directly in the eyes, but at the same time, I was trying not show my fear.

"What's that?" I said faintly.

"If you ask me, you're much prettier than that other girl. He'd be stupid to turn you down."

I froze for a split second. Then I looked at him squarely in the eyes. I couldn't help but smile. "He won't," I said. "He loves me."

He nodded and smiled back. "And you love him?"

I nodded. "Yeah," I said. "More than he knows."

"All right," he said with a smile.

He opened the exit door, and I followed him out.

An ambulance was parked just a few feet from the door.

I watched as the driver stepped out, walked around to the back, and opened the two doors. "Hey, Red," he said as we approached.

"Steve," Red said. "What's up?"

He shrugged as he pulled the stretcher from the back of the ambulance. "Another day, another dollar," he said.

"Yup," Red said, shaking his head.

"Miss," the driver said to me, "I know you can walk fine and all, but I have to place you on the stretcher. It's policy."

I nodded, not saying anything. I stood by as the driver unfolded the legs so that the stretcher was about waist height. He motioned to me, and I went over and sat down.

"Just lie down, and I'll roll you in. After that, if you want to sit up, just make sure your feet don't leave the stretcher," he said, and I nodded.

I did as I was told. I felt a jolt as the legs of the stretcher folded up, and he rolled me into the back of the ambulance. Red came in after me and sat on a small bench to my left.

"Should be a fun ride," he said with a smile.

I shrugged and sat up on the stretcher.

We remained silent as Steve closed the doors, walked around to the driver's seat, and got in. I was able to see him through a small window. He was filling out some paperwork, and then he started the ambulance. We drove off.

Red slid his hand into his back pocket and pulled out his cell phone. He rested back in his seat and folded his legs. I figured that was my cue to stay quiet for a while—not altogether a bad thing, considering I was about to kill myself. I focused on my plan. I thought it was a pretty good one. But, of course, many things could and likely would go wrong. I needed Carl to come through in a big way. My stomach turned the more I thought about it.

We arrived at the hospital a few minutes later. I'd been in the same spot a few times before—in the back of an ambulance, about to be wheeled through the emergency room entrance.

The doors of the ambulance opened with a small gust of air. Steve was standing by with a wheelchair. I lay on the stretcher, he wheeled me out, and then he helped me into the wheelchair.

Steve pushed me while Red followed. For an instant just before the hospital's double doors slid open, I felt like running.

We entered the hospital, and Steve checked me in. After a short wait in the lobby, he wheeled me to an elevator, and we went up to the sixth floor. Steve pushed me along, obviously well acquainted with the hospital, and stopped in front of room 633. I was put into a private room. This was a bit of good luck.

"I'll be right outside," Red said as I surveyed the room.

"Sure." I nodded.

Red went outside, and I went to the window and looked outside. I was facing Redwood Street. This was another bit of luck, because Carl would be scanning that side of the building first with his binoculars. I looked through one of the closets and found a stack of plastic coffee cups and an empty water pitcher, both wrapped in plastic. I took the three cups out of their wrapper and placed them on the windowsill side by side. I placed the empty water pitcher in front of them, still in its plastic. Between the plastic cups and the window, I placed a playing card, the two of hearts, which I had swiped from the game room the day before. Carl would see that card against the white of the cups and know exactly what room I would be in.

I took off my clothes and bunched them up in front of the apparatus I had constructed on the windowsill, blocking it from view. I put on my gown and lay down on the bed.

My nurse came in a few minutes later. She was a pudgy older woman. Her name tag read Mandy.

"Hello. How are you feeling?" she asked.

"Good," I said.

"That's good. We have you set up for an MRI in about an hour. I have to start an IV for you in the meantime. Is that OK?"

I nodded yes.

I was no stranger to IVs, but I still cringed as she put it in.

After she left, I watched the clock. We didn't have much time, and we needed everything to go perfectly.

Ten minutes turned into twenty, and nothing happened. Red came in twice in those twenty minutes to check on me, asking if everything was OK. I gave him a pleasant, unassuming smile each time.

Five more minutes passed, and then I started to worry. Maybe Carl hadn't seen the card. Maybe it had fallen down when I walked away. I looked over at the windowsill, and then I heard the screaming.

That was my cue to run. I unhooked the IV and ran out the door. As expected, Red was busy with Carl, who was yelling all kinds of obscenities. There were three nurses right outside my room, all of whom were watching Red detain Carl. I turned right in the first hallway, and then I turned left.

In the time that I had spent at the hospital working as a laundry girl, I had learned every nook and cranny of that place. I also knew the laundry transit system. For starters, dirty towels and sheets were placed in a big bin marked with a black stripe. That bin was taken to a laundry chute that was inside a room near the elevator shaft on each floor. The room was accessible only by a code, which I knew. With luck, it was one of the things that hadn't changed after my time travel.

Three-six-four-seven, I said to myself as I found the room and typed in the code. I was filled with relief when the green light above the keypad blinked twice and the door unlocked.

I went into the room and found the laundry chute. I had told Carl the code, and right before he created the diversion, he'd gone into that room and left a small bag containing some essentials. I opened the bag. Inside was a change of clothes, a hat, sunglasses, and my father's gun. I stared at the gun for a minute. Its small barrel opening seemed to stare right back at me coldly.

I took off my gown and quickly put on the jeans, shirt, glasses, and hat. At the bottom of the bag were two suction cups. These I would need to descend the laundry chute. I tucked the gun into my back pocket.

I lifted the door to the laundry chute and stuck my head and torso in.

I barely fit, and the sheet metal was slippery. Using all the strength I had, I held myself in place, a suction cup in each hand, as I got my whole body into the chute. Now the hard part. I would need to work my way down two floors. Manuel was on the fourth floor. I had decided that if I was assigned to a room above him, I would go down to his floor; but if I was below him, I would go down one floor and then use the elevator to go up to his floor. This was the better of the two routes, since I would not run into any hospital employees on the way to his floor.

Slowly, I worked my way down the chute. My elbows banged against the metal as I held on as tightly as I could to the suction cups. Inch by inch I arrived at the fifth floor. I took a second to rest, holding on to the edge of the opening to the fifth-floor laundry room.

After the rest, I went back to it. The suction cups gripped the sheet metal firmly, and I slowly descended. I was at the fourth floor when I heard some noise above me. An alarm, I thought. They must have discovered I was gone. I figured this was good luck, since I was about to exit into the fourth-floor laundry room.

A few more shifts of the suction cups, and I was there. I pushed open the fourth-floor laundry door and crawled out. Actually, I fell out headfirst. No matter; I was safely on the fourth floor, and I had plenty of time before they would figure out where I'd gone.

I collected myself, brushed off my shirt, and straightened my hat. I took a deep breath and stood for a minute, looking through the small rectangular window in the door to the hallway. I tried my best to see if anyone was coming from either direction. I was more concerned with hospital staff than with patients or visitors. After a second, I opened the door and walked out. A young woman was standing at the elevator, just outside the door. She looked at me and then looked away. Down the hall from her was a nurse on a computer. She didn't even look in my direction, as she was engaged with whatever she was doing. Behind me was the hallway I would need to travel down to reach Manuel. Before I could get to him, however, I would have to find a way to get through the security doors.

I walked down the hallway, following signs to the ICU. I reached the double security doors and stood far enough away so that I would not be in view of the camera. After a minute, a couple walked out, and I walked in.

Without any hesitation, I walked briskly down the hall. I had to be quick, and I couldn't make any mistakes.

I turned right and then turned right again. At the end of the hallway, I saw the police officer outside Manuel's room. A nurse walked out of a room to my right and gave me a glance. I put my head down and walked past her, toward Manuel's room.

As I walked, I looked into the rooms on either side of me.

The nurse I had passed must have taken notice of this, as I heard her call out behind me, "Miss, can I help you find something?"

I paid her no attention, as I'd found what I was looking for.

A few rooms before Manuel's room, on the opposite side of the hallway, I found an empty room. I walked into it.

The nurse behind me called out again, this time a little louder. "Miss, that room is empty."

She was wrong. It wasn't empty—at least to me it wasn't. Azrael stood in the corner, his face grim as he stared down at his gold watch. In the opposite corner was the woman with the white face. She looked at me with her expressionless gaze.

Knowing the nurse would be coming after me, I faced the door and put the gun to my temple. From my front left pocket, I produced the note that I'd had Carl prepare.

Just as I pulled out the note, the nurse walked in. Her hands immediately went to her face and she gasped. I pulled back the hammer with my thumb, cocking the gun. The nurse screamed. Calmly, I placed the note on the bed next to me and held my breath.

This was it, I thought. I cleared my head. The nurse let out another scream; I think she was telling me to stop. I heard the officer running down the hall. He suddenly appeared in the doorway, but he was too late. I pulled the trigger.

First came a flash of bright-white light. Darkness followed.

For a brief moment, darkness was all there was. When that moment passed, I felt the pain. It came from my left side. It seemed to start just under my left arm and then spread all through my body. There was a smell of iron and burning rubber. I heard the crying, a faint whimper at first, and then it became louder. The pain reached the base of my neck and shot down through my legs. It was as if every nerve ending in my body had been set on fire. My breathing slowed as I tried to withstand the agony. I could feel my heart pumping in my chest. I tried to move my hands, but I couldn't. I tried to open my eyes, but I couldn't do that, either.

I heard the voices. They were distant, but they were there. I tried to talk back to them, but I couldn't move my lips. The pain started to fade. I felt my heartbeat slowing down. I took a few more breaths, and then I stopped. The pain was gone.

His footsteps were all I heard next. The gravel crunched beneath his shoes with every footfall. Step by step, he approached, and as he neared, I heard the ticking of his pocket watch.

"Alexandra Drummond," he said softly. His voice was soothing and made me feel as if a silk cloak were being draped over me.

"Your hour has arrived. Do you accept?"

Able to move, I lifted my head to face him. His eyes were the first thing I noticed. They were no longer black but the color of the sky on the clearest day. His face was delicate, and he smiled a beautiful smile. The hair that once had been greasy was now silky smooth. He was exquisite, and as I stared into his eyes, I had no fear. Suddenly, as if awakened from a dream, I was filled with a rush of awareness that had lain dormant in me since my conception.

Then I understood.

To his question, I replied, "I accept."

Epilogue

D ANIEL GRIMES WAS A GOOD man. Many called him friend, some called him neighbor, but most everyone just called him Danny. He was born in a rural town in Iowa called Norwalk. Back in those days, Norwalk had a population of fewer than five hundred. Danny was three shy of being resident number five hundred when he was born.

Danny's father was a military man. They traveled a great deal in Danny's early years but eventually found themselves back in Norwalk, where Danny's father was stationed at Fort Des Moines, just outside of town. That was where Danny spent most of his adolescence, all the way through high school.

Danny went on to college after high school. He attended Iowa University, just a few hours' drive from his hometown. There, as a sophomore, he met the love of his life, Judy. They both pursued degrees in liberal arts and had a passion for politics. They both graduated with honors and were married just weeks after they walked off the stage at their college graduation.

Danny and Judy had two children and spent most of their life in Des Moines. They had a boy and girl, who grew up and had kids of their own. After Danny's parents passed away and his kids were married, he and Judy moved to southeast Michigan. Danny took a job as an economist for Ford Motor Company, and Judy stayed at home, wrote short stories for a literary magazine, and painted.

Shortly after Danny and Judy had their third grandkid, Judy was diagnosed with cancer. It was stage four and far beyond any medical treatment. She passed away, leaving Danny alone in their small ranch home in Michigan.

After that, Danny retired from Ford and collected a pension for about a decade. He found solace in living alone with his pets, his garden, and his memories of his beloved wife to keep him company.

Before my last time travel, Danny would die of a massive heart attack in his living room on the morning of my family's accident. In fact, his heart attack occurred at exactly the same moment that the accident did. This time around, he was in his truck, heading in our direction as we exited the freeway. How did he get there? Well, the day before, he was at a cell phone store and ran into a very enthusiastic salesman. The salesman's name was Manuel. He was the same Manuel who once was a felon, fleeing the police. But this time around, his life took a very different path.

Before my last time travel, Danny would have walked out of that cell phone store without buying anything. This time, thanks to Manuel, he walked out with the latest and greatest product the tech world had to offer. Since he had his new cell phone in his pocket while working in his garden the morning of the accident, he was able to receive a phone call from his daughter, asking him to meet her and the kids for a late breakfast. Just before he crossed the intersection and collided with our minivan, his heart gave way. He never made it to breakfast, and I never made it to the park. That would be the headline story on the evening news that night. Luckily, Danny hit only my side of the van. My family walked away unharmed.

I would find out that they mourned me for a long while. My parents would have another girl two years after the accident and name her Sarah, after my late grandmother from my father's side. Bailey would grow up to become a doctor and save countless lives. Kate and Carl would marry and have one child, a boy they named Alexander. Sure, they missed me, but we would meet again someday. That, I was sure of.

There was no pain or regret where I went because after Azrael took me, the first thing I was able to do was relive every moment in my life that I wished I had back. Every single birthday, every hug from my parents, every kiss from Carl, and every second I spent with Bailey. I would also live out all the scenarios that could have been if things had been different. Carl and I would marry. I would grow up with Bailey and my parents by my side and live a full life. Not a single memory would go unrealized as I lived through a collection of life's greatest moments.

After that, I would learn that as much as I thought I had changed things, I had not changed a single thing. Everything that happened to me—every breath, every movement, all of it—happened just the way it was supposed to. Knowing what I know now, I wouldn't have it any other way.

Tragedy Strikes Crescent City

Crescent City Hospital confirmed that two people died in an auto accident just outside the city limits this morning. Daniel Grimes, 76 and a resident of Baker City, died of a severe heart attack. Authorities cannot confirm whether the heart attack happened before or after the accident. The other victim was Alexandra Drummond, 18, of Crescent City. Authorities believe that she died instantly when Grimes's truck struck the van in which she was riding with her family.

Officer David Reynolds, the lead investigator at the scene, said it was possible that Grimes did not see the stop sign as he passed through the intersection. Due to trees and shrubs on the right side of the road, Grimes's vehicle was not visible to the Drummonds as they passed through the intersection, and they were unable to avoid the collision. Other passengers in the car were Alexandra's parents, Victor and Patricia Drummond, and her 6-year-old sister, Bailey.

Young Bailey Drummond may have her deceased sister to thank for her walking away from the accident unharmed. Victor Drummond tearfully told investigators that he found Alexandra draped over her sister, her arms wrapped around the child as if shielding her from the impact.

A source close to the investigation of the accident estimated that Alexandra would have had very little notice that Grimes's vehicle was about to strike their car. Based on where the vehicles were found, it appeared that the vehicles collided right after the Drummonds' minivan passed through the intersection.

The source went on to say that in 20 years of responding to car crashes, he had never seen such a selfless act of bravery. "Alexandra's first impulse apparently was not to save herself but to protect her sister," he said.

One of Alexandra Drummond's best friends, Kate Thompson, said, "Crescent City will surely miss Alexandra. She meant a lot to a lot of people, and her memory will live on forever in all our hearts."

A candlelight vigil is scheduled for Tuesday night at nine in the evening at Crescent City High School, where Drummond would have been a senior. All are welcome.

—Kiley Steele, *Crescent City Free Press*

Made in United States
North Haven, CT
09 November 2024

60052422R00188